BEGUILED BY NIGHT

A VAMPIRE TALE

NICOLE EIGENER

POLIDORI
PRESS

POLIDORI
PRESS

First Edition: October 2020
Also available in ebook and hardcover

Book and jacket design by Stacie Herndon
Cover art courtesy of The National Gallery of Art, Washington, D.C.

Library of Congress Control Number: 2020916734

ISBN: 978-1-7354639-1-9

To Franco, my eternal love

to Bijoux … RIP mon petite monstre

to Sheila, who lit my imagination

"Some men never die
and some men never live
But we're all alive tonight"

CHARLES BUKOWSKI

"For the dead travel fast"

BRAM STOKER

IN WHICH WE MEET LOUIS DE VAUQUELIN
(AN EXTRAORDINARY MAN)

LOS ANGELES, CALIFORNIA | NOW

History is history — closed, permanent, uneditable — or so it may seem, for those of us without hope for redemption.

Vauquelin is immersed in his past: much more so than any average man. He is a vagabond of time, drifting and drowning in seas of centuries, adapting to whatever life casts his way. And the time has come for him to unadapt, though he is not yet aware of this.

It won't be long now.

Tonight, he is making a rare public appearance at a museum reception for his collection of ancient garments: the sartorial chronicle of his life. He was anxious to send them out into the world, to sever one of his many oppressive ties to the past. They deserve a better fate than one spent languishing away in his closets, reduced to moth food.

They took up far too much space in his mind, anyhow.

Now he stands at the perimeter of the enormous crowd gathered for the collection's unveiling. He worked in absentia with the curators for months to create this spectacular exhibit: *The Well-Heeled Aristocrat: A Survey of Men's Clothing and Accessories from 1668 to 2018.*

Media around the world covered it as one of the most important historic textile discoveries of the twenty-first century.

His elegant wardrobe will be displayed on mannequins for all the world to see, yet the particulars behind the museum's acquisition of the collection will remain an enigma.

Officials work the room, fawning over certain attendees and prattling on and on as Vauquelin toes the edges of the throng. The hall is packed to capacity with journalists, hipsters, and fashionistas, mostly women with a smattering of pompous men in ridiculously avant-garde glasses.

They all look so self-important: guzzling champagne, emitting ear-splitting squeals of fake laughter, looking down their noses, holding their smartphones up and snapping selfies. The women, pretentious and affected, teeter on towering platform heels like newborn giraffes. Every person in this hall is identical in their efforts to be unique.

By instinct, Vauquelin is drawn to freaks, artists, and eccentric outcasts who feel at home on the outskirts of acceptable society. He has long been a master of detecting impostors ... after all, he is a skilled impostor himself. But fashion people are a whole other breed, and he finds them artificial and distasteful.

As the evening wears on, it becomes clear that these people are here for the open bar and free food, and to be seen on the red carpet — not because they have a deep love and appreciation for the exquisite antique clothing of some obscure Frenchman.

The venue, the audience, and the presentation fill him with regret and dissatisfaction. Perhaps he had been careless in his choice of beneficiaries.

The museum hired a baroque quintet to perform, which he thinks adds a dreamy ambiance. It was his idea, but no one is paying the slightest attention to them ... a DJ pumping obnoxious house music would have been a better choice for this crowd.

Even though no one in this building has the slightest indication of who he is, or that he is the reason they are here tonight, everyone is aware of his presence: the tall, blanched loner on the perimeter. It is impossible to not notice him, but his aura is spiteful, foreboding. No one dares approach him. Throughout the night, he deflects come-hither glances from both women and men, always staring straight ahead.

Stock-still, aloof, and unyielding: it is his usual demeanor.

He flits back and forth from moments of losing himself among the masses and being forced back into awareness.

It is an erratic, splintered evening.

"This rare and important collection is an anonymous bequest to The Institute. Never before have we encountered its equivalent: a pristine accumulation of garments from generations of the same family, spanning almost four hundred years of history. It is an honor and a privilege for us to be the designated caretakers of this incomparable archive," the curator says, "to be able to study and preserve these garments, to put them on view for our patrons, and to make them available for our students to study and appreciate. To our undisclosed donor, whoever he or she may be, we thank you for offering your collection to the world."

The crowd applauds and murmurs when the curtain is pulled, at last revealing the display, and they disperse like obedient ants toward the mannequins.

Vauquelin remains in the back at a suitable distance. As soon as there is space, he steps up to one particular ensemble, the one that was the most difficult for him to surrender.

It is a seventeenth-century court suit: a pink watered-silk *justaucorps* embroidered with silver threads and embellished patterns of paste stones and metallic seed beads, and matching petticoat breeches — a lavish confection that was the height of fashion in the late 1660s.

White, beaded gauntlet gloves encase the hands of the mannequin. An ermine fur cape is suspended on one shoulder. Ivory silk stockings lead down to silver-and-diamond-buckled black leather shoes. A hand-forged and jeweled *rapier* in a tooled hilt completes the look. The outfit is a magnificent spectacle, befitting of a noble gentleman of the baroque era.

He leans in, noticing that blood droplets remain on the lapel of the justaucorps. He supposes they had not tried to remove them since the fabric was so fragile. Even so, the stains provide a layer of authenticity.

His existence was irreversibly altered the night he wore that suit. He succumbs to a desire to touch the coat, but yanks his arm back: he does not dare. It is no longer his.

The vision of his garments, spread out and detached from him in the cold light of the museum, eyeballed and passed over by complete strangers, *these* strangers in particular, has an unanticipated effect on Vauquelin: it plunges him into the depths of pathos.

He thought they were no longer important to him.

He was mistaken.

His precious collection has lost all its meaning.

For centuries, it had been exiled from human eyes, as he himself had been. Now it is tarnished, diminished by the very nature of its public accessibility.

Blood begins to pulse in his ears, drowning out all other sounds in the hall. He pushes his way through the milling crowd, jostling anyone in his path and agitating their champagne glasses, and strides out into the night. He snatches his keys, crushing some bills into the valet's chest without a word, and peels out as he exits the parking garage.

Speeding up Mulholland, he finds some solace in the powerful asylum of his topless car and in being away from humans, with only the sky and towering palms above him.

He parks and sits on the hood. High on his perch, he gazes down at the expanse of Los Angeles twinkling in the night, teeming with life. He is a million miles away from his own universe, condemned to observe.

He is astonished that he is still alive.

It is a night like any other night until it is not.

Vauquelin stands a moment on the porch, looking at a map on his phone, keys dangling from one finger. He begins the descent down his imposing front steps on the way to his car, engrossed in the phone. He looks up when he presses the unlock button on the remote and gets no response.

This is when it all begins.

When life slips into discord, the mind seeks logical explanations. His first thought is that some delinquent stole the car (a brand-new, blacked-out Pagani Huayra roadster, his most recent extravagance). After returning home from the exhibit last night, he parked in the driveway where he always parked.

But maybe he parked under the porte-cochere and forgot ... except the car is not there, either, and he never forgets anything, not even the most insignificant detail.

He is certain that he did not park in the carriage house. He hasn't parked there in years. Dismay enshrouds his brain.

The knowing of things, of familiarity where none existed before, is common for him. Bewilderment is not.

The remote swings in his hand, powerless, useless.

A sudden movement startles him and he jerks his head toward the sound. The massive old palm trees and birds of paradise in his front yard make a hasty retreat into the ground and vanish before his eyes. The tire shop across the street twists, groans, and crunches. Metal braces whine and walls collapse, heaving up heavy, choking clouds of dust and exposing menacing rebar.

At last, the building completes its regression into its glorious predecessor: a grandiose Gothic Romanesque mansion, which had looked much like his own before falling into shameful disrepair and being torn down in the 1970s.

After this unholy reversal, the atmosphere is silent and serene, as if time has stopped. There is not a single solitary sound until the frantic pounding of his heartbeat begins to thrum in his ears. He drops the key ring on the lawn and sprints back into the house, leaving the front door wide open.

His parlor has also suffered retrogression. The *Los Angeles Times* he was reading on the sofa yesterday evening is missing. The large flat-screen television has disappeared, and in its place is a long-discarded Philco cabinet model. The wireless speakers are gone and his old hi-fi stereo is back, along with shelves containing the hundreds of records he had once collected.

He glances at the phone — no service — swallows hard and rubs his eyes.

I must be hallucinating.

From deep within the bowels of the house, the old grandfather clock chimes six. It is a wretched time stamp for these bizarre events. He turned the clocks back just last night, bidding welcome to the earlier departure of the sun.

He returns to the porch. The passing cars on the street are old. Much older. It is quiet. Much quieter than normal.

A black dread begins in his toes and creeps upwards, settling into his heart and causing it to flutter, dizzying him. It was dusk when he first walked out the door. Now the moon is beginning its ascent over the mountains and the street lights are flickering on in unison, giving the sky its familiar amber Los Angeles glow. The accelerated nightfall is comforting, but still, his hands quiver with trepidation. His mind begins to work robotically.

A glass of wine. I must steady my nerves.

He hurries into the kitchen, uncorks, and guzzles straight from the bottle, his body calming at once, responding to the warmth.

In the backyard, he is relieved to find his rabbit pens still there, quiet and undisturbed. He has kept them for more than a century. Rabbits are tranquil creatures, effortless to conceal. They reproduce fast (sometimes *too* fast). They are quiet, docile. They arouse no suspicions.

He drains one rabbit, then another, gazing over the rooftops of the neighboring houses that stretch for miles across this sprawling wasteland. His lot stands higher than most in the neighborhood. The roofs all have antennae: decades ago, the advent of digital television made them obsolete.

What is happening?

Depositing the rabbit carcasses in the incinerator, he crosses the lawn to the carriage house, past the swimming pool and waterfall, and through the night garden. The garden is his prized outdoor haven, encircled by a stone wall. It is landscaped with night-blooming plants: day blooms are of no use to him.

Last night, the garden was illuminated by remote-control

pathway lights and floodlights shined up into the trees.

Now the garden is dark and somber ... the Italian cypress and palm trees are considerably shorter.

Yesterday they were reaching for the skies.

Vauquelin rubs the back of his neck as he stands outside the carriage house doors. His missing car will be there: it has to be. He heaves the doors open, hinges creaking and groaning, doors dragging the gravel driveway. Inside is an altogether different black car: a 1955 Mercedes that he sold to an overseas collector for a tidy sum, give or take thirty years ago.

He never expected to lay eyes on it again, and yet there it sits, awaiting him. The chrome fender catches a gleam from the carriage house lamp, giving him a rush of butterflies.

No, no, NO.

He removes the phone from his pocket.

Still no service.

The butterflies explode into panic, eviscerating his nerves.

His brain floods with a hundred thoughts in a millisecond, a frantic attempt to pinpoint a reason for all this.

The internet must be down. This is all an illusion ... someone is fucking with me. Or maybe they're filming in the neighborhood, yes, that must be it ... that makes sense. But how in the hell did they find that car?

There is a rationale for this ... he just needs to identify it.

Maybe someone is filming a movie or a television show.

That makes sense.

Location scouts pester him all the time, begging and pleading to use his house. It is one of the few surviving Gothic mansions in Los Angeles — so desirable for film. He ignores every request.

The last thing he wants is disruption and scrutiny. But it has been months since anyone has contacted him.

He stomps out to the front yard, expecting to find film crew trucks lining the street.

The street is empty.

There are no trucks, no trailers.

No permits posted, no directional signs.

What. The. Fuck.

A block over from his house, he reaches the shops. As he walks, the cars on the road begin to regress. One by one, they become altered, transformed. They mutate into mostly 1950s models, many of them even older. The traffic is light on the surface streets, but whizzes by on the 110 Interstate bridge above his head.

The façades of the buildings fade and revert, revealing bygone signage. The convenience store, the tattoo parlor, the fried chicken restaurant — the seedy establishments that had sprung up around his house over the years — all of them have disappeared. Most of the remaining businesses are shuttered for the night: unheard of in modern-day Los Angeles, a city that never closes.

A woman gawks at him from a passing car window.

Vauquelin twists his long hair into his fists, eyes widening as he glances down to his attire. He must look as though he just stepped off a flying saucer from an androgynous goth planet.

And just like that the city stops changing, like a vehicle that flipped over and over and over again, landing on its tires and continuing to drive on as if an earth-shattering accident had not just occurred.

The air itself is sinister.

He turns on his heel and sprints back to his house, slamming the door and leaning against it. He can't breathe: he rips his shirt open, gasping for air, sending the buttons into a rattling scurry across the vestibule floor. He lived through this time once before. Why on earth would he expect to be back?

Ages ago he harmonized himself with the passage of time and reconciled with a life lived in solitude, but the past two decades were by far the easiest of his life. He could live as he pleased, unburdened by any need to conceal himself. Now time is going in reverse, and he is caught in the in-between.

It is a terrifying revelation, akin to waking up and finding oneself descending a greased pole.

"Fuck, fuck, fuck, fuck, FUCK!" he yells, sliding down the door. The muscles in his back clench as he bumps down and lands hard on the floor.

There is only one person he can talk to about this, to help him sort it out or make sense of it, or just listen. But he does not know if that person will even be alive in this chaos. He glances at his phone again.

Now it's just a useless little sphinx.

Nevertheless, he shoves it into his pocket.

He isn't ready to give up on it yet.

He retreats into his bedroom, his dark sanctuary. It is entirely unchanged. The room is painted a sooty charcoal, a shade just shy of black, the same as it has been since the turn of the twentieth century. It was a most unusual choice at that time. The walls are paneled in gilded *boiserie* moldings and mortises in the baroque style that was in fashion at his inception.

It has been two lifetimes since he swore off the coffin, preferring luxurious bedding, feather pillows, and his own design of midnight darkness. Instead, he sleeps in an elaborately carved antique canopy bed. He can draw the curtains tight and rest in manufactured nightfall.

His portrait, painted by Charles Le Brun in 1668, still hangs on the wall. Imagine a grand aristocratic bedchamber in Versailles designed in diabolic baroque splendor ... it is perfection. Yet here in this room, which has seen scant modification in over a century, he stands dismayed, not knowing what year this is, consumed by anxiety in his own shadowy shelter.

He cautiously opens the doors to his dressing room. It is filled-to-overflowing with apparel and shoes he discarded at least fifty years ago.

His brow furrows. He looks down once again to the clothing on his body, one of his only ties to the present — or his futurepast or futurepastpresent. He always looks weird, but with the reversal of time, he looks even weirder. His jacket is made from fabric that once lined a coffin, the one in which he slumbered during his journey to the New World.

How effortless it had been for him to assimilate in the future! No one gave him a second glance — he looked like any other artsy, pale hipster. Los Angeles welcomed misfits with open arms, even celebrated them. He was able to emerge from the shadows after centuries of self-exile. It has not always been this way, though. His physical appearance is off-putting, and there is little he can do to alter it: nor does he have the desire.

If he has learned anything in his interminable lifetime, it is that nonconformity is frowned upon. Humans are hard-wired to fear any anomaly, to be suspicious of any who dare to stray from the herd. That has never changed, and likely never will. The longer he lives, the more he realizes that humans evolve with leaden steps.

In L.A. he always has a number of Hollywood falsehoods to fall back on, to explain his oddities away. He is a virtuoso of deceit. He disguises himself as an actor, writer, or producer. It is a line people always greedily devour. Lies get lapped up like honey in a city of unfulfilled dreams.

Of all the cities he has traveled to, he loves Los Angeles the most — other than Paris, it has been his continuous home longer than any other city. The mild winters are a miracle for his cold bones. In futurepast L.A., it was at long last possible for him to be himself, to feel like a human being again for the first time in his interminable life, and now what? His fabricated normalcy is in danger, and fear snakes along the edges of his psyche.

A woman whispers his name.

His cocks his head and looks around the room — there is nothing. No one.

This is madness.

Perhaps he is losing his mind.

He trudges back downstairs and flops down on the sofa, scrutinizing the few yet mighty revisions in the room. This house has been his home since 1900 and has changed little, aside from the modern devices that are now missing. He loves his bittersweet refuge. Its walls and antiquated artifacts form the temple to his unorthodox history.

Fresh flowers, a necessary luxury, festoon every room. Dozens upon dozens are delivered without fail each Wednesday. Since he cannot enjoy them outside, in their proper daylit glory, he surrounds himself with them indoors, and in the night garden.

His most devoted hobby is ornamenting his domain with beauty, particularly beauty that is denied him by the presence of the sun.

Once upon a time, this house belonged to Maeve, his beloved human consort, and because he could not fully reveal himself to her, she slipped through his grasp to the other side.

She left the house and her inherited wealth to him, and he has lived here ever since.

The house was one of the most resplendent in L.A. at the time, and the third three-story house constructed on Pearl Street. Now it is known as Figueroa. The city was untamed and primitive then. It was not so long ago, in his memory, that Sunset Boulevard was merely a dirt road.

The metropolis sprung up around them overnight.

The house is a shrine to Maeve and the inestimable legacy she left him. She was an eccentric, a free spirit ahead of her time, and she loved him.

The two of them had contributed to the budding splendor of Los Angeles when it was still a fledgling city, cavorting among the new breed of wealth and the hangers-on who reached for glittering heights of L.A. society, such as it was at the cusp of the twentieth century.

They were legendary Angelenos for a time. But now, save himself, there is no one alive to remember them.

He misses her. Her death was the hefty price exacted upon him for his audacity at attempting the human experience, for allowing himself to become attached to her and suffer her loss.

It was a doomed passion. And so he continued his life without her ... he had no other choice.

It is proving impossible for him to relax. He returns to the dressing room, still baffled by the mid-century wardrobe in the closet. Across the room is a wide antique armoire, which he used to store his invaluable collection of bespoke antique clothing ... the collection he viewed, just last night, on exhibit in a museum.

He selects a wild black lurex pullover and an old pair of Levis. He bought the Levis new in 1901 for $1.50. In 1998 a vintage clothing dealer paid him $350 for them, so desirable with their genuine patina, buckle back, and redline selvedges.

Slipping his feet into a pair of black and red leather boots, he searches his memory for what his story had been in the middle of the twentieth century — there have been so many, though the basic facts always remain the same.

Keep your lies close to the truth, and you'll be a triumphant liar, he tells himself repeatedly over the years.

If this is indeed mid-twentieth-century Los Angeles, his place is with the beatniks, the bohemians. They accepted him and took his peculiarities in stride.

He pins up his dark, curly mass of exceptionally non-1950s hair, covers it with a stingy-brim straw hat, and heads for the carriage house.

It is now midnight. He eases the car down the long driveway and floors the gas pedal *(my god, how I missed this car)*, enjoying the sumptuous floating sensation of the classic Mercedes, appreciating the comfort of flying across the freeway in a red leather cocoon with the throaty reverberation of the engine vibrating up into the seat. His long fingers caress the slick, grooved steering wheel.

He loves this; it assuages, somewhat, the missing Pagani.

Hanging a left on Fairfax, he sees an empty spot in front of

Canter's Delicatessen, one of his favorite late-night haunts, and parks the car. Unlike the majority of survivor businesses in Los Angeles, it has seen few changes over the years. It is not the best choice if one wants to confirm that one's time period has indeed inexplicably shifted, but once he walks through the doors, it all begins to sink in.

The customers all look like they just stepped off the set of *Leave it to Beaver* for a quick bite. The waitresses move through the restaurant in dresses, white shoes, and stockings, lacy napkin name tags bobbing below their shoulders. Could he have wandered onto a city-wide movie set after all? Anything is possible in Hollywood, but he just wants some proof.

As he walks to a table, he grabs a discarded newspaper next to an empty plate.

The date is November 1, 1959.

He sits blinking at the year, rattling the treacherous paper with his trembling hands.

The waitress takes a subtle step backward as he orders coffee (black), keeping his lips tight. When she places it on the table, he grips the cup, absorbing its warmth. His thin, pale hands are even paler in the unforgiving diner lights.

Coming here was a bad idea.

The humans are staring at him, and this he does *not* like. Now he will be forced back into exile, and his gorge rises with long-suppressed emotions.

He glares out the window, his mind bereft of words or thoughts, and slams his fists on the table, disrupting the silverware and spilling his coffee as he grinds out "Why?" like rock salt between his teeth.

The coffee sits before him, cold and undrunk.

A waitress hears his uproar and doubles back. "More coffee? Ready for some food?"

"No, no, thank you," he murmurs.

Her intrusion has vexed him even further.

Vauquelin has gotten what he came for — an acid test of time. This is not the place for him: not anymore.

The restaurant occupants move about him at warp speed. Idle chit-chat, obnoxious laughter, and the clatter of silverware and plates intensify in volume until they become deafening.

He pays his ten-cent check with a twenty-dollar bill, and tells the wide-eyed waitress to keep the change.

Twenty minutes later, he arrives on a street far away from his own and knocks on the blood-red door of an old friend.

There is no answer.

Vauquelin has no idea what to expect. Perhaps she no longer exists ... perhaps the time-shift has obliterated his only remaining human connection and a stranger will open the door.

He knocks harder.

Footsteps grow louder behind the door followed by a husky, French, female voice: "Who is it?"

It is *her* voice. He closes his eyes and exhales, leaning his head against the door.

"C'est moi, c'est Vauquelin," he says.

Many locks clatter, the door flies open, and there stands Delphine: the queen of the Los Angeles beatniks, and, like Vauquelin, a Parisian expatriate. Her house, once splendid, is an absolute dump. The neighborhood was on the lower side of downhill, even in 1959.

"Get in here, you beast," she says, taking his elbow and leading him inside. She re-locks the door as he collapses on the sofa in a daze. The room is an artist's den — dark and cozy, with candles ablaze on all available surfaces. The candles provide a tranquil ambiance, but the truth is she probably just forgot to pay her electric bill.

Sitting in this familiar room with the living, breathing Delphine, who, twenty-four hours ago had been dead for forty-two years, gives him an immense measure of comfort. It took decades for her memory to fade for him. He loves her and he believes she loves him in return, which is miraculous.

Orphaned at the age of five and left in the care of a geriatric aunt, Vauquelin's attitude toward relationships in his human life was defined by loss. His mother died in childbirth, and his father was killed on the battlefield when Vauquelin was five. The death of his parents at such a young age had instilled in him a permanent sense of fragility and fear of making connections. If one loves, and especially if one is loved in return, that love will surely be taken away. Everyone he had ever allowed himself to love had vanished from his life.

Only once before had he been convinced that anyone could love him in his de facto incarnation: a veiled monster, undeserving of love when it is rooted in lies. For a vampire, love is most often won by deception. By the time he got to know Delphine, he was weary of telling lies, and so he revealed everything to her.

She is the only human who met him and survived beyond learning that he is vampire. He trusts her. And indeed, she had taken his secret to her grave. In his original past, he wanted to turn her. He had been begged time and again by humans, who instead received his obligatory death blow.

Delphine never once asked him for it and refused him when he offered. In fact, she laughed at him.

"Why would anyone want to live forever? The world will be

unbearable in a few more years," she said. "I can scarcely tolerate it now! And it will only get worse."

She enjoys hearing Vauquelin's fanciful stories — but are they just stories or the truth? A guarded spot of disbelief lingers in her soul. But she will gladly fuck him, anytime. Her feelings for him come as close to love as she will allow herself. She craves his presence. He is a bonafide addiction, even with his many eccentricities. He is so solitary, so reclusive and distrustful of people, and she covets the fact that he chose her and trusts her above all others.

It is a vanity — she has few, but this one is a constant.

"I haven't heard from you in almost three weeks. Where have you been? I've been sick with worry," she says, lighting two cigarettes, one for each of them.

He takes the cigarette and drags deeply. *Three weeks?*

"More like four decades," he mumbles.

"What did you say?"

He does not have the language to describe what has transpired … not yet. He looks at the floor.

"I went on a trip," he says. "I went to Paris."

"Liar. You would have told me if you were leaving the country. You never even leave this city, except to go out to the god-forsaken desert." She flicks an ash in his direction.

He squeezes her hand, thankful he does not have to continue the deception. "Delphine, something terrible has happened to me. I don't know how to begin telling you this."

Her Siamese cat, Henri, curls around his ankle.

Vauquelin's mind buzzes with erratic thoughts: how can he put them together, how can he make sense of everything?

For a moment he gets lost in the satisfying crackle of the Serge Gainsbourg LP spinning on her hi-fi.

"Oh, it can't be all that bad." She pours a glass of wine and shoves it into his hand. "Here. You look like you need this."

He gulps it down, and at last, he speaks.

"You said you haven't seen me in weeks. But less than twenty-four hours ago I was in the twenty-first century," he says, cutting his eyes toward her.

Delphine thinks for a moment, then tilts her head.

"But that's impossible."

"For me, it's been sixty years, not three weeks, and you've been dead for forty-two years. You should have let me turn you when I offered it."

He does not want to tell her about the night he found her dead of an overdose in his futurepast, while he continued living on and on, but she probably would not have minded given her dismal outlook on the future — her future, anyway.

"Your voice sounds different," she says.

Anxiety takes root in the pit of her stomach. Perhaps he is an impostor and not the true Vauquelin — someone is playing a trick on her. But no one else looks like him, or could mimic his strange mannerisms or the timbre of his voice with such precision.

She tries to disguise her trepidation, but her nerves tremble in rampant alarm. This is just another one of his elaborate fabrications, yes?

"My accent has weakened with time," Vauquelin replies, his expression falling. "You don't believe me?"

Delphine's face betrays her skepticism. Her foot shakes back and forth and she retreats deeper into her chair, gripping the armrests until the blood vanishes from her knuckles.

He remains silent, his brain tormented by thoughts of how to bring her around, to make her understand. Maybe even to make *himself* understand. He is desperate for some assurance, no matter how minuscule, that he is not going mad.

He pats the loveseat, beckoning her to sit next to him, and she reluctantly obeys, leaning into him. He nuzzles her cheek, clasping her waist.

The softness and chill of his skin reassure her that this is the one, true Vauquelin.

A flash of inspiration strikes him — he extracts his mobile phone from his pocket, pressing it into her hands. She stares at it, dumbfounded, holding it out from her body as if it might explode at any moment.

"Relax ... it's only a telephone," he explains, powering it on.

Her eyes widen as he uses his fingerprint to unlock the device. It is just like the clever little machines she has seen in science fiction movies.

"It can't make calls because there's no technology for this now. I can play music on it, send messages, order things I need from stores, read books ... " He trails off. How can he explain to someone, in 1959, that this is no ordinary telephone: it is a computer, a jukebox, a servant — a portal to all the information in the world?

There is little he can show her without service, so he opens his translation app and speaks into it: *"Dis à Delphine que tout c'est vrai et que je suis vraiment emmerdée."*

The phone speaks back: "Tell Delphine that it's all true and I'm really fucked up."

22

Delphine's jaw drops.

She has always taken everything Vauquelin told her with a grain of salt, with cautious yet guarded belief, but this is a mind-bender. And he is holding physical, visible proof of his wild adventure right in his hands.

Swiping on the screen he shows her photographs of the sleek black Pagani and its beguiling red interior, sitting in the driveway next to his house. It was hand-built in Italy to his exact specifications. There is no other car identical to it — and now it is gone, lost in the ether. It *looks* futuristic in the photos: enough, he hopes, to convince her.

"I received this car about a week ago ... that is, a week before this happened. Now it's missing."

"This is space-age! This is wonderful!" she exclaims, joy spreading across her face.

"No, it isn't. It's the polar opposite of wonderful. It's disorienting and frightening. Look. Watch this."

He takes a selfie and shows it to her. She claps with childlike glee. They pose for a few more pictures, mugging for the camera, and then he makes a video, moving the device around the room and zooming in on Henri.

She covers her mouth, laughing and shaking her head as she gazes at the phone. The fascinating little instrument has erased her turmoil and replaced it with delight.

Vauquelin relaxes at last. She believes him!

This is what he needed.

When he first got a mobile phone, he was enraptured by the possibility of a self-portrait. Mirrors repel his transcendental appearance, but the magic of a camera lens can capture his true likeness. Aside from the few photos he possesses, he has the portrait of himself that hangs in his bedroom, painted the year of his creation. He carried it with him from France.

It is a perfect semblance of him, and one of the few visual confirmations of his appearance.

Delphine cannot keep her hands off the revolutionary device. She swipes back and forth, as Vauquelin had demonstrated, until she opens an app by accident — music blasts forth from the small speakers, loud, harsh, industrial, and foreign to her ears. She panics and hurls the phone to Vauquelin.

The moment he catches it, it abruptly dies. The charger did not survive the time-shift. He frowns and crushes the phone into pieces with his hands, startling her even more.

"But why ... *why* did you destroy it?" she asks.

"It's dead. The battery is dead. There's no way to revive it. Like everything else that has been taken from me today, now it's just a worthless relic of a future that no longer exists."

"My poor darling, if what you say is true, you were without me for so long, and I without you."

"I missed you terribly," he says, pulling her into an embrace.

"Well, we're together now. I'll take care of you."

Vauquelin slips a hand under her top and kisses her neck.

She is wearing a fuzzy angora sweater, braless as always. The angora rises over her breasts, framing them, encasing them.

The sweetness of the sweater thrills him. He pulls it over her head, drawing it across his face. The material is feral and soft, a conflicted lushness that is altogether animal and cruel and erotic. He lifts his own shirt off, knocking his hat to the floor and spilling his hair across his shoulders.

Electricity surges through him, sending him into shivers when their skin comes together. It has been ages since anyone held him like this. He has been alone, and celibate, for decades.

He lifts her onto his hips as if she weighs nothing. He has a flash of Maeve, the only other human he ever allowed to get this close to him. The time-shift is bringing out the specters.

Delphine drags her fingertip down his lower lip and kisses him. She is a master at maneuvering around his teeth ... she knows every centimeter of his body. She adores him, this odd misfit soul. She makes no claims on him, though he wishes that she would.

She always knows what Vauquelin needs.

She needs him, too.

"What will you do now?" she asks.

"I have no idea," he says. "Everything is upside down."

They lie on the narrow divan she uses as a bed, smoking cigarettes under a coverlet. Delphine is obsessed with velvet — every textile in her house is soft, begging to be caressed. It is a tactile paradise, a sanctuary for the senses.

The room is filled with myriad fragrances that are at once repulsive and enticing: lusty sandalwood crossbred with turpentine fumes, sweaty sheets, Delphine's perfume, stale cigarette smoke ... heady cocktail ingredients with top notes of cat piss, spent joints, and old wax from candles that had been burned a few too many times.

They are complete opposites in this regard: Vauquelin is a slave to cleanliness and order.

Delphine is bohemian through and through, with the enigmatic charm that so many French women possess. She is bony and built like a boy. She survives on nicotine, marijuana, wine, and occasionally bread and cheese.

Vauquelin prefers fleshy bodies, the opposite of his own rail-thinness, but he had fallen for her spirit and her body is inconsequential. Her hair is dark like his, with just the beginning whisperings of gray, cropped into a pageboy.

She is at least forty, maybe older (it's anyone's guess, really: she refuses to reveal her actual age), and delights in having a strange younger man in her life, one who is devoted to her and viciously protective of her. For years, he was just another weirdo she had added to her collection.

He was drawn to her right away when they first met in his futurepast, at a downtown L.A. jazz bar in 1952. He sensed an otherworldly wisdom about her that few humans have.

When he first took her hand all those years ago, an energy passed between them that sealed his bond to her, and it was unbreakable until the day she departed the earth.

The passage of time goaded him into an irrational act: he began to trust her. His emotions took control and he unmasked himself, revealing his true identity. He broke an ancient vampire maxim in doing so, namely the act of self-revelation, but the enormous relief he gained from his honesty was worth the betrayal.

"Do you want to drink?" She drapes her arm across his chest.

He parts his lips — it has been at least thirty years since he last consumed human blood.

In his futurepast, the kill was risky in the extreme, with the police having so much technology and advanced forensics at their disposal. Modern humans were reckless and untrustworthy. Their blood was polluted with god-knows-what substances, and there were too many vegans in Los Angeles. Dull. Lifeless. The rabbits were a superior alternative to tainted human blood.

He hesitates, bringing her wrist up to his mouth in fits and starts, and with a deep breath drives his teeth into her skin. His eyes roll back in ecstasy when the metallic thrill of iron hits his throat, hot and sharp.

Delphine's blood is pure, crimson, meaty life.

The rabbits pale in comparison.

She arches her back. She loves the exquisite *douleur* of this, loves nurturing him. As he drinks, she gazes at the ceiling and, despite herself, surrenders into self-analysis. There is a persistent part of her soul that triggers disbelief in him. The allure of the vampire is undeniable. She is enchanted by the idea, but even the act of giving him her blood does not confirm it.

Vampires are fiction.

She is too pragmatic for such tales — she is a practicing nihilist. It might be true, or it might be a fantasy in which she is an absolute willing participant. But it could also be that he's just a sick bastard with malformed teeth and a fetish for drinking blood.

Tonight: the phone, the glimpses of the future ... all of it makes her believe in him more, and mollifies the rising terror in her gut. She runs her hand over her face, biting the inside of her cheek, absorbing the seductive pain of the bloodletting.

Since fantasy is becoming reality, she decides to let it flow. Vauquelin is a sensuous and intriguing man and the fact is she will never encounter anyone like him again, whether his stories are real or not. And at this moment the sensation of his teeth emerging from her flesh is very, very real.

Vauquelin licks her arm and ties it up with the sleeve of his discarded shirt, applying pressure to stop the bleeding. He never acquired the gift of healing that his maker had possessed, and he regrets it; she has little scars all over her body because of him.

"Better than any wine," he says, raising an eyebrow as he sneaks another Gitane from the package on the floor.

This is good, so good. The blood, the sex — two of his greatest pleasures in life — he had long relinquished them, buried them away, because it is imperative for his own sanity that he remain solitary.

He glances across the cluttered room to her easel, which holds an unfinished painting of him. She started it a few weeks before she last saw him.

He likes it. It is abstract. It suits him.

Delphine has captured an ironic depiction of Vauquelin: his face is fractured, his individual parts dismembered like a Picasso married to a Dalí. Surrealism could not be more appropriate for his current state of mind.

She flips onto her stomach, taking languid drags from her cigarette and tracing imaginary designs across his chest with a fingertip. She loves his dark hair, which is the absolute negative of his alabaster skin. His lips are full and luscious, better suited to a woman in her opinion, but so delightful to kiss. His slender body is absent of hair, his skin cold, like a sculpture: rigid, with a contradictory softness.

Pale, greenish rivulets of veinery map his body ... minuscule surface capillaries that one would not notice unless one was as close as she is now. His heart beats like any ordinary heart, but it is so subdued it might as well be missing. He is altogether ethereal, which eases her doubts — sometimes. Now.

He leans up and kisses her. She can taste her blood on his tongue, twinged with a hint of spent tobacco.

"Tell me what to do," he says.

"Go on living. What else?"

Vauquelin drives home, thrusting the engine to beat the emerging sun. He runs his unwashed fingers across his face over and over again, inhaling Delphine's musky fragrance.

As of tonight his twenty-first-century life is extinct.

He is further away from himself than ever before, and he is stuck in 1959.

The evening newspaper appears through his mail slot.

The date: November 2, 1959.

So Vauquelin is going forward again ... but for how long?

He is bored stiff.

Before the time-shift, he had settled into an impenetrable ennui bred from fatigue and the rotting predictability of his lifespan. That ennui has followed him back to 1959, minus a multitude of ways to assuage it. The entirety of the entertainment he had come to rely on is now uninvented technology. Cursed by his intense power of recall, he is perpetually fixated on experiences he can no longer have.

Vauquelin owns more than twelve thousand books, yet all of them have been read, many multiple times, and memorized.

His memory is eidetic — a gift of the vampire, along with an abundance of heightened senses. A vast library is his mind, volumes upon volumes of memories and exploits. A shame that he had never written them down ... but who would believe him?

He wanders up to his art studio in the turret of the house. Painting is something he has dabbled in on and off since

World War II. A sketch on canvas — a Belle Époque woman coming to life stroke by stroke — is perched on his easel. He completed this piece in oils during his original 1959.

He picks up a paintbrush and breaks it in half. Inspiration isn't forthcoming. He is a phantom, outside himself, as if he's living someone else's life.

It's too bloody quiet in the house, for one thing.

He walks out to the terrace to check on the rabbits. Some are sleeping, some peacefully nibbling their vegetables.

Roaming around the house, he ends up standing before his gargantuan antique armoire. No doubt the entirety of his donated garment collection will be inside, right where he had left it — exactly as it was before the museum curators cataloged each piece and took everything away in bins.

He takes a deep breath and opens the doors.

Shoes, weaponry, waistcoats, hats, breeches ... all are accounted for. It is a relief to have them back in his possession. He should never have given them up in the first place. It was a botched attempt to shake things up.

He begins to walk away but stops with one foot off the ground, listening to a strange, insistent beckoning emanating from the armoire. When he surrendered the wardrobe to the museum, there was no hesitation or melancholy. It was merely a collection of relics. Now, the garments whisper to him from behind the doors.

He reopens the armoire and rifles through its contents.

There is his beloved pink justaucorps. There are the blood stains. He eases his arms into the sleeves, and his body is at once seized by a paralyzing surge of menacing energy.

His mind explodes with music and laughter and flashes of faces in a dark room. Coffins occupy multiple crypts on all sides of him. And then a scream — his own, escaping from his lips as he is overcome by violence.

The horror of that fateful night washes over him, and he cannot get the coat off fast enough. The instant it leaves his body, the noises stop and the diabolical energy dissipates.

With trembling hands, he returns the coat to its hanger and clicks the lock on the doors. He backs away from the armoire, keeping it firmly in his gaze, and it falls silent once more.

Did the museum handlers feel that same surging malevolence? *Doubtful.*

When Vauquelin was created vampire it was the year 1668, and he was thirty years old. In his human era, he was born two days after the dauphin, the future king Louis XIV, and given his name. He has been thirty for over three centuries. It is a vexing age for perpetuity — he is too old for young people and too young for old people. In the twenty-first century, it was a good age. In 1959, it is an odd age for an eccentric bachelor.

He turns on his old TV, lamenting the pitiable picture quality and its lack of channels and on-demand films. A live quiz show is in progress. He glues his eyes to the small screen, shaking his head from time to time in profound disbelief.

This is fucking surreal.

The past is no place to live.

A longing for his now non-existent music collection overwhelms him. In his futurepast, he spent countless hours building a library of digital music, hundreds of thousands of songs and pieces available at a touch. He cultivated a newfound passion for French goth music. Now it is all unattainable, lost in time. He altered his modern life to embrace technology, and without it he is bereft.

Playing an actual record is yet another thing he has not done in at least thirty years, but he walks over to the hi-fi cabinet and puts on Gilles' *Requiem*. It's a fitting choice for his mood. The angry, foreboding percussion of the Introit's opening bars resolves itself into peaceful acceptance.

The act of setting the needle down on the record, and the resulting hiss of the old vinyl, is rather nice — even though the sound quality is inferior to his still-modernist ears.

Revisiting these activities of the past are equal parts amusing and depressing, but his longing for futurepast conveniences overwrites his transient joy.

He sits at the desk in his library. An antique inkwell and quill, circa 1650, stands ready in the corner. He received it as a gift when he was still a child, and writing with the quill is a habit he has never been able to shake. It is the most sincere method of composition, and no modern implement can provide such satisfaction. It is one of many reminders that his soul is an old one, despite his eternal youth.

Now is the moment Vauquelin has been dreading: he must appraise his finances. He had over five million dollars across his accounts before the time-shift — what would that amount be in 1959? He opens his bank book and drags a hand down his face. It is even more dismal than he had anticipated.

His long-term stability is dwindling.

If only he had the internet — he could click a button to calculate exactly how much destruction the time shift has wrought upon his wealth. He hates numbers and math: there's far too much infinity in his life as it is.

Over the centuries, he has been a philanthropist: he has given vast sums to causes and humans that interested him. He has always been fascinated by science and technology.

Despite his countless years, he never managed to cultivate the skills to do and invent himself, aside from dabbling: he throws cash around instead. But many worthy projects got off the ground because of his anonymous patronage, and the world will never know that certain conveniences and art and achievements they enjoy were partially funded by a vampire.

Having no occupation to speak of, he had grown his fortune by virtue of time and solid investments. Wealth is an ethereal concept to him: it has always been at his disposal. Now he is apprehensive about it for the first time in his long history.

Like many things in his life, perhaps he has squandered it, along with his time. It is astonishingly easy to do: time *and* money have a way of vanishing under one's nose.

But all of these heavy thoughts are sending him into blistering anxiety. He shoves the bank book back in the drawer, suffocated by the need to get numbers out of his head.

Accustomed to digital music, he neglects to turn off the record player. The needle thunks against the record label.

He takes a book outside and leaves it on a bench in his garden, strips off his clothes, and dives into the ice-cold pool. It does not affect him ... his bones are eternally chilled.

At the end of the pool is a tall stone wall encasing a sculpture of the Devil as a fallen angel. The moody setting is a replica of his reflecting pool at Rueil, Château de Renonçeau — a little piece of France in the middle of the City of Angels.

Floating on his back, he looks up at the handful of scattered stars puncturing the sky. Even in 1959, there is already severe light pollution in Los Angeles — it was much worse in his futurepast.

Before electricity, the world was righteously dark at night, blanketed by impenetrable silence. The night sky in ancient times was velvet black and thick with stars. Now it is hazy with the beginnings of smog and not black at all, but a muddy orange from the millions of street lights and parking lots.

He hears the constant hum of traffic, even in this peaceful little paradise. His tranquility was shattered in the late 1940s when construction for the 110 Interstate began, disemboweling his neighborhood, ruining his clear view of the downtown skyline, and bringing the monstrous freeway mere meters away from his front door.

There are few genuinely silent outdoor spaces in Los Angeles.

Emerging from the water, he walks around to the garden. He adores being naked in the moonlight. It is primal. He lies down on the cool grass lawn and reads until he can sense the sun is about to rise. His eyes drift from the book to the sky to the book and back again. He cannot clear his mind.

The reversal of time brings with it more frequent thoughts of Maeve. Thinking of her is an indulgence he has denied himself across the years. Both the thoughts themselves and their denial are pure self-punishment. He cannot bear the shadow of her preventable death hanging over him for all of his nights.

His memories of her must remain entombed. Day(night)

dreams are dysfunctional in his (un)reality.

The clock chimes five as he goes to his slumber, and his brain decides to punish him by adding up the number of days he has been alive (could he not just go to sleep like a normal person for once in his life? Only this once?).

Great. Just fucking great.

His immortality is not a subject that crosses his mind often, but the illogical events of late have caused it to bleed into the edges of his psyche. Life everlasting is fascinating in concept and crippling in reality.

Before the time-shift, he lived his life as any other nyctophile: he woke, bathed, dressed, went about his night, slept, and then did it all over again. Ad nauseam.

His daily amusements are inadequate at best. He strives (usually in vain) to liven things up for himself: buying outrageous clothes and objects, digging up obscure movies and books, seeking out art or anything slightly progressive and offbeat ... anything that might spark his curiosity and brighten his dark entries.

Unfortunately, humans have a penchant for repeating themselves, and, as all who are born human, so does he.

There is nothing new anymore.

He has witnessed the modern advancement (and subsequent cultural deterioration) of humankind. He has withstood the best of humanity, and indeed the worst.

Many people are convinced they want eternal life, but it is impossible for them to fully comprehend its consequences.

How romantic FOREVER sounds, until one realizes that day-to-day existence is violently mundane and monotonous — even more so for an immortal. Seconds and minutes and days accumulate like snow, burying one without warning. Eternity loses all meaning when life ceases to offer wonder and curiosity.

To a vampire, FOREVER is a frivolous word, an empty human concept. A world without end is beyond a mortal's endurance. "I'll love you forever" — or until someone better comes along, or you die, or I die of boredom.

Mistakes will inevitably be made, human mistakes or vampire mistakes (no matter, really), and someone will die because of them. The difference for him is that there is no end in sight, no promise of death or heaven or hell or even fucking oblivion.

Death will not come for Vauquelin.

Then there is the unromantic, violent side of vampirism, inconceivable to a human, or at least to a non-criminal human: finding a perfect kill, disposing of the corpse, cleaning up the aftermath, avoiding detection. It is messy and unglamorous at times, and nothing like the movies.

Vauquelin faced substantially greater challenges than in the old days, when science was primitive and religion and superstition ruled society.

Discarded bodies and missing persons are an insurmountable problem when detectives, forensics teams, and hidden security cameras are everywhere. He is a criminal by default, by his nature, incapable of reconciling the shadow version of himself.

Before the time-shift, his long life was taking a toll on him, although he loved modern conveniences at times, and certainly their technological benefits.

Respect for history was reduced to a trickle. Old buildings became irrelevant. He witnessed them being torn down or "remodeled" into vanilla oblivion on a daily basis in L.A., replaced with hideous, soulless structures. The systematic erasure of outmoded buildings, constructed during his early days in the city, crushed his spirit.

In his futurepast, the last of the Southern California orange groves had finally been removed, because L.A. had an unquenchable thirst for more strip malls and condominiums to complete the whitewashing that threatens to make it indistinguishable from any other American city. Stucco begets stucco: the scourge of modern-day architecture.

The iconic palms that made L.A. instantly recognizable were dying and/or being cut down all over the city, and they were not replaced. "Unsustainable!" barked the real estate developers. "We need shade, not palm trees."

Fickle Americans have so little regard for preservation.

They want only the latest shiny object, taking selfish, maniacal pleasure in destroying the features that draw them to a new city in the first place. Los Angeles had once held such promise for him: he believed it would be inventive and bold, creating new wonders upon the traditions of the past.

He could not have been more naïve.

Instead, it became a hotbed of bland uniformity, driven by purposeful chaos, vulgarity, and gluttony rather than preservation and beauty.

It was painful to stand by and watch it unfold.

As Los Angeles ballooned from a Wild West hamlet into the epicenter of filmmaking, culminating into its modern incarnation — a plastic city of insatiable greed and snuffed-out dreams — it dawned on him that he had made the perfect choice for his permanent home in the new world. Los Angeles was an illusion: seductive on its surface and sinister below.

The city was a beast: it swallowed people whole and spit out their bones. Its body count far outnumbered his own.

It was a reflection of his vampire life.

Now they were both empty.

And the way people dressed in his futurepast — *oh, holy hell, it was appalling!* He cringed at what he saw some people wearing out in public. The mode was vulgar, garish, and slovenly, resulting in a population of diffident, careless slobs.

His hatred for it is a side effect, he supposes, of living across centuries. He is traditional, old-fashioned, an antique being: the dimension of time, though it marches forward in the same manner it does for humans, is vastly different for him.

He carries within him the colossal, suffocating weight of his past remembrances, and as his experience of life ever grows and expands, his memory remains unscathed by the passage of time. His mind is active, but his spirit is detached; he is a voyeur to his own dream state.

The natural evolution of humans takes place slowly, generation by generation, making it easier to absorb the blows of change. For someone who has been alive for hundreds of years, the remembrance of how things USED TO BE is inescapable.

Vauquelin was born into nobility in an era when one's personal appearance defined every aspect of life. He grew into manhood surrounded by living, breathing works of art.

And in his futurepast, he saw people wearing house slippers and pajamas out on the streets. Stained, vulgar t-shirts, cheap disposable clothing ... it was mortifying. His memory of women dressed like frosted confections and unable to show their ankles without causing a scandal is as crisp as any childhood memory for the average human.

It makes adjustment complicated, and it is a vital characteristic that separates him and makes it difficult for him to relate to human society as a whole. Indeed, it facilitates his reclusion. Living in extreme isolation is more comfortable for him than facing the fiasco that is modern humanity.

With his slower process of adaptation, and the plethora of disappointments humans deliver up daily, nothing truly surprises him anymore. In any case, the time-shift has rippled his waters up enough to add some interest back to his day-to-day life.

For once things are less predictable.

Slumber does not come ... his mind is fitful.

He lies still, indulging himself with the rare luxury of reminiscing about the long, convoluted road that led him to a life in Los Angeles.

PARIS, FRANCE | 1900

Vauquelin took delivery of an elaborate customized coffin, carved in dark walnut and lined with red silk velvet over an eiderdown-filled center. The coffin was equipped with a lever mechanism, allowing him to lock it from the interior. The undertaker was curious as to why a coffin needed locks, but a satchel full of gold and a bit of enchantment put an end to his questions.

It was not foolproof, but neither was relocating his entire existence to the other side of a vast new land, of which he knew nothing — other than that it was wild and unfettered and just what he needed. Something new and youthful, far removed from the fetid history of Europe.

He had existed as a vampire for two hundred and sixty years, and France loosened her grip on him at last. It was time for a different landscape, to have another language in his ears.

Running his fingers over the fine wood, he marveled at the exceptional craftsmanship. It was exquisite: like himself.

He opened the hinged lid and caressed the red silk velvet. Inside was a plaque, painted with his favorite quote by Voltaire, in French:

The human species is the only one
which knows that it must die.

Vauquelin stretched out inside and drew the lid closed, engaging the internal lock. Its movements were smooth, and of utmost importance, silent. It would be impossible to open from the exterior, aside from prying it open with a crowbar, and he relied on human fear of the morbid not to attempt it.

The coffin would be his luxurious shelter for a long, self-imposed slumber, when he would cast his fate to the winds, relying on his plans going off without a hitch.

If he was discovered?

So be it.

He was prepared to accept whatever destiny awaited him on the other side of the sea. Either he would awaken in the American West, his plans vindicated, or he would meet his destruction. It mattered not.

Vauquelin unlocked the coffin and emerged, eager to embark upon his adventure and the vast changes it promised.

This was a new beginning for him, and he would transport only what he deemed essential. A great many large crates were already packed, awaiting the journey. His portrait, encased in excelsior and wood. A staggering quantity of extravagant clothing, much of it already quite antique. A generous selection of books, and a few crates of curios.

Jewels and gold were concealed in panels along the sides of the coffin, buried beneath the velvet.

Everything else he would leave behind. Perhaps he would return someday to reclaim it, but at that moment he could only afford to look forward, not back.

His latest attorney, a well-respected man named Antoine Duclos, would accompany Vauquelin's coffin and possessions on the voyage, conveying additional well-concealed currency and letters of credit.

The attorney was obedient and compliant: his discretion was rewarded with a substantial advance.

At daybreak, transport carriages arrived outside the house. A train would take them to Le Havre, where they would board a ship for New York City. The transatlantic voyage would take just over five days. With Vauquelin still in slumber, they would board a train for San Francisco, California, which would take four days, followed by another all-day train to Los Angeles.

Choosing a new city in a different country was no small undertaking. New York was his first thought, but he read that the city was overcrowded and cramped with people living on top of one another, crowned by dismal winters.

He wanted wide spaces, open views.

He settled on Los Angeles for the genial climate and the rugged beauty of its Pacific coastline, and he was intrigued by the possibility of living in a city at its genesis.

Having been alive so long, he had had quite enough of history. His only regret in making this journey was that he would be denied the views of America that cross-country train travel would have afforded a mortal, but there was no alternative.

SAN FRANCISCO, CALIFORNIA | 1900

Vauquelin was dead to the world. When he was in prolonged slumber his heart did not beat and he did not breathe, though his mind remained alert.

As he traveled over the sea and across North America, it would be impossible for him to know where he was at any given point in time, or what was being done with his body and his belongings. He placed his trust and destiny in the hands of humans.

Throughout the journey dozens of men had handled him in his coffin, removing their hats and holding them over their hearts in respect for the dead, unaware that they were transporting the *un*dead. Vauquelin could rely only upon their superstition and sentimentality. He was confident they would not disturb him, and thus far they had not.

Duclos exited the train station and stood on the platform, clutching a leather satchel containing Vauquelin's financial assets and explicit written instructions:

> *The remains of M. Louis-Augustin du Cavernay*
> *de Vauquelin and accompanying impedimenta are*
> *to be delivered to The Palace Hotel at 2 Montgomery*
> *Street, San Francisco, Calif., and will be received*
> *in the rear of the building at the designated dock.*
> *All crates shall be placed in secure hotel storage.*
> *The remaining trunks will be moved to a room*
> *registered in the name of M. Louis de Vauquelin,*

the nephew of the deceased. His lodgings must be kept completely dark, as said nephew has a severe disorder causing acute sensitivity to natural light (refer to the enclosed physician's documentation).

M. de Vauquelin will meet you in the hotel restaurant at approximately half-past seven o'clock the following evening to finalize all remaining details.

The physician's letter (forged) confirmed the medical necessity. Duclos ascended the hired carriage and began the journey to the hotel. It was late afternoon. After ensuring the delivery was made to his satisfaction, he checked in and ordered a sumptuous room-service supper, gourmandizing on his wealthy client's generous allowance.

At sundown, Vauquelin's eyes flew open. By his calculations, the correct number of days had passed. He inched open the coffin lid and surveyed the room. It was a storage facility, full of luggage and crates. The room was unlit, abandoned for the evening.

Good. He could plan. He would wait a few hours so that the hotel lobby might be less populated.

A cat meowed and hissed, startling him.

"Be quiet, little cat," he whispered, "... the rats are all yours."

It was unlikely that any back-of-house workers would be on duty; even so, he moved with measured stealth. He was weakened and starved, but he could not hazard any mishaps. After an extended period of slumber, his self-control was nonexistent, his hunger rapacious. If any human were to be present, his instincts would manifest and nothing could stop him.

He checked his pocket watch. It was time. He closed the coffin and locked it, smoothing his garments and his hair. Regardless of how still he had been these past few weeks, he was, in effect, a corpse. Due to his lack of blood sustenance, small capillaries had erupted across his skin in a slight, hive-like rise. He would have to do his best to avoid frightening people or eliciting questions.

Opening the door of the storage room a crack, he peered out into an empty hallway. He made it this far on pure luck and faith. Now he must depend on that faith, and his powers of charm, if necessary, to get himself safely into his room.

Vauquelin located an entrance marked MAIN LOBBY AND RECEPTION and approached the registration desk.

The hotel was opulent, and this time of night, the lobby was dim, illuminated by gaslights.

Perhaps he would not look so frightful.

The desk clerk was writing in a ledger.

Vauquelin pressed the bell, and the clerk looked up.

"Good evening, sir. How may I be of assistance?"

So far, so good.

Vauquelin's nails had grown long as he slumbered on the journey. Bitter alarm spread across his face as he noticed them. He plunged his hands into his pockets.

"I would like to check in, please. The name is Vauquelin."

"Of course, sir." The clerk held out the key.

Vauquelin made no move to take it.

The clerk overlooked this and placed the key on the desk.

"Welcome to San Francisco," he said. "You must be looking forward to refreshing yourself after your journey!"

You haven't the slightest idea, Vauquelin thought, conjuring an artificial smile as he signed his name in the ledger. He flashed a hand out and snatched the key. "I thank you. Good night."

Lingering awhile in the lobby, he admired the luxurious surroundings. He took a cage elevator up to the third floor and unlocked the door to his room. It faced west, and a second set of curtains had been mounted over the windows. His portmanteau awaited him. His demands and expectations had been met, so far, to perfection.

The first order of business was to trim his nails. They disgusted him. He bathed, changed his clothes, and went out into the night. He was revived, but not restored, and he moved like an old man. It was time to assuage his ravenous hunger and explore this novel world in which he had awakened.

The streets were sparse of people, and the fog from the bay crept in amongst the buildings.

It was delightfully macabre.

As he walked, his silk top hat catching occasional glimmers from the street lamps, the lone sounds were of his footsteps and his staff striking the ground.

So this is California.

He had expected to see forty-niners and saloon girls, but instead was surrounded by elaborate architecture, a few scattered pedestrians, and the occasional horse-drawn carriage.

It reminded him of Europe, and was far from being the Wild West. What a bitter disappointment!

His prospects for the night were looking slim, and he was

growing weaker. He found himself at the entrance to a tavern and went inside, seating himself at the only unoccupied table.

A barman appeared to take his order.

"A bottle of dry red wine, please."

Aside from blood and water, wine was the only liquid his sensitive body could swallow.

He swirled the sanguine liquid, watching legs form on the inside of the glass, and taking slow sips as he studied the bar patrons. They were an intellectual, well-to-do lot ... not a single cowboy in sight. He rolled a cigarette and as he licked the endpaper, a natty young man appeared at his table.

"Good evening," the man said. "May I sit? There are no other tables available, I'm afraid."

He was English or some such; Vauquelin had never had an ear for British accents. He looked the man up and down, motioning to a chair as he lit his cigarette.

The man dragged the chair back, scraping it across the floor with an ear-splitting screech, and said, "It certainly is a quiet night to be alone."

Bile rocketed up Vauquelin's throat. He was seldom inclined toward idle chit-chat, but he was incapable of being impolite.

"Indeed. Louis de Vauquelin," he replied, offering forth his slender hand.

The man took it and recoiled at its frigidity.

"I've been walking, I've only just sat down," Vauquelin said, his shoulders stiffening. "This city is quite cold."

"Sinclair Jarvis. It is my pleasure to make your acquaintance. You must be a visitor, then."

"No, an immigrant. I've just arrived by train. I leave tomorrow to make my permanent residence in Los Angeles."

Vauquelin's accent was thick, but his English was impeccable. There had been plenty of time for him to learn it, of course.

"Los Angeles? Good lord! There's nothing there, save dirt roads and orange groves. You strike me as the type of man who would be much better suited to San Francisco or New York, especially being European. Why on earth Los Angeles?"

"I am an undertaker by trade. Los Angeles is a burgeoning city, *n'est-ce pas?* It seems an ideal location to establish oneself in such an evergreen business."

"An undertaker! I daresay you might rather have a shot, then."

They sat in silence, drinking and smoking, looking around the bar. He thought it odd that this random young gentleman would approach him, merely pursuing conversation, until the man brushed his fingers along his thigh.

Ah, there it is, Vauquelin thought.

He dropped some coins on the table, donned his hat, and exited the tavern, beginning the trek back to the hotel. He knew the man would follow, and sure enough, rapid footsteps rang out close behind.

Vauquelin sped his pace, and at last, Jarvis caught up.

"I know who you are," Jarvis said, his voice a wheezing whisper.

"I sincerely doubt that, monsieur." Vauquelin stopped and looked down at him. He stood a good head and a half over the man. He resumed his brisk step, anxious to get back to the hotel and be rid of his new disciple: one way or another.

The long-winded Jarvis chattered throughout the short journey.

"Yes, sir, you are quite extraordinary, you are. When I saw you walk into the tavern, I said to myself, now there's a right elegant gentleman. It's quite obvious you're not American. You have the look of the elegant European written all over you. I must say, since arriving in San Francisco myself a mere three months ago, my observation is that this fair city is populated by charlatans and get-rich-quick types, but you, sir, I knew you were the genuine article, a true Old World gentleman, the instant you entered the door of that tavern. I continued studying you, so upright and so splendidly solitary. And then, realization overtook me. You are vastly alone, more alone than humanly possible. I thought, it cannot be. It simply cannot *be!* Loneliness is etched into your soul. And there is a purpose to our encounter tonight. That has become quite clear to me now."

Vauquelin came to a stop at the revolving doors of The Palace.

"Will you take me to your room?" Jarvis asked. He was hunched over, wheezing, with his hands on his knees.

"Now tell me," Vauquelin said, looking down his nose, "why the devil would I do that?"

Jarvis grasped Vauquelin's gloved hand, his eyes brimming over with anticipated dejection.

Throughout his existence, Vauquelin had been a sexually fluid being. His life was far too long to taste only one flavor. Although his predilection was for women, he was above all an admirer of beauty in all its incarnations. Jarvis was not an attractive man, but blood was blood. Vauquelin correctly surmised that he was about to have to sing for his supper.

"I see," said Vauquelin, prying the man's fingers off his own. "Wait in the lobby and come to Room 315 in ten minutes."

By the clock, a soft knock rapped on the door. Vauquelin was sitting in a chair, smoking another cigarette. "Enter," he said.

Jarvis locked the door behind him. He sank at Vauquelin's feet, placing his hands on his knees.

"I know who you are," he repeated. "I know *what* you are."

Vauquelin's eyebrow shot up. At this point, he was unsure whether Jarvis had pegged him as a vampire or a homosexual. He may have been obliged to put on an act, but he did not intend to make it easy.

Whatever his motivation, Jarvis signed his own death warrant by inviting himself into a vampire's domain.

Vauquelin removed a bit of tobacco from his tongue with his fingertips. "Please, enlighten me," he said, his voice cold as ice.

"You're a dark creature, a creature of the night. When you shook my hand, I knew." Jarvis trailed a finger down Vauquelin's cheek. "Your eyes! They are the most exquisite shade of blue, like melting ice — the unmistakable gaze of the undead."

He seized Jarvis's wrist and pushed his arm into his chest.

"If what you say is true, you should be terrified of me, no?" Vauquelin said, releasing him as he fell back into his chair. He had been in this predicament a thousand times. Looking to the ceiling, he wagged his fingers and said, "Go on...I await your inevitable request with bated breath."

"I want it. Make me as you are! I beg you! I am gravely ill, sir. Soon, I will be dead. I do not wish to die ... I wish to live forever. Please! You must do it!"

Vauquelin burst out laughing, and his laughter culminated in a vicious smirk.

The man rose, brushing Vauquelin's ear with his lips, and whispered, "Give me your unholy embrace."

In a flash, Vauquelin had the man bent forward on the bed.

"It never ceases to amaze me how easily humans ask for this, as if it is so freely given. Who are you to demand eternal life from me? I do not give life — I take."

"You do not have to take," Jarvis stammered. "I offer myself to you willingly."

Vauquelin pushed the man's face further into the bed and leaned over him. "Be silent," he growled.

Jarvis gave the slightest, struggling nod.

Vauquelin's strength was vanishing at an alarming rate, rendering him enfeebled. He relied on his body weight to hold Jarvis down as he locked his teeth into his neck. It was all he could manage, but he invigorated swallow by swallow.

When Jarvis unclenched Vauquelin withdrew, spilling blood on the bedspread. In normal circumstances, he would have been tidier.

He disliked wasting the merest drop.

Robust once more, he wrapped the body in the quilt and crept out the window, taking the fire escape up the side of the building. He deposited the body on the roof and lunged onto the landing to his room.

After ensuring the doubled curtains were pulled tight and overlapped, he rolled another cigarette and read until it came time for his mandated dormancy, as if nothing had happened.

A clock pierced the silence a moment after he laid his head on the pillow, growing louder and louder with each menacing tick.

He leapt up and smashed it with his fist.

Ticking clocks were high atop the list of his most-hated objects … they were a cruel narrative of the infinite number of seconds that lay ahead of him. He pitched the battered clock out the window, drew the curtains, and went to his rest.

The next evening, Vauquelin met his attorney half-past seven as promised. It was the first time they laid eyes upon each other.

They spoke only in French.

"*Bonsoir*, Monsieur de Vauquelin. I am Antoine Duclos. Allow me to extend my condolences for the loss of your dear uncle. I understand you were close."

"I thank you. Yes, quite close. He raised me. I bring him to California because this is my new home, and I could not bear to have him so far from me, nor to lay his body in a country that despised him. I should like to visit his grave on occasion, you see, and I shall not be returning to France. Your stewardship in this venture is most humbly appreciated."

Lies, all lies.

How weary he was of lying.

"It is my honor to ensure his safe delivery to you, Monsieur."

The attorney handed him a leather satchel filled with gold and jewels. He had more than passed the arduous tests presented to him thus far.

Vauquelin extracted a small gold bar from the bag and slid it across the table with his fingertip.

"*Alors*, Monsieur Duclos. I have a business proposition for you. Would you consider staying on in America in my employ? I will provide for your lodging, and of course a generous salary. I have very specific needs that must be tended, and being a newcomer to this country, I naturally trust few people. I would prefer to work with a fellow countryman. But I will be relocating to Los Angeles, which is a developing city and not quite as sophisticated as Paris ... or even San Francisco for that matter."

Duclos was nonplussed. He had not anticipated this turn of events. "Monsieur, this is most unexpected."

"Must you return to France straightaway? Have you a family?"

"No, I have not," Duclos said. "I am rather married to my profession, one might say."

"Superb. I will give you until tomorrow evening to consider my proposal. Until then, I bid you adieu."

Vauquelin signed the check, took the satchel, and vacated the dining room, leaving the attorney to finish his meal alone.

Duclos was early for his appointment with his mysterious client the following evening.

"Monsieur de Vauquelin," he said, "it is with great pleasure that I accept your generous offer."

"I am most honored." Vauquelin bowed. He was relieved that the transaction was completed without enchantment. "You needn't concern yourself with the burial of my uncle ... arrangements have already been made."

Duclos got to work straightaway. First, he secured lodgings in Los Angeles for himself and Vauquelin. He would again accompany the coffin of his new client's "dear uncle," this time to its final destination.

Vauquelin gave the diminutive attorney five hundred American dollars to complete the journey.

"As you know from my letters, I have a severe sensitivity to light. All my business is conducted during the evening hours.

I will need you to be free to consult with me at night. During the day, your time is yours to do as you please, as long as my needs are addressed. Is this agreeable to you?"

"Without a doubt, Monsieur. I am grateful, and I look forward to a long partnership."

They shook hands. Duclos did not react to his new client's chilled skin: he merely took Vauquelin's right hand in both his own with the enthusiastic respect any man would give to another. Another plus. Or else he was a damned fine actor: an excellent quality in an attorney.

And so Vauquelin forged one of the few human relationships he would have in this new world. Duclos would remain devoted to him until his natural death in 1926 at the age of seventy-four, and Vauquelin would mourn him.

Duclos never learned that his generous, eccentric client was vampire. Vauquelin fought with might and main to protect him from this knowledge.

It was in both of their interests to keep it that way.

As for Vauquelin never appearing to age, that was another issue. Vauquelin saw him less and less as the years passed, conducting most of their business via telegram or over the telephone, and the one time it came up Vauquelin dismissed it as a combination of his zealous vanity and exceptional ancestry.

At the exact moment Vauquelin's coffin and possessions were being loaded on the train at the station, police officers swarmed the rooftop of The Palace, responding to the discovery of a body.

IN WHICH WE MEET MAEVE
(AN EXTRAORDINARY WOMAN)

LOS ANGELES, CALIFORNIA | 1900

Vauquelin saw her for the first time at the theatre.

He had been living in Los Angeles for just over two weeks. He sensed he was being watched, and indeed, he was: a woman stood alone, sipping champagne in the lobby during intermission, and she held him in her unwavering gaze.

She was tall, taller than most of the men in the room. Dazzling shades of emerald and peacock swathed over her curves, multiple strands of pearls bound her neck. Her hair was a mass of flaming red twists and turns, piled high on her head, and her eyes black as a starless night.

He was thoroughly entranced. Redheads were uncommon in France, and in fact, taboo. He was raised to believe that women with red hair were the spawn of the Devil, conceived from coupling during menses: they were bad luck and evil.

Naturally, this was attractive to Vauquelin.

They each stood out in the crowd.

She was transcendent. He was bizarre. It was inevitable that they should be drawn to one another.

Vauquelin looked quite anachronistic, so statuesque and alluring with his long hair cascading below his collar when other men wore close-cropped hairstyles. His face was clean-shaven, absent of any mustache or mutton side whiskers that were so popular.

He met her eyes and she thrust her chin in the air, looking at him out of the corner of her eyes.

Perhaps she was a loner like him. He could not stop himself, and he began to approach her. Her cheeks flushed crimson, despite her attempts to remain aloof.

This woman was not beautiful: she was harsh, striking and unusual, which Vauquelin found more alluring than any ordinary beauty. The typical held no appeal for him. He preferred the exotic, the ferociously uncommon, with details he could drink in and unmask.

It was the same for her. There stood a man who she thought lived only in her reveries. His appearance disoriented her, deep into her bones, and her fingers began to twitch, longing to touch something unknown.

She regained her composure upon seeing that he was an actual living, breathing man, albeit a magnificent one.

Her air was intimidating; still, as an unescorted woman, she was often accosted by men — she had become an expert at subduing them. But something about this particular man softened her, and she could not fathom the reason.

"Good evening," he said, bowing and kissing her hand. "I am Louis-Augustin du Cavernay de Vauquelin."

"A Frenchman! How exciting! *Enchantée*, monsieur. My name is Maeve Sullivan."

"And are you enjoying the performance, Madame Sullivan?"

It was a terrible show, a burlesque comedy with some lukewarm East Coast touring act.

She smiled and crinkled her nose. "Well ... no. But I suppose it is the best we can hope for in terms of culture in this city. I surely hope that our artistic offerings continue to grow, and I do my own small part to support them. Are you a tourist?"

"No, Madame," he said. "I have immigrated from Paris."

"Paris! Oh, how I adore France! I was not born in Los Angeles, but I am a permanent resident now. I have built a wonderful house that I am in love with, and I plan to live out my days here."

The chimes sounded for the patrons to return to the auditorium for the second act.

"May I invite you to join me in my box seats, Monsieur de Vauquelin?" she asked.

Maeve was elegant, brash, forward, and refined, all rolled into one. This combination sent Vauquelin's blood into rhapsody.

"Nothing could delight me more," he said, taking her hand and placing it in the crook of his arm.

After the burlesque, they stood for a few moments on the steps outside the hall gossiping about the departing patrons: a shallow attempt at delaying their separation from one another. Upon learning he did not have transportation of his own, she insisted on dropping him home in her carriage, and he accepted.

This lady had an elegant coach and a driver she called by name. She was Somebody, and therefore could not be his victim for the evening.

Nevertheless, he was enjoying her, and he had fed on a railroad worker the previous night. She was in no danger.

When the carriage stopped, she invited him to dinner at her house the next evening, which he also accepted.

"Charles will pick you up at eight o'clock. *Bonsoir!*"

Vauquelin tipped his hat to her and the carriage drove on.

He walked up the steps to his spartan, one-room cottage. It was in a busy area and far from ideal, but it had been arranged in haste and it would have to do for the time being.

Vauquelin dressed in a black waistcoat, a deep blue velvet vest, and some outrageous trousers he had recently purchased. They were white, covered in tiny black houndstooth. His shoes were brilliantly shined. He clipped a gardenia from the bouquet that Duclos had purchased for him that afternoon and tucked it into his buttonhole.

At eight o'clock on the nose the driver, Charles, arrived at the corner where Vauquelin stood waiting. He navigated the coach across the uneven dirt roads with skill, at last pulling into the elongated drive of a Romanesque manor house. The entire neighborhood radiated affluence. It was far more elegant than the roughshod regions of the city that he had toured so far, especially when compared to his humble street.

Charles opened the carriage door and unhinged the retractable steps for Vauquelin. A uniformed maid opened the door, welcoming him inside.

He stalled a moment at the threshold, clenching his jaw and

twirling the bouquet of flowers. Now that he had arrived, he was baffled by his curious, giddy behavior. What on earth was he doing, exactly? Was he *courting* this woman? Throughout his life, he had been accustomed to seeking comfort in the arms of strangers: strangers that invariably became his victims. For him, there existed no purpose for companionship other than for sustenance.

Before his creation as a vampire he successfully staved off marriage, preferring the unbridled bachelor life. As the sole surviving heir, there was no one alive to pressure him to live in any other manner than how he pleased. He had never entertained the idea of an actual relationship, let alone one with a *human*.

It would be impossible.

He had alighted upon Maeve's elegant little web without even noticing. And now he stood in her foyer, unsure of his motives.

She burst forth from a doorway in a cerulean and black silk gown. Around her neck was a choker of sapphires and diamonds. The combination of colors in the ensemble set her red hair aflame. She was completely *outrée* and he found her irresistible.

"*Mon cher* Monsieur de Vauquelin! I'm beyond thrilled to have the pleasure of your company tonight!"

It was a rare occasion for Vauquelin to be greeted with such enthusiasm by a human, and a bemused laugh escaped his lips.

She took the gardenias into her arms and buried her face in the petals. "Divine, absolutely divine." She handed them to the waiting maid, who disappeared with them. Taking Vauquelin's elbow she guided him into her library, ringing a small bell as they sat.

A butler entered with a silver tray, presenting a bottle of golden liqueur and two cut crystal glasses.

Maeve said, "I figured you for a cognac man. Did I guess

correctly, monsieur?"

"I am not inclined towards spirits, Madame, but I will accept a glass of red wine if it is not an inconvenience."

Maeve nodded at the butler, who bowed slightly and departed.

"I like a man who knows what he wants," she said. She drained her cognac in one dainty gulp — and poured herself another. Her shyness from the theatre had evaporated. Here, in her own home, she was fully herself and confident.

Vauquelin sat on her elegant sofa, his long legs crossed like a woman as always, she across from him in a silk armchair. They sat merely looking at one another and the electricity between them was palpable.

Despite the silence, Vauquelin was relaxed and at peace there with her, as if he had at last found a place to attach his long-sequestered heart. Had he chosen to read her mind, he would know that Maeve was experiencing the identical unfamiliar sensation: it frightened and delighted each of them in unison.

Comfort in silence with another being is a rare thing indeed.

The butler returned with the wine, poured a glass for Vauquelin, and closed the library doors behind him.

Vauquelin struggled to find his English, surprising himself with his lack of confidence. Mere speech was inadequate; complimenting her would have to suffice. In truth, he was unpracticed in seducing women, let alone conversing with them in a foreign tongue, but he was fluent in the language of beauty.

"Your dress is exquisite, Madame. What refined taste you have!"

"Oh, thank you! I had it made it in Paris last year, at the House of Worth. It's my favorite souvenir of my voyage!"

At her utterance of Paris, his heart quickened. The dress was of the latest fashion: she had been in Paris, then, at the same time as he. How odd ... what if their paths had crossed there? They would not be sitting here in her house at this moment. He would likely have killed her, and not given her a second thought.

What a strange new world.

The awkwardness between them began to fall away as the libations flowed. They discussed the art hanging in her library. Their conversation became natural, even excited.

Maeve asked him endless questions about France and he obliged her with a few choice tales, adhering to recent history and his titular lineage, editing the timeline ever-so-slightly.

The butler returned and announced dinner.

As they walked to the dining room, he prepared an excuse for why he would not be eating tonight.

A maid began serving the meal, beginning with the mistress of the house, and Vauquelin held up a hand as she approached his plate. He explained that he was following a special diet mandated by his physician in France to help him adjust to the differences in American food — he had eaten before his visit.

His excuse did not fluster Maeve in the least, nor did it hinder her from devouring her supper. She ate with orgasmic, mannered decadence. He finished an entire carafe of wine.

It occurred to him that, in the many years since his creation as vampire, he had not once observed a human eat a meal. He sunk his jaw into his hand and watched her with envy. In his brief human state he was a notorious gormandizer, and Maeve was clearly in the midst of a love affair with food as he once had been.

The lavish meal ignited his bittersweet memories.

After dinner they retired to the parlor for coffee, which

Vauquelin would not take, and the butler offered him a cigar. He had smoked many a small cigar in France, but nothing like this unwieldy American torpedo.

"This is an odd — and monstrous — cigar," he marveled, turning it round and round in his fingers.

"Oh! That is a Punch," she said. "I import them from Cuba."

The butler clipped and lit it for him.

"You mustn't inhale the smoke, though! Just puff and taste!"

Maeve fired up a cigar for herself.

Vauquelin brought his fingers to his lips: he had never seen a woman of quality smoke.

She kicked her shoes across the room and put her feet up on an ottoman. He was discovering that Maeve did what she liked and was quite unapologetic about it.

Vauquelin puffed away. The smoke singed his taste buds. He liked it. It was strong: malodorous and delicious and thick and heavy.

He listened as Maeve explained that her father had invested his entire small savings in American steel, moving the family from Galway to Pittsburgh, and prospered from his ventures. She was an only child, an heiress. Her mother died when she was three. She was married at nineteen, to an equally wealthy American steel man, and widowed at twenty-three. Now, she was the same age as he: thirty. She had decided to remain a widow.

"I treasure my freedom," she said, exhaling a blue cloud of smoke. "No one can order me around or make my decisions for me," she said. "Few women have that luxury."

"Indeed ... once one has tasted freedom, it becomes impossible to surrender it, no?" Vauquelin replied.

Liberty was a conviction he esteemed above all else.

Human men of this era would scoff at a woman wanting her independence, but Vauquelin was in a unique position to appreciate this.

He had been threatened by tyranny at multiple stages of his life, and he would never begrudge any individual, man or woman, wanting to protect and preserve an unfettered existence.

He could not give her specifics without betraying his implausibly long history, so he said, "My own freedom has been threatened many times. Suffice it to say I have a deep appreciation for the value and fragility of liberty."

He carried the cigar and ashtray to her piano and began playing Liszt, which delighted her.

The hour was growing late, and he did not want to overstay his welcome. When the cigar was near its end he said, "I would be most delighted to see the remainder of your magnificent home before I depart, Madame Sullivan."

"Please, call me Maeve. And shall I call you Louis?"

"Maeve, I prefer to be called Vauquelin," he said, standing and offering his elbow.

She thrilled at the sound of her name on his lips: "Mev." Her name had never once sounded exotic. It was a rusty old Irish name. But hearing it pronounced this way, and not its harsh normal pronunciation, *Mayve*, opened a window in her soul.

She escorted him throughout the house, drawing his attention to her favorite objects and architectural details along the way, and up to the grand turret.

It afforded a magnificent moonlit view of the mountains and orange groves stretched across the landscape in the distance, as far as the eye could see.

"Isn't it splendid?" she whispered. "I much prefer Los Angeles over Pittsburgh. Are you very familiar with the United States, Vauquelin?"

"In truth, I know very little of it outside of my recent train journey," he replied.

It was an alteration of fact: while he had indeed traveled across the country, he was trapped in a box in the cargo car. He saw neither the port of New York City nor the train stations in San Francisco and Los Angeles. He saw nothing in between.

"Pittsburgh is in Pennsylvania, in the Northeast. So much snow and ice. The damp winters there were destroying my health. I read about the California winters being perfection, ideal for those with frailer sensibilities. I sold my properties in Pittsburgh and moved my entire life here, and I cannot ever imagine regretting it."

Los Angeles was his country now, and all he knew of America. Southern California was a wild paradise and he was enamored with it. That night amplified his conviction.

The tour ended in her bedroom. Her bed was enormous; it was an early Georgian heirloom brought over from Ireland.

Vauquelin was dismayed. This was a turning point in the evening, and he found himself in a quandary.

He wanted her, but he could not have her … not in the manner he was accustomed to having women. He was besotted by her manner and intelligence, and seldom had rapport with a human been so facile for him. His soul hungered for a different flavor, one that was not so easily quenched.

For him, sexual union was merely the means to an end — the glorious satisfaction of his body, followed by the taking of the blood that kept him animated. Seduction that did not end in bloodletting was not his forté; he was quite feral.

He loved sex. It was his sole physical connection to his humanity, but it was also a loathsome reminder that he was denied the finish, one of his most vital functions as a human man.

Maeve sat on the bed and held out her hand.

Vauquelin was unacquainted with females being so direct and bypassing formalities, and this further complicated his feelings. Perhaps it was a trait unique to American women. Yet he was unsurprised by her candor: it was completely in character, based on his knowledge of her thus far.

Even so, he was hesitant. "*Ma chère* Maeve, you have not yet inquired as to my marital state."

"Oh, goodness," she chirped in a falsetto voice. "You aren't a married man, are you, Vauquelin?"

Mon dieu, she could rival the stage actresses! Her humor annihilated his reticence, and he could not help laughing.

"Indeed, I am not."

"Well, then," she said, unclasping her necklace.

He pulled her up from the bed and turned her around, fumbling with the back of her dress.

Again, he hesitated.

She reached behind her back and loosened the dress herself, letting it fall. The taffeta made audible crinkles as it dropped to the floor. Her skin was pale and soft as velvet. Its delicacy thrilled him.

She was fleshy and round, his favorite. He caressed her, brushing her lips with his own, ensuring she would not feel his teeth and become alarmed.

Maeve untied his cravat, running her fingers underneath his collar, and she gasped. "You have caught a chill," she whispered.

It was the height of summer.

The room was warm ... the windows were closed.

He ignored her remark.

Her flesh was the opposite of his: so radiant, so inviting. He had to control himself, but there was only so much he could do. Because he could not take her life and must keep his cruelty at bay, he was obliged to let loose his lust and let that be his only satisfaction.

This was a critical juncture in his relations with Maeve. She would either reject him, or she would become completely enamored: there was no middle ground in his experience.

But she, unlike her precedents, would not die that night.

Vauquelin was still fully clothed. He threw open the bedcovers and picked her up, tossing her on her back. She squealed in surprise. He undressed in front of her as if he had all the time in the world (after all, didn't he?).

He untied his neck stock and removed it with a snap, giving her a sharp jolt.

She drew her knees up, scrutinizing his every move.

He dropped his jacket, unbuttoned his shirt, disengaged his suspenders. He slipped out of his shoes, sliding each silken sock off with one toe, and let his trousers slide to the floor.

He kicked his clothes aside and moved toward her with panther-like grace, pushing her back on the bed, opening her legs with his shoulders.

As he teased her she grasped his backside, trying to pull him up. He drew his shoulders back and touched a fingertip to her breastbone, murmuring, "Not yet." He wanted to savor and prolong this serendipitous pleasure.

She thrust out a petulant pink lip, but still he would not budge. He ran his hands over her body and sunk his face between her legs, inhaling her scent.

She took fistfuls of his hair, running her fingers through it, and pulled his head in harder. He curled his tongue up the junction of her thighs and closed his eyes.

"My god, you taste like sunlight," he said.

She grasped his shoulder and went still as a statue.

No man had ever spoken to her with such poetry.

"Please, let me touch you," she breathed.

He relented and heaved his body up, lying to her side. He guided her hand to his cock and she caressed it.

"How can this be so warm when the rest of your body is still so cold?" she whispered. "I want you inside me."

Her body quivered beneath him as he entered, and she moved her hips in unison with his slow, slow tempo that escalated into brutal thrusts.

A scream blossomed in her throat and he clamped his hand over her mouth. That moment was torture for him ... traditionally, that was when he would go in for his kill.

Maeve would never know how much self-control he was exerting. When her body relaxed from her climax, he slowed his hips and delayed his withdrawal, yearning to prolong their joining.

He maneuvered onto his stomach and buried his face in his

hands, and as his heart hammered in his chest, he prayed that he would not break into a blood sweat.

Their lovemaking was exquisite, unmatched in his lifetime. Long-dormant currents of eloquent rapture had awakened in his soul ... he received almost as much pleasure as he would from taking her blood.

Almost.

Maeve was wide-eyed on her back, panting, her skin shining with perspiration. She was quiet for a while.

They both appreciated the silence.

Before long she rolled onto her side and said, "You didn't reach completion. You were left unsatisfied," she said, thrusting out her bottom lip. She reached for his cock, beckoning.

He grasped her wrist with two fingers and moved her arm onto her hip. "Maeve, it is just the way of my body. I cannot ejaculate. It will never happen. This is no fault of your own. Please do not think otherwise."

She had not been repulsed by his peculiar physique: on the contrary, she seemed to embrace his oddities. He pulled her toward him, enclosing her in his arms, silently vowing that he would never harm her.

The earth trembled beneath the bed.

Vauquelin's axis shifted.

He was entering perilous waters, trifling with a human in this manner, but he plunged into their depths. There was something about her that made him feel like he was home, and he desired to possess it, no matter the cost, no matter what multitude of vampire maxims he violated.

He ran his fingers up and down her arm, nestling his face in her mussed curls. Her hair was fresh with the fragrance of vetiver, and it brought him a memory of the grasses that grew in the meadows of his château in Évreux. He pulled her leg back towards him, enclosing it between his, and she fell asleep.

It was still his daytime — he was wide awake. He lay there, enveloping this human, dropping delicate kisses on her shoulder, entwining her hair in his fingers. "I have been waiting for you all my life without knowing it," he whispered in French.

Somewhere in the house, a clock chimed four times.

The hour had come for him to depart.

He carefully disentangled himself, trying not to wake her, and dressed. He dropped a shoe on the hardwood floor and panicked: but she did not stir.

She slept hard, emitting tiny snores.

Her quirks merely amplified his infatuation.

Vauquelin's leave-taking of her was unhurried. As he sat on the edge of her bed, tying his shoelaces, an unexpected pang of regret struck his chest. He had never before taken issue with parting from his lovers: he had hastened them all to their graves.

The emotion was bitter and disconcerting, but the morning sun would soon be approaching. To stay would mean putting himself in harm's way.

He could not hear Charles, figuring him asleep for the night. He covered her with her lush blankets and crept out the window, alighting cleanly on the lawn.

The streets were abandoned, silent. He was in no danger of being observed, so he flashed himself at lightning speed back to his shabby little house.

He dropped his clothing on the floor and eased himself into his coffin, hearkening the evening over and over in his mind. The mere thought of Maeve and her fleshy curves, her ivory skin and its tenderness, brought his cock alive again. He moved his hand over it, missing her luxurious bed and body, dreaming of his release which would never come.

A few days later, there was a scented letter in Vauquelin's letterbox. He ran it beneath his nose, intoxicating himself with the fragrance.

Her handwriting was exquisite.

> *Ma cher Vauquelin ... Vous me manquez.*
> *Whenever will I see you again?*
> *Yours, Maeve*

He needed no further incentive. He flagged a carriage down on the street and rang her bell.

Maeve answered the door herself. "There are no servants. I hired them just for that evening. I was hoping to impress you."

She pulled him inside, and they sprinted up the two flights of stairs to her bedroom.

Once again, they lay naked and delighted. He nuzzled her ear and said there were some things they needed to discuss if they were to continue romancing each other.

She sat up in the bed, alarm flushing her cheeks.

"No, no, dearest. You needn't be frightened. It is just that I have some features and idiosyncrasies you may find odd. I merely want you to be at ease, to be confident in me ... yes?"

"Tell me," she said. "I have a few peculiarities myself."

"I want no surprises between us. You have not yet noticed some of my physical deformities."

He began with his teeth. Vampire legends were, in 1900 America, still fairly obscured in European superstitions and old wives' tales, though Vauquelin himself already owned a great deal of vampire literature. Bram Stoker's *Dracula* had not yet found its international audience.

"I have malformed teeth. I was born this way. But I am very aware of them and I would never harm you."

As he parted his lips she reached out, her eyes growing wide as she prodded each menacing tooth with a fingertip.

"My, but they're sharp," she said.

"I did not hurt you last night nor tonight, and I assure you I never will."

"Now I understand why you move your lips so little when you speak," she said. "You're ashamed."

"No, I am not ashamed. They are part of me, but I abhor answering questions about myself from curious strangers."

"I sympathize with that ... I don't enjoy answering questions about why I refuse to remarry." She pointed to the top of one ear and leaned toward him. "My ears look as though someone took a bite out of them," she said. "Papa once said that an angel must have bitten me when I was born, because I was so sweet. But I dislike it when people notice this." She covered them with her hair.

"Your ears are lovely, *bien-aimée*," Vauquelin said, caressing them as he smoothed her hair back. This small imperfection endeared her to him all the more.

"But there are others yet," he stammered.

She sat up and took his hands in hers, folding her legs under her hips.

He could feel something akin to trust growing for her, but it was much too soon for him to reveal the truth to her. He was in love, hovering on the edge between joy and despair.

He wanted to land on the side of joy.

So he used his traditional story.

"I have a rare disorder. Sunlight is deadly for me. I have adapted my life to be awake only during the night. Therefore, I can only meet you in the evenings."

He was not lying to her, except by omission. He crafted his words so that he was telling her the essential truth. How he survived and how long he had been alive: that would remain his noxious secret.

"How devastating that you can't feel the sun upon your face, especially in this golden land! But I would like to be with you anytime that I could," she said.

The empathy in her eyes was killing him.

She was so kind-hearted.

"I'm not done yet ... you'll learn that I'm quite a challenge, my darling. I dislike eating in front of other people. I simply will not do it. I cannot explain why, but please, never attempt to force food upon me or draw attention to my issues with it."

"Alright. You have my word," she said.

"And you already know of my other ... well, defect. I would live to please you, but do not be troubled that I cannot achieve climax. It is a mere physical blight, and nothing more."

"I am saddened for you. But if our few meetings are proof, you certainly are enthusiastic about lovemaking. As long as we both gain our pleasures, we shall be well-suited." she said.

He was humbled by her.

Perhaps humans were not so bad — or perhaps he had just been blessed with this one. He struggled to comprehend how he deserved such treatment.

He took her neck in his hand and tilted his head, gazing at her.

"You have beguiled me," he said. "You have taken ownership over my heart and soul."

Vauquelin walked away from her house, hiring a coach on the street, feeling lighter now that the partial truth was out, and that he could see her without harming himself.

After several months of courtship, or whatever it was they were doing, Vauquelin relented to Maeve's constant inquiries and invited her to his little cottage. Her carriage arrived driven by Charles, the one servant in her permanent employ.

Vauquelin helped her down and led her inside, while Charles made himself comfortable on the front stoop and lit a pipe.

An open door led to the only other room in the house, crowded floor-to-ceiling with his unpacked trunks and crates. He kept the coffin hidden in a locked closet during the day ... he hoped her curiosity would not get the best of her.

She halted just outside the door and peeked inside, her eyes darting about the room, then turned to face him. "I frankly do not believe you are living this way," she said, peeling off her gloves.

"I beg your pardon?"

"You were born a Marquis, were you not? Perhaps you have not been truthful with me. Surely you can afford something more dignified. This house is desolate and dismal! I am horrified that this is where you are living. You deserve better."

She began to cry.

Her tears unraveled him.

There he stood, a Frenchman of noble origin, living in a hovel in a rough, untamed American city. He had not even once considered the appearance of his current lodging. He and Duclos were both ignorant of American ways.

The abode itself was only temporary in his plans. His new experiences, and the life that lay ahead of him, were all he cared about ... until Maeve so harshly dissected the room before him, exposing its festering sadness.

For the first time, he noticed the missing plaster, warped floorboards, and cobwebs. It was ghastly.

How had this escaped him?

If it looked this downtrodden at night, he hated to think how the room would look during the light of the day. He was one step away from living in a squalid crypt.

How (in)appropriate for a vampire such as himself!

Vauquelin gave her a handkerchief from his pocket and grasped her shoulders. "Maeve, I know so little of this country. I have been in Los Angeles for less than three months. I need only a place to store my possessions and to lay my head until I can find something permanent. I am a man. I require few luxuries. I have been touring the city to determine where I would like to live, and I have not yet decided."

"Well," she said, "this will not do. You don't even have a bed!"

Her stubborn streak was practically electrifying the room.

She sat on the sofa, which had come with the house and was more than a little bit shabby, erupting a small dust cloud that made her cough.

"Is this where you're sleeping?" she asked, bringing the

handkerchief up to her nose.

He could not tell her the truth. He shrugged.

"There are no two ways about it," she said. "You must come and live with me."

Vauquelin's jaw dropped and he swayed back on his heels. He could never have predicted this! It took him a moment to regain his composure. He let her words wash over him like waves on the shore: *Live. With. Me.*

"I could not fathom imposing upon you. And now that you have seen my humble abode, how can you be sure I am not lying to you?" he asked, "Or is it that you desire my worthless title? I could be a penniless aristocrat, looking to benefit off the good fortune of an innocent woman! This is a very common practice on the Continent, you realize."

Another test had begun.

She regarded him with righteous side-eye. "Ha! You are much too refined for that. Besides, titles are immaterial in America, Vauquelin! I would like you to trust me, though ... if it will reassure you, show me some proof."

He went to a cupboard and extracted his bank book. Duclos had opened the accounts for him. His balance was $385,350 plus receipts for five safety deposit boxes.

He was $1,000 poorer from a cash contribution he had made to a charity house on Skid Row, but she did not need to know about that. His good deed would come off as pretentious, and he had always preferred for his altruism to be anonymous.

In truth, this particular offering was to assuage his guilt for feeding there so often. It was too perfect a location to find victims.

Vauquelin handed her the bank book. "Lest you think I'm after your money," he said, raising an eyebrow and smiling. "I could build a house to rival yours tomorrow. In fact, perhaps it's time to begin. Duclos has already located an architect."

"Nonsense! I've a perfectly good house already," she said, rapping him on the chest with her gloves. "And furthermore," she said, slowly raising her face to meet his eyes, "I love you."

Vauquelin stopped breathing for a moment. She certainly did not hesitate when she wanted something, did she?

His powerful attraction to her was perplexing. He never thought that he could be loved in his wicked state, yet a human revealed — without prompting, without enchantment — that *she loved him*. HIM. It was a revelation.

I love you ... in his memory, no one, not even his own mother, had uttered this exact phrase to him.

His rational mind said this was impetuous, a fool's errand ... but spontaneity is always intoxicating. There he stood, in a brand-new country, embarking on a brand-new life, considering an offer to live in sin with a mortal. It was kismet.

He could not deny that he loved her too: why should they not start a life together without delay? If it meant deception, if it meant editing his existence away, if it meant fettering his lips against the truth to win her love, he would do it.

Vauquelin had the luxury of knowing he would persevere, no matter the outcome. So he threw caution to the wind.

"I have only two requirements," he said. "Occasionally I will want to go out at night by myself. You must never question me. I beg you to respect the fact that I must be solitary sometimes, and if you can agree to this, I will pledge my loyalty to you."

"Alright ... provided you extend me the same respect. I, too, appreciate solitude and not being questioned about my activities. You'll have your freedom, as long as you allow me mine. That is *my* only requirement. I must live without restrictions. I'll not take orders from any man, not even you."

He clasped her waist and pulled her to him.

"I am quite sure you will take certain orders," he said, a devilish grin curling his lips.

Before she left, Vauquelin pointed out the thick, doubled-up curtains on the single window in the room, and gave his second requirement: that he must have an enclosed canopy bed.

He could not bring his coffin into her house ... that was a quirk that could not be explained away. But oh, how he longed for a real bed again! He had not regularly slept in a coffin for over two hundred years, and it was, thankfully, only a temporary misery.

"And you shall not pay for this, my sweet. I will meet with a builder and have him begin my design at once."

Two weeks later, Vauquelin removed the ruched velvet from his coffin and folded it up, tucking it into one of his trunks. He wanted to keep it as a souvenir of his journey. He broke up the wood with a hatchet and dropped it in the alleyway.

It was a shame, all that fine timber and craftsmanship chopped into kindling, but the act of destroying it was a rite of passage, a repudiation of a life that kept him in the bondage of obscurity. He had been given the opportunity to explore a way of life he had never before been able to consider.

He packed a satchel with necessities and Charles drove

him to Maeve's house. The rest of his belongings would be collected the next day.

On the carriage ride, Vauquelin considered the distinct possibility that he might have taken leave of his senses.

He was flouting his vampiric legacy, but his bravado had prevailed, leading him to feel impulsive and (*could it truly be?*) happy. Happiness was unsettling — and he was in danger of becoming its slave.

When he arrived, Maeve rushed him upstairs. The heirloom bed was gone, and in its place was a herculean carved bed with peacock-blue velvet curtains edged in golden silk fringe.

Vauquelin circled the bed, lifting the curtains, his eyes widened in veneration. He had drawn it on a piece of paper and given it to Duclos, who ordered the design from a furniture builder. Now it stood before him, eclipsing his own original vision.

"Oh, please do go inside," she said, clasping her hands with nervous anticipation. "If it is not sufficiently dark, I'll recall the carpenter to correct it at once."

He removed his shoes, leapt into the bed, and drew the curtains.

Not even the merest speck of light shined through.

He poked his head out. "There's only one way to find out. We must exhaust each other, and if I am still alive in the morning, we will have triumphed."

He pulled her into the bed, and they tossed their clothes out, laughing like children.

While Maeve slept, Vauquelin put on his dressing gown and read in the library until daybreak. He crept back into bed, ensuring the curtains were secure. After an hour had passed, there was still not a trace of light. He drifted off with his hands folded across his chest like a corpse.

Maeve rose and began her day, ensuring the curtains were carefully closed behind her.

And thus began their accursed time together. She lived her daytime life as she pleased, and spent her evenings with Vauquelin until she fell asleep.

They took excursions, attended balls and theatre performances, and picnicked in Elysian Park after sundown. They provided an endowment to a small orchestra, which eventually became the Los Angeles Philharmonic.

It was glorious — while it lasted.

One fine, Southern California evening, they were riding through an orange grove in their topless carriage. It was one of the many delights of California: there was ripe fruit on the trees along with blossoms. Their fragrance permeated the air.

"Such a magical life we are living," she said, bringing his hand to her lips. "Sometimes I ask myself if I'm imagining it all."

Vauquelin could not have agreed more. His new life, with its fanciful landscape and Maeve's unanticipated appearance in it, was delivering one breathless joy after another.

He plucked an orange off a tree and peeled it for her with his Opinel pocket knife. Although the landscape was lovely, he was overcome by the desire to be riding with her in a carriage in Paris and not in this crude, unpolished city.

How delightful it would be to travel to Europe with her, or perhaps to some exotic island ... alas, it was impossible.

He could travel alone, but not with her.

As he gazed upon her bouncing in the carriage, he wished that he could have had her with him throughout all his years, that he could have taken her to a ball at Versailles in the era of the Sun King, built up his hôtel for her, not for himself alone, and taken her to his châteaux so she could be his proper Duchesse — but these things could never be.

He was living under the protection of a beautiful lie, one that ate away at his soul.

"You look so troubled, my love," Maeve said.

She was attuned to his moods at all times; she could always lift the weighty veil of his melancholy.

For Vauquelin, the difference between happiness and despair was as subtle and unpredictable as a wave reaching for the shore and vanishing back into the deep.

He took her hand and said, "I am terrified that this euphoria will end. My fevered love has blinded me."

His face darkened, imprinted with the black reality he could not share with her, and with another thought he could not admit: *I am unworthy.*

She pressed her cheek to his. "We must always make the best of the time we have," she said. "We are mere mortals. Our appointment on earth is fragile and uncertain."

Her words sent ice through his veins.

Her time was uncertain. His was not.

Far from it.

He glowered at her. The temptation to tell her everything quivered on his lips, but the words would not come forth.

Maeve puzzled to interpret what was brewing in his mind.

She would never know that a vampire held her in his embrace, one who anguished for her to be alive.

When they arrived home, Vauquelin asked a favor. Might he hang a portrait of his ancestor in their bedchamber?

Maeve was delighted for him to make his presence known in the house. Charles retrieved the painting from the cellar and removed it from its wooden crate, trying and failing to contain the wild mess of excelsior. The painting was colossal, almost life-size.

As the excelsior fell away and the painting was fully revealed, Maeve went pale. "When was this painted?" she asked.

"In 1668. It was painted by Charles Le Brun. Are you familiar with his work?"

"I have seen his paintings in museums," she said, "and his work at Versailles." She looked from Vauquelin back to the portrait. "The likeness between you and your ancestor is astounding."

She brushed her fingers against the elaborate gilded frame.

Vauquelin remained silent as a sphinx.

A few minutes later, the portrait was hung in the exact spot where it would remain for well over one hundred years.

They stood arm-in-arm, gazing upon it.

"I am amazed, my love," she said. "It is as if I am standing next to your ancestor, come alive again."

Vauquelin loved looking at it.

It was beyond mere vanity. It was visual proof of his longevity, documentation of the extraordinary events that had afforded him the great fortune of standing in this very room in a strange, young country. And now it bore a new significance: had he not been created a vampire, he would never have met Maeve.

He would already have been dead for centuries.

Reaching in his pocket, he extracted a garnet, diamond, and pearl-encrusted choker and clasped it on her neck.

"These jewels belonged to my mother, passed down from generations before her," he said, "and now they will adorn the neck of the only other woman I have ever loved."

Her hand moved up to touch the necklace, and she kissed him.

He leaned back and admired her. How beautifully it accentuated her long neck! The choker was heavy, and it drew his eyes to her jugular vein pulsating under the jewels.

What extravagant euphoria would he taste in her blood — the rich Celtic blood coursing beneath her milky skin? He could hear the thrum of her heart in his ears, and his cock swelled in anticipation.

Bloodlust must give way to his other, considerably less lethal lust. He would give her *la petite mort* instead.

He pushed himself against her, urging her over toward the wall, and stripped her down: leaving her clothed only in the necklace. He took her with her legs wrapped around his waist, knocking pictures crooked in his frenzy.

There had been no such beckoning from Maeve's blood before. He would never allow himself to harm her, but this instinctual response disturbed him. His intense power of self-control was the only trait keeping him inside this beautiful life, and he would not relinquish it.

He was left with no choice but to go out and make a kill.

Leaving her breathless on the floor, he vanished into the night.

Over the coming days, the remainder of Vauquelin's belongings were brought up from their crates in the cellar.

Maeve delighted in their unpacking, emitting murmurs of joy at the extraordinary objects that had made the long journey from France. Soon, the house was truly theirs together, a melding of both their fine tastes.

They had the bedroom painted a near-black charcoal, the color it would remain until Vauquelin was ripped out of his futurepast. The color was Maeve's idea. "Now it will be even closer to nighttime while you rest, my love."

Evermore, Maeve also became nocturnal. She insisted on spending as many waking hours as possible with Vauquelin. Like him, she was a seeker of solitude, and they seldom had visitors. There were few people Maeve enjoyed spending time with. In Vauquelin she found she had all the companionship she could ever want: a friend, with whom she could be her unedited self, and a lover.

Vauquelin went out alone once a week.

True to her word as always, Maeve never questioned him about his ventures. She was confident in their love: she had no reason to believe he was ever unfaithful to her. He would leave her for an hour or two at most, and promptly return.

Her former marriage had been one of social placement. Once it registered that there would be no children, her husband became a philanderer: he turned a cold eye on her. She might as well have not existed. When he died in a steelwork accident, she was not the slightest bit sorrowful.

The existence of a broad-minded man like Vauquelin was a marvel, and this time, she had chosen for herself. Until he came into her life, she was unaware that it was possible to love someone with such ferocity, to exist as she pleased with another being in her life.

She needed no one else, nor did he. They each found themselves completed in one other. Their rarified compatibility astonished them both. But Maeve's voluntary surrender of sunlight would be a detriment to her before long.

Once per season a tailor visited them after dark, and they would order dozens of bespoke ensembles. It was an activity they both looked forward to with half-starved impatience.

Maeve indulged Vauquelin's dandy tendencies, and likewise, he encouraged her affinity for outright whimsy.

She designed her own dresses, peculiar visions which Vauquelin would one day appreciate as being far ahead of their time.

She was a skillful artist.

Her concoctions always raised eyebrows and garnered

open stares when they went out into the city. It never affected her. She was fearless and independent — like him — and he adored her for it.

"It amuses me to shock those stuffy old prigs!" she said one night, sticking a pin into a hat that added a foot-and-a-half to her height. The hat was sculpted red felt with yards of black netting. A taxidermied California raven sat upon its crown.

Vauquelin shook his head and laughed. Maeve was an endless source of joy for him. Being with her was infinitely superior to being in the sunlight.

It was rare for them to appear in public, aside from attending musical performances and plays, but when they did tongues would wag. They were both so extraordinary-looking that people could not help but gawk. Had they not had money and reputation no one would have spoken to them, so different were they from everyone else.

The earliest years of the twentieth century brought technology to Vauquelin's life, and he was hooked. When Talley's Electric Theater opened in Los Angeles, he and Maeve were present at its debut screening: *The Great Train Robbery*. The sorcery of "the flickers" mystified them both.

Any new invention that became available found its way into their home: a Victrola, a vacuum cleaner, a telegraph machine. Vauquelin taught himself how to use it and it became his primary method for sending messages to Duclos.

In 1906, a shiny new Packard appeared in their driveway. It was the first motorcar he ever owned, and it ignited his love affair with the horseless carriage.

He was fascinated by the concept of horsepower, and the sleek

Packard boasted the power of twenty-four. Maeve learned to drive and often took it out on her own.

Soon, funny little electric and gas-powered cars became all the rage in the city, editing horse-and-buggy out of the picture.

Twice a year, they threw lavish dinner soirées. The guest lists were populated with their fellow eccentrics: artists, actors, directors, musicians, oddballs. Each soirée had a theme.

Charlie Chaplin was their first Hollywood guest, though at the time he was fresh off the boat from England and well ahead of the massive fame he would achieve as The Little Tramp. Vauquelin was shocked by Chaplin's diminutive stature in person: all the actors appeared remarkably taller on the silver screen.

There were few society types invited to their events; Maeve thought them too tedious. Even on the wild west coast, she was still considered *nouveau riche*. She was growing into herself as a true bohemian, and though her wealth was plentiful, it was clear that she found joy in low company.

A small army of servants was hired for the dinners. Chefs were brought in from San Francisco and the endless courses, each of which Vauquelin supervised from a purely aesthetic (and envious) standpoint, dazzled and delighted the guests. No one noticed that Vauquelin did not partake: there were so many other spectacular distractions that his queer behavior was the least interesting part of the evening.

The first one was based on a new cabaret concept in Paris, The Moulin Rouge, which had debuted in 1889. Their home was outfitted in reds and pinks, and the entertainment was provided by can-can dancers from the burlesque.

Maeve's impossibly long dining table was spread stern-to-bow with Parisian delicacies and sinful desserts, and the champagne flowed without end. Voluptuous bouquets of roses, thick ostrich feathers tucked within, were scattered across the expanse of the house.

The soirée carried on until the wee hours. The guests were reluctant to depart, and an exasperated Vauquelin ordered them all out just before sunrise.

Their second soirée was dear to Vauquelin: they held a fête in the style of the Sun King. He brought out a ravishing red velvet court ensemble from his collection and sported a baroque wig with red-heeled black leather shoes upon his feet. He wore full makeup and carried his *rapier* upon his waist.

Maeve was dressed in a resplendent costume outfitted by their tailor. She wore an off-shoulder golden gossamer dress topped with scarlet bows, a long brocade train spilling down her back and onto the floor. The garnet choker graced her neck. Her hair was braided and curled into a wide Titian crown, sprinkled with pearls. She carried an elaborate hand-painted fan which had also belonged to his mother.

Vauquelin was overcome with emotion when she first descended the staircase and landed before him like a queen.

If only she shared this history with him.

The company that evening marveled over the authenticity of their costumes and swooned over the Versailles-worthy cuisine. Stuffed pheasants in full plumage were placed upon the dining table, and silver tray after silver tray was passed, bearing puffed savory pastries, truffles, and frilly sweet cakes.

Each member of the hired staff wore elaborate livery, and a harpsichordist and soprano performed music of the era. Vauquelin imported candlelit crystal chandeliers on pulleys just for this evening, and they remained hanging over the dining table after the party — Maeve fell in love with them and their beguiling light.

Despite his comfort and joy, he was disappointed by the guests. For them, it was all fantasy, and the event fell far short of the true opulence of seventeenth-century France. He focused instead on Maeve, and the delight she gave him in her aristocratic finery.

She was the embodiment of elegance.

Another legendary evening was based on the occult and dark arts. Vauquelin was able to let his guard down a bit, and everyone was impressed by his convincing portrayal of an ancient soothsayer. They were mystified by his factual and detailed recollections of the past. His inspiration was Count Cagliostro, whom he had once met, but he was pure Vauquelin. Still, he kept his lips tight.

Tarot cards were read, their sensational new Ouija board was placed on a table, and guests could see their futures in a crystal ball, with an appropriately appointed Romani madam — Maeve, in an elaborate costume of her own invention — at its helm.

They burned incense and the spooky menu included an array of fantastical foods in the shape of body parts, including a human brain replicated in aspic with veins of saffron.

Between the two of them, there was a bottomless wellspring of ideas and concepts, and they spent a great deal of time planning and creating.

Word about the dinners soon spread, and the elites were

incredulous at being denied invitation. Snobbery had sunk its teeth into the formerly undomesticated city of Los Angeles.

Maeve's generosity and constant presence in the world of the arts precluded them from outright snubbing her in public. They thought her impertinent for flaunting her eccentricities, but this just encouraged her further.

Maeve grew up ensconced in the old-money *hauteur* of New England, and she rebelled against elitism: even more so when it infested her chosen hometown, whose wildness and lack of social convention had attracted her in the first place.

Vauquelin himself, having lived out a couple of centuries among the French aristocracy, found this all endlessly entertaining and was elated to flaunt his eccentricities right by her side.

At long last, he had found his kindred spirit!

One evening in the kitchen, Maeve was cutting lemons into slices. She enjoyed them in her water and tea. "Lemons were once so exotic, and here, I can pick one right off my very own tree! I never would have imagined this as a girl!"

Their just-installed telephone rang, startling her, and she impaled her finger on the knife.

She gasped. It was a deep cut — thick ribbons of crimson branched out across her fingers, dripping into a pool on the countertop.

The damnable telephone continued ringing, further distressing them both, and the heady fragrance of her blood perfumed the air.

Vauquelin ripped the phone out by its roots and stumbled

against the cabinet, panting. She could not pick up the scent of the blood as he could.

"Worry not, dearest. I think I shall live," she said, laughing as she wrapped her hand in a linen towel. She kicked the broken telephone with her foot. "Good riddance! I never liked this ridiculous thing, anyway."

He fled through the back door and sat trembling on a bench, senses throbbing, enshrouded by shame. He could not control himself in the presence of living blood, particularly not hers, which he had never experienced — he had only imagined its spice.

She followed him outside.

"Are you quite alright?" he stuttered, covering his nose and mouth with his handkerchief. His shoulders sank as his masculinity withered in one fell swoop.

"I am fine! Vauquelin ... are you frightened of blood?"

An incredulous snort escaped his throat.

How could he possibly justify his behavior?

"Please forgive me. I abandoned you when you were injured. You must think me a coward, but my darling ... I panicked. I haven't the words to say what I mean."

Maeve began to approach him and he held up a hand, backing away from her. The bleeding had stopped, but her wound was now unwrapped and the fragrance of iron still hung thick in the air. Her figure was enshrouded by a foreboding, flowing red aura, which could only be seen by the eyes of a revenant.

"*Bien-aimée*, if you are truly well, I must go out for my walk. At once." Vauquelin left her standing in the garden and slipped away into the darkened city.

He could not trust himself to be near her.

He was not in need of blood, but its unexpected appearance tonight had unleashed his hunger.

It must be satisfied, regardless of the cost.

He had made a kill only yesterday, and that, under normal circumstances, would have sustained him for a full week.

Now his diminished aplomb alarmed him.

He wandered the streets in desperation. He had partaken too frequently on Skid Row as well as the train tracks. Policemen now patrolled both areas after nightfall.

Vauquelin continued walking until he reached an orange grove. Workers were setting out smudge pots, rushing to protect the trees from a sudden cold snap. A group of three men stood huddled against one another, fueling and lighting a pot. He enchanted them all and killed each one, drinking with a black fury until he could almost feel the last man's skin begin to contract.

It had been ages since he had killed with such ferocity.

The exsanguination of humans was necessary ... he must do it to survive, but the extreme violence was shocking even to himself. For Vauquelin, taking a life was no different than a human man eating a steak. Rarely was hatred behind it. He knew this barbarity was borne from his accidental proximity to Maeve's blood.

He gorged himself, inflicting savagery about the tranquil orange grove, taking more than he needed — it was out of character for him.

With his Opinel he cut all their throats. There was not a drop of blood spilt ... he had taken it all. This would bewilder the poor souls who discovered the three bloodless corpses in the morning.

On his way back, he washed his hands and face at a neighbor's faucet at the end of their street. He hoped by the time he walked through the door that the scent of Maeve's blood would have faded. He stood on the porch a moment, gulping in deep breaths, willing himself to be calm and still.

She was sitting in the parlor reading when he entered.

"I hope your walk replenished you, my love. I am fine now. Just the slightest throbbing. For such a strong man, Vauquelin, I must say your aversion to blood amuses me!" she said, bringing her fingertips to her mouth to suppress a laugh.

Vauquelin knitted his brows. Her ridicule was well-founded, and he mustered a half-hearted laugh at his own expense. The recollection of his swift departure while she was in pain heaped additional agony upon him.

He knelt at her feet, burying his face in her lap, believing more than ever that he did not deserve this life she was giving him.

He would never, ever deserve it.

As Vauquelin's time passed with Maeve, she developed recurring bouts of illness which became his *bête noire*. He was powerless to help her. Whenever she was ill, he was tormented by thoughts of turning her.

Maeve's renunciation of sunlight was crippling her, causing a return of the lung weakness that inspired her to move to California and thus put them in the right place and time to meet. Few things could harm him, but as a human, many, many things could harm her.

He wrestled with his truth, wondering if the time had

come to tell her that he could save her from her afflictions and end them forever.

But the infallible Maeve always rebounded stronger than before, and he pushed her poor health — and thoughts of turning her — far into his subconscious.

He continued living his exquisite lie.

LOS ANGELES, CALIFORNIA | 1918

Vauquelin's hunting field eroded night by night.

Police patrols were increased all over the city, due not only to his occasional nocturnal jaunts but to recent outbreaks of violence among its inhabitants.

It was incumbent upon him to change his course. Los Angeles Harbor became his primary reserve, where an abundance of seamen, disembarking ships and returning late at night, provided him with a steady stream of victims for months.

In October, fear erupted across Los Angeles. The Spanish Influenza, which had devastated Europe, had found its way to the West coast of the United States.

Vauquelin was horrified by the news from abroad and apprehensive about Maeve's safety. He ordered her to stay within the bounds of their property at all times until further notice.

She was beyond furious.

His demands resulted in their first — and only — argument.

"But you are still going out at night whenever you please, and I have said *nothing!*" She stamped her foot and clamped her hands into fists. "Give me one good reason why I should be imprisoned in this house, when you are free to wander the city as you please!"

Because you could be taken from me. "Because it is too dangerous. The contagion is rampant and Los Angeles is closing down."

"Then you shall not leave this house, either!" She ran upstairs and slammed the door to their bedroom.

Vauquelin was panic-stricken. He did not wish to disobey her, but without his blood sustenance, he would endure hellish suffering. He sat for hours wracking his brain for a way to survive this and, at the same time, to keep her safe.

At last, inspiration struck.

He picked up the telephone and rang Duclos.

Two days later, large pens and ten rabbits, half of them pregnant, were installed in the back garden.

"They shall give us a bit of joy and distraction while we are confined," he explained. A book on their safekeeping was included in the delivery, and Vauquelin read it aloud to Maeve that night.

She was captivated, but when the rabbits occasionally died, she was distraught. Vauquelin had an explanation for this, as well.

"Perhaps they were not hardy," he said. "Perhaps their diet was inadequate."

But then new litters were born and the tiny kits enraptured her anew, allowing her to forget about the dearly departed.

Two rabbits per week sustained him, but minimally.

He had to ration them to sustain their gestation period and growth.

He was wasting away, but he was surviving.

Barely.

He moved as if his bones were rusted; his cheeks became hollow. Dark circles developed under his eyes, and his hair lost its luster.

The greatest irony was that Maeve feared he had contracted the dreaded disease. She fussed over him like a mother hen.

Los Angeles was crazed and terrified by an invisible killer. The streets were emptied: businesses, churches, theaters, and gathering places were all shuttered by decree of the health commissioner.

The few citizens brave enough to emerge from their doors did so with improvised fabric masking their faces, crossing the street or stepping into the gutters to avoid others in their paths.

It was surreal and bizarre ... even having lived through multiple health crises in Europe, Vauquelin was flummoxed by the disease's aggression. He had supposed that medical advancements would have brought the world beyond such tragedy.

The newspapers delivered fear and grim reporting from across the globe.

The city death toll climbed.

Vauquelin continued to have faith that by sequestering Maeve, he was keeping her out of harm's way.

How wrong he was.

Maeve was living a lie of her own, sneaking out of the house after Vauquelin went to his rest and making regular calls on her physician.

She was confident that her gauzy lace veil was adequate protection. Like Vauquelin, she pushed illness far away from her thoughts. She wanted nothing but happiness, and she refused to let anything steal joyful moments from her.

With an artificial brave face, she stubbornly moved forward, forcing herself to appear robust even when she was not.

She frequently pinched her cheeks to force color into them.

In November she fell gravely ill, decimated by fever, unable to speak. Vauquelin sat bedside in a chair, tapping his fingers together and twitching his foot as the physician attended her.

One evening she began thrashing, drenched in sweat. Her face was darkened and blue. The doctor strong-armed him out of the room. Outside the door, he could hear her screaming and gasping for air while he stood despondent and fearful, every slight noise fraying his nerves.

The physician opened the door a crack and yelled for his nurse, who dashed into the room and slammed the door in Vauquelin's face.

He was too shocked to even summon the strength to knock the door down, something he would later regret. He was altogether unversed in ordinary human response, and the unfolding scene disturbed him to the depths of his soul.

After an hour her screams faded and the physician emerged, tailed by the nurse. "Sir, I'm very sorry indeed, but it is doubtful she will live the night. I've done all I can do for her, and I've given her some laudanum. She is sleeping now. Keep out of this room, lest you risk the same fate. She is in God's hands now. You must trust in him. I will show myself out."

Vauquelin stood stock-still, merely nodding his head in numb acknowledgment. When the front door closed, he paced up and down the hallway, frantic. The situation was alarmingly human. He had strayed far, far from his vampire existence and into a life which was an elegant sham.

He had pretended to be something he was not, and at what price? The time had arrived for him to tell her the truth. He must turn her, end her illness, so they could be together for eternity.

He agonized over this decision.

But if she could not reply, at least she would know his true nature at last, and if need be, he would turn her against her will. There was no other option left for him.

The room was dank, the air heavy with the fetid, drowning odor of contagion. He sat next to her on the bed and took her hand. It was cold, as cold as his own flesh, and it set horror into his heart. The icy feel of expiration was upon her body, when it was once so soft and warm.

Her breath was reduced to rattled, sporadic, gasps.

He was running out of time.

"*Bien-aimée* ... I must tell you the truth." Language failed him, as it so often did. "I am the undead," he struggled out. He knew they were on the verge of being parted forever.

"I am vampire," he blurted, a sob sucking the last word back into his throat.

She squeezed his hand with a decisive force that took him aback. His face brightened, but his long-overdue admission had come too late.

Feathers fluttered against his face.

His arms flew out, grasping.

An ominous gloom enveloped him, creeping down his chest as the Angel of Death fled with her prize, looking back over her shoulder with an air of absolute victory, leaving a filmy black smoke in her wake.

"You have let this one evade your grasp, Vampire," the Angel screeched, emitting a spine-chilling cackle as she spread her glossy, obsidian wings. She swanned out the window as surreptitiously as she had entered.

He rushed to follow but the night sky was empty, leaving him defenseless, hopeless, broken.

Maeve was dead.

Vauquelin was devastated.

He fell to his knees.

And what right had he now, to sit here so vigorous, his lungs easily bringing in air while she lay suffocated, needlessly and irrevocably dead?

None. None. None.

He rocked to and fro, begging for answers in silence.

He would give his life, all of the hundreds of years of it, to have her quicken again. To give her all the hours that had devoured him before she settled in his heart and convinced him that he could be loved.

He bit his wrist and pried Maeve's mouth open, letting his blood drip in.

It resulted in naught.

Vauquelin was no necromancer.

Death's calamitous skill was one he could give — but could never receive himself. He was as in love with Death as he was powerless over her.

Death was not the Grim Reaper, so immortalized in literature: Death was a black angel, a feminine god — exquisite and unforgiving, capricious and unprejudiced. She had her orders, and she carried them out without fail despite (or in spite of) prayers and (un)holy cries and despair. Throughout his life as a vampire, not once during any of his kills had Death appeared. No one came for their souls. He was the reaper, delivering them to their afterlives.

Where their souls went, he did not know.

Vauquelin lay prostrate on the floor. It had been over two hundred years since he shed any tears ... the last time was the night of his creation as a vampire. Any emotion, especially — fiercely — love, was nonexistent, UNTIL.

Until Maeve came into his life.

His eyes began to burn and he clawed at them, bringing forth streams of blood that engulfed him in their despairing undertow.

"Christ," he whispered, and fell to his back, his body ravaged by ruthless sobs.

When blood stopped, he lay staring at the ceiling.

Without warning he rose and strode out of the room, unable to bring himself to look at her. He washed his face in the bathroom sink, grateful for once that his reflection was absent from mirror that hung above. It would be a portrait of grief. He smashed it with his fists and went through the expanse of the house, smashing each remaining looking glass.

He left a gory trail in his wake, staining the polished herringboned floors with crimson shards and his cursed blood.

It took all his self-control to not destroy everything in his path and burn the house down.

At last, he stood seething in the foyer, calming himself by filling and re-filling his lungs with the air of the too-empty house. Loneliness washed over him, drowning him in its abyss, and he thought he could never move one foot in front of the other again.

Yet I must face this.

Vauquelin returned to the bedroom, his chin on his chest. His head weighed a thousand pounds, yet he somehow managed to lift his face.

Maeve was angelic and childlike in the candlelight. She had aged little since the day they met.

His breath came in staccato convulsions, as he struggled to mute his lamentations.

Her disease-afflicted body had relaxed, no longer brutalized by the lack of oxygen. Her legendary strength had vanished, replaced by frailty.

She was so pale.

He cleansed his fruitless blood from her lips and climbed into bed next to her. He laid there for hours, arranging her hair, caressing her face. He straightened her body, smoothing out her bloody nightdress and folding her hands on her chest.

"My love, my sweet. I should not have hesitated."

Vauquelin kissed her shoulders, her lips, her neck.

He had never, in all his years of solitude, been so alone. This solitude would sink into the marrow of his bones, deepen across the years still ahead of him, and envelop him like the sea takes a ship.

Perhaps it was the cruelest fate of the vampire: empowered to take life, yet powerless to restore it once it had vanished.

He half-slept, his arm draped across her ribcage.

At some point in his fitful slumber, he had a clear vision of the doctor in the room with Maeve. He was certain that the doctor had hastened her death with the laudanum.

She might not have survived regardless, but the doctor had numbed her into oblivion, robbing Vauquelin of his last chance to speak with her, either to tell her goodbye and that he loved her, or to save her.

A torrent of overpowering anger pushed him to rise. He knew who his next victim would be. That would come later. For now, he willed his rage to subside until it could be dealt with properly.

He had to think of Maeve, and Maeve only.

At four o'clock, he went down to the carriage house and knocked on the door of Charles's apartment.

"Our darling Maeve has left us," he said. "You must go and fetch the undertaker."

Eighteen years.

Eighteen years was but a drop in the fathomless ocean of his existence, yet she had given him more love than he had ever known, either as human or vampire, love that he had neither earned nor merited.

Dear god, how he wanted her with him.

If only he could bring her back to the beginning and live for a thousand or more years with her — that was what he wanted.

And now that could never happen.

Vauquelin sat at the desk in the library and wrote out pages of specific instructions for Charles. He telephoned Duclos, who would handle the daylight business of Maeve's death for him and speak to her attorney on his behalf.

When the clock chimed five, he sprang into action. He flashed himself upstairs and went into her dressing room, selecting his favorite of her gowns. He chose jewels, gloves, and shoes for her.

He only had a few minutes left.

The sun would rise ... it always did.

As an afterthought, he fetched Maeve's rosary from her jewel box. She was a rebellious Catholic, but her father was a dyed-in-the-wool papist. She was attracted more by the morbidity and ritual of the religion than any other quality.

He picked up her body and floated down the stairs with her enclosed in his arms. He laid her down on the sofa in the parlor and dressed her. He brought the rosary to his lips and placed it in her hands, caressing her fingers, kissing her forehead and lips.

"Good night, my love," he whispered, covering her with a mink blanket and placing his instructions on the table next to her. He stoked the fire and fed her besmirched nightdress into it with the poker. Fleeing back upstairs, he encased himself in bed at the exact moment the sun began to emerge.

His eyes refused to close.

Maeve's body was gone when he rose.

There was no question of her wanting a funeral. She did not believe in them. She once said she wanted to be cremated but it was controversial at the time and, even so, Vauquelin could not bear to hasten her body to ashes.

Regardless of anyone's wishes, funerals during a pandemic were thrice as dismal. No mourners could be present.

Closure was forbidden: the despair of contagion was compounded by the pitiable robbery of farewells.

A knock rapped upon the door, startling him.

He rushed to open it. There stood Maeve's attorney, with Duclos close on his heels. Their presence hoisted the grim reality of her death onto his face.

They read documents stating that Mrs. Sullivan had been entombed in her crypt at Evergreen as decreed, followed by her last will and testament.

Her home at 2421 Pearl Street would be transferred in title and deed, along with its interior contents and all Mrs. Sullivan's material possessions, accounts, and stocks to Louis-Augustin du Cavernay de Vauquelin.

Lastly, there was a clause bequeathing Charles $100,000 and a request for him to remain in Vauquelin's employ. Duclos read everything, and Vauquelin wordlessly signed the papers, his jaw set to lock away his pain.

It was done.

Los Angeles was unusually cold that night.

Vauquelin haunted the hallways, aimless, feeling her presence at every turn, expecting her smile to illuminate his face as she ran down the stairs, full of the joy of being alive. She had kept him well-fed daily with life, and now he was starved.

The sounds of her voice and laughter echoed throughout his subconscious, while the malignant silence in the house reverberated up the walls from the foundation to the ceilings. Each surface bore the ghostly imprint of her touch, her tread, her verve.

Countless times per day, sharp pains struck within the void of his heart. Barbaric jolts of grief caught him by surprise and shattered his soul, stole his breath at any moment he dared to feel quite normal again.

He walked to the backyard and looked at the garden they had designed together, looming half-done in the moonlight: workers' spades and shovels laid to the side, flats of plants waiting. He dropped into a wicker chaise by the unfinished swimming pool she had never gotten to enjoy. The broken ground glared at him like an open grave, and he allowed his bloody emotions to stream down his cheeks.

A deluge of beautifully-written letters of sympathy arrived for him. The house should have been filled with flowers, but in the middle of a pandemic, there was no one available to deliver them. It made his detachment from Maeve even bleaker.

When ... if ... life outside his doors resumed its normal pace, the presence of flowers would become a habit for him. He would fill the house with blooms forever — the blooms she deserved, and did not rightfully receive.

Vauquelin flitted through the house like a restless specter, unsure what to do with himself. His life with Maeve had been authentic and fraudulent in concert. He had survived under the mandate of the vampire, hunting at night away from her realization, while he existed with her as a human: visiting the theatre, reading with her in the library, making love, hosting magnificent parties in the land of the living.

Yet he had failed her — and himself. He was submerged under the asphyxiating guilt of his inaction, a guilt that would never leave him for the rest of his days.

He rang Duclos.

He had a plan.

The next day as he slept, masked workers descended upon the cellar, laboring off the detailed orders issued by Vauquelin.

Massive shelves were constructed throughout the cellar, with one in particular inlaid in mahogany and bearing a glass door.

A heavy steel bank vault door was installed at the entry, equipped with a wheel lock.

The laborers dug a six-foot deep pit in the center of the floor and affixed a hinged door to cover the opening.

They asked no questions.

They were grateful for the work, besieged as they were by pandemic-induced unemployment. Duclos paid them double what they had quoted to complete the project.

Vauquelin descended to inspect the work.

It was now a crypt: or it would be, later tonight.

At midnight, he visited her tomb at Evergreen Cemetery. He heaved the substantial stone cover off — it would have taken three human men to lift it.

"I'm taking you home, dearest," he said, "so that we may be together still."

He eased Maeve's rosewood coffin to the ground and loaded it onto the undertaker's carriage, replacing the stone cover. When he arrived at the house, he verified that Charles's light was out for the night. He dragged her coffin down the cellar steps and opened the lid.

There she lay, in rest, just as he had dressed her. Her jewels were intact and her gloved hands clasped the rosary. He kissed her lips and brought forth his Opinel, severing a crimson curl from her hair which he placed in his handkerchief and rolled up with great care.

He kept vigil over her until exhaustion took him in its clutches, at last bringing down the lid of the coffin and placing it into its designated chamber. He left the candles burning, as they would continue to burn for decades more, and slowly ascended the stairs, closing and locking the vault door.

Down on the street, he slapped the rump of one of the horses, sending them galloping away with the empty carriage tottering behind them.

Before resigning himself to sleep, he placed the lock of Maeve's hair inside the leather case that held their only photograph, clasped the hinge, and hid it away in his drawer. It would be many years before he found the strength to open it again.

The flu took Charles a month later.

Vauquelin left the quarantine sign on the front of the house for years to come, a reminder that the devil's luck had diseased the marrow of its bones.

And thus ended one of the shortest — not to mention one of the most influential — chapters of his life.

LOS ANGELES, CALIFORNIA | 1959

At sunrise, still encased in the safety of his velvety bed-tomb, Vauquelin calls his attorney and instructs him to go to the bank to retrieve a sum from his security boxes. They are filled to their brims with gold coins, precious stones and jewelry, bricks of bouillon.

Everything is starting to feel a little pointless. At the rate things are going, who knows where, or when, he will end up?

If another time-shift occurs, and his Los Angeles bank is not yet established in the time period in which he haphazardly lands, his American accounts will all be lost.

Vauquelin had been paying all of Maeve's charitable causes up until the time-shift, and even endowed some new ones for her. There was a Maeve Sullivan Scholarship for Emerging Designers at the largest fashion school in Los Angeles, and a wing in the new opera theatre bore her name, or the name he wished for her to have: Maeve Sullivan de Vauquelin.

Both institutions, along with his financial endowments, are lost to his futurepast.

The attorney drops off his statements and a full briefcase later that evening. He is dismayed to discover that his accounts are down to \$800,000, though it is still a fortune in 1959.

Nevertheless, it is reassuring to have some hard currency in his hands, currency that will have a value no matter the time, but never has he been so doubtful of what lies ahead.

The past is history, over and done, and the future will keep unfolding — until it doesn't.

Vauquelin's hair is a problem. It is the same as it was when he was turned in 1668: a long, sacrosanct mass of dark waves hanging just below his shoulders. He is stuck with it. Cutting it is pointless: it will always return to its original length while he sleeps.

In the twenty-first century, he got by with it — indeed, it was even fashionable, but it had caused difficulty at multiple stages of his life with the ebb and flow of trends. And in 1959, a man simply does not wear his hair long, even in Los Angeles. It is just another of the many symbols of his eccentricity.

He forces it up into a hat and drives to an industry costume shop in Hollywood. He has a story ready to go. There are so many, perpetually ready at a moment's notice for any occasion when he needs to conceal his truth.

"I'm auditioning for a role and I need a wig. I'd like something contemporary," he tells the shop girl. He removes the hat, letting his hair tumble down to his shoulders, and positions himself in a chair so the mirrors will not be an issue.

"Why don't you just get a haircut? Men ain't s'posed to wear their hair long anyways," she says with narrowed eyes, chewing gum like a cud, ogling his every action.

"Mind your own business and show me something."

"I mean, it's a lotta hair to cram under a wig, mister. I ain't even sure I could get a woman's hair flattened down enough for a male wig."

He shoots her a dirty look, but she brings out several models, laboring in great melodrama to arrange his hair under a wig cap.

He tries on five different ones with the shop girl staring at him the entire time.

"How can you tell if you like it or not? Don't you want a mirror?" she asks, grappling to place one in his hand.

"No," he says, pushing it away.

"You're a pale one, ain't ya? Must not be from California. Are ya puttin' on that fancy accent for your role?"

She is on the verge of pissing him off. His mind vibrates with thoughts of ending her; she is there alone. But is it worth the effort he would need to expend? He would have to take the body back to his house to dispose of it. Instead, he gives her a death glare until she takes the hint and leaves him be.

It is her lucky night, and she will never know it. In all likelihood, she will take the bus home to a dismal studio apartment, or perhaps a small house she shares with other girls or her parents, and watch television ... never realizing that she had barely escaped the grasp of a reaper.

Whenever he goes to ordinary human places like this, self-awareness throbs in him like a drum. In the early years after his creation, he basked in being vampire, and exulted in working up theatrical climaxes for his victims. As time passed, he grew weary of proving himself, and being vampire became more of a hidden, internalized condition for him, like having a disease or a secret birthmark.

Now he lives just beyond reach of human perception, with his vast difference and separation from them weighing on his shoulders. He will never be able, let alone want, to integrate himself and of this he is painfully aware.

Over the last hundred-odd years, his ancient braggadocio evolved into a desire to go unnoticed, which, in this time warp, is a mounting challenge. And now, due to his bright idea of procuring a simple disguise, he must prevent this nosy shop girl from noticing his absence in the mirrors.

He claws his face in vexation.

"Have I seen you in any pictures?" she asks, tilting her head. *He's just gotta be somebody,* she thinks. *He's too interesting-looking.*

"Maybe," he says, leaning toward her and digging his fingers into the armrest. "Or maybe it was just someone who looks like me. I get that a lot."

Vauquelin leers at her until she moves behind the cash register, still watching him with side-eye. He selects a rather mediocre short wig, pays, and leaves with it upon his head.

He needs to talk to Delphine.

She answers the door, leaning on the jamb like a cat.

Vauquelin starts inside, but then he hears voices jabbering in the background.

"François and Kibby are here," she says. "I tried to call you, but you didn't answer. What on earth have you done to your hair?

It looks ridiculous."

He hesitates. His skirmish with the shop girl has left him in a foul temper, and the last thing he needs is an encounter with Delphine's strung-out friends.

"Shh ..." he says, "come over later. I need you."

He kisses her and trudges back to his car.

Panic is setting in again — it is a raw, unfamiliar emotion for him and he does not like it.

She closes the door as he speeds off.

"It was Vauquelin, but he didn't want to stay," she says, flopping down on the sofa between François, another French expatriate, and her American friend Kibby.

"Oh, how unfair of him to deny us his presence," François says. "I don't see nearly enough of his nightmarish beauty."

"Pffft. Why do you all like that cat? He gives me the heebie jeebies," Kibby says.

Delphine's face contorts. "What do you mean?"

"I don't know, man, like he's not genuine."

"*Pourquoi?* He is not weird enough for you?" François asks.

"No, man, he's too weird. Like too weird to be genuine. Aw, hell ... I can't explain it. You Frenchies really stick together no matter what, huh?"

"*Tais-toi*, Kibby," she says. "You do not know him."

"Yeah, but therein lies the problem, chicky," Kibby replies, poking her cheek with a freshly-rolled joint. "You don't really know him, either ... do you?"

"Stop this. I mean it," Delphine leaps up from the sofa.

Hearing someone else express distrust in Vauquelin does not help her fragile mental state. It adds to her stockpile of red flags, and she must stomp them down before they engulf her.

"Okay, okay, don't blow a gasket," Kibby says. "I just hope we don't come over here someday and find you strangled or something, is all I'm saying."

François laughs and shoves Kibby off the sofa.

"You are just jealous that Delphine is fucking Vauquelin instead of you. Now that I say it, I am jealous that he is fucking Delphine instead of me."

Delphine narrows her eyes, working her jaw side to side. She snatches Kibby's joint and tells François to show him out.

Kibby will never be invited to her house again.

For hours, Vauquelin drives around the city. His recent sampling of Delphine opened a vein, so to speak. The only way he can calm himself now is to go back to his old ways.

Rabbits cannot placate the furious craving rising in his throat.

He scours the downtown streets.

He is on the hunt.

Prostitutes are too cliché for his taste, but they are easy prey and he is not in the mood to split hairs tonight. He turns down a side street and scans the parade of flesh.

No redheads — he will never select a redhead. He pulls up to a blonde and opens the passenger door.

"Where we headed, doll?" she asks.

As the woman sits, she fumbles with Vauquelin's fanciful gull-wing door.

Exasperation swells in his chest.

He clenches his teeth as he gets out and closes it for her, slamming it a little harder than necessary.

She is cheap.

She talks cheap, smells cheap.

Her perfume pollutes the air of the car with its dime-store tang.

But he does not care just now.

"My house. It's just a short distance," he says.

"Fine by me," she says, plumping up her bosom. "You Italian or something? What's your name, sweetheart?"

"Vauquelin. I am French."

His smile fades into a frown.

The chit-chat period is officially over, and he casts a deep enchantment over her.

No more talking, he wills.

She remains silent all the way to his house and inside, though her eyes bulge at the expanse of the place. Her rabbit fur coat falls off her shoulder as she gapes at the living room. She walks over to admire one of the floral arrangements and reaches out to it, moving the vase a centimeter out of place.

"Don't touch my things," he whispers, returning the vase to its original position. He motions to a chaise and makes her a drink.

"Aren't you having anything?" she whispers.

"I have a different thirst," he says.

She takes little sips and glances around the room until Vauquelin takes the glass from her hand, placing it on the table.

He refuses to put on a performance tonight: this is all business. Sitting next to her he crosses his long legs, draping his arm across the back of the chaise.

Even in ordinary circumstances, Vauquelin is a spectacle.

She looks him over, head to toe. He is elegant and handsome in his own bizarre way, but there is something off about him, something she cannot place. So incredibly pale, and those eyes ... she has never seen such light-colored eyes.

"So what's your pleasure tonight?" she asks, swallowing hard.

As he leans toward her and opens his mouth wide the blood vanishes from her face, making her look already ghastly dead. In one swift motion, he clamps a hand over her mouth, jerks her head to the side, and drains her until her life fades. She never makes a sound, not even the merest squeak or moan.

Vauquelin's face is engulfed in ecstasy as he spirals to the floor, his head lolling to his shoulder. This is his first full measure of human blood in over twenty years.

God, that was good.

He strokes his erection. It happens every time.

Regardless, he is physically incapable of climax.

The nature of the vampire. No matter — the aftermath of a kill is far superior to any orgasm he ever had as a human.

The blood of a victim coursing through his veins, warming his body, electrifying his senses, giving him life, satisfying all his hungers — it is the pinnacle of eroticism.

He arranges her corpse on the chaise, crossing her hands on her chest with the skill of a seasoned funeral director. He may be a killer, but he will forever be a slave to aesthetics.

Vauquelin never got her name ... he preferred it that way.

He admires his handiwork with a tilt of his head, marveling at how much classier and at ease she looks dead rather than alive, and descends the steps to his cellar.

He has not been down here in decades, since the night he took his last human victim. It has the musty scent of a mausoleum, and it is soothing to be back: it has been much too long.

He lights a candle at the foot of the stairs and walks the perimeter of the room, illuminating the others. Hulking eight-arm candelabras fill the room with cozy, morbid light.

This is his catacombs: stacked ground-to-rafters with bones … the osteo-archive of his Southern California victims who had involuntarily surrendered their lives so that he could go on living.

In its special cabinet in the wall, in pride of place, is Maeve's exquisite rosewood coffin behind a glass door. He once kept candles burning for her night and day. When he no longer needed the catacombs, the candles snuffed out.

Vauquelin summons his finest seventeenth-century aristocrat, extends a gallant leg, and bows deeply to her. She had afforded him deep love and a beautiful twentieth-century life and beyond, and he will be forever joined to her.

He unlocks the wooden door on the floor and flashes himself back upstairs to retrieve the lifeless woman from the chaise. He feeds her body inch-by-inch into the bubbling acid that fills the pit. Her coat and handbag go in last, followed by his stupid new wig. He hated it, anyway.

She will be reduced to bones in a matter of minutes, and hence will become part of his eternal collection.

Breathing in the comforting, moldering fragrance of the catacombs he relaxes at last, sinking into a velvet chair at the exact moment an earthquake rolls across the floor, startling the many bones, jostling them into a percussive clatter.

Earthquakes are a never-ending source of fascination for him, and one of his favorite things about California. He loves their unpredictability, their colossal force that causes the restless earth to convulse beneath his feet.

The house sustained minor damage from the 1994 Northridge quake, and although the potential for utter destruction is no laughing matter, each earthquake still gives him a thrill. Mother Earth is flexing her muscles, keeping humans in check, and he has an immense appreciation for that.

On the other hand, he could get trapped beneath piles of rubble for days or weeks, and wither without his blood sustenance.

Perhaps it would finish him off with a glorious Final Death.

He would welcome it ... or any death.

He sits a moment, waiting, hoping for an aftershock.

When it comes, he lies face down on the floor, feeling it in his soul, stretching his arms to embrace it.

As Vauquelin emerges and locks the vault, he thinks of how difficult it had been to designate the cellar as off-limits without arousing the curiosity of prying servants and his rare, occasional guests. They could never resist asking what was behind that mysterious door.

A few months after Maeve and Charles died, he experimented with keeping domestics again. It was convenient to have someone on standby for daylight tasks he could not complete himself. But the arrangement was a failure and after a string of egregiously bad choices, he dismissed them altogether. It was tiresome adjusting his life to accommodate them and he was sick to death of self-editing for strangers.

Maids always troubled him about eating. He is so thin that women, in the old days, were fanatical about plying him with food. It exasperated him to conjure creative excuses for why he never wanted to eat. The male servants were a hair more discreet.

When he was growing up, domestics were less curious — at least to his face. They followed orders and said nothing. As the years progressed, they became bolder: and the longer they stayed on, the more meddlesome and invasive they became.

Centuries of human curiosity had hardened him, but when he befriended Delphine, he inherited her circle of beatniks. None of them knew the truth about him. They accepted him as a well-off eccentric and bought his story about being the last in the line of an ancient aristocratic French family (well, *that* part was true). Their natural inclination was to embrace society's rejects, with few exceptions: weirdos, freaks, dissidents — they were more than willing to welcome him and cast away any suspicions.

Because they accepted him, he resolved to do them no harm. He craved their sanction, their human connection, but he never carried on with the illusion that these people were his friends.

Aside from Delphine, he has no friends — friendship is an impossible concept.

In the kitchen, he opens a bottle of wine. He replaced the purposeless icebox with wine racks in the early 1920s. However, the now-antique Victorian stove remained in its place.

The stove is just something else for him to dust, but he has treasured memories of Maeve standing before it, cooking, laughing, joyous, and so it stays.

He washes the woman's cocktail glass and puts it away, waiting for Delphine in the living room.

Everything is once again as tidy as the moments before he arrived with his victim less than an hour ago.

With the passage of time and his apparent resumption of foraging for humans, he senses he is on the brink of lapsing, with ease, right back into his old brand of elegant savagery.

Well, so be it.

If he is being forced to go backward, then he will go all the way.

Why should he restrain himself now?

He hears the doorbell and snaps himself to the front door. Delphine, his faithful misfit, stands on his porch.

"Let's take a drive," he says.

They jump in his car and motor to Surfrider Beach.

He wants to breathe the ocean's fragrance, feel the magnetic pull of the waves. The sea is never more beautiful than it is at night, and with no buildings to obscure one's view and no street lights to compete with the moon, the universe seems timeless.

There is only darkness ahead.

It is a perfect place to think.

When they arrive, the beach is deserted and quiet. In a few more years, it will become the playground of the surf craze, and many scenes from *Beach Blanket Bingo* will be filmed on the precise spot where they sit. By and by, it will be renamed Malibu Beach.

As they sit facing the waves, the moon casts its soothing beams of illumination across the sea.

"What if it happens again?" he asks. He takes her hands and blows on them. It is chilly for her. "I must prepare myself."

"I've never known you to be paranoid, my pet," she replies.

"I never have been, but this has shaken me to my core. I have to go to Paris and I want you to come with me."

"No. Fuck Paris. I love it here in California."

"Just for a week or so," he says. "We'll come back, I promise. I love it here, too. There is nothing France can offer me now."

"But why? Why do you want to go back?"

"I need to see my attorney and have him take care of the financial reserves I still have there. If there's another time-shift, I'll lose my money. My bank here in Los Angeles only opened in

1924. Think about it. I could lose everything."

It is another (partial) lie. He does want to safeguard his wealth, but the real reason is that he needs answers — and in order to get them, he must try to locate his maker, Yvain, who had been curiously silent for centuries. Yvain would have an explanation for Vauquelin's reversal in time.

Despite breaking a few rules with Delphine, Vauquelin refuses to speak aloud about his elder. Insubordinate as he is, certain rules must remain unbroken.

"I told you I would never go back, remember?" she says. "Keep it in your house."

Vauquelin lists off the many modern items stolen from him by the time-shift. Goodbye, three-million-dollar Pagani.

"If an object is not on my person, it will not follow me. I only had the phone because it was in my hand," he says. "Right now, my house and its contents are just as they were in my original 1959. Sixty years of changes, erased in the wink of an eye."

She chews on her thumb, deconstructing the reality of what he is saying: that he could vanish from her life at any moment. The thought leaves her feeling sick and bereft.

"This is heavy," she says, "it's cracking my skull."

"I know, I know. I cannot explain it even to myself. But can you understand why I need to do this? And I want you with me. I'll feel less ... foreign. It's been three lifetimes since I've been in Paris. I need you to show me around, be my anchor."

Delphine squeezes his hand. "I get it. You'll be helpless in Paris without my expertise, no? Fine. I'll go. But only for one week."

All things considered, she has to admit she will do almost anything for him, despite her protests and misgivings.

He stands, holding out his hand to help her up.

Just as they arrive at Delphine's house, the sun begins to peek over the horizon, edging the sky in pink-orange flames.

"I don't have time to get home," Vauquelin says, slumping down in the car seat.

He sleeps in her closet, wrapped in blankets. After she closes the door for him, she tacks up another blanket outside the closet door. As ever, that grain of doubt is inside her, but she does not want to take any chances on harming him.

The additional precaution will not hurt anything, regardless.

PARIS, FRANCE | DECEMBER 1959

When the airplane lands at four in the morning, an angry sky is pouring down rain. Scheduling a flight that departed L.A. after dusk and arrived in Paris before dawn was a great challenge for Vauquelin, and he wasted hours on the phone with travel agents until he found one willing to work with him.

Even so, it was less complicated than packing himself into a coffin and traveling cross-country and over the sea in a wooden crate. Besides ... Delphine would never have consented to travel with him that way.

They are soaked as they scramble into a taxi.

"*Bienvenue à Paris,*" Delphine says with a crooked grin.

"Le Meurice," he tells the driver.

Their suite is sumptuous. They enter into a lush sitting room, with panoramic views of the city. They wander about, and Delphine whistles when she sees the Italian marble bathroom. She trails Vauquelin into the bedroom, while he closes the curtains.

Delphine has never had money, and she thinks this sort of place is one thousand percent bourgeois. She drops her bag on the floor and jumps on the bed, bouncing up and down and singing "La Marseillaise" at the top of her lungs, reveling in behaving like a naughty child for a moment.

He clasps his hands on his head and watches her.

"You are a raving lunatic!" he yells. But this is what he loves about her: she is nonconformist, irreverent, and fun.

The suite had been carefully modified prior to their arrival. When money is no object, demands are met without question. Vauquelin's instructions read:

> *The guest has extreme light sensitivity. No sunlight must penetrate the room at any time. Artificial light (lamps), fire, and candlelight are of no concern. The guests are not to be disturbed under any circumstances between sunrise and sundown.*

Most of the time, people obey such demands at face value. But if they do not, or if he is met with skepticism, he enchants them into obeying his wishes, and they are none the wiser.

Once they are settled, they head straight for bed. Delphine is jet-lagged and Vauquelin is on his normal schedule, exhausted and in need of his rest.

He nuzzles her face, wishing she would change her mind and let him turn her. Why must she be so resistant?

"Maybe I could get used to this kind of life," she says.

"I wish you would."

It rains all day as they sleep.

At nightfall they dress and go out into the city.

There has been no communication from Yvain, yet Vauquelin

is plagued by the caustic presence of vampires. So why are they not showing themselves? Their relentless thrumming makes him trepidatious and edgy: he glances over his shoulder at every turn, trying not to alarm Delphine.

Everyone knows there are revenants in Paris.

They cannot have all vanished, yet none have appeared.

In all the places he visited, and in almost one hundred and thirty years of living in California, he had never encountered another vampire outside of Paris and Venice, where he sought refuge during the French Revolution.

The majority of the Venetian vampires were Parisian expatriates who, like himself, fled during the Reign of Terror, and a small sect of clandestine, sequestered Elders, who did not associate with the younger generations.

He had never visited New Orleans, the vampire capital of the United States according to multiple novels and films. Allegedly New Orleans is brimming over with vampires.

He wonders if it is true, but his curiosity has never been that great. He has no need or desire to meet other haemovores, and he long ago shunned the idea of belonging to a coterie and being subjected to their rules. He must live without constraint.

As for the other cities he had visited, why were there no signs? Had none traveled, like him, to the new world?

Vauquelin's thoughts are interrupted by a bizarre premonition spreading across his back. He freezes in place as the building where he had been damned comes into his view.

Taking Delphine by the hand, he crosses the street and stops in front of an archway leading to a small shop, closed for the night. His former portal to hell is now a cheerful, highbrow *parfumerie*.

Still, he keeps Delphine close by his side. His need to protect her is overwhelming. She has no idea how much danger she is in and he aims to keep it that way.

Next to the shop is a charming café.

There is an accordionist.

A perfect Parisian movie moment is unfolding before his eyes, and he grasps her by the shoulders and steers her toward the chairs.

"Oh, come on ... this is such a stereotype," she says.

"How can you resist this? If you admit it that you love it, I'll buy you a beret," he smirks.

The sky is aromatic with petrichor and the dampened pavement glistens, casting reflections from the scattered neon and illuminated TABAC signs. The rain slows into a fine mist, blurring and intensifying the scrolled street lamps. They walk huddled together against the chill.

Paris is dressed to the nines in such beautiful yuletide finery. Evergreen wreaths hang on the shop doors and electric candles glow softly in their windows.

Vauquelin oohs and ahhs at every step.

Delphine is an atheist. She does not like Christmas, not even the kitschy, nonreligious side of it, but Vauquelin adores it.

During his short stint as a once-devout Catholic human, Christmas was a time of reflection, a somber occasion to acknowledge the birth of Christ and little more.

Paris was never decorated like this in his era. It makes him feel as though he is visiting the city for the first time, which in many ways he is. Contemporary Paris enthralls him.

He is grateful to have Delphine with him; he has not returned since he left for the United States in 1900. But the spirit and joy of *his* old Paris still endure, and the city's heart still beats within his own.

Melancholy nips at him, and he says, "I feel like a stranger."

"Well, you *are* strange," she replies.

They stop in front of a magnificent *hôtel particulier*.

"This was my home," he whispers.

The three-floor hôtel looms ahead of them, its many windows darkened for the night. The juniper boughs stretched across the iron gates waft their lusty fragrance into the air. A stone walkway bordered by manicured topiary leads to the front entrance, framed by arches and Corinthian columns. Eight life-size marble statues, illuminated by electric lights, keep guard from the mansard rooflines.

Delphine glances from the façade back to his face.

His house in L.A. is palatial, enormous and beautiful, but this? *C'est la connerie.*

"I grew up thinking of this as a government building," she says, "not a house. I have been inside. It is smothered floor to ceiling by its opulence."

Again, the doubt creeps in. How could this have possibly been his house? He cannot be serious.

"It was falling apart when I inherited it," he says. "It was one of our family homes. I spent a great deal of money to restore it. It was constructed in 1532."

His mind is filled with visual postcards of his seventeenth-century life in Paris.

In his imagination, he hears the sounds that once filled this house, the ancient sounds of his origins … he runs his fingers over its delicate moldings, lays his face on the cold parquet floor, listens to the creaking wood doors and sniffs the horsey luxury of his carriages. He had not really missed it, until now. Misery had taken root within those walls and drained its bliss.

He presses his face between the iron balustrades, straining his neck to peer inside, wishing he could enter.

Delphine lays her hand on his shoulder, coaxing him away.

The resonances of his reverie seep out into his consciousness — a distinct clatter of horse hooves rings out on the street, but there are only passing cars. (Delphine hears nothing ... the ghosts are his, not hers.) A church bell chimes ... a deep, moody tone that Vauquelin greatly missed hearing in Los Angeles, and he stretches his arms over his head, trying to force his mood.

He wants her to enjoy herself. He does not want to drag her down or, worse, frighten her.

"Show me the house where you grew up," he suggests.

She leads him to a neighborhood in Montmartre, high above the city. The Sacré Coeur sits atop the hill like a crown.

Delphine points to the second floor of a small pink building with green shutters on a steep street.

"That was my window. It used to have geraniums in the planters. I once loved to beg bits of cheese from the shopkeeper downstairs. He always indulged me," she says with a wistful smile.

"So charming. I can see you living there."

She shrugs. "It's just a regular old apartment. Nothing special. Certainly not like yours."

It is a great relief for him to be away from the oldest part of Paris, far from his past experiences.

He kisses her.

Delphine's presence has a calming effect on him.

For the moment, he worries about nothing, pushing thoughts of vampires to the furthest corner of his mind.

He cannot feel them now.

At ten o'clock, Vauquelin meets his attorney at the bank.

Over the centuries, dozens of attorneys have been secured to maintain his various legal connections.

Before he and Delphine flew out of Los Angeles, he transferred approximately $500,000 to his accounts at the Banque du Courtois, which was established in 1760. For all they know, he is a descendant of the original account holder, Louis-Augustin du Cavernay de Vauquelin, bearing the same family name of his ancient ancestor.

The attorney is given orders to distribute the majority of the currency to charities in Paris. Vauquelin has witnessed desperate poverty throughout the duration of his long life, and it troubles him. His affluence is in jeopardy, and rather than waste it or have it disappear in time, he wants it to have a purpose.

He regrets, for a fleeting second, dropping so much cash on the Pagani, which he had gotten to enjoy for six whole days.

It still had the paper plates on it.

He has always had money, and never had to think about it before now. Infinite money. He is accustomed to having it at his disposal. The threat of becoming destitute terrifies him. What could he do? Sell everything he owns? Get a job?

Few jobs exist that would befit a vampire.

From the security box, he selects one of his mother's necklaces, a silk velvet ribbon with a solitary pearl drop. He wants to give Delphine a gift. She is the opposite of materialistic, and she dresses simply. But this will be from him, a reminder. There had been only one other recipient of his mother's jewels: Maeve.

Lost in nostalgia, he saunters back to the hotel, and, once in their room, is careful not to wake her — not just yet.

He sits by the fire a while, twirling the necklace in his fingers like a rosary, until his eyes become narrow and gritty. He crawls into bed next to her, delighted by the mandated blackout.

Vauquelin has not nourished himself in six days. He can go for a maximum of seven, but if he waits much longer he will be rendered defenseless.

His body is already in the throes of trauma, so he informed Delphine that he will soon go out alone — and that she is to remain in their room and unlock the door to no one.

He told her why he is leaving her: he has never concealed his reasons. But perhaps she does not believe that he actually kills people. After all, she has never witnessed him do it.

"Take my blood," she says. "I can see that you're nervous in Paris, and you look like shit. Stay here with me so you can be safe."

"No. It's not enough for me. All it does is make you suffer, and I don't want that. I won't be gone long ... I promise."

He waits until four o'clock, his golden hour of sorts, when the city will be quiet and pose fewer obstacles.

Behind a *patisserie*, he assumes a position by the back door. Patisseries always have early employees. They bake the day's bread while the city sleeps.

At last a man emerges and Vauquelin seizes him, pulling him up along the wall to the top of the building, drinking as they rise.

There is no struggle.

It is his preferred method — quick and neat. He drops the body on the roof and slides back down the wall.

By the time it is discovered, Vauquelin will be long gone.

A few blocks from the hotel, he passes a narrow alleyway. A long arm reaches out and pulls him in, planting him face to face at last with another vampire.

She is dressed like a prostitute, tattered and hideous, and reeks of spent blood and body odor. She grabs his chin in her filthy hand and hisses, "There is blood on your lips. Introduce yourself, beautiful one."

"Who are you?" he snarls, throwing her to the ground.

Whoever she is, she is a poor match for his strength. She is young for a vampire, maybe fifty years old if that.

"Where is your coterie?" he demands. "Why have you been stalking me and not identifying yourselves?"

"You are a stranger to us. We must be cautious."

Vauquelin clutches her by the throat. "Where is Yvain?"

Her eyes narrow. "How do you know this name?"

"He is my maker!" he snarls, digging further into her throat. "I demand to know his location!"

"You are Vauquelin!" she gasps, struggling against him.

"Indeed I am ... and whoever you are, vile *salope*, you are no threat to me."

The narrow space begins to darken as shadows choke out what little light remains. Their presence enfolds him in a black dread, and he is at once surrounded. He dares not move or break eye contact with the one in his clutches.

He is intimidated by their approach, but it is imperative that he does not lose his composure. Two and a half centuries stand between him and his last encounter with vampires, and he can rely only on instinct.

Soon, there are seven other revenants around him, all of them unkempt and ragged.

Yvain's silence must have something to do with this. His coterie would never have become so downtrodden.

Where the fuck is he?

Fingers dig into the back of his neck and he whirls around.

"Keep your distance!" she rasps. "He is the vampire Vauquelin!"

At her utterance of his name, the entire brood recoils, slinking against the walls.

He is the forbidden one.

It is legend.

Unbeknownst to Vauquelin, Yvain has been missing for centuries and his survivors still worship him as a god. His power remains unmatched.

This wretched lot had clearly not carried on his traditions and standards. The tenants of Yvain's coterie had always been bizarre, but at least they had been educated in elegance.

"Where is Yvain?" Vauquelin demands again, with gritted teeth.

The vampires are silent.

"Can none of you besides this harlot speak? Have you no tongues? Where is he?"

But still they do not answer. They are too shocked to reply.

The woman stands, her injuries from Vauquelin's rough treatment now healed. "Yvain is no more," she says. "But his decree was clear: you must not be touched. We never believed you would appear to us. We thought you had reached another plane, like Yvain.""

As she speaks, a male vampire approaches Vauquelin from behind, reaching for his head.

"TURN BACK!" she screams.

Vauquelin flings himself around and snaps the neck of his attacker. This will not deliver death, so he tears open the vampire's shirt, ripping the flesh and ribcage apart with an agile, heinous crunch and extracts the heart.

"Stay away from me!" he screeches, thrusting it toward them like a trophy — dripping blood and still beating.

With their curiosity about the legendary Vauquelin satisfied, the entire coterie evaporates, screaming into the night.

And Yvain? He refuses to believe that Yvain is extinct. This must be a group of rogue vampires who take orders like gospel, believing any and all tales they are told.

At one time, Yvain's house had been full of such creatures: followers, lemmings. They were undistinguished in their human existence, and their creation as vampires amplified their natural sensibilities: mediocre humans became exponentially mediocre vampires.

Vauquelin emerges from the alley with wild eyes, panting and frantic as a madman, still holding the vampire's heart.

He pitches it behind him like a piece of garbage.

The heart shrivels and hisses as it hits the ground, melting away into a paltry pile of ash.

The city is still quiet. Just a few passing cars, and even fewer pedestrians. It will come alive soon.

Yvain, where can you be? Show yourself to me. I beg you.

There is only silence.

Despondent, he reaches a fountain and washes the blood from his hands. Nothing can frighten him, but the night has turned eerie. When he lived here he was too nervous to relax: his ancient anxiety abides.

He quickens his pace, at last bursting through the brass-framed entrance to his hotel.

It's time to get the hell out of Paris.

LOS ANGELES, CALIFORNIA | 1959

Christmas Eve is a wonderful time to go hunting.

After Vauquelin arrived in America, he witnessed the holiday evolve into a pinnacle of commercial frenzy. He rather enjoys all the colorful lights, painted windows, and beautiful decorations. The constant search for beauty is his avocation — only his reaction to it is often lethal.

Houses illuminated with holiday spirit enthrall him, and he drives around for hours looking at them every Christmas — alone. Perhaps it is just that, with the absence of sunlight in his life, Christmas affords him a wealth of light as no other time of year can.

He enjoys taking short trips to small towns on the outskirts of Los Angeles, the type of small towns that still have main squares with lighted boughs stretching across the streets, almost as far as the eye can see. But his sentimentality always prevails: he refuses to hunt there. His feast is in L.A., among the lost souls that no one will miss.

Tonight, with his current state of mind and the erratic chaos of the time-shift, he intends to get obliterated.

Direct consumption of alcohol does not affect his blood. He can drink twenty bottles of wine and not feel a thing. He adores a good burgundy or cabernet sauvignon. But drinking the blood of an intoxicated human will anesthetize him, and that is what he wants now.

Outside a dive bar, he parks the car and waits, chain-smoking. By and by couples emerge, tottering off in all directions full of holiday cheer.

A couple would be nice ... he could drink two tonight in a snap. But couples are hard to get. They are suspicious. The circumstances must be perfect and they rarely are, especially on Christmas Eve in 1959. A rueful smile curls his lips as he thinks of how easily he could have gotten a couple back to his house in the twenty-first century. All it would have taken was a scant purchase of a few drinks and the proposition of a threesome. Perhaps he should have eased up on his no-humans rule in his futurepast.

Five cigarettes later, the ideal victim emerges: a man wearing a tattered Santa hat, zigzagging across the parking lot.

Vauquelin leaps from the car.

"Are you alright, sir?" he asks, steadying the man's elbow.

"Oh yeah, sure, sure," the man slurs, reaching in his pocket for his keys, which plummet to the ground.

"I believe you are unfit for driving," Vauquelin says.

He considers that he is applying his futurepast mentality to the current calendar: in this era, no one gives a damn about driving drunk.

What if he has blown his cover?

But it is irrelevant, anyhow: the man is exceptionally intoxicated.

He falls, landing on a knee, and says, "You know, mister, I think you might be right."

"Allow me to drive you home," Vauquelin says. "You can retrieve your car tomorrow."

He leads the man to his car and helps him sit, bringing the gull-wing door down. As it seals shut, a pungent fist of malodorous air smacks him in the face. He sits behind the wheel and hesitates a moment, wondering if the promise of inebriation is worth this particular kill, then starts the engine.

Oppressive body odor fills the car.

Filthy Santa passes out right away, piercing Vauquelin's eardrums with his vulgar snores. His head thunks against the passenger window.

This is the essence of Vauquelin's frustration: it is difficult to find fresh blood. So, so difficult. His futurepast experiences are tattooed on his psyche. He retains his disdain for the police, for bodies being discovered, for leaving evidence of his vampirism.

Looking at this poor bastard, he realizes he does not want to exert the effort to drag him into his house and dispose of his bones.

This is humiliating.

Vauquelin drives a few blocks and then abruptly pulls up to a deserted side street, opens the passenger door, and shoves the man out, squealing his tires as he departs.

Stopped at a traffic light, he slams his head on the steering wheel over and over again. Life had been so much less complicated in the future.

Fuck me, I've gone soft.

The car reeks of rank perspiration and cheap booze.

A resolve rises in his gut.

He makes a U-turn and rushes back to the spot where he dropped the man.

He is still there.

"There, there ... into the car now, that's it ... " Vauquelin shoves the drunkard back in and takes off. He holds his breath in increments, as long as he can bear it.

He drags him through his kitchen door and straight down into the cellar, guiding him down the stairs. The man is as limp and uncooperative as a sleepy toddler.

He opens the pit and drains him right next to the opening. His nostrils flare at the man's physical funk: a deadly brew of body odor, cigarettes, and bottom-shelf liquor.

Despite this nastiness, as the last of the blood slides down his throat, Vauquelin's clockwork erection comes to call. He ignores it and slips the body into the acid, Santa hat and all, closing the lid.

He stumbles as he stands.

The man's blood-alcohol level must have been staggering.

Vauquelin has gotten just what he needed: sweet, sweet intoxication. Numbness ... the gift of forgetting his current troubles, if only for a few fleeting hours.

He closes the heavy vault door behind him and careens up the two flights of stairs to his bathroom.

Vauquelin is meticulous about his bed. Drunk as he is, he refuses to carry the stench of his unenviable victim into his sheets. He runs a hot bath and fires up the jets. Peeling off his clothes, he submerges himself, stroking his forlorn cock, so engorged with new, boozy blood.

He is sanguinated and exquisitely wasted.

The soak mellows him even further.

He has always loved baths ... their warmth is a tonic for his cold bones. He scrubs the foulness off of himself and lies in the tub awhile, smoking.

Tomorrow night he will clean the car, absolving it of the horrible fumes inflicted by his wretched victim.

In his clean, soft bed he pulls the curtains and descends into a velvety-black, dreamless void.

It is early March, Los Angeles is erupting into Spring, and Vauquelin has been back in 1959 for almost four months. He is fearful of getting too comfortable. Preparing himself for a sudden change (or perhaps just a return to his real life) is a constant in the corners of his mind.

Delphine and Vauquelin are having dinner at his long, old-world table, capable of seating twenty people. It is completely extra and over the top, but what in his life is not? Maeve had imported it from Venice and Vauquelin loved it, along with all the other relics of his life with her.

He would never dream of changing it.

Delphine is wearing the necklace he gave her in Paris and dressed in a shabby antique Japanese kimono. She has a way of bringing elegance to clothes that others would toss away. It gives her a timeless quality which he finds irresistible.

Despite her dismal everyday diet, she is an excellent cook.

Her talents are wasted on Vauquelin, however: not one morsel of food has touched his tongue since his last night as a human in the year 1668.

He sits a distance away from her. The aroma of her cooking makes him nauseous, although he is quite sure it is delicious. The longer he lives, the more intolerant he grows to the pungency of human food.

She is having *coq au vin*, and he is drinking from two crystal glasses: one filled with wine and one with blood.

This is Vauquelin's typical two-course meal: there are decanters of each in front of him on the table.

Delphine decides to indulge Vauquelin's future fancy, to let him talk it out. "Tell me what it was like. Were you accepted? Did people know about you?"

"Oh, no, no, no. It was easier to blend in. But no one knew. And I did not hunt in my future."

"But why? How did you survive?" she asks.

He points to the darker of the two decanters.

"Rabbits. Come, now … you've seen my pens. Surely you did not think I was keeping them as pets?"

"Rabbits, Vauquelin? Really?" she sneers. She cannot help her sarcastic tone.

"There's a reason I stopped hunting humans. In the year 2000, I went to a nightclub. I lured a young woman back to my house and made my kill. She had taken some sort of drug, and it rendered me delirious for weeks. I thought I would perish. The rabbits are pure, so pure."

He runs his finger around the rim of the glass, lost in thought.

As he had done with the drunken man at Christmas, he does not mind being intoxicated by a victim on occasion, and his infrequent snacks of Delphine's cannabis-infused blood used to mellow him out. But narcotics are an altogether different matter.

Imagine the effect of recreational drugs on a human and multiply that times one thousand for the heightened senses of a vampire's body.

He *abhors* losing control of himself.

Throughout his existence, he had never been attracted to pharmaceutical substances of any kind. In the seventeenth century, elixirs and powders were prevalent amongst the aristocracy. They were a distraction, a balm to soothe the tedium of empty lives filled with doldrum, vapid parties, endless card games, and inane conversation.

These "remedies" are not something a vampire needs.

"Everyone in Los Angeles is obsessed with health food in the future ... so I guess I'm no different," he says.

During the pandemic of 1918, Vauquelin became an accidental farmer of rabbits. He cultivated them for his emergency sustenance during that dismal era. After Maeve's death, he returned to the human hunt. But that changed again after another fateful night further into his futurepast.

"There were nightclubs all over the city in the future ... many people claimed to be vampires. They wore fake fangs and colored lenses in their eyes. Some of them were quite convincing, but there's more to identifying another vampire than the visual," he explains. "I went to one of these clubs so I could draw my own conclusions."

He had yet to conceive of a way to describe the internet to her. If only he could show her pictures of the poseurs, or the websites with the alleged vampire rules listed for the entire human world to read, or the pages and pages of faux fangs for sale.

She would get a kick out of it.

And the modern-day movies — *holy shit, the sparkling, virginal pretty boy* — how could he possibly explain them? So many horrible, horrible films. Daywalkers, vampires eating regular human meals, teenage slayers ... it was all just too insulting.

He was glad Bela Lugosi did not live to witness the utter farce that vampires would become in mainstream culture, although the role had consumed his life. He was forced to poke a little fun at himself and the character merely to survive. That was when the public perception of vampires went downhill. Lugosi created the archetypal vampire with his Dracula, but he himself became just another of Dracula's victims.

Vampires had been reduced to caricature.

No wonder Vauquelin chose to retreat from human society.

"They did this every day, and not just on Halloween? They were pretending to be actual vampires?"

"Yes. There were stores that sold the teeth. There were costly ticketed events, masquerades, balls. It was a mockery."

"Please tell me you're joking."

"If only. It became a fashion trend. If they had ever faced the true, bloody gore of the vampire's existence, those phonies would have wilted on the spot."

At that moment, Vauquelin decides to tell her about the girl. Maybe it will help him articulate the absurdity of it all.

"I have a story to illustrate all this. But will you be upset if I talk about having sex with another woman?" he asks, cautiously.

"Of course not," Delphine says.

She does not *think* she'll be jealous.

Let's find out.

LOS ANGELES, CALIFORNIA | 2000

It was the first — and last — time he went to a goth club.

He wanted to break up the monotony, and perhaps to prove to himself that he was right about the frauds.

The club was called Vortex 13 and floated around to various locations in Los Angeles.

When he first arrived, he recoiled in the entryway, hesitant to go any further. The music was angry, deafening, but it had an unexpected effect on his ears: it spoke to him. He took a deep breath and walked through the door with a cigarette dangling from his mouth.

It cost $20 to get in, and he had to show his ID.

It amused him.

Three hundred and thirty-two years old and still getting carded.

Nice, he thought.

The room was filled with goths, unclassified societal rejects, punks, and a smattering of squares attempting to broaden their colorless horizons and take a walk on the wild side.

They stuck out the most.

He studied faces as he began to move through the crowd.

So. Much. Black. Eyeliner.

So many facial piercings.

So many red and white contacts. He went up to the bar and ordered his customary wine next to a gigantic Viking of a goth guy, who jerked his head at him. Vauquelin's height is two meters, but this man stood head and shoulders above him.

"Good evening," Vauquelin said, keeping his lips as close together as possible, as he was always wont to do.

"What's up?" asked the Viking, flashing his store-bought fangs.

Vauquelin was speechless.

"Well done," he blurted, raising his glass.

He thrust his chin out. He considered baring his own (quite real) teeth but thought better of it and said, "Enjoy yourself, *mon ami,*" vanishing into the crowd.

On a stage at the end of the room, a live dominatrix show was in progress. He never understood how these worlds had merged. Bondage, goths, "vampires," steel spikes, Neo-nazis, quiffs, piercings, greasers, death metal, pseudo-Satanists.

It was a mélange of concepts that did not quite fit together but had nowhere else to go. They had all blended into a parody of themselves. Or maybe he was just too different, too discriminating, and this lifestyle simply did not appeal to him.

Regardless, Vortex 13 was not meant for a real vampire. It was imaginary, make-believe. As hard as these people fronted their "vampirism," he struggled twice as hard to remain hidden from sight.

He continued on, walking and observing, and as he moved through the bar he received dozens of dirty looks. It occurred to him that these people were lumping him in with the squares and thought he did not belong there.

Oh, the irony.

It was hilarious: an authentic revenant in a club designed for the children of the night was being summarily rejected! He laughed out loud, tilting his head back. Bewildered by the spectacle, he did not notice the small goth girl sidling up to him.

She was staring at his teeth, which were exposed by his laughter.

"Those are really good fangs," she said.

"WHAT?" Vauquelin yelled, leaning down. His acute vampire hearing was no match for the stultifying industrial music.

She stood on tiptoe and screamed into his ear.

"I SAID, THOSE ARE REALLY GOOD FANGS. WHERE DID YOU BUY THEM?"

She smiled and pointed to her adhesive fangs.

As he reached toward them someone bumped into him, causing him to knock one off. It tumbled to the floor.

"I BEG YOUR PARDON," he yelled.

They looked down in unison.

It would be absurd to attempt its retrieval from the mucky floor. He could feel the soles of his shoes sticking with each step. He forced himself to not think about what filth he was walking upon: a hellish recipe of vomit, spilled liquor, sweat, and god-knows-what-else.

She glanced up at him and placed a hand on his chest.

He was moved by her gentleness and parted his lips.

She prodded his elongated canines one by one, having no idea that she was handling the weaponry of a true vampire, pricking her finger upon a point.

A bead of blood appeared on her fingertip.

Vauquelin's nostrils splayed.

Her eyes widened, and she plunged her ruptured finger into her mouth.

She was elfen: skin the color of moonlight, with jet black hair framing her face. It rose high on her crown into a slight bouffant, and sharp bangs came to a point in the center of her forehead.

He gazed down her body. She wore a black dress, ripped fishnets, and heavy, unfeminine boots. Intermingled in the scent of her blood was the distinct fragrance of lilies: the heady aroma of death, an odor undetectable by humans.

He was enraptured.

Come home with me, he willed.

Her lips mouthed "Yeah," but it was inaudible to anyone besides Vauquelin. She began to move toward the door.

He grasped her elbow and steered her through the crowd.

In the parking lot, she popped her remaining faux fang off, flicking it across the pavement.

He opened the car door for her and she froze, glancing sideways at him. She was young, but whatever her age, she was not of a generation where men opened car doors for women.

The drive to his house took almost an hour in the congested Saturday-night L.A. traffic. The entire time, she stared straight ahead, saying nothing.

His enchantment was potent.

There was classical music on the car stereo. If she had her senses about her, she would think that this guy was really, *really* weird. Who would choose to listen to music like this on purpose?

When they pulled up in his driveway, he decided he wanted

to have a bit of fun with this one. It was turning out to be his favorite type of evening: a fuck followed by a kill. This was a rare treat. There was a lot more killing than fucking in his life. It was an indulgence, and he aimed to enjoy it to the fullest.

Now the true performance could commence.

He snapped his fingers and broke the spell.

"Here we are," he said.

"Wow, what is this place?" she asked, wide-eyed.

Vauquelin laughed. "This is my home."

He took her hand and lifted it into the air, leading her into the house like a lady of the court.

This impressed her; she had never been treated this way before. She looked down at his hand, startled by the chill of his flesh.

He opened the front door and guided her inside with his hand on the small of her back.

"Oh my god, so beautiful," she breathed, marveling at the interior of the house.

"Thank you ... I inherited it from a loved one." He had long gotten over sullying Maeve's memory by bringing victims to the house. It was safer for him than killing on the streets.

He led her to the sofa. "What's your name, *mon ange?*"

"Michelle," she said. "What's yours?"

"Louis-Augustin de Vauquelin."

"Um, that's a pretty fancy name," she said.

"Is it? Well, you can thank my French ancestry," he replied, raising an eyebrow. "Would you like a glass of wine?"

"Okay," she said.

He went to the kitchen and brought back two glasses and a bottle. He was enjoying himself immensely. He put Miles Davis on the stereo. It was a benediction for his ears after the harsh music at the bar.

"So tell me, Mademoiselle Michelle, why this fascination with darkness and vampires?"

Though she had been slumped-shouldered and morose, at the mention of vampires she sat upright and her voice became effervescent. "Dude, I fucking love vampires. I've read a lot of books, and I've seen all the movies. Vampires are super rad."

"And which do you most admire?"

"Gary Oldman as Dracula. And Lestat, obviously. I guess those two movies are what made me love vampires so much. I didn't like the original Dracula, the old one. I thought it was totally boring. Whatever. He didn't even have any fangs."

Vauquelin suppressed a smile. "Very good ... respectable vampires, the both of them," he said, twirling a lock of her hair in his fingers.

"What about you? You don't look like the rest of the guys that go to Vortex. Were you slumming?"

He was unfamiliar with the term "slumming," but he got the gist. "Oh, my sweet, I am most *definitely* not like those guys."

"So where did you get those great fangs? Are you with the studios? They're good enough to be in a movie."

"As a matter of fact, I am. I'm a writer."

She smiled. "Holy shit, that's so cool! Are you writing a vampire script for a movie?"

"Well, I am dabbling a bit with one in particular," he said. "It's a work in progress, although it may take me an eternity to finish it. One might say I'm still doing my research. So that's why I was at the club tonight ... was it that obvious I was an outsider?"

"Yeah, totally. You're dressed too nice."

Vauquelin was quite taken with this woman. She was a delight. He had chosen well. He would almost hate taking her life.

"Please, satisfy my curiosity ... it isn't every day I get to speak to such a passionate vampire fan. What else is it about them that intrigues you so?" he asked.

"I love that they get to live forever. It's like, so dark and romantic. I'm jealous of them. It's way more exciting than the boring way people live now."

"True, very true. But the vampire leads such a lonely existence, does he not? And what about the killing? Delivering humans to their deaths, drinking their life force ... surely you find that unappealing. Do you drink blood?"

She squirmed in the chair.

That question *always* made mortals uncomfortable.

"No, I've only tasted my own. I've never really thought about that. They're just movies. I go to the club because I feel accepted there. I don't really fit in anywhere else. You don't drink it ... do you?"

"I've had my fair share. It's an acquired taste, for sure."

He softened toward her. He knew all too well how it felt to be an outcast, to scrounge the dark fringes of society for a fleeting fragment of acceptance.

"Can I use your bathroom?" she asked.

"Of course, mademoiselle."

Vauquelin led her to the door and returned to the living room. This was the problem with acting. He should have no feelings for her whatsoever. He should regard her as mere sustenance ... but then she had to go and be adorable.

He tapped his fingers on the back of the chaise like a metronome, losing himself in the music. When she returned, he noticed that her pupils were constricted. As he puzzled over it, she sat on the floor in front of him and ran her hands up his thighs, tilting her head as she met his gaze, and his brain went adrift.

That was the opening he needed. He stood abruptly, offering his hand, and led her upstairs into his bedroom.

"Whoa, this room is so sexy. It's beautiful," she said.

"I'm glad it pleases you," he said. He kissed her neck and ran a finger down her cleavage, his hand on the small of her back.

She tilted her head back and pressed into him.

"Run your tongue over my teeth," he said.

She obeyed: blood fanned across her tongue. He drew his finger across and licked it, stripping off his clothes. That minuscule sample of blood had taken him too far to go back now.

"This feels like a dream," she murmured.

"How can you be sure it isn't?" Vauquelin asked, pulling her dress over her head. He held the canopy aside, inviting her in.

They sat facing each other, both on their knees. He crawled across the bed, pushing himself between her legs as she kissed his cold neck, bit his shoulders. He took a fistful of her tights, ripping them apart at the seam between her legs. She groaned, grinding her hips against his hand.

Clutching her neck, he inched his cock against her, just shy of entering her. Her body quaked, and the hothouse, musky smell of her was driving him mad.

"Do you want a bit of death? *La petite mort?*" he whispered in her ear. "That is what you came here for, yes?"

"Please," she whispered back.

Vauquelin arched his back in ecstasy once he was inside her. He brought her to climax again and again in relentless waves — until the breath vanished from his lungs.

He had to claim his own satisfaction.

Still buried deep inside her, he plunged his teeth into her neck. Her screams delighted him, made his blood twitch in his veins. No one would hear her in his fortress. There was no need to worry about that. He drank her down, and his cock swelled even more.

She should have been dead, but no: her voice penetrated the room's silent darkness. "You're real ... take me, make me like you ... a vampire." She gurgled the last word. Blood was coming up in her throat, oozing out of the corners of her mouth.

He had perforated her esophagus.

Her heart slowed — he pulled out.

Leaning his mouth next to her ear, he whispered, "No, *chérie* ... you are a delight, but this is not the life for you."

He lapped the blood from her lips as she writhed on the bed. There was more life yet to take from her yet. He gnawed into her femoral artery and placed his hand on her heart, waiting for the tell-tale moment. Before her heart delivered its last beat, he withdrew his daggers and she went still.

There was no remorse. At least this girl, who loved the idea of vampires, had met her death at one's hand.

Vauquelin picked her up and carried her downstairs. When he reached the kitchen with her body in his arms he faltered, stricken by a sudden, visceral weakness.

Every muscle in his body began to spasm, causing him to fall to his knees ... he cratered on top of her. He left her lying on the floor and crawled back upstairs to his bedroom.

What have I done?

Vauquelin was annihilated.

It was a struggle to get himself up onto the mattress — with the violent shaking in his arms, he could not support himself. At last he made it up and lay still, panting. A blood sweat began to prickle his skin, seeping from his eye sockets.

His body was rejecting the blood.

He was long accustomed to being cold, but a harrowing frigidity burrowed into the depths of his soul. Gooseflesh erupted across his skin and his teeth began to chatter.

Perhaps this was The Final Death.

With great difficulty, he managed to maneuver himself under the covers. There was no relief. His chills vibrated the enormous bed. Then he was consumed by heat, but so enfeebled that he could not lift the covers off himself.

Bloody steam oozed from his pores.

He fought the covers off, and the steam emanated off his body, permeating the air, filling it with the scent of iron.

Convulsions wracked him, and he rolled to the side of the bed, retching out endless buckets of blood.

Once again, he was seized by chills. Hot and cold, back and forth. His teeth resumed their hellish chattering, rattling his skull to pieces, and what little blood he had left pulsed in his temples. It knifed through his veins, boiled over in his ears.

Time slowed as he dragged himself into the bathroom by his elbows and struggled to reach up to the tub. He extended a shaking arm to turn on the water but the tremors were so intense that he lost his balance, slamming his head on the marble.

The blow knocked him out, enfolding him in a black void.

When he came to, he was disoriented, wet, and cold. The tub had overflowed, and he found himself lying in several inches of blood-tainted water on the bathroom floor. The shock of this gave him a bit of clarity, and something, perhaps adrenaline, empowered him to push himself up by his arms. He turned off the water and pulled the plug.

His mind was foggy, so foggy.

What is happening to me?

On his knees, he gripped the side of the tub and held himself there a moment, trying to reassure himself that he could stand. He slipped on the wet tile and collapsed in a shivering heap on the floor.

He was a naked, bloody, pathetic mess.

A distinct voice from his ancient past whispered in his subconscious: "You shall live free from harm." Well, that was a ruse ... because he *was* harmed, possibly beyond repair.

His fractured mind called out, *Yvain. Help me.*

There was only silence.

No one could (or would) come to his aid.

He trudged across the floor, making small splashes as he stepped. The water was tinted pink from the blood he had sweated out. He made it to the bed and sat on its edge, gripping the duvet with his hands. Fighting his way into a dressing gown, his body still vibrating, he made it to the bedroom door, leaning on the jamb. His breath was reduced to pitiful, ragged spurts.

He thought he could make it downstairs — maybe. He pressed himself against the wall, gripping the banister for dear life, and descended the stairs.

In the kitchen lay the dead vampire lover in an advanced state of decomposition. The stench of her decay assaulted him as he entered.

Fuck ... how long had he been up there?

He knelt by the body. She must have been dead for weeks. He tried to step over her and lost his balance, landing on her head. It collapsed like a melon. He was half-drenched in rotting human muck.

Holy fucking shit.

There, laid out before him in revolting technicolor, was the hideous reality of being vampire. He took off his dressing gown and dropped it on her, struggling to pull open the massive vault door. He dragged the putrefying corpse down the stairs and, with all effort he could muster, managed to heave open the heavy lid of the vat. He slid her in and lay panting as the acid consumed the remains.

The acrid, vile odor punched him thick and fast.

As he lay there, listening to the sizzling and bubbling of her flesh, he had an epiphany.

In over three hundred years of his existence as a vampire, was his lowest point. There was a hideous disaster left in his wake, a gargantuan mess like no other he had ever experienced.

He would have to clean the festering detritus himself.

There was no possibility of calling in a restoration service. The police would be notified: it was a ghastly crime scene, even by L.A. standards.

And still he was baffled by what had caused this to happen to him. He was weak, so weak. A full portion of human blood, which should have strengthened him and given him life for days, had nearly destroyed him.

Vauquelin walked to the living room as if his body was ninety years old, not the robust body of an eternally thirty-year-old man, his skin shrinking and desiccating.

He seized the girl's purse, rifling through it. He found her driver's license — she was Michelle Anderson, she was twenty-seven years old, and she lived in Encino.

He continued digging, and found another pair of fake vampire fangs. He hurled them across the floor. His fingers latched onto a small plastic packet. He removed it from the purse and fumbled it open. Even this trivial task was an uphill battle. The packet split apart, sending multi-colored pills scattering over his rug.

There was no doubt in his mind that this was what had decimated him. The girl had gone into his bathroom, he recalled now, and she must have taken these.

What the fuck is this evil elixir?

A few days later, after spending every waking hour dragging the murky waters of the internet, he figured it out: Ecstasy, a drug that was wholly unfamiliar to him.

For several months afterward, there was a rash of murders at the various locations where Vortex 13 popped up. The cases all went cold, but the common thread was that each victim was a known drug dealer. It was all over the L.A. news stations, and stories appeared in the paper for weeks. Vauquelin did not drink them — he wasted them, snapping their necks and leaving them beside dumpsters where they could be easily spotted.

He would have eliminated every single one had he been able to track them all down. The club ceased operations within a year ... good riddance, in his book, but he knew they were like cockroaches. There were many other clubs, and the street pharmacists would continue to thrive on humans' unquenchable thirst for self-medication.

They had done so throughout history.

"The end," he says. "I know that was explicit," Vauquelin says, "but it was one of the defining moments of my modern life."

Recounting the dismal tale has made him weary. He wants to elicit some sort of response from Delphine, but her eyes are wide as saucers; she's biting her fingers.

Maybe I went too far, he thinks.

She wonders why or if Vauquelin would make something like this up. Maybe he's only trying to scare her. An acid pit in the cellar? *Right.* Or was his goal to make her jealous? The truth is she did not, not one little bit, like hearing about Vauquelin fucking another woman.

This sudden, irrational envy supersedes her ability to even feel sorry for the desperate anguish and misery he experienced, and she cannot muster a single ounce of sympathy for the pitiful girl who had met her demise in his demented story.

If he had even killed her!

It was ridiculously far-fetched.

Vauquelin is pansexual ... he has never hidden that fact from her. It's a given that he had been with many other lovers. He is far from a saint ... but did he have to be so detailed?

No wonder he always tells people he is a writer.

She is conflicted, aroused, and angry all at once. No other man has ever ignited such a poisonous combination of feelings in her. She has to ask herself: what does this say about her own ego? And the girl had begged him for eternal life.

He refused her.

Delphine had refused *him*.

Could it really be? she wonders.

Her eyes go blank as she drifts into a fantasy. She and Vauquelin are both vampires — dressed in some sort of outrageous, unidentifiable, ephemeral fashion — and they terrorize the night, feasting upon an out-of-luck human, laughing, frenzied, blood streaming down their chins. Then they fuck, climaxing together in their bloodlust. Her face becomes wild as she falls deeper into the reverie.

Maybe I should ask to see the cellar, she thinks.

"Delphine," he says, placing his hand on hers. "Are you alright?"

She jerks at his touch. Her heart is pounding so fast that her breath catches in her throat. Here in front of her is the real Vauquelin, and he is in love with her. But she cannot fathom why his gruesome confession is turning her on so.

All she can think — at this moment — is that she wants more.

Delphine leans in, unsure if she is ready for this, but she must test herself. She must test *him*. She decides it is time for her to hear all he has to say, or is willing to say, *now*.

Right now.

She twists her glass on the table. "Tell me how it happened ... how you became a vampire."

Vauquelin squints at her as he stubs out his cigarette and immediately lights another, puffing out perfect smoke rings.

He's not convinced she needs to hear more tonight. As the years passed, he thought of the act of his creation less and less, and he isn't primed for opening that chapter tonight.

In his original 1959, he had known Delphine for seven years. At the time of her death in the late sixties, they had known one another for almost twenty years. Throughout their relationship in the futurepast, she was satisfied with what he gave her: entertaining bits and pieces, stories. She listened to him talk about what he had experienced and lived through, but for her, it was merely storytelling, fantasy. She never asked for his secrets.

But things are different now. It is rare for her to ask him about his history, and he takes notice.

"Why so inquisitive tonight?" he murmurs. "Why are you asking me now?"

She gives him a wry smile and shrugs.

The ancient vampire maxims are simple and few. Breaking them means punishment, banishment, or even death, depending on the severity of the transgression. Many vampires through the ages had disobeyed, and they — or their familiars — all suffered dearly for it. He violated a paramount law with Delphine long ago: self-revelation.

He always offered her his whole truth, something he had not offered Maeve. He ruined his chance for a life with her, and in his futurepast, he hoped to redeem himself with Delphine. There is a possibility he still can ... but perhaps his policy of truthfulness with her is why he is in this time-shift predicament.

Well, too late to stop now, he thinks.

If he is struck down, fine.

He is ready.

He stands up with his back to her, facing the fireplace, and runs his hands through his hair, mussing it up into a wild mane. He has something to say to her that he cannot say out loud.

He has never once forced himself into Delphine's mind.

Now is the time.

Vauquelin turns to face her. He spreads his arms wide on the table, and holds her fast in his gaze: *By telling you this I am facing the utmost danger.*

She hears his silent words and panics.

This is more than she bargained for — she is not, in fact, prepared. Despite seeing his teeth, despite allowing him to feed on her, there has always been that persistent corner of her mind that believed he could not truly be a vampire.

They do not exist! It is impossible!

It is why she had been so flippant when he asked to turn her. But she lingers on with him in self-defiance. Hearing his thoughts now changes everything. Or did she only imagine that he spoke just now, though his lips did not move?

Am I spooking myself? she wonders.

A gathering darkness envelops her, as if the walls are being covered in a black shroud, and fear ripples across her spine.

Her skin turns to gooseflesh.

"Don't … don't … please stop. I have changed my mind. I don't want to hear it," she says.

"But I must. I cannot stop now."

Vauquelin *hungers* to tell her. He has never told his creation story to anyone, vampire or human. He has carried its burdensome weight within him through the centuries.

He takes her hands in his.

"It was in 1668. I was thirty years old. It began at the Palais Royal in Paris. I attended a three-day entertainment given by the Duc d'Orléans. Are you familiar with his life?"

Delphine shakes her head and whispers, "Not really."

"The Duc was the brother of the King. He was flamboyant and openly homosexual. He threw savage fêtes. It was not easy to secure an invitation. His affairs were untamed, scandalous ... endless champagne, mind-boggling quantities of food ... dogs running loose throughout the palace and gardens ... unbridled wantonness that defied any possible imagination. His friends were the misfits of the aristocracy. It was nothing short of an orgy in every room. There were men having sex with men, women with women, three men with one woman, one woman with three men. Nothing was forbidden."

"And were you participating?" she says, fluttering her eyelashes.

"But of course I was! How could I not?"

"Great, just what I needed ... more lurid tales of Vauquelin, the Vampire Sex God," she says.

His back stiffens.

"If you intend to ridicule me, I will go no further."

"I'm sorry. Please continue," she says.

PARIS, FRANCE | NOVEMBER 10, 1668

Vauquelin stood on a balcony, amusing himself by eavesdropping on the debauchery unfolding in the gardens below with his spyglass, a new whimsy imported from Amsterdam.

It afforded him the ability to be a clandestine voyeur to the wanton mischief, and he moved the small eyepiece to and fro, zooming in and out on the jeweled décolletés of the ladies and the glistening, sweaty waists of the half-naked men.

A silk-clad woman caught him looking at her and flipped open her fan, peeking over its edge. Vauquelin lowered the spyglass and delivered her a dazzling smile, which caused her to erupt into a fit of giggles and run the fan faster, wagging a coquettish finger at him.

He shook his head, still smiling as he mouthed, "No."

It was atypical for him to be so disheveled: breeches missing several buttons, chemise ripped at the shoulder, and one shoe had lost its buckle. His hair was a tangled disaster and his *maquillage* was smeared and intermingled with rouges and lip stains from the countless hedonists he had been kissing all night.

His extravagant pink justaucorps was draped over his arm..

Throughout the evening, he could not shake the feeling that someone was watching him, yet he did not see any other spyglasses. They were still uncommon, even amongst this affluent crowd, and he was the first to have one.

He had drunk so much champagne, bedded so many people, and snorted so many powders that night that he could scarcely walk a straight line.

Three days of such revelry had caught up with him at last.

It was time to go.

He was nearly home when a wheel slipped, and while the coachman attended to it he sat with the door open, fanning himself, with one stockinged long leg draped outside the carriage. The cool autumn air was a balm for his sodden composure. He noticed another coach stopped at a distance behind him but paid it no mind. Other people had departed the Palais Royal at the same time as he.

A sharp whistle pierced the air from behind and a rotund, heavily rouged girl beckoned to him from an archway.

"I thank you, mademoiselle, but I'm off to my bed," he said, touching the brim of his feathered hat. He glanced at his coachman, who gave him a slight nod. The clocktower in the nearby cathedral chimed three.

"Please help me, Monsieur," she beckoned, "I would just need a moment of your time."

In truth, he was longing for his bed and a bath to soothe his drunken stupor, and he was sure he smelled quite atrocious by now, but she was hypnotic and tantalizing: raven ringlets framed her face, and her skin reflected so pale in the moonlight ... her mouth was as pink as a rosebud.

Vauquelin could not refuse this exquisite creature. He followed her into the passageway and through a door into a small apartment. The room was petite yet inviting, with Turkish carpets spread upon the floor. A vase of dead flowers (how odd!) was placed atop the chiffonier, and a narrow daybed with a velvet canopy angled out from a corner.

She backed him toward the bed, pressing his face into her bosom. The fragrance of sex crept across her skin and into his nose, and he sniffed her, running his tongue across her plump breasts.

A door opened in the room with a flourish and two hostile men appeared, their faces hidden by black carnival masks. They strong-armed Vauquelin away from the girl.

All at once his drunkenness dissipated, replaced by fear and trepidation. Perhaps they meant to rob him … or perhaps he had seduced someone's wife. Whatever his trespass, he surmised that it was in his best interest to comply.

They led him down a long stone stairwell lit by torches. Given the time it took to reach the last step, they must have been a kilometer under the city by the time they landed.

The stairs terminated into a vast, circular room. The candles had burned low. In the corner was an elegant man, tall and imposing, seated like an emperor on a large chair. He wore a suit of luminescent black silk, with an outmoded, stiff, white ruff thronging his neck and an ominous ruby amulet dangling below its folds. He rested his chin on one hand. Every finger bore golden, thick rings.

His air was one of venerable decay.

The man was surrounded by beautiful figures, male and female, sitting in a semicircle, framing him.

The scene resembled a fine, fiendish painting.

"Come closer," the man said.

"What is this place? Where am I?" Vauquelin demanded. Beyond his own control, his feet propelled him forward.

The man gave no reply, merely smiling and bringing his hands up to his face as if in prayer.

Vauquelin attempted to take stock of the room, though his vision was compromised in the low light. Elaborate, grotesque coffins surrounded the perimeter. His heart began to pound, rushing blood into his head. The chamber absolutely blossomed with evil. Why the devil had he been brought to a crypt?

"I am Yvain," the man said.

Ever the gentleman, Vauquelin bowed and gave his full name.

"I know who you are. And you will know me."

Vauquelin was confused — and mesmerized.

"Which of my chimerical darlings pleases you most?" the man asked, gesturing around his gathering.

Vauquelin scrutinized the sea of faces: at least thirty pairs of eyes were fixed upon him. He had to admit it was an eerily beautiful horde, but why should this man care about his desires? All he could think was that he wanted to flee, but still, he was seized by mysterious compulsions.

He wanted the girl with the raven ringlets and the lavender-fragranced bosom, but she had vanished. His eyes settled on a fragile young woman with flaxen hair. She was meek and frightened: the others were downright ravenous.

He nodded to her, and she nodded back.

A creeping dread spread across him, fueled by the urge to bolt.

The dread settled in his stomach, and he crept backwards towards the stairwell. The timid blonde cowered in the corner.

The man lifted a finger and Vauquelin was overcome in a flash. The creatures held him down, groping him, caressing his entire body, and the man was all of a sudden next to him, breathing in his ear.

Vauquelin had not seen him move from the chair across the room. He fought to rise, but he was trapped.

"I wish to bestow upon you a gift," Yvain said. "Your beauty is necessary for me. You are extraordinary, too sublime to wrinkle and die as a mere human man. I have been observing you for quite some time, and tonight is the night you become mine. It was destined for you to stand before me now. You shall be my emissary, and facilitate the expansion of our population."

He stood and dispersed the coterie with his hands.

They hissed and hit the walls.

Vauquelin went stiff with panic. This must be a nightmare or a hallucination from the powders. Soon he would wake and forget the entire horrid scene.

"I do not understand," he whispered.

"You must live forever. Our survival demands it," Yvain declared, drawing a long-nailed finger down Vauquelin's cheek. "You will never age, you will never die. You will be preserved in this exquisite shell, exactly as you are now, for as long as time endures. You shall live free from harm, free from the struggles of humanity."

He removed Vauquelin's hat, sailing it over to a chaise, and dipped his hands into his thick hair, bringing their eyes level.

"You will survive on living blood alone ... you will be a god ... humans will relinquish their vital fluids so that you may live.

For eternity, so you shall be. This is my gift. Do you accept?"

In the depths of his soul, Vauquelin took the meaning of Yvain's words and his hands flew to his face. These creatures were vampires, and they meant to make him immortal.

He sank to the ground, his face contorting as his brain was suffused with images of diabolical grandeur and unfettered power.

His lips trembled, disabled from speech. He wanted to refuse but he knew that if he did, he would die on this floor.

He had been given options.

Both meant death: one meant salvation.

"Yes ... yes ... " he whispered.

Yvain grasped Vauquelin's shoulders and plunged his teeth into his neck, extracting his blood in swinish gulps.

Vauquelin screamed.

"Ah, the gourmet saltiness of Sicily runs through your veins," Yvain said, throwing his head back. "A rare delight, indeed."

He struggled against Yvain's chest and tried to push him away, but the man might as well have been made of iron. His lips were pried apart — a hot liquid cascaded down his throat, and he choked on its alien tang.

He began sinking, sinking, sinking. He sank through the floor, to a floor below, and a floor below that. As he descended, he saw swirls of an entertainment, blurred faces. Music, breaking glass, ecstatic moans, demonic laughter.

When he landed, it was pitch black.

There was no light.

There was nothing but silence.

He had never known such terror, such hopelessness, such blackness. He was drowning in an immeasurable sea, black as ink, and he knew this was death: oblivion. There was nothing on the other side. No purgatory — not even hell.

He was ensnared in a vortex of naught: no sound, no feeling.

He screamed, and still there was no sound. He screamed until his throat was raw. It was the only sensation he could feel. In desperation, he curled up like an infant and plunged even further into his despair.

When he stopped moving at last, tears flooded his eyes and would not cease. An infernal coldness seeped into his bones that would remain with him for the rest of his days.

How long he lay there, he did not know.

Vauquelin quickened and bolted upright.

At once he was back in the room with Yvain and the creatures. The candlelight jabbed his eyes with bright pain, and he hastened to cover them with his hands.

The noise was deafening, although no one was speaking and the room was silent.

"Come," said Yvain, crooking his finger.

Abruptly the horrific din was replaced with enigmatic peace.

Vauquelin dragged himself across the floor and knelt at the fiend's feet. "What is this malignant sorrow you have inflicted upon me?" he pleaded, his face drenched with tears.

Yvain gave him a long box covered in silk. "Open this," he said.

Vauquelin's hands quivered and he dropped the box, powerless to break Yvain's gaze. He fumbled on the floor to retrieve it.

The box contained a menacing stiletto.

"The gift you have been given is Darkness ... and it is also Light. Many years will pass before you will come to appreciate this, but once you achieve your glory, you will revel in it."

Yvain removed the stiletto and pierced his own neck.

He clutched Vauquelin's head, forcing his mouth open on the streaming blood. "Swallow," he commanded.

Yvain's blood slid down his throat like fire.

He was repulsed, and he gagged.

A fierce paroxysm tortured his body.

Still, he drank.

And as he drank, he was possessed by overpowering greed. His strength returned, amplified, exploded. He grasped Yvain's shoulders and bore down on his neck.

"*Arrêtez!*" Yvain screeched, flinging Vauquelin across the room.

He crumpled against the wall, panting and sweating.

Yvain dragged a finger across his wounds and they dutifully closed. One of the men licked the remaining blood from his neck.

"My creature, come," he beckoned.

Vauquelin returned to him.

"The gift is eternal life. Perpetual power. You have the strength of my blood: few others can claim that. Now you may leave us to arrange your affairs. The sun will rise soon, and you must never greet the sun. Never."

Vauquelin turned on his heel and bolted up the nefarious staircase, knocking the scattered creatures over in his flight.

His coachmen were asleep on the front steps, awaiting him.

He leapt into the carriage, shouting "*Maintenant! Vite, vite!*"

They clattered off into the night, the footman barely keeping his balance on the back.

Something was eating his face.

Devouring his skin, licking his bones clean.

His hearing was shredded by moribund wails.

The air was siphoned from his lungs, forcing him awake.

Vauquelin sat grasping his head, gulping greedy breaths in his own luxurious bed.

The whole hideous vision, the darkest night he could recall, had only been a nightmare after all. His arm shook violently as he caught hold of the servants' sash on the wall.

Olivier, his valet, arrived in an instant and flung open the bed curtains, flooding the room with abundant sunlight. Vauquelin screamed when the light hit his eyes.

"Close them! The light afflicts me!"

Olivier was terrified. Monsieur de Vauquelin was mild-mannered and courteous to a fault: quite the libertine, but still an admirable master. It was a rare day that he lost his temper or his senses. He must be ill.

"Shall I call the surgeon, Monsieur?"

"No, Olivier, that will not be necessary. I must apologize for my behavior. I was ... I *am* ill, but I will be alright. Please, just leave me be. Do not return unless I call you."

Alone, he tossed on the bed, his arms and legs restless and skittish. He wanted sleep, but it refused to come. He was tormented by visions from the nightmare. Fleeting moments of rest teased him until he sank into slumber at last.

The nightmare returned and Yvain appeared next to him in the bed, laughing like a demon as he stroked the naked newborn vampire, running his hands over his body. Harsh, peculiar echoes of his transformation reverberated through his subconscious until the sounds forced him awake. He was quite alone.

"*Aïe!*" Vauquelin's head jerked as a sharp sting pricked his lips. He raised his fingers and squeezed. Blood gushed forth, spiraling into a thick crimson stream down his arm, staining his bed linens.

He sprung from the bed and crossed the room to his dressing table. In the massive looking glass that hung above, he could see his bed reflected behind him — but he could not see himself.

He clamped his hand over his mouth and stifled a pitiful squeak. Pools of blood amassed in the corners of his eyes and sped down his cheeks. He splashed water on his face and returned to bed, enclosing himself in its sanctuary, where he lay staring into the dark.

If what Yvain said was true, then yesterday was his last experience of sunlight. Never again would he be warmed by the sun. If only he had known; he would have savored its final shine upon his face.

He opened his mouth and brought his trembling hand towards his teeth: they were now foreign to him. His canines had distended into four sharp daggers. His jaw ached with profound, vengeful pain. He collapsed on the pillows and wept, punctuating them with blood.

Dry of tears, he vacated the bed with trepidation.

The room was pitch black, night having draped her inky velvet cloak across the city. To his astonishment, every object in the room was distinguishable. Nevertheless, he lit a solitary candle at his bedside table.

Olivier, true as always, had not disturbed him.

A wicked voice whispered, "You must regain your composure. Dress as if you were meeting the King."

Vauquelin rang for Olivier.

"I am ready to be dressed for the evening," he said.

"But of course, Monsieur."

The valet paced the room, lighting the many remaining candles in the night-darkened room. He disappeared and returned a moment later with water, refilling the ewer next to the dressing table and the mirror.

"No, not there. By the bed," Vauquelin insisted.

Olivier noticed the blood. "But Monsieur is injured!"

"It was only a nosebleed," he said, placing a hand on Olivier's arm. It was the first of what would be many lies for the duration of his lifespan. "You need not worry."

The valet summoned the staff to perform his master's toilette and dress him. The procedure took hours, and Vauquelin's stomach began to growl and heave.

"Would Monsieur like his supper?" Olivier asked.

"Yes, please. I thank you."

Olivier bowed and left the room, returning with a prepared tray. When he lifted the first cloche, the aroma of the food engulfed Vauquelin like a wave, and he fought back the urge to vomit.

"It appears I have no stomach for this. Please, take it all away."

Vauquelin, hollow as a shell, went to his library and sank into a chair. A harsh screech scraped across the window and he lurched toward the sound.

It was only a tree branch raking the glass.

His nerves were raw; he was outright jumpy.

He poured a glass of wine and brought it to his lips in fits and starts, fearful of his recent nausea. Relief washed over him as he drank. His body accepted it and the pleasing liquid slid down his throat, calming him.

The doors opened and Olivier entered. "There are some odd gentlemen calling for Monsieur. I informed them you were not at home, but they are quite insistent."

"Show them in," Vauquelin said.

He was frightened, but he needed answers, and he could not shun this opportunity for confrontation.

Yvain appeared in the doorway paler than death, tall and ethereal. It was the first time Vauquelin could get a decent look at this bizarre man. Olivier had been generous in describing the visitors as "odd."

Behind Yvain stood a considerably younger and much more handsome man — his paramour, Vauquelin assumed. He nodded to Olivier, who closed the doors as he departed, and motioned the men into the room.

Yvain appeared to have just emerged from a coffin. His attire was resplendent and of the latest fashion, but the lace at his wrists was dirty and ragged. His demeanor was repulsive.

Vauquelin would not have wanted to encounter him on a dark street, and he hoped that he did not now appear as ghastly as these two.

"My creature," Yvain bowed.

"I most certainly am *not* your creature," Vauquelin said through gritted teeth. The very word made him recoil.

"Oh, but you are indeed my creature. My *finest* creature. Vauquelin is dead. I alone allowed you to live in your present incarnation. You belong to me."

Vauquelin thought about strangling this fiend, this thing. His fantasy took his body hostage. Before he knew it, galvanized by a new, untested strength, his fingers were fastened on Yvain's throat.

Yvain shrugged Vauquelin off and pushed him across the room, with a wicked laugh. The other man grinned, bringing two fingers to his lips in a dandyish attempt to suppress his amusement.

"My darling, you must learn to control yourself."

Vauquelin dropped into a chair, panting.

"What have I become?"

Yvain kneeled in front of him. "You are vampire. You are like me, and like Clément." He gestured toward his pet, stroking Vauquelin's cheek with the back of his other hand. "And now, your presence is required by my coterie. A ceremony awaits you, to usher you into your superior state of being."

They rode in Yvain's funereal black carriage outside the gates of Paris, to a small château. "You are welcome here, dear Vauquelin. Consider this your home."

Yvain took his elbow and guided him through the door. Inside, a large gathering of the creatures stood waiting. They slithered toward him, twittering and cooing as they looked him over head-to-toe, parting as he and Yvain entered with Clément trailing them.

"My friends, this is Vauquelin. Welcome him."

He was surrounded in an instant.

They all strained to lay their hands on him, vibrating about him like bees in a hive.

Yvain took his hand and led him to a dais on the opposite side of the room. "No one shall partake of Vauquelin. He is mine."

Vauquelin regarded his audience, panic burgeoning across his abdomen. The fair-haired beauty from the nightmare appeared from behind a curtain, dressed in scarlet.

The room fell silent.

She crossed the dais as if in a trance, and Yvain yanked her head back, exposing her neck.

"Take her," he ordered.

Vauquelin gawked in horror and confusion: what did Yvain mean for him to do? He glanced at the sea of bizarre faces. They all nodded and gestured to him, and he flinched.

Take her blood. Drain her, Yvain willed. *She will be your own creation, your thrall, your bride.*

Yvain's lips did not move, yet his instructions found their way into Vauquelin's consciousness.

He stood frozen in place, squinting in terror at the crowd. They were all still as statues, awaiting his performance. He averted his eyes from the woman. Last night, she had been frightened. Now her eyes were full of lust, and they were locked on him.

Her hand moved to her neck, her fingertips coming to rest on fresh puncture marks.

He was overwhelmed by an emotion he could only describe as cruelty. Anger and irrepressible hunger swelled in his chest. He strode across the dais, seized her by the waist, and sunk his teeth into her throbbing jugular.

She issued forth breathless little cries as blood streamed down her neck, disappearing into the scarlet of her dress.

"STOP!" Yvain thundered.

The woman turned chalky white and fainted.

He dropped her to the floor with a sickening flump.

Yvain draped an arm about Vauquelin's shoulder, and his voice became tender. "The last drop is a sacred offering to our ancestors and must not be consumed. You must never drink beyond the moment the heart has ceased its beating. You will learn to feel the last cadence a human heart has to offer."

The woman lay crumpled on the floor, emitting small, shallow breaths. Yvain opened the vein atop Vauquelin's hand and hastened his blood into her open mouth. Her cheeks became ruddy, and her eyes flew open.

"Pick her up," Yvain ordered.

Vauquelin obeyed. His strength bewildered him. She might as well have been a feather. They were led into a room and the doors were closed behind them, the lock clicking into place.

Yvain's distinctive voice found its way into his head: *Finish it.*

He laid the woman on the bed and she began to thrash about, panting and sweating.

Her tortured screams lacerated the silence. Vauquelin gritted his teeth and clawed at his face in anguish. His ears ached from the shrill reverberations of her screeching.

She was dying, as he had died.

At last she stopped moving, and Vauquelin began pacing about the room with his hands laced behind his head, glancing at her now and then.

She was lifeless.

The clock chimed ... two, three, four o'clock ...

Still, she did not move.

He lost all sense of space and time and became obsessed with the foreign hunger that grew within him.

He rattled the doors. They would not budge. He paced a bit more, then pounded on them with all his might.

"Let me out!" he cried.

The doors flew open and there stood Yvain.

"You must be patient."

Vauquelin's face darkened with unfathomable fury.

Yvain pushed a young man inside and said, "Your bride will need nourishment soon, as you will."

The doors slammed shut and the lock clicked back into place.

The young man was entranced. He made no effort to fight or even move. Vauquelin grasped him by the throat and dragged him towards the bed. He pulled the boy's head aside, tormented by his desire to bite and repulsion at the thought of doing so.

Something animal inflamed him, a foreign and wild compulsion. The animal took over and he plunged his teeth into the condemned boy's neck. He drank as much as he could and threw his head back. A forceful erection arose, and he moved his hand over it as he drank more.

The fragrance of hot iron filled the room.

Vauquelin snarled as the blood thickened his vocal chords.

The woman began to stir and he pulled her toward him.

She ripped open the boy's coat and sank her teeth into his abdomen, suckling on him with wild abandon.

Vauquelin was ensnared by an overwhelming lust, fueled by blood. He seized the girl and kissed her, hoisting her skirts up with both hands. He took her with unprecedented yearning. She returned his ferocious advances, and he thought they might tear each other apart. He flipped her onto his hips and yanked her hair as far back as it would go. She panted like a beast and rode him like a horse.

He thrust into her with such force he thought he would explode. But he was unable to achieve climax — he had to stop from the rawness and unyielding exhaustion.

They lay breathless and spent on the bed. She draped an arm over his stomach, and they slept.

When he woke the candles had all snuffed out; even so, his newly-acquired gifts afforded him clear vision in the dark-as-pitch room. He drew his knees up to his chest and stared at his new bride. In her slumber, she looked like a child.

"What will become of us?" he whispered.

He was a prisoner.

He was bloody and filthy.

The dark presence of the young man's body, dead and discarded on the floor, made his flesh crawl.

Vauquelin put on his fouled chemise and tried the doors, finding them now unlocked. He assumed that the vampires had been waiting outside, listening for proof of consummation, unlocking them after they received their satisfaction.

He opened the doors as slow as possible, though their hinges creaked in grim protest.

The house was dark and silent, empty of its creatures, as he skulked barefoot through one passageway and then another.

The halls were heavy with silence.

Vauquelin found himself in a large vestibule.

A scream welled up in his throat, dying to be let loose, but it would not rise forth. His stomach began to rebel.

The great quantity of blood he had consumed coursed through his bowels and into his veins, setting them ablaze. The pain was excruciating. He doubled over and fell to his knees, rocking back and forth.

Over his head was a fresco of angels floating in clouds, the sun shining as the night sky choked out its light.

Angels! Ha!

His hands clamped together to pray, but no words would form. There was no god in this place: he had been forsaken.

Vauquelin stood and found his way back to the room where the woman slept. She was awake when he returned, and he refused to look at her despite her beckoning. He located the remainder of his clothing and dressed. The moment he emerged from the room he was enveloped by the creatures.

He saw them through different eyes now.

They were grotesque, beautiful: they were hallucinatory.

And he was now one of them.

They let him pass. Yvain stood on the other side of the room. Vauquelin took flight out the front door and ascended a waiting carriage. No one attempted to stop him.

It took the carriage two hours to reach his house in Paris. The road was empty, sodden from rain. It was a menacing night. Low, fast-moving clouds clung to the horizon.

Inconceivable perception assaulted his senses.

The damp grass, horses' hair, the beastly odors emanating from his own body, the leather of the coachman's boots, fecund earth — all smothered him with exaggerated pungency.

His eyes darted about his phantasmagorical new landscape.

It was too much.

At last, he stumbled through the doors of his own house.

"Monsieur, that odd gentleman is waiting for you," Olivier said.

Vauquelin could not fathom how Yvain had arrived before him.

"So ... you've abandoned your bride."

"I do not want her."

"You have no choice. You are her maker. You are bound to her."

"You chose her. You forced me!" Vauquelin's voice escalated into a scream. His acidic anger flashed him to the other side of the room and his hand fixed itself upon Yvain's throat. He was stunned by this power, by his ability to move this way.

He backed off in surprise.

Yvain strode toward Vauquelin and jammed a forefinger into his chest. "I require you to surrender this domicile and live among your kind, with my coterie of revenants. We are now your kindred, your protectors. Vampires are forbidden to live among humans. I will see you — and your bride — at our château tomorrow night. You shall not return here. Have I been heard?"

Before Vauquelin could respond, Yvain smiled and vanished.

Not for the world would he give up his homes and live in Yvain's decrepit pit, amongst his brood of blood creatures. He would retain his liberty at any cost.

He strode out of the library and was startled when he saw the woman at the top of his stairs.

She was fully dressed — and radiant.

He softened for a moment as he looked at her.

"I do not even know your name," he said.

"Arsinée," she whispered.

Vauquelin was filled with portent, and hatred for her surged in his chest. He was now tethered to her. His freedom, which he had just so vehemently defended in his mind, was in peril. He regarded her with disgust, turned his back, and walked away.

She ran down the stairs, following him.

LOS ANGELES, CALIFORNIA | 1959

Vauquelin ends the story there.

Soon he will learn the full depth of the treachery he just committed. Now he folds his hands, awaiting Delphine's reaction to his extraordinary tale.

Her face is devoid of emotion.

Vauquelin had never before mentioned a wife, and he never told her how he came to own this house. She suspected it had something to do with the old painting of an elegant Titian-haired beauty hanging in his library. But he had described Arsinée as a blonde. The woman in the painting could not be her.

And where are they now? Dead?

"Do you believe me?" he asks.

"Why would I doubt you?" she whispers, unable to bring herself to look at him.

But he can feel her doubt, her fear: it is charging the atmosphere. She has never been frightened of him before — that he is aware of.

"Where there's belief, there should be doubt. I could be making this all up, you know," he says.

He is challenging her, placing her skepticism on the table.

In time he will discover that she has her own designs for his entrapment.

Delphine looks up and meets his pleading countenance at last.

Keep going, she thinks, trying to will him. *I do want to hear more. I do. Tell me everything.*

His face flushes and he leaps from his chair. He heard her thoughts without trying. This unsettles him.

No human has ever penetrated his mind. Perhaps Delphine has a strange hold over him that no other human ever had throughout his history, not even Maeve.

Now he is unsure if he should continue.

The recollection of his creation, not one word of which he had even once uttered aloud, has depleted his energy. Despite Delphine's mental subterfuge he decides to pull the reins back, reminding himself that these are just stories to her, not reality.

"Another time. I think I've scandalized you enough for one evening. Stay here with me awhile and then I'll take you home."

They sit on the lawn by Vauquelin's pool, both of them destitute of words. Delphine smokes a joint and falls asleep in his arms, comfortably numb for the time being.

He grazes her temples with his fingertips, a tender thing he once loved to do with Maeve, and a hiss — the voice of a man — skewers the stillness.

Vauquelin is at once on his guard.

Delphine does not stir.

"Vauquelin ... you betrayed me."

The hairs on his neck prickle.

The repercussions have begun.

It is an undeniable violation to reveal so much to a mortal, and there is no doubt in his mind that he will suffer for his transgression. His mind reels with the myriad ways he could be punished or destroyed, or fall from his vampiric grace.

But maybe that is what he deserves now.

Vauquelin glances at Delphine, his love, his innocently sleeping human, and lets her down to the grass.

He could take her blood and force her to drink from him — yet she would despise him for it. He could save her from her dreadful fate, and she would live forever, with him.

She loves him: he is confident of this. She trusts him.

But if she hated him, it would destroy him.

He had not created another vampire since that night in 1668. Arsinée was his only issue, forced upon him. Time and again he had been discovered, begged, pleaded with, and still, he only took — he never once gave. Those who asked him received the full brunt of his savagery without fail.

Vauquelin is a misanthrope and always has been, even dating to his pre-vampire days. He is content to stay within the confines of his luxurious walls: solitude is preferable to vapid companionship for its own sake. He finds other beings loathsome, both human and undead. He craves being alone.

It is an absolute necessity for him.

The last thing he wants is insoluble ties and obligations to another vampire — the act of creation is an eternal bond. Only twice in his existence had he wanted to do it, and both of those times proved ill-fated.

He falls back on the lawn, thunderstruck by a new realization.

What if it is not love and trust Delphine is projecting,

but disbelief? Disbelief in him, that he is vampire? Perhaps that was why she asked so many questions tonight ... because she does not think he is truly capable of inflicting such violence.

His mind begins to flutter like a fish on a deck. How could this human make him feel so insecure? How could he have lived this long and been deceived by a mortal?

He is abruptly obsessed with the desire to prove himself.

Conflicted emotions rush at him, angering him.

He pushes them away.

He must summon his self-control when it comes to her.

Soon, the sun will rise.

Vauquelin nudges her until she wakes and he grasps her shoulders in his hands. "Delphine ..."

Let me take you. Live with me. Live with me. Live with me. You're my love ... I cannot bear to lose you again. Please. Please.

He is unaccustomed to begging — he never begs. He takes. He takes what he wants, does what he wants — but not with her.

She reaches up and caresses his face.

"No, my love ... no."

A fury rises in him, a black fury he has not suffered in centuries. "Do not call me that." He turns his back to her.

He drives her home in silence and returns to his silent house, racing up the steps as the sun begins to rise over the mountains. The slight burn he begins to feel on his back as he ascends cannot compete with his emptiness, his void, his numbness.

Coming back to this time is breaking him little by little, and it is all because of her. He had adjusted to life alone, and now her very presence is wrecking him.

Their future has grown dim.

At nine o'clock, on a whim, Vauquelin tosses a bag in the car and speeds across the 10, driving with a death wish. He wants to get out of L.A., and away from Delphine, as fast as possible.

He needs some peace, some open space, and he knows he can find it in the god-forsaken desert.

Near the exit for Joshua Tree, a California Highway Patrol officer pulls him over. He skids off the road, his tires kicking up sand and gravel.

Vauquelin is in a horrid mood. He grips the steering wheel, realizing one of two things can happen: it all depends on the officer's behavior.

He monitors the patrolman's approach in his side-view mirror. When he gets close enough, Vauquelin lifts the door. The desert heat assaults him like opening an oven. He loves its intensity and turns his face toward it.

It is the closest he can get to feeling the sun.

The desert is harsh and beautiful and deadly.

Like him.

"License and registration, please," the officer says.

In a split second, Vauquelin decides to play nice and extracts the paperwork from his glove box. The insurance is real, the license fake, yet undetectably authentic in appearance. There is no record of him at the DMV: he does not exist. He has shelled out a great deal of money over the years for such documents.

He hands them over, and the officer looks from the license to him, back and forth.

"In a hurry tonight? The speed limit is fifty-five miles per hour. You were going eighty-five."

"My apologies, officer. I'm late for a film location meeting in Desert Hot Springs," Vauquelin replied. His accent has grown more French and less Americanized with the reversal of time.

"I see. Not from here, huh? Please step out of the vehicle, sir."

The officer makes Vauquelin walk back and forth a bit to rule out intoxication. When he is ordered to recite the alphabet backward, he begins to lose his patience.

"I have lived in this country for decades. I assure you, officer, that unlike most Hollywood executives, I am quite sober."

The officer thinks, *There's something strange about this one*, and continues looking him up and down.

Vauquelin is fed up with the officer's scrutiny.

The situation grows more trepidatious by the second.

It can go either way.

"May I look in your trunk?"

"By all means."

Inside is a briefcase containing a script. Vauquelin always thinks ahead; he is ever-equipped to protect himself.

The officer unlocks the trunk and rifles through the script.

An approving expression spreads across his face.

"Alright. I'll let you go with a warning. But listen here ... we don't like you Hollywood types thinking you can drive like a bat out of hell here in the desert. This isn't Los Angeles. Slow down and drive safe."

Vauquelin slams the trunk shut and pulls his door down, starting the car. He waits for the patrolman to disappear from sight, organizing his papers in the glove box to kill time, and drives the speed limit for a few miles, resuming his preferred death speed when the highway is once again empty.

The motor howls. He still marvels at gas-powered vehicles, even after so many decades of driving them. How strange it is to ride around in a small metal box, when it seemed only yesterday he relied on horse and carriage for transportation.

He pulls to a stop at Two Bunch Palms, a hot mineral water spa north of Palm Springs. He has been coming here since it opened in the 1920s, though it was remodeled multiple times in his futurepast.

Al Capone had once used it as a hideaway. Allegedly, there are tunnels underneath the property where Capone stowed contraband liquor during Prohibition.

In his futurepast it evolved into a haven for hipsters, but in 1959, it is still a well-kept secret retreat for movie stars who want a moment out of the spotlight.

After signing the register for the night, he follows the hostess down a palm-lined walkway, arriving at a secluded room with a private pool. When the door closes behind him, he strips down and eases himself into the steaming mineral water.

It is absolute heaven ... or as close as he can imagine.

Even when the weather is cold, the temperature never affects him. He has long been accustomed to his perpetual chill, but he craves warmth.

The water is like a womb, embracing him, its mineral heat commingling with his bones.

He floats on his back awhile, looking up at the stars. Far away from the smog and light-pollution of L.A., the Milky Way burns bright in the night sky over the mountains.

Vauquelin senses the end is coming with Delphine.

She is different this time.

He hates it.

Her rejections are cutting him afresh.

Maneuvering to the corner of the pool, he stretches his arms out. The concrete edge is still hot from baking in the desert sun all day and he closes his eyes, basking in its delicious warmth on his sepulchral skin.

He emerges only when he is struck by a brilliant idea.

He walks inside, dripping along his path, picks up the phone, and requests a massage in his room.

A few minutes later a masseuse arrives, an older woman in a white uniform. She sets up her table and Vauquelin stretches himself out on his back.

There is only one small lamp aglow in the room.

He wants it dark, so she will be unable to see his veins.

"Do you speak English?" he asks.

She shakes her head no.

Excellent, he thinks. No conversation.

He radiates warmth from his soak. For once, a human will neither recoil nor comment on his coldness.

She presses her hands into his body, loosening his sinewy,

pent-up muscles. He tries to keep his mind clear, but it is difficult with relentless human touch palpating his skin.

He plays a little game, daring himself to behave alone in a quiet, isolated room with a human, resulting in no bloodshed.

She indicates he should roll over onto his stomach.

He is impressed by his willpower.

There is no blood desire, no erection.

He is slick with oil, his skin shiny and supple. He lets his arms hang down and he goes limp.

Yes ... this is good ... so very fucking good.

The woman makes no eye contact with him the entire time. The massage lasts an hour and a half. At the end, she places hot stones in a row down his spine. It is a completely new experience for him and it is a revelation.

All his rage rises up and out of his body. This is by far the best idea he has had in ages. She rubs oil on his temples, and his nostrils flare. He cannot place the soothing fragrance — bergamot? Lavender? Both? He breathes it in.

The masseuse clasps her hands behind her back and Vauquelin rises from the table, extending his hand.

She accepts it.

"My most gracious thanks," he says.

When the masseuse departs with her equipment and a generous tip, he takes his pack of Gitanes and steps back into the mineral bath. He soaks, smokes, and thinks of nothing, blowing smoke rings as the palms undulate in gentle swirls over his head. His oiled-up skin creates a slick on the surface of the water.

His mind drifts to Maeve. In their later years together, they often made the trek to the hot mineral waters of the desert.

These brief excursions were the only times they traveled outside the confines of Los Angeles together. It eased her ailments and brought her temporary relief.

If only those waters could have cured her and bought him some additional time with her ... but it was not to be.

By the position of the moon, he calculates that it is now three o'clock. He cannot stay here.

The room has too many windows, and the staff would be unable to accommodate his intricate needs at this late hour. It is the downside to the desert: the desert-dwellers worship the plentiful sun.

He wrenches himself from the bath and dresses.

He has just enough time to get back to L.A. before dawn.

As he climbs into his bed, the sun begins its ascent.

His brief, spontaneous, and surreal adventure has stifled his evolving anger ... for now.

They do not speak of the chasm that has materialized between them. It grows wider with each passing moment, threatening to swallow them both.

Vauquelin plans a gathering, a diversion to break the layer of ice that he created. Delphine will plan the menu and handle the guest list: a delicious population of intellectuals, weirdos, artists, and other assorted creative detritus.

His rare parties are legendary, though they cannot hold a candle to the extravagant spectacles he threw with Maeve. Without her, he never had the urge to plan events of that caliber, especially not now. But at the very least he can provide unlimited wine, food, and an intriguing venue.

On the appointed evening, his living room is thronged with people and filled with smoke, music, and laughter, all perfumed by doom.

He feels a bit like he had at the museum exhibit of his clothing: here, but not here. He remains on the edges while Delphine spreads her social butterfly wings. Aside from those he has met in her close circle, he keeps his distance.

The perimeter is always his place.

He prefers to observe — and listen.

He smokes cigarettes and drags his eyes across the dregs.

No one can resist talking about him.

Across the room, where they assume he cannot possibly hear, they gossip with wild abandon.

He hears it all, and it amuses him.

They are weird ... but he is weirder by far.

"He looks like a character from a horror movie," a girl said.

"Maybe he's a vampire!"

"Have you noticed how he never blinks?"

Oh, how they laugh at him.

All of a sudden the room is populated not with guests but victims. A wry smile lifts the corner of his mouth as he begins to make his selection.

So many worthy options.

A beautiful, effete young man sits down at the piano and begins playing, and soon other instruments appear. Despite Vauquelin's heavy state of mind, he enjoys the music. It is a seedier version of the salons in Paris. Snippets of conversation mingle over the music, mixed in with inane druggie jive.

He is still determining who the winner will be.

The party fizzles out around three in the morning and Delphine begins tidying up. Only the man who played the piano remains, flaunting his reluctance to leave. He loiters, ogling all the artwork in the house, fingering every little thing, asking Vauquelin where he got this or that.

He is just a little *too* curious.

The sheer audacity of this man, picking up and running his

fingers over Vauquelin's precious objects! He follows him step-for-step, stiff-backed and agitated, readjusting each trinket the man touches.

But it is uncommon for Vauquelin to be such a nervous wreck.

Thirst is upon him.

It was foolish of him to have not fed prior to the party ...

He knows better.

He flits about the room, knitting and unknitting his fingers.

Who is he? he asks Delphine in their new silent language.

She shrugs. *I didn't invite him.*

Vauquelin jerks his head, indicating that she should leave.

Go. Go home NOW.

She hesitates. She is dying to catch Vauquelin in the act.

She wants proof, and this is her chance.

He locks her out from seeing this, his darkest side — if he even really is a murderer. But the thought of spying on him arouses her. Now she can confirm that it is all pretense, that he just wants her out of the way so he can fuck this guy and, later, tell her a gruesome story about killing him.

She is surprised by how this is affecting her, yet she obeys — to a point. She makes a grand pretense of yelling "Goodbye!" and slamming the front door, then waits in the vestibule with her heart punching its way out of her chest.

After a few silent minutes, she sneaks behind a large parlor palm, obscuring herself from their view.

Vauquelin is behind the man like a shot.

Delphine flinches, astonished by his speed.

He has never moved this way in front of her before.

Vauquelin kisses the man's neck, licks it. He inhales his scent and grasps his backside, swaying his hips against him.

"I've been trying to catch your eye all night, hoping you'd swing my way," the man whispers, biting his earlobe. "I'm glad I stayed to find out. My name is —"

"No. Be quiet. I don't want to know."

"Okay, okay … I can dig it," the man demurs, unbuttoning Vauquelin's shirt. He slips his hand inside, gasping when he feels the chill of a vampire's skin.

Delphine watches through narrowed eyes — it is all she can do to stay hunkered down in her secret spot.

How dare you touch Vauquelin this way!

She bites her knuckles, unable to look away.

Her heart thrums; her blood screams in her ears.

As the man unzips his pants, Vauquelin rears his head back and plunges his teeth into his neck.

He screams and strains, trying and failing to push him away until he loses his strength and faints.

Vauquelin's head vibrates at the finish and he throws his chin back, licking blood from his lips as he drops the dead man to the floor and collapses on the couch, his eyes squeezed shut.

Delphine moves like a ghost, out of control of her own body. She tiptoes across the floor and kneels at his feet. The night has pushed her into a complex jungle of emotions: astonishment, fascination, repulsion, lust.

She has never wanted him so badly.

"Why didn't you fuck him first?" she whispers. She lays her hand on his swollen cock, jolting him back into reality.

"What?" He is woozy, intoxicated by his kill and by the fresh, inebriated blood keening through his body.

Indignation spreads across his face as he realizes Delphine eavesdropped — she saw it all.

She slithers up next to him on the chaise, still stroking him.

Bereft of words, he clutches her wrist and moves her arm away, unable to look her in the eye.

Vauquelin is always vulnerable and moody after a kill. And as a matter of principle, he is always alone, able to recover and luxuriate in his own way. But this time, Delphine is sitting next to him, her eyes full of questions and judgment — it is almost more than he can take.

She has unveiled him.

Something cracks inside him, like a bone about to splinter, and her deception prickles his skin. His self-restraint is in danger of succumbing to an angry red tide.

The dead man lies motionless on the floor mere feet away.

At last Delphine believes, and she unravels.

"But this is who you are. You have let me in so little. How can you expect me to love you, or even to understand you, unless you give me everything you have?"

"I have begged you — *begged* you ... to let me make you as I am. I want you. I never wanted to be without you. Instead, you repeatedly refused me when I could have saved you!"

"Saved me? This is your vanity speaking. What about what I want? I adore you, but I don't want to live forever, not like this!"

She begins pacing.

Her desire for Vauquelin evaporates.

"I found you dead in my futurepast! Stiff and ashen-faced with a dirty needle in your arm," he says, his voice breaking. "One of your pathetic junkie friends was comatose in the corner, unaware and not even caring that you were gone! I snapped his neck and left you both there for the police to sort out. It devastated me to be the spectator of your wasted life ... *devastated me!* It's not that you don't want to live forever ... you don't want to live forever with ME. Just speak the truth: you don't want me. Shall I leave you to your inevitable narcotic death, then, my sweet?"

Her mind twists with anguish.

"Vauquelin, I do want you, but ... "

"But not enough," he finishes.

"No, I ... I pity you."

His eyes bulge.

"Pity? *Pity* me? Pray-tell, why?" he asks, half laughing.

He thinks of the myriad advantages this life has afforded him, that he has centuries of history on his pages. He is (quasi) indestructible. He never has to shave.

She stares at him in icy defiance, her chin jutted out.

"You are bored. You are lonely. You've built your walls so high you can't let anyone in ... not even me."

This slams him in the gut.

"Delphine. For half a century, you were the only being I have ever wanted to be a part of my life. I would not have been lonely in the future if you had agreed to stay with me forever. I am not lonely now."

Vauquelin curls his fingers into hers.

He wants to fix this, to reroute the conversation.

She yanks her hand away, angry tears welling up, and leaps to her feet. The veracity of what he had just said becomes clear. She does the math, based on his stories. Half a century? So what if there had been another great love in his allegedly long life ...

why should she care now? Or is this proof that he cannot even keep a story straight? Her thoughts hum as if a million bees have entered her brain.

"If that is true, you've forgotten what it is to love, if you ever knew! It was a hell of a choice you gave me. Live and kill with you forever, or not at all! What choice did you give the other one?"

She stands seething, fists clenched at her side.

The room falls quiet as a tomb.

Vauquelin closes his eyes as his blunder sinks in. He has never discussed Maeve with Delphine, and refuses to do so now. He had treasured and guarded her memory for so long, and in the presence of such deception, even more so. He holds her in his thoughts like the fragment of a fragile seashell.

Would Maeve have said yes? He never once doubted her love for him, but then again, he kept himself behind a curtain, shielding her from his true identity. Would she have accepted him?

We can never know.

He proved himself incapable of protecting either Delphine or Maeve from meeting their mortal deaths.

Delphine gestures at the dead man on the floor. "Tell me, what kind of life is this that you're offering me?" she wails.

"Perhaps I should have proven myself sooner," he says, his voice hard as stone, "but I could never bring myself to subject you to it. Please, just admit it — you were hiding over there, spying on me. You betrayed my privacy and my trust!"

"I did not believe you. I thought it was all an act. I was playing along! So you want me to live with you forever, but you have concealed the true cost of it from me," she says. "This is not a gift you were given, Vauquelin. *Tu est maudit!* And you want to damn me, too?"

Delphine bursts into tears, falling to her knees.

The ship is sinking.

"You are reducing my entire existence to shameful irrelevancy," he whispers.

He is unversed in humiliation.

His life, his glamorous vampire life, has been exposed as a farce. A never-ending farce.

She is right — he is a fraud at love.

As he did with everything in his life, excluding Maeve, he is merely going through the motions of it.

Almost four hundred years have passed and here he stands being systematically invalidated by a mortal, fooled into thinking he was loved again. By someone who had been merely acting a part, humoring him.

Not only is his life a sham, but the love he had allowed himself to feel for this particular human is a sham. Delphine pulled him into her orbit, and he entered it without hesitation.

In the first days after his creation, he declared himself tarnished, polluted. Centimeter by bloody centimeter, he metamorphosed into his new life as a murderous, merciless miscreant ... but the centuries softened him and his violence receded. He remembered those early years, just as Delphine spells it out now, as damnation: not something to be glorified.

In fact, he had taken his bestowal for granted.

Everything is so fucked up now that he doesn't know whether he's coming or going, or what would happen to Delphine even if he turned her. This is his burden, not hers.

But the poison has risen to the surface, and he is unable to stop himself. He grasps her shoulder and jerks her chin up, forcing her to look at him.

"You lied to me … you said you believed me! You let me drink from you! Now you have all of my lurid truth. You think I'm just a murderer, is that it? That I made it all up? Do you think I have no soul, that nothing else matters to me?"

She begins to cry again, wailing.

This is too much for her.

He should never have exposed her, but it is far too late. A tsunami of despair washes over him. He presses himself against her, crushing her, feeling her heart beating through his shirt. "What a fool I've been! I trusted you … I convinced myself that you loved me."

"Yes, my pet … I did, once upon a time. But not anymore."

She places her hands on his chest. Her face is written over with certainty.

Their illusions of each other shatter in that instant.

The façade crumbles into dust, and they move apart.

Her gallant, once-imaginary vampire stands before her, no longer a figment. The corpse lying on the floor is the cruel, conspicuous proof.

"What will you do with him?" she stammers.

Prior to this night, Vauquelin had not once been violent with Delphine. She inspired tenderness in him, not fury. But she has irrevocably broken him. Her soul is now laid bare to him, and he sees her for what she is: a morbid, mortal ghoul, who had gotten a thrill from fucking a "vampire" and letting him feed on her. Nothing more.

How wrong he had been.

This has gone on too long.

He must finish it.

He pushes her down on the sofa and shoves his fingers against her breastbone, baring his teeth: "Don't ... you ... dare ... move."

He picks up the body of his victim and vanishes.

Delphine sits quivering on the sofa, too frightened to disobey him. Vauquelin had never scared her before this night.

She thought she was strong enough to handle him.

How wrong *she* had been.

After a few moments her instincts materialize and she makes a run for the front door.

In the blink of an eye he is behind her, digging his fingers into her elbow, pulling her through the kitchen.

He heaves open the vault, the forbidden entry, revealing a stairwell enshrouded by an eerie black void.

Soon, Delphine will wonder about the door no longer.

He rushes her down the stairs and into chamber alight with candles. The dead man lies next to the opening in the floor, his hands folded across his chest as if he has been embalmed and is now ready to be placed in a coffin for a viewing.

Delphine cries in silence, hugging herself. Terror spreads across her face as it registers that she is standing in a catacombs ... hundreds upon thousands of bones surround her. Patterns made from skulls spread floor to ceiling. There are so many that they lose all meaning for her and become mere objects, no longer the woeful remnants of actual human lives.

Dozens of gilt-framed oil paintings cover one wall in a collage, each one a depiction of the redhead from upstairs: figure studies, details of her voluptuous breasts, an unfinished oil of a man's porcelain hand plunged in a mass of titian hair. Above them hangs a framed canvas of her. It is enormous, greater than life-size.

No one was ever meant to see any of this.

It has always been for him and him alone.

Delphine squirms toward the wall, wishing she could disappear. She leans on the only glass door among the shelves, pressing her hands against it, fogging it up with her breath, overwhelmed by the many secrets of Vauquelin that have been exposed to her in the span of an hour.

"Get away from her," he barks, lunging toward Delphine.

She snatches her hands away as if the glass is on fire, and turns on her heel to face him. This must be the final resting place of Vauquelin's greatest love. Did he kill her, too?

He slides his victim into the tank, and the acid devours the flesh with hideous and vengeful bubbling and hissing.

Delphine screams and sinks to her knees.

She begins to hyperventilate.

Vauquelin is so enraged that his eyeballs are vibrating in their sockets. He cannot look at her. His voice deepens.

"Do you dare to toy with me? Do you think this is a fucking movie, with a convenient fade-to-black for the parts you do not wish to see? You gave me your blood. You listened to my outlandish adventures. So this whole time, you just turned a blind eye and pretended to love and understand me, playing your little games with me?" He lets forth a disgusted laugh. "And you think I am the one who is damned!"

Still kneeling by the tank, he meets her frightened eyes at last.

"You wanted me to let you in and now I have. So you have seen all of me — is it quite what you were expecting, my love?"

She stares at him, quivering.

"Answer me, *putain!* Is it?" he bellows.

Delphine backs away, mouthing, "No, no, no, no, no ..."

A profound rage bubbles into a crescendo in his chest.

The last remaining ember of love he had for her extinguishes.

His eyes narrow and a wrathful vein erupts on his forehead.

There stands one of the two loves of his interminable life — terrified, ruined, decimated — and the full breadth of his horror has been unfurled like a bolt of sinister silk.

There is no changing her at this point. He had not given her enough truth, he can see that now. And one of the few mortals he ever allowed himself to trust had been lying to him all this time.

He seizes her by the neck. "I have had quite enough of your refusals," he hisses, vitriol dripping in his voice, his mouth pressed against her ear, "and of your fucking pity. *C'est fini.*"

Vauquelin lacerates her neck with a vicious pop and drinks her down, drinks until her heart pumps its precious liquid slower and slower past his lips.

"You punish me for not wanting what you want," her empty voice gurgles as blood fills her mouth. "Nothing human or animal could ever satisfy the longing in your soul. But I did love you ... once."

He stops, gasping. It is far too late for those words.

Her perfume writhes into his nostrils. The ensuing pang of her scent vexes him, but he sinks in even further, determined to finish her. He gazes up to the ceiling, relishing this very expensive swallow as it rolls down his throat.

"It appears we never knew each other after all," he says, his voice thick with her gore.

Delphine stiffens, then withers soft as a rag doll in his arms.

Vauquelin's cheeks flush red, the heat surge of saenguination giving him life, strengthening him, easing the shock.

His inevitable erection rises once more, and it makes him sick. He does not want to savor it or even touch it.

This is not the climax he had anticipated.

His callousness towards her demise appalls him, and he stumbles as he rises with her body still in his arms.

There is no Angel of Death for Delphine. In this death he is the reaper, and he snuffed her soul into oblivion.

Love had wrought him nothing but cinders.

He is done trifling with humans and their fragile emotions.

"Your ruin was your fraudulent love for me," he breathes, and drops her unceremoniously on the floor with a dull thunk.

He sits under the massive portrait of Maeve and imagines her reaction to what he has just done. Her arms enfold his neck, filling him with an inexplicable serenity.

It is almost forgiveness — almost.

He stands on unsteady legs and glides around the catacombs, lighting all the remaining candles for Maeve.

He had been foolish to ever let them go dark.

He must let her illuminate his path once again.

He ambles up the stairs, flipping the light off behind him as he throws the heavy lock on the door. He must go to his rest, even though he just caused his world, or what is left of it, to crumble around him.

The moment Vauquelin snaps into consciousness, his mind is deluged at once by odious visions of the previous night.

Delivering death to humans is his ethos. His long life had begun in a baptism of blood, and has been one infinite string of horrors great and small. Violence is part and parcel of his existence, but now, his latest vicious exploit assaults his spirit.

An inhuman French voice, not quite male and not quite female, whispers into the darkness: *Or it could be your fault that she died in her other life as an addict. Did this never occur to you?*

"Who is there?"

He flings himself to the edge of the bed.

Silence.

In his futurepast, things had been much different. Delphine had refused him then too, but they had many happy years together regardless. Nothing unpleasant had passed between them, and she died by her own hand. Maybe that was how things were supposed to happen again, and he fucked it up.

If he had to guess, he would say that approximately half of his victims had sussed out his vampire identity and begged him to make them immortal. The agony! So many other humans coveted this life ... why did she not?

All this time he thought Delphine was wronging him by refusing to give him what he wanted. He never once considered her feelings. Her last rejection was deadly.

Vauquelin rises and strides down to the catacombs.

He presses a button and a platform rises, bringing up the bones of last night's first victim to the surface. He removes them with a large set of tongs and sets them aside, replacing them with Delphine's body. He closes his eyes as she submerges, forever still. He will keep her bones separated from the others.

Despite his newborn hatred for her, which courses through him blended with her blood, he is determined that her bones will have a special place in his catacombs.

She is perhaps his greatest trophy — the one mortal who had almost torn him down. The only despair he feels is for himself.

He sits for hours, glowering into the open acid pit, his mind fissured by all these new revelations.

Perhaps he should kill Kibby, Delphine's suspicious little friend, but what can he do now? Locate and assassinate each of her many friends who will be concerned about her disappearance, inviting the police to his very door?

He must get out of this house, take a requisite drive to clear his head. He flings open the carriage house doors.

The Mercedes is gone and in its place is a much older Bugatti Type 55, imported from France in 1928 for a small fortune and sold in 1943 at scrap metal prices for the war effort.

It glints shiny black in the reflection of the full moon.

He sinks onto his knees.

At least it is less of a shock than the first time, and he is (a trifle) more prepared. Beyond question, he was sent back to 1959 to alter things with Delphine. Well ... he had altered them, alright, and now he is going even further.

He rifles in the glovebox of the car. The vehicle registration confirms the date: it is 1936. His heart thrashes against his breastbone, stealing his breath away.

Now Delphine is alive again, but she is a schoolgirl living above a cheese shop in Montmartre, innocent of the future American wiles that will send her down a path to destruction.

Scorn coils inside him like a viper. Immortality is something he is accustomed to: time travel is not. He expects to go forward throughout perpetuity, as one does, not backward. There must be a reason he is retreading his history. Still he cannot get his head around the reasons behind his backward traversal, or why he had allowed himself to be tortured so by Delphine.

He settles into the Bugatti and sniffs its delectable leather interior, starting the engine. It rumbles with throaty power. Wrapping his fingers around the steering wheel, he fights the urge to rip it off its base.

A vein pops out on his forehead.

That vein is never a good sign.

"FUCK!" He lets forth a primal growl and slams his fists through the soft top, all but shearing it clean off the car.

He returns to the house to inspect the damage inflicted by the latest reversal. His Philco television is gone, replaced by a cabinet radio. A horned Victrola, one of his last purchases with Maeve when she was still alive, sits upon its former perch with dozens of 78 RPM records standing upright on the shelves below.

In the dressing room, his reacquired mid-century attire has been replaced by rows and rows of elegantly art deco black jackets with embroidered lapels, slacks, and crisp white shirts.

An army of bizarre, bespoke boots with pointed toes awaits him, perfectly shined and polished, each pair organized in meticulous cubbyholes.

Dubious of his own reality, Vauquelin manages to piece together an outfit. He attempts to tame his hair, which proves to be more anachronistic day by day. He surrenders in defeat, mumbling curses under his breath.

Back in the carriage house he puts the top down on the car, ragged edges and all, and tears out onto the streets, ending up in front of a decrepit little second-run cinema.

He is overrun by nostalgia.

Decades have passed since he last set foot in a movie theater. Films were something he and Maeve had enjoyed together toward the end of her life. He adored looking at her face in the darkness, set alight by joy in the exquisite magical luminance of the silver screen.

In his original 1936, she had been dead for eighteen years, but in his deteriorating timeline he has existed over one hundred years without her. Her memory is still just as fresh to him as the day she departed.

So now he stands alone, peering up at the marquee, and what is the feature presentation?

Mark of the Vampire.

"Of. Fucking. Course," he mutters.

How can he resist? He buys a ticket and watches Bela Lugosi play the vampire lead, carrying on the style that would define all vampires throughout his futurepast years. Even as Count Mora, Lugosi channels his own suave, polished Dracula. THE Vampire.

How could he have ever explained away their similarities to Maeve if she had lived to view vampires on the silver screen? But in 1936 she would have been sixty-six years old…surely he would have found his footing and revealed himself to her before she reached such an advanced age.

Seeing all the vampire movies, the good and the bad, has been his habit ever since the advent of cinema. It fascinates him how humans interpret, manipulate, and outright dismiss the lore. A common thread is the discovery of a human woman who looks exactly like the vampire antagonist's long-lost love.

Pure sentimental sap.

He will never find Maeve's face in another.

It is inconceivable.

After the film lets out, Vauquelin drives around the city, vignettes of Delphine's death bursting in his head like flashes of a camera. He tries in vain to drown the black fury that once again thunders in his soul.

Loneliness cannot touch him: he had constructed his life to avoid companionship. It never worked out well. But now Delphine's absence is a vacuum for the second time in his life, and this time he is responsible. He had been so grateful to have someone in his life who knew his secrets. Perhaps he destroyed her by making her carry his cross.

The strain of sorting out his two futures is mind-bending.

Delphine is the reason he had re-appeared in 1959, but nothing significant had happened to him in the 1930s.

So why is he here?

Could he go far enough to return to Maeve, so that he might have her alive again?

The way things are going, he thinks, *it's more likely that I'll be transported back to the day after her death so I can live it over again.*

The 1930s were not among his favorite eras, yet the decade's desolate atmosphere is uncannily appropriate for his current mood. The United States is emerging from grievous despair and poverty, the world is on the verge of exploding into warfare, and here he is, living in a city whose fundamental industry churns out picture after picture to help people forget their mundane woes. By giving them vampires and monsters and fantastical stories to take their minds off of reality. Ah, well ... vampires are a figment of the imagination, are they not?

Let's put this to the test.

Vauquelin cruises the streets, his arm hanging over the car door, scowling at the passers-by. Some of them are coupled up and laughing ... most are alone, heads hung down, aimless, their minds god-knows-where.

The air of a late night in 1936 Los Angeles is perfumed by the fragrance of loneliness and severed dreams, and the sky is illuminated by ceaseless flashing marquees selling artificially-flavored hope for something bigger and brighter.

He pulls up in front of what would be, one day in his futurepast, Delphine's house. Will she ever live here again? Decrepit in 1959, in 1936 it is a quaint family home. There are children's toys strewn about the lawn. The blood-red door is its natural oak.

A few miles over he passes the exact spot where Elizabeth Short, The Black Dahlia, will be found in another decade. At this time, there are no houses here: only empty lots. Former orange groves, he supposes. He had ended dozens of aspiring starlets just like the Dahlia, the difference being that their remains are at rest in his catacombs — not left in a field to be discovered and exploited by morbid humans. Elizabeth's killer was obviously not looking to be discreet.

With this new awareness of Delphine, of her being both dead and alive in his chronology, he cultivates a malignant brutality, a darkness that he had long abandoned. He is like a pot that has been set to boil, and it is his ancient cruelty that is swirling and bubbling inside him.

He can conceive of no justification to hold back now.

Vauquelin's twenty-first century ennui is about to be obliterated: he will surrender, allow his authentic disposition to reclaim him. He will resume his former role: a ruthless, promiscuous assassin, a *sauvage*. He will cast away human emotions as easily as he slides empty bodies into his vat of acid, and never give them a second thought. He is what he is ... it is imperative that he stops pretending to deny it.

He arrives at his last destination for the night: the Greyhound bus station. There is always fresh blood to be found there.

Potential victims pour into Los Angeles by the hundreds, daily, with their fragile dreams of stardom. The Depression increased their numbers a hundredfold. The softened, futurepast Vauquelin might have felt sympathy for these wretched folk. Now he merely sees opportunity.

He parks a block away and walks to the back of the building.

His nostrils tweak as he picks up the scent of a nearby man leaning against the wall, smoking a cigarette. A human would not have noticed him: only the slight orange glow from the cigarette tip gives him away, but Vauquelin can outline the man's figure as if it were daylight.

Under the protection of the night, he flashes himself inches away from the man. "Have you a match?" he asks.

The poor man nearly jumps out of his skin.

"Jesus Christ, fella ... I didn't even hear you come up. Sure, sure."

He fumbles in his coat pocket, and while his head is down, Vauquelin latches onto his neck, willing silence.

The man thrashes and strains, trying to fight, but he is pinned against the brick wall. The lit cigarette falls to the ground, and Vauquelin snuffs it out with the toe of his shoe.

He drinks until the symbolic moment — the second to the last heartbeat — then eases the body to the ground, slashing over his bite marks with his Opinel and giving silent gratitude.

He carries his shame in his survival, always erasing any evidence of his presence.

The next morning Vauquelin sits enclosed in his bed and calls the imported car dealership as the clock chimes half past seven.

"I need my Bugatti top repaired. It is torn up to pieces. Must have been an animal. 2421 South Figueroa. The car will be in the drive and the keys will be under the mat. I need it back before nightfall this evening without fail. Send me the bill."

He hangs up and goes to sleep.

When the doorbell rings that night, he speaks only through the heavy door. He is not in the mood to answer the questions he knows are forthcoming.

"I have your automobile, Mister Vack ... Vocklin?"

Splendid, Vauquelin thinks, banging his head against the door. *I do so love having my name butchered.* "Drop the keys through the slot, please. That will be all, thank you."

"We were pretty amazed at the condition of that top, sir. Tain't a man nor animal around here what could do that kind of damage from the inside."

Vauquelin bristles. It appears he cannot avoid idle chit-chat, even behind a closed door. The further he moves back through time, the more he mourns the loss of independence that the technology of the future had afforded him, to obtain the goods and services he required without having to speak to a soul.

In the past, he was obliged to rely on the kindness (or control) of humans for certain tasks.

The future made it possible for him to have anything he needed brought right to his door: toiletries, food for the rabbits, even wine deliveries. He rarely needed to leave his house or speak to anyone.

He says, "No? Well, how else do you suppose it could have happened? A monster, perhaps? Shall I alert the authorities?"

Vauquelin's French accent chokes out his Americanized voice like a creeping vine: it is more pronounced than it was even yesterday when he was in 1959. For a split-second, his own voice sounds to him as if someone else is speaking.

The man emits a nervous laugh and clears his throat. "Well, we appreciate your business, sir. You have yourself a good night, now."

The keys fall through the slot, followed by the bill.

LOS ANGELES, CALIFORNIA | 1936

Vauquelin cuts his hair short, dropping long curly black locks into the sink, and slicks it back with Brylcreem, shiny as a record.

It will revert to its original state as he sleeps, but for now, he must put on airs for his appointment at Bullock's Wilshire — the sales manager remembered him when he called.

Tonight he will have a private fashion show, to choose a wardrobe for a trip abroad.

His first time around, he had a reputation for spending large amounts of money to satisfy his voracious sartorial appetite, and the Bullock's salesmen would open the store at night anytime he called: no questions asked. They are gladly doing it again tonight. It will boost their paychecks, and sales of this level are few and far between these days.

As a rule, his clothing has always been tailor-made to his own unique designs and measurements. He prefers shopping when there are no other customers and adores having salesmen and shop girls waiting on him hand and foot.

A valet meets him at the door and parks the Bugatti.

In the men's department salon, male models parade in front of him, presenting suits for both evening and day ("No day suits," he says, dismissing them with a wave of his hand, "I'm only interested in evening attire."), dressing gowns and smoking robes, ties, shoes, hats, and a few pieces of jewelry. He chooses a new pocket watch, a pinky ring, and several tie clips. He selects and rejects at will, and writes out a check for $12,500.

In 1936, it is the fiscal equivalent of buying a large house. The sum of the bill, as all financial matters have become to him, is immaterial.

His order will be delivered to his house tomorrow evening.

Vauquelin packs a steamer trunk with his new wardrobe and calls a taxi. From Union Air Terminal, he takes an evening flight to New York and boards the *SS Normandie* just before dawn, bound for France. His love for the expanse of the sea overwrites the complication of long-distance travel.

His last sea voyage was when he first came to the United States over two hundred years ago, or thirty-six years ago if he goes by the current calendar.

Might as well see Paris before the Nazis ruin it again.

The first time-shift left him feeling robbed; now he is permitting himself to enjoy it. Rather than letting anger get the best of him, he decides it is the ideal cure for his self-inflicted loss.

When he emerges on deck the first night he marvels at the elegance of the passengers, all of them dressed to the nines for the evening. The only ship he had set foot aboard since his original voyage was the *Queen Mary*, where, in his futurepast, she sat docked as a hotel in Long Beach, California, her decks teeming with terminally boring mortals in their atrocious shorts, flip flops, and fanny packs, allowing their screaming, snotty offspring to run amok.

Sailing the *Normandie* in all her art deco glory, with her sophisticated, mannered passengers, is magnificent.

This is how it should be.

He sits in the dark that first night, aloof, smoking cigarettes and watching the beautiful humans stroll by, his long legs crossed like a woman as always, the portrait of refinement and elegance. The passage will take just over four days.

He mulls over what has transpired in the last week.

The two distinct sides of his personality have suffered a collision: his recent savagery battles with his relaxed, comfortable, futurepast lassitude, where he was soft and (somewhat) unthreatening and unaffected.

Time is proving to be a tricky mistress.

His recent memories of Delphine begin to gnaw at him, bringing vile acid to rise in his throat, eating away at his sensibilities.

Her misdeeds and her rejection eviscerate him afresh.

What gall she had to refuse him!

Now she is alive again ... on the other side of the ocean from him, but very much alive. Her current age is sixteen. Should he ever encounter her again, he will walk right past her.

Vauquelin flicks his spent cigarette into the sea, and studies the ship's unrelenting movement as it disturbs the tranquil surface of the water. Gripping the rails, he absorbs the immense force of the ship, surging ahead through the sea as all ships must do, fulfilling her destiny.

He beckons that power into himself, a prayer of sorts.

Let me be as this ship ... let me savagely plunge through the waves of mortals, and live as I am meant to live.

At once it strikes him: had he been brought back to 1936 because Delphine is alive at this time? What is he meant to do? End the life of a child?

It is another strict entry in the vampire edicts: no children.

No — that cannot be the reason.

He begins to pace on the deck. He had been a malevolent devil for hundreds of years and he had merely given up, or else he had just given in. Perhaps humanity is the true curse.

His time spent isolated from them eroded his inclinations toward his own wrathful brutality. As powerful as he is, he had not been strong enough to resist the one who almost vanquished him, and his self-imposed exile had backfired.

Being around humans is toxic.

A woman in a maid's uniform walks by, alone.

Without hesitation he pulls her to him and pierces her neck, drinking her down as she screams. He did not have time to enchant her. He presses his hand over her mouth, muting her, willing her to be silent.

There is not much time.

At any moment someone who heard her scream will appear.

He takes as much as he can, until he hears rapid footsteps and urgent, shouting male voices.

She is not near death, nor is he finished.

He snaps her neck and heaves her body over the rails, shooting upwards and alighting on a lifeboat just as a group of men round the corner.

He snakes along a walkway, and flashes over to the end of the deck. Not once has he come this close to being caught in the act. Adrenaline throttles his senses: beads of sweat erupt across his forehead.

The kill was unnecessary — he fed himself well prior to embarking on this journey. He merely surrendered to his instincts, trying on his hypothetical cloak of savagery.

With shaking hands he extracts his handkerchief and wipes his face, sucking the blood from his teeth.

He descends a staircase, steadying his gait.

"Good evening," Vauquelin says, tucking the handkerchief back into his pocket. "Is there trouble? May I be of assistance?"

A couple of men are peering over the railing.

Vauquelin's aristocratic demeanor immediately absolves him of any suspicion in their eyes.

"A lady screamed, but there's no one on the deck. Very odd," one of the men says.

"That is indeed odd," Vauquelin says. He looks to the balcony above. "Perhaps a lovers' quarrel." He nods, touching the brim of his hat. "Gentlemen."

They scratch their heads and continue their survey, not giving him a second thought.

Vauquelin returns to his cabin and sits at the desk.

He puts pen to paper and writes a letter.

He remembers the address of Delphine's childhood home from their trip to Paris.

17 March 1936
Mademoiselle Delphine Boisseau
2 Rue de l'Abreuvoir, Paris

Dear Mlle Boisseau,

You have not met me, and god willing, you never
will. I can only tell you this: someday a desire will
overcome you to leave France and travel to America.
You must not.

All that awaits you there is horror, a disaster you
cannot possibly imagine. You may choose to ignore this
advice or dismiss it as mere superstition. I urge you to
heed it.

You are so young, and a better life will be yours by
remaining in Paris. Stay there and flourish. Leave
and meet your destruction. Do not tempt fate.

Louis de Vauquelin

He seals the letter and drops it in the passageway mail chute.

The ship will dock in Le Havre in the morning well after
sunrise, but he has his plan in place. When he boarded he checked,
among his luggage, a large crate. Inside the crate is a mahogany
coffin lined with red velvet, embedded in excelsior: identical in
every way to the one from his first journey.

He summons the yeoman purser and gives him his explicit

instructions for dealing with his belongings. The purser is to nail up the crate and deliver it, along with his luggage, to an address in Paris. He should not be alarmed by the contents. The coffin is empty; it is a family heirloom he is returning to France.

Traveling this way is much more dangerous compared to his 1900 overseas journey, but it is his only option. Air travel is still too primitive. This entire trip was thrown together with little forethought. He can only hope the purser will respect a passenger's wishes and not get his curiosity up.

Besides, who would dare pry open a coffin?

It worked once before, and he is counting on it working again. Should he be discovered and destroyed, he is at peace with whatever the fates have in store for him, just as he was the first time.

Before sunrise, Vauquelin descends to the cargo hold.

It will be a bumpy ride, but once he is in slumber, he will not feel a thing. He winds his pocket watch and climbs into the coffin, pulling the crate top down along with the lid. He locks it from inside and crosses his arms.

Tonight he resurfaces in Paris.

Part II

Vauquelin is startled awake by the sound of a crowbar and creaking wood. He hears men speaking muffled French ... he is lifted, then dropped, head first.

"Dear god! It is a coffin!"

The top of the crate bangs back down.

They have opened it!

"You bastard! You dropped it on my foot! You should have more respect for the dead!"

"He won't mind."

Vauquelin is picked up and carried for several meters, then smashed to the ground. The resounding impact reverberates into his bones. The crate is dragged across the floor, landing hard and knocking his skull against the top of the coffin.

Only two voices find their way into his ears — it is impossible for him to verify if there are more. Nevertheless, he does not appreciate such harsh treatment.

He unlocks the coffin and hurls open the lid, bursting the side of the crate off. Wood splinters, excelsior, and nails fly through the air.

It is dramatic in the extreme, and exactly the type of scene he had wielded in his original past.

Both the men's jaws fall open.

Vauquelin glances about the room. It is just the three of them in an otherwise deserted warehouse.

"Which of you has the injured foot?" he bellows.

One of the men raises a trembling finger ... he is holding a baguette stuffed with ham in his second hand.

Vauquelin flashes himself to the other man.

"Your friend is correct. You should have a little respect for the dead." He breaks the man's neck and seizes the other one by the elbow. "And as for you, I thank you."

He shoves his hand in the second man's mouth, preventing him from screaming, and rips his shirt open, sinking his teeth directly into the heart.

Vauquelin's spirits lift at once.

It was a shame he had to waste the one human, but the joy of snapping his disrespectful neck cancels out his regret.

He rifles around in the pockets of his blood victim and finds a knife, which he plunges into the man's chest, concealing the marks of his teeth and leaving it quivering in the wound.

Whoever finds him can sort out the mystery of there being no blood left in a stabbing victim.

He locks the coffin and snatches his bills of lading from the crate and trunks. Tipping his hat to the dead men, he vanishes out a side door into the night.

When he emerges onto the street, he is dismayed to discover he is in Le Havre, not Paris as he expected.

As he walks, the motorized vehicles disappear one by one, metamorphosing into horse-drawn carriages.

The streamlined art deco ocean liner on which he just arrived is now a clipper: its graceful canvas sails oscillate in the wind.

Déjà vu.

He has a flash of standing on the streets in Los Angeles when this all began, and the sinking sensation of the present dissolving into the past pulls him down once more.

He fumbles for his pocket watch. It is nearly midnight.

He continues strolling, searching for the only hotel he knows of in Le Havre. He approaches a man on a corner and asks for L'Hôtel Barrière Le Normandy.

Sartorially, the man appears to have stepped out of a Victor Hugo novel. He replies that there is no such hotel as he gawks at the mysterious stranger.

Vauquelin purses his lips and thanks the man, absorbing the familiar feeling that things are not as they ought to be, and enters the first tavern he sees. He asks for the day's journal. The barkeep hands him a single sheet.

The date is 29 June 1900.

It is the same day he emigrated to the United States.

His first thought is that he is weeks away from meeting Maeve, and that she is now alive.

His heart begins to hammer in his chest.

With trembling hands he rips the paper to shreds, and inquires where one might arrange transportation.

"One may catch the delivery wagons in the morning, but there is nothing tonight. It is too late, Monsieur," says the barkeep, moving to the furthermost corner of the bar.

Vauquelin looks a fright. With his 1930s suit, gaunt face, and pallid complexion, his guise is quite apparitional.

As he exits, the barkeep crosses himself three times.

Panic careens through his veins. Even if he were able to find a bed to sleep in, it would not be sufficient to protect him. He dares not return to the warehouse for his belongings and the safety of his coffin ... not with the corpses he left behind.

Vauquelin paces up and down the road in front of the tavern, riddling over what he should do. He cannot stay in this town — the sudden appearance at midnight of a strange, pale man? An empty, lived-in coffin? Bloodless murder victims? Abandoned trunks containing mysterious attire and jewelry from the future? This is the stuff old wives' tales are made of!

It would take the average human almost forty hours to walk to Évreux, perhaps ten on horseback or carriage, but he does not have the luxury of such time.

Outside a stable he wakes a man sleeping on a chair by the gate, willing him to remain silent and still, and moments later he tears the hell out of Le Havre on the back of a saddled stallion.

Several hours into the ride, the moon begins to sink. He has two, maybe three hours before sunrise. In the commune of Bourneville he locates a cemetery and leads the horse around until he finds a large, crumbling crypt. BOISSEAU is etched over the seal.

A shudder ignites across his back.

These could very well be Delphine's ancestors.

He tethers the horse to an iron fence and removes the heavy stone door. Fighting off cobwebs, he descends the many steps down into the earth. At the bottom of the crypt are five coffins on shelves. It is musty, damp, and frigid, but it is also dark as pitch: his only true necessity. It will have to do. He reclines on the floor and forces himself into slumber.

As he emerges the next evening the stone door collapses and smashes into three large pieces, startling a caretaker standing a few meters away. The crash, however, is not near as terrifying as the vision of a strangely-dressed man exiting a crypt that had been sealed for more than one hundred years.

Vauquelin flashes over to the caretaker and empties him post-haste, pitching the body down the steps. "My apologies for the fright, monsieur, and I thank you," he says.

The horse has vanished, causing his heart to sink.

There are only two courses of action for him: pilfer another horse from town and repeat this cemetery routine for two more nights, or try to find a hotel and proper carriage transportation. The latter is not ideal. It would be difficult — if not impossible — to adequately darken any available room.

Shabbiness has overtaken him.

He is offending himself. He can only imagine what humans will make of his appearance now.

The only currency on his person is a wallet full of American banknotes and a thin book of checks. Perfectly worthless, since it is all from 1936. No matter. He notices a men's clothier, shuttered for the night. He flashes to the back and forces open the door.

Theft is not his forté, but this is a desperate time.

He removes his filthy suit, folds it up neatly, cobwebs and all, and ransacks the racks until he finds an ensemble that fits, finishing it with a period-correct starched high collar, cravat, and a top hat.

He places his futurist suit in a leather satchel.

At least now he will appear as if he belongs in this time, and rather less terrifying.

He leaves the banknotes on the counter.

At the desk of an inn, Vauquelin inquires once more about transportation. Would he be able to hire a carriage to take him to Évreux tonight?

Not at this hour, he is told, but there are stables around the corner and he can speak to the proprietor in the morning.

Ah. There is to be more larceny in his future.

Behind the stables he twists open the lock on the gate, breaking it into pieces with his fist. Inside is a phaeton and four horses. During his privileged youth, he had learned how to saddle horses, but never how to secure them to a carriage.

How hard could it be, though?

He walks around to the front of the phaeton but can only recognize the shaft. The wall is hung with hundreds of pieces of tack, and the phaeton requires the use of all four horses.

He will never be able to sort this out.

Fuck, fuck, FUCK!

He blasts out of the stable on a white mare.

He can only hope she will survive the journey, given how he plans to ride her.

He has traveled maybe twenty kilometers in full gallop when

the poor horse begins to lather and cough. He must stop, but he is in the middle of the French countryside with one to two hours left before sunrise.

He unsaddles the horse, lets her go by a stream, and sprints with his satchel tucked under his arm. He will come across a village or a cemetery before sunrise — he hopes.

The situation is fraught with peril, but he has no recourse.

His body flows into a movement akin to that of an Olympic sprinter. He thinks of movies he had seen where vampires could fly or turn into bats, and pierces the night air with uproarious laughter. How convenient that skill would be!

Nevertheless, he is not fast enough. The sky morphs from midnight black to pale violet as he approaches a village at last.

He has perhaps a half-hour remaining, if that, to find shelter.

As he slows his pace and ambles through the gates, he is mystified by the early risers walking about, all markedly ancient in dress. On the opposite end of the village is an imposing cathedral: the spire reverts to scaffolding before his eyes.

A swarm of butterflies is set aflight in his stomach.

It is the same, familiar phenomena he experienced when his pages first began turning backward.

Vauquelin sprints to the cathedral, upsetting a few marketeers, running through the doors and down the first subterranean stone steps he encounters, his skin prickling with the temperature drop.

He reaches a heavy wooden door with a chamber beyond.

It is empty, containing only a single chair and miscellaneous religious artifacts.

He can only hope it is not a room frequented by humans.

He closes the door and lets his exhaustion carry him away.

Vauquelin finds his way back to the sanctuary and lights a candle for Maeve, who is now even more sequestered from him by time. He bows and kneels down on a prie-dieu.

How unpracticed in worship he is!

God cannot love vampires — or can he? Did not all creatures who walk the earth belong to god?

Like the vast majority of the French populace, Vauquelin was raised Catholic. He was an altar boy and sang in the choir, with a crystalline soprano voice. But as he grew into manhood and expanded his readings, he began to summarily reject his religion. He read the entire bible and, upon its completion, declared it a manual of hypocrisy and contradiction.

And after he was vampire, he lashed out at god — for if he had ever truly been a creature of god, that god had forsaken him. Lore and literature before and after his creation condemned him as evil, the spawn of the devil.

The candles reflect on Vauquelin's eyes as he genuflects on the prie-dieu, his fingers entwined for prayer.

He feels nothing.

Hears nothing.

If only prayers could truly be answered.

He stands, hands laced behind his back, and strolls around the sanctuary. He does love the artifice of the Roman Catholic Church. One cannot deny that they put on a glorious show.

How he wishes he could glimpse the sunlight streaming through the stained glass windows, illuminating his tread with brilliant color ... alas, they are all darkened, their hues hushed by the sullen virtue of the night.

He gazes up at the Christ figure on the colossal crucifix in the Gothic nave.

He esteems Christ as a benevolent figure, but he finds organized religion deplorable. In three hundred and fifty years of existence, Vauquelin has witnessed more evil at the hands of humans, much of it in the name of dogma, than he could ever conceive.

Christ was the original Immortal, sent to absolve humankind of its sins. Perhaps he *was* in fact a chosen man, the son of god … or was he just an exceptional human man with a kind, pure heart, who inspired legends simply because his soul was a little cleaner than those around him?

Vampires are evidence of eternal life, yet Vauquelin abandoned his duty to bequeath the gift of immortality and create more of his kind.

Maybe, much like himself, Christ did not want the job, either.

A priest emerges from a curtain and approaches him.

"Welcome," he says. "I bid you a good evening. Are you here to confess, my son?"

Vauquelin sways his head back.

Confession?

Where would one even start?

"Oh, most assuredly not, Father. The summation of my sins would set your confessional, as well as the expanse of this majestic cathedral, alight with hellfire."

The priest pats Vauquelin's shoulder and takes his elbow.

"Come," he urges.

Vauquelin stiffens. Why is this man being so kind to him?

He hangs his head and follows the priest into the confessional.

The ancient rite had not been uttered by his lips in centuries. The words had fallen from his pre-vampire memory, so he recalled the modern line repeated so often in movies.

"Bless me, Father, for I have sinned. It has been three hundred and sixty years since my last confession."

His chin quivers.

He turns his head as the priest's eyes bore upon him through the wooden screen.

"I beg your pardon ... do you jest with me?" the priest asks.

"I do not. It has been at least three hundred and sixty years ... perhaps three hundred and seventy ... I have lost count. You must understand: I have traveled from far beyond this time. No doubt you took notice of my strange garb."

"It is late, my son," the priest says. "I can offer you God's forgiveness if you will only be truthful with me."

Vauquelin slumps back in the confessional, his mind wrought with these problematic concepts. Truth has long ceased to exist for him, and forgiveness is unnecessary.

He could kill this priest with little effort ... it is quiet and there is no one else present. But he has never taken a priest, and he will not do it now — it is too fucking cliché. He rarely makes choices that would be at home in a B-movie.

He gets a bigger kick out of his candid confession of his time on earth, which is implausible anyway. Maybe he should have been more vocal in his futurepast.

Nobody would have believed him!

But this is a very different era. He cannot risk being committed to an asylum or thrown into prison or, worse, brutalized and buried alive with a rock shoved into his jaw, marked as a vampire for eternity, unable to rise again.

He must remain veiled in secrecy.

However, merely saying the words "three hundred and sixty years" aloud to another being in this time has given him the smallest measure of relief.

At long last the words begin to pour forth, as if a dam in his soul has been breached, and he cannot stop their force.

"Father, you are ill-prepared to grasp my truth. I take my communion from humans. Their blood is my wine. I drink their life force and send their souls to hell. So it is decreed, and so it shall always be. Your god can give me no solace, and you certainly cannot be his emissary," Vauquelin says. "There can be no contrition for me. Your words are mere platitudes that might soothe the soul of an average man, but no one, not a deity and certainly not a human man, can save me."

The priest keeps silent for some time and then says, "Surely you speak in metaphor, but I hear your despair, and so, I assure you, does our benevolent Lord. Expel the anger that resides in your heart, my son. No burden of sin is too great for our savior to absolve, should you ask for his forgiveness. Let God provide you with the redemption you seek. Perhaps we should pray for patience, that God may grant you the time you need to surrender to your path."

"Patience? *Time?* Ha! Father, I have nothing but time. I am swimming in it, sinking. The pressure of it suffocates me as if I were at the deepest point in the ocean, counting the grains of sand beneath my weight. I have more in common with the listless son of Neptune than your god."

Vauquelin buries his face in his hands, and then is struck by a passage he read in his youth and never forgot. Never had it been more appropriate to utter aloud.

He stands tall, imposing, his head nearly striking the ceiling of the confessional.

" '*Verily I say unto you, there be some standing here which shall not taste of death,*'" Vauquelin whispers. "It is in your Bible, Father. Surely you recall the verse? Again, I assure you — no redemption exists for me."

He throws back the curtain and strides out of the sanctuary, looking back over his shoulder at the candle he lit for Maeve.

The priest remains hidden in the confessional.

Vauquelin departs like the Wandering Jew, condemned to shed his skin and rejuvenate over and over again to the age of thirty, throughout eternity.

He arrives at the front gates of his château in Évreux on another stolen horse. He stables the stallion and ascends the dark stairs to his bedchamber.

The house is quiet; only a solitary caretaker remains in his employ. He lights a candle and strips off his bizarre clothing, collapsing into the dusty comfort of his own bed.

The wild journey has drained him.

Vauquelin wakes with blurred vision. He does not recognize his location straightaway. The atmosphere gives him the satisfying sensation that he is back in Los Angeles.

Was that a police siren? A helicopter floodlight?

No.

There is only silence.

He rubs his eyes and thinks, *Wait ... this is not my bed.*

He is most assuredly not in L.A., nor is he in his château at Évreux — he is in his ancient bedchamber in Paris. This house was stolen from him by the King in 1687 and he has not set foot inside it since.

He opens a tiny slit in the bed curtains.

The room is dark, yet light bleeds around the edges of the shuttered windows. He tiptoes across the room, peeking through the wooden shutters. His fingers rest on the latch and it pops open, thrusting the panels apart and flooding the room with abundant sunlight.

His eyes begin to water, and he digs his fingers into his face, panicking, fearful of the sun's slow burn. But there is no pain.

How curious!

He looks out the window, still half-asleep ... he must be dreaming, *but damn, this is far too detailed for a dream!*

There is a coach-and-six stopped in the cobblestoned courtyard below. Several men in ancient livery dress walk its perimeter, checking the mechanicals and tending the horses.

There is a strange lump in his bed, the shape of a sleeping dog. He flings the linens back and finds the leather satchel, containing the suit he had purchased at Bullock's department store in Los Angeles in 1936.

He had fallen asleep with his arms around it.

The horses whinny and stamp outside.

This is bizarre.

A bolt from the blue strikes him wide-awake.

It is daytime, he is inside the Paris house whose gates he stood outside with Delphine, and the sun is not harming him.

He is vampire no more.

It must be Death. The afterlife, perhaps.

Vauquelin lets forth a long, heart-rending howl.

The howl startles the horses and the men — they peer up at the window where he stands howling.

He hunches over, rubbing his arms as his eyes dart about the room. They land on the servant's bell-sash, and he rushes to pull it. He glances down at his naked body and seizes a banyan from a chair next to the bed, hands shaking as he struggles into it. He stands in place panting, hair wild, eyes dilated.

At once the room erupts in pandemonium as the door flies open and Vauquelin's valet Olivier enters, shocked and concerned to find Monsieur in such a state.

Olivier rushes to fill the ewer with water.

Vauquelin glances at the clock as it chimes on the fireplace mantle. It is a quarter to noon.

Noon! The middle of the day!

His face is etched in terror as he regards his faithful valet, whom he has not seen in three hundred and fifty years — at least.

He died in 1681.

Vauquelin blurts, "Tell me, Olivier ... what did I do yesterday?"

Olivier is amused by the question and turns his head to hide a grin. Perhaps Monsieur le Duc had overindulged last night. It was not the first time nor would it be the last, yet he answers without hesitation.

"Monsieur went to purchase a stallion in the morning and had luncheon at the Château d'Écouen. Monsieur returned home for his supper. Is Monsieur unwell? Shall I call for the surgeon?"

"No, that will not be necessary," Vauquelin stammers. "I would like my toilette now."

"As Monsieur wishes."

Olivier begins setting up the dressing table, arranging many jars of creams, powders, and sterling silver-handled implements.

Vauquelin clasps his hands together until his knuckles turn white, hoping Olivier will not notice how badly they are shaking. His eyes flutter and continue to water, so unaccustomed are they to such abundant light.

After his shaving ritual is complete, he picks up a looking glass from the dressing table. Anger swirls in his chest. The looking glasses had all been destroyed, had they not?

He fumbles and it falls to the floor. As he picks it up, he holds it out as far as he can, but it catches his reflection. His reflection!

He smiles in awe, running his hand over his jaw, and parts his lips. His teeth are ordinary human teeth ... the daggers are gone. He bares them, tilting his head back and forth.

Vauquelin's face had endured significant transformation after his creation as a vampire. His eyes, azure at his birth, turned an icy, cold blue. To accommodate his elongated teeth, the jawbone had moved forward, giving him a haughty appearance. His speech was altered. He taught himself to move his lips as little as possible when he spoke.

No one need ever see his teeth unless he wanted them to.

He runs his fingers across them and along his chin.

His entire body relaxes.

A chambermaid enters with a silver tray, laden with a lavish seven-course meal and a large crystal decanter of wine. She places the tray on a table and curtsies, departing without a word.

Olivier bows and closes the doors behind him.

Vauquelin recoils at the tray, but his stomach responds by growling with ravenous hunger.

The food smells delectable, not repugnant!

He attacks the plates, reveling in thick slabs of roast beef, allowing their rare juices to dribble down his chin. He dips his finger in the vat of butter, tears bread apart and gobbles up cheese — it is orgasmic.

He washes it all down with insatiable gulps of wine and polishes off everything on the tray, licking his fingertips to grab each minuscule crumb and tiniest shard of meat, leaving the plates clean. At the end, a luscious sweet confection awaits him: a *chou à la crème* dusted with granules of sugar and candied orange zest, drizzled with decadent violet syrup.

In his futurepast, with its abundance of gourmet dining, this would not have been possible. He did not go to the finest restaurants. He never went grocery shopping. He was deprived of one of his earliest passions in life: food. He was, with food as with a multitude of other of life's pleasures, forever from the outside looking in.

When it is all finished, he leans back in his chair, kneading his protruding belly. Suddenly, his mind is overtaken by a flash of Maeve's thighs, her fiery red curls — his head in the crook of her arm, kissing her inner elbow, his fingertips caressing her cheek.

He buries his face in his hands. She is unborn, unattainable, and so is the futurepast he had lived and loved.

How long can this go on? Shall I continue going backwards until I am a mere infant, a seed, a wish in my mother's womb?

When the chambermaid returns for the dishes, he seizes her by the wrist, twirling her into the room, and locks the door behind her. "Madeleine," he whispers, picking her up and laying her on his bed.

She hikes up her skirts at once. Monsieur is so handsome. She has been pining in secret for him since the day she arrived to work in his house. He has never once made any indication that he wanted her, but she dares not protest now, not at this moment when it is quite clear that he does. And by no means has he called her by her name ... she is surprised that he knows it.

Vauquelin drops his banyan, reaching up under her skirts and into the dampness between her legs.

He conjures more visions of Maeve, yearning to retain the flashes that had just pierced him, memories of her velvet fleshiness getting his blood up. It takes no time at all to work himself into full hardness. The chambermaid is a mere surrogate.

He sinks into her with a subdued resolve and thrusts his hips with accelerating ecstasy, until he is dizzied by the pulsing, foreign freneticism of orgasm.

Oh god, oh god, oh god.

He withdraws and tumbles onto his back, ejaculating in hard spasms, silky white and volatile. Sticky bursts spew across his stomach, surging through the air as his hand pumps. It seems that it will never stop, yet the entire event lasts two, maybe three minutes. He groans with each pulse, his body at last growing still, aftershocks of joy electrifying his blood.

Running his hand across his stomach, he besmirches his skin with ejaculate, releasing its earthy, fervid fragrance into the air. He breathes it in, inhaling it.

It is at once familiar, preternatural, and marvelous.

He regards his sodden hand as if it belongs to someone else, turning it to and fro. It glimmers in the light of the windows.

How I have missed the glorious act of the release.

Madeleine has ceased to exist in his mind. When she sits up, smoothing her skirts down, his shoulders jerk.

He does not have even the slightest urge to kill her.

Incredible!

"I thank you," he says, "oh, how I thank you."

She curtsies, takes the tray, and leaves him.

He does not notice that she has forgotten her coif on the bed.

Vauquelin wanders about the chamber, reacquainting himself

with his ancient objects and possessions. The case of his mother's jewels sits beckoning on a table. He opens it, and there are all of her sparkling baubles, including the velvet ribbon with the pearl drop he had given to Delphine and the garnets he had given to Maeve.

He lifts them out one by one. They are now bewitched for him, each at different points in time gracing the necks of women he had loved, none of whom, at this time, are alive.

Closing the case, he places his fingers on his lips, unable to bring himself to look away. At last he wraps himself back up in the banyan and rings for Olivier again.

"My bath," is all he can muster.

The valet returns with a throng of servants including Madeleine. She maneuvers herself about the room, attempting to catch Vauquelin's eye.

He gasps when he spots her bare head.

There the coif lays on his rumpled bed. He snatches it up, shoving it into his pocket. He is careful not to look at her, not wanting to give her false hope or bring attention to his indiscretion.

When no one is looking, he tosses it into the fireplace.

Vauquelin is the master of his domain. As custom dictates, he can have her or any servant whenever he wants, but his modern sensibilities fill him with shame. He has done nothing out of the ordinary, yet he feels reprehensible. In his original past, he never once laid with staff.

This is a shocking turn of events.

His copper bathtub, draped with a linen sheet, is filled with hot water, lavender sprigs, and juniper. The servants swish out of the room, with the exception of a solitary musician who remains to accompany Vauquelin's bath on a viola da gamba.

He sits in the bath for over an hour, soothed by the fine music and the savory fragrances of the water. He polishes off another bottle of wine and puffs on a long pipe, until the water becomes chilled and wrinkles his skin.

He misses cigarettes and running water and his marble tub with jets in Los Angeles, but this is the zenith of seventeenth-century luxury and for that he is grateful.

Olivier initiates the elaborate ritual of dressing Vauquelin, accompanied by the male servants. He conducts each step as if he is leading an orchestra, finely-tuned down to the last note, and not a single participant ever misses a beat.

It has been performed daily, with only one modification, since Vauquelin's thirteenth birthday. Although the ritual became routine for the staff, Olivier once wrote out the details of the entire spectacle for their reference.

PROCEDURE FOR CONDUCTING THE LEVER
OF MONSIEUR LE DUC DE VAUQUELIN

23 August 1651
Signed Olivier Boucher
1er Valet de Chambre and Head of Household
L'hôtel des Coquillages, Paris

Begin with a gentle whisper in Monsieur's ear to awaken him at ~~dawn~~ sunset

The copper bath, filled with hot water and fragrances of the season, will be wheeled into Monsieur's bedchamber

Monsieur will be undressed and assisted into the bath, where he will remain for one to two hours at his pleasure

A full carafe of wine and a goblet will be placed within Monsieur's reach

At the conclusion of Monsieur's bath, the house musician will be invited into the bedchamber by the first valet de chambre to perform during Monsieur's toilette

Monsieur's person will be dried with linen and massaged with oil of lavender

While seated, Monsieur's feet will be massaged, and the nails of each toe trimmed if needed and filed, repeated on Monsieur's hands

A hot linen will be placed upon Monsieur's face for approximately five minutes: no more, no less

Any hairs in Monsieur's nose will be removed with a pince à épiler

Monsieur's face will then be shaved with a razor. A light layer of lanolin is to be applied after shaving is complete

Monsieur's person will be spritzed with perfume

Monsieur will be dressed in a laundered chemise

Ten suits of clothing and ten boxes of shoes will be presented to Monsieur for his selection

The third Valet de Chambre will bring the appropriately matched silk stockings

Monsieur's blouse will be tucked into his breeches and they will be buttoned. Next, his vest, waistcoat and lace cuffs

Monsieur's jewel box will be brought forth, from which he will make his selection of rings and buckles

Monsieur's chosen buckles will be placed upon his shoes, and the shoes fitted upon his feet

The second Valet de Chambre will attach Monsieur's hilt and rapier about his waist and the third Valet de Chambre will place Monsieur's walking staff in his hand

At the conclusion, Olivier opens a small velvet box full of *mouches* and presents it to his master, who selects a crescent moon and a star.

The valet dampens the backs, placing them on his master's cheekbone, just below his right eye.

Vauquelin has rather missed this.

Having a staff to attend his every need makes the earlier nostalgia for his jacuzzi tub feather away into oblivion.

The entire ritual, bath included, consumes three to four hours of Vauquelin's time each morning. The only time it was altered was after he became vampire, when the ritual was performed after sundown instead.

At last, he turns to the large, full-length looking glass and beholds his majestic reflection. His cadaverous pallor has been replaced by the olive complexion of his birth: robust and healthy, the skin of his mother's Sicilian lineage.

His cheeks are flushed with their natural blush.

He assumes a wide stance and joy bubbles up inside him, placing him on the verge of tears with so many conflicted emotions assaulting him. A quivering smile spreads across his lips, and it occurs to him how rarely he smiles.

He is serene, comfortable in his own skin again, unedited in his primeval body. His hair, his clothing, his surroundings: it is all genuine. This is his origin: the authentic Vauquelin, the Vauquelin he was born to be.

He has never been able to shake the dandyism he had embraced while still a human man. He continued to cultivate these tendencies throughout his vampire existence.

Olivier fusses with his master's garments, finishing the details.

Vauquelin's reflection has been eclipsed for over three hundred and fifty years: he cannot stop looking at himself.

He is wearing the ensemble that drew him in his museum exhibit, the same one that captivated him when he removed it from the armoire during his first time-shift.

His fascination with his appearance turns to dread.

This day bears significance — and now he knows he is human again for a malignant reason.

Tonight he has an rendezvous with destiny and he will not stop himself, even though he can.

He is made for this life.

Scrutinizing himself in the mirror, he certainly looks the part.

It is his destiny, and he will fulfill it.

Vauquelin dabs some rouge across his cheeks and lips as a parting gesture and emerges into the courtyard, pleased at how easily he re-embraces his original way of life.

It is congenial, sublime.

"This is my time," he ponders aloud in English.

A footman hears him speak and approaches him, asking, "*Pardonnez-moi, Monsieur?*"

Vauquelin scowls, waving the footman away.

Before he was vampire, he was a Duc. A bon vivant. A peacock. A legendary *enfant terrible* who delighted in devilry. And after he was vampire, he was all those things still, only amplified and with the addition of an unquenchable thirst for blood.

The carriage is waiting, but he is not quite ready to make his departure. He takes a leisurely turn around his courtyard, enjoying the pleasing sound of his walking staff striking the cobblestones. He walks to his fountain and gazes upon the flowers in his gardens, illuminated by the setting sun, the golden hour.

The entire setting is an intrinsic part of Vauquelin — indeed, he had carried it into his futurepast, incorporating it into his new life in California.

He is still draped in the evanescent sensation of a dreamstate, but the dream is interrupted when one of the coachmen clears his throat and says, "Monsieur will not want to arrive late to Monsieur le Duc d'Orléans entertainment."

"Ah, yes ... the entertainment," Vauquelin replies, ascending the carriage. Appointed with lush, overstuffed, silk velvet upholstery, it is the ancestor of the Pagani — crafted in Italy with Venetian glass windows. He sinks into the seat with his legs splayed wide and raps on the ceiling with his staff.

The carriage begins its sluggish dispatch and rumbles over the cobblestones, out Vauquelin's gates into Paris.

It is indeed 1668 — there is no uncertainty. People traipse through the busy roads on foot and in carriages or the occasional sedan chair.

Repugnant odors penetrate the seams of the carriage windows. He draws forth a perfumed linen handkerchief to cover his mouth and nose.

Peasants surround the carriage, impeding its speed.

Cathedral bells ring out, resonating the hour of six in mellifluous tones that echo across the walls.

As if he needs further visual confirmation, a multitude of printed Decrees of the King are pasted across the walls and obelisks he passes.

PAR LE ROY

LOUIS XIV

ANNO DOMINI 1668

He clenches his fists.

By now he is a master at bouncing around the decades, but how long can he count on staying in this era?

The carriage arrives at the Palais Royal and Vauquelin dashes into the crowded, exquisite debauchery that is the patent hallmark of His Royal Highness, Monsieur le Duc d'Orléans.

Vauquelin lingers by a small orchestra performing a rowdy Jean-Baptiste Lully march. In his futurepast, he had Lully, along with many other baroque composers, in his digital collection.

He never lost his love for the music of this time.

The raucous notes swelling through the room fill him with a rapturous ecstasy. Certain music stabs him right in the heart.

He had been in this spot and witnessed this very performance once before: the night he became vampire.

Gooseflesh erupts across his body and his throat clenches in and overwhelming volume of pleasure and pain.

He approaches a balcony and removes his spyglass from his pocket, surveying the people in the gardens below. There is the bejeweled morsel he had teased on this selfsame night.

History is unfolding as it had before, to the letter.

His heart stutters. He can stop this. He can escape.

But he knows good and well he will not.

He continues moving the spyglass across the half-dressed throngs and this time notices an unattractive man staring at him from across the ballroom, which gives him pause. He resumes spanning the spyglass across, abruptly swinging his arm back to the man in a dreadful moment of recognition.

Bringing the glass down he whispers, "Yvain."

The man stands erect, his arms crossed, with Vauquelin fixed in his unwavering, ominous gaze.

Vauquelin does not recall Yvain's presence at the fête the first time. But this proves that his maker was there that fateful night. That was when it all began, when he was chosen: and it was Yvain stopped in the carriage behind his own.

In an instant, Yvain appears at his side on the balcony.

Vauquelin does not flinch.

"Alas, my exalted creature has returned, human once more," Yvain whispers, caressing Vauquelin's cheek. "A mere fragment of a mortal, yet as magnificent as you ever were."

"Evidently." As the word leaves his lips a deluge of memories of Maeve floods him, killing his bravado and sending his shoulders into a slump.

"And now you yearn for your stolen future."

Yvain smooths his hands over Vauquelin as if he were a toy come to life: his shoulders, his hair, his arms, his hips.

"So it was because of you," Vauquelin hisses, digging his fingers into Yvain's wrist. "I should have known! Why have you uprooted me? Why must you persecute me?"

"We shall not discuss it here," Yvain says.

He seizes Vauquelin roughly by the arm, pulling him away from the stone balustrade.

At once they are barreling through Paris in Yvain's demented, luxurious black coach. The plump, beckoning beauty is absent from the archway. There is no need for her role to be reprised ... because this time, the maker has Vauquelin just where he wants him.

Yvain places a hand on his back and guides him through a doorway, down, down, down to the ignoble chamber where Vauquelin was damned so many centuries ago, the one from which he emerged a revenant.

Dark walls with ornate golden moulding ... *boiserie* ... red velvet curtains ... the consummate vampire den. Glittering chandeliers hang from the ceiling, casting an eerie yet inviting glow.

Men in various states of undress recline on the furniture, their garments filmy, gauzy, as if they were refugees from a nightmare. They rise and surround Vauquelin like curious, carnivorous butterflies.

He crosses his arms in exhausted annoyance. He is ill-disposed for the vampiric drama that threatens to play out in front of him if he does not put a halt to it.

"Get rid of them," he commands.

With a flash of his hands Yvain indulges Vauquelin, dispersing the vampires against the walls.

They hiss and evaporate from the room.

Yvain sits on a sofa, motioning for Vauquelin to join him.

Defiant for perpetuity, Vauquelin remains standing.

"You knew you would be back here, standing before me once again, in this very instant," Yvain says. "It was your decision."

"Well, then?"

"You made errors, dearest. Grave errors."

With his fingers, Yvain counts off the litany of Vauquelin's alleged trespasses. "You turned your back on your destiny and gave your sartorial legacy to a public museum: that was the final straw. You did not create vampires, as you were decreed to do. You divulged your identity to mortals yet mercifully allowed them to live. You ... shall I go on?"

Vauquelin glares at his maker like a scolded child.

"Delphine," Yvain snarls, drawing out the name.

"I am being punished because of *Delphine*?" he sneers, half-laughing. "You cannot be serious."

His hatred for her is still a gaping wound. He had killed her less than a month ago, though time is now utterly meaningless.

"On your original journey, you revealed yourself to her, yet you kept her alive."

"Even so, why did you not smite me at the moment of my alleged infractions, instead of letting me live out my miserable existence?" Vauquelin said. "A pitiful excuse for a vengeful vampire god, you are. Nevertheless, I loved her once. She was loyal to me. She was innocent."

"Innocent? Loyal? Ha! Another mistake: compassion for mortals!" Yvain snorts. "You let your most faithful human die, when you could have made her immortal and lived out your existence with her, instead of withering into a void of your own creation ... and a worthless waste of my blood."

Yvain flashes behind Vauquelin's back, whispering in his ear.

"*Un vampire compatissant ... tellement charmant.* The future softened you, mon cher Vauquelin. You became ... dull. What happened to the mighty murdering bastard I created?"

Vauquelin stares straight ahead, mistrustful of what is transpiring. He is uncertain what he had expected from this encounter, but a lecture is definitely not on his list. Did Yvain destroy his life and wrestle him back through the aeons merely to chastise him?

He turns his back and speaks into the fireplace.

"I cannot deny that you are correct. I am jaded. I am weary. I exist, nothing more."

"At last, you admit it! That is why you are here, my creature. I needed to hear those words from your lips. But I can offer you deliverance."

Vauquelin turns and faces Yvain, suspicion spreading across his countenance. "I beg your pardon?"

"A redemption, of sorts. But the choice to accept it is yours."

Vauquelin's brow furrows.

"When I made you vampire, you were reluctant to accept my bestowal. And as I kept watch over you through the centuries, I began to realize that I did not gift you. I condemned you," Yvain says. "I sentenced you to perpetual unhappiness by not educating you to use your bestowal in the manner it was decreed to be used. So here you stand before me, human once more, and I ask you ... do you desire atonement? Or will you continue to live as a pathetic, insignificant human, tormented until the end of your days by visions of the one you love but can never hold, bedeviled by your tastes of the future which are unattainable in your present state? Do you want to die an ordinary, diseased mortal death? This is the decision I give you."

"But why? Why do you offer me this now?"

Yvain approaches him. "It is quite simple, *mon cher*. I love you. I wronged you. Perhaps I should have given you a proper mortal death the very first night you appeared before me. Instead I have witnessed your interminable suffering, which has been my burden, my curse. It was I who placed you back with Delphine again. I hoped you might overcome her and right your wrongs. And so you did. You redeemed yourself. But I have pulled you further back through the centuries because you must save me, and thereby save yourself from this wicked ennui you have cultivated. You must begin again."

"*Save* you? How can I save *you*? You are my maker. You are older and stronger than me. Surely I cannot save you."

"Oh, but you can, as I will explain in due time. If you survive and behave, you can have another go-round with your little human — if you still want to toy with her, that is. I am remiss in not educating you properly about meddling with mortals."

Vauquelin's mind crackles. Is Yvain talking about Delphine, or Maeve? Or both?

"Delphine is the only one I ever ... toyed with."

"But why did you allow her to live? Your failures puzzle me. You retained too much of your human sensibility, Vauquelin. Perhaps I taught you nothing ... or is it that you ceased to listen? As for this particular human, you gave her too much power over you."

"There was something about her, something extraordinary. She penetrated my thoughts the night I told her about my creation. No other human has ever done that."

Yvain considers this. "Because you surrendered yourself to her completely and made yourself vulnerable. As for the other one — well, what can one say about her? You concealed your identity as you should have. But you deceived yourself, which is an egregious crime, my darling one. It is clear to me who you really allowed yourself to love. The latter was a scant substitute." His voice deepens into a frightening bellow. "You cannot deny this!"

The severity of Yvain's statement strikes Vauquelin at his core. It is an accurate assessment, one that had not occurred to him before. He begins to pace.

"Yvain, why did you abandon me? You became silent, unreachable. I could no longer hear you. You left me alone ... it bred within me a hatred for you, and for myself. I was wretched and forsaken."

A half-year after his creation, Vauquelin escaped Paris and the misery of his grim life and his new bride, retreating to his ancestral château in Annecy, Provence. After several months had passed, he could no longer hear any vampires, not even Yvain, beckoning to him. There was only silence, and he found short-lived contentment. He crossed the border once a week and hunted his victims in small Italian villages.

The other vampires in Yvain's coterie had no connection to Vauquelin — they could not locate him.

During the months leading up to his departure, Vauquelin called on Yvain constantly, begging his maker to guide him and help him with Arsinée. As a fledgling vampire, he could scarcely take care of himself, let alone the foul succubus that had been thrust upon him.

She had no grace or integrity. And since he was her maker,

he had an indelible bond with her.

The mere thought of her ignited flames of anger in him.

When he complained to Yvain, the old master offered no guidance. He said Vauquelin must learn to dominate her, and that it had been his choice to live outside the coterie — where Yvain's influence would have been stronger.

Vauquelin must live with the consequences.

He tried his damnedest to make her hate him, but still she lapped at his heels like a rejected puppy. The crueler he was to her, the deeper grew her resolve.

She was a nuisance: sloppy, vindictive, and murderous.

Her body count was astonishing, and it was he who had to clean up her messes.

Before his creation, he had been restoring his family's *hôtel particulier*, L'hôtel du Coquillage, located at 17 quai Malaquais in the 6th arrondissement of Paris.

Yvain had at least educated him on the vital importance of retaining trustworthy legal advocates. "You must above all ensure that your funds are maintained, and that you have a loyal human to rely upon for deeds you cannot accomplish yourself. As a human you had financial security. You must keep the illusion intact."

Trustworthy humans were challenging to find, but money and enchantment worked wonders. Loyalty is an easy purchase.

It was the best advice Yvain had ever given him, and he had not given him much.

With the assistance of a lawyer, he completed the restoration of the hôtel. The lawyer made all the daytime appointments, met with the artisans, and ordered the materials.

But Arsinée was not only bloodthirsty: she was draining

Vauquelin's accounts at an alarming pace.

When the hôtel was finished, it was impossible for him to enjoy it. The magnificent *esprit* of the house was tainted by the presence of Arsinée.

Vauquelin sent Olivier away to Annecy for his own protection when it became impossible for him to disguise the truth of what was unfolding.

Arsinée killed all the other servants in his employ.

Olivier, it seemed, was just lucky.

One night, with little forethought, he filled two leather pouches with gold and took his carriage rip-shod to the lawyer's house. He ordered the lawyer to deliver the larger pouch to Arsinée, change the locks on the hôtel, and give her the sealed letter he pressed into his hands:

> *Arsinée, you are a blight upon my soul. I do not love*
> *you. I will never love you. We are united only in*
> *darkness. The most wretched part of this tale is that*
> *we will both live forever, and consequently, the day*
> *that you can no longer torture me may never come.*
> *I renounce you. I regret creating you, though it was*
> *not my choice. I can only hope that when I next lay*
> *my eyes upon your face, it will be illuminated by the*
> *flames of hell.*

He did not sign the letter. There could be no question in its authorship. With that, he boarded his carriage followed by three others loaded with his belongings, and departed for Annecy.

Even self-exiled in the provinces, Vauquelin's problems with Arsinée persisted. She continued living in his Paris house, ruining his life from afar.

For months, he was tormented by her calling to him. He had not a single moment awake when she was not penetrating his mind. It nearly drove him insane. He was accursed, and abandoned by his maker. His life was shattered.

At long last, she stopped. He could not determine the reason but, to his consternation, it coincided with Yvain's absence and silence. He did not question it.

Anxiety settled into his marrow.

Vauquelin feared her retribution. She would in all likelihood burn the hôtel to the ground, but it would be worth it to be rid of her if that was what it took (he knew now that she had not. He saw it with Delphine in his second 1959).

He had no doubt that she would haunt him. Most of all, he feared never having a moment without her presence for the infinite numbers of years he had yet to live.

Now Yvain hears all these thoughts, and they immerse him in Vauquelin's deep grief. He moves behind Vauquelin and places his hands on his shoulders.

"I failed you in myriad ways. I did not prepare you. I made a fatal mistake, one with which I burdened you. I should never have forced you to create Arsinée. I should have allowed you to choose for yourself. You were not the only one she wronged. But now we must address the problem with Delphine," he says. "You were strong enough to escape from Arsinée, but you let an irrelevant mortal plaything tear you down. How slow-witted you can be at times, Vauquelin! She did not love you … she did not even believe you! I brought you back to her so you could recognize this at last. You are an obedient boy after all, my pet. You did what you should have done when you first encountered her, and you learned the truth about her peculiar attachment to you."

Obedient boy?

Vauquelin's cheek begins to twitch.

Between Delphine and Yvain, Vauquelin's ego has taken a beating these past few weeks. His maker speaks so dismissively of this worthless mortal, so undeserving of his attention, that Vauquelin begins to question himself even further for letting such a creature best him.

"She was too sensible. She did not want it. She did not want me," Vauquelin says, "not forever."

"But another did. I never expected you to be a coward, Vauquelin. What have you become? You were a Chosen One. It was your destiny to create vampires. Instead, you were determined to isolate yourself and live as a hermit. You have squandered all you have been given!" Yvain strides over to face Vauquelin, catapulting aside a chair in his path. "It was my own mistake for granting you your independence, for not insisting that you live with my coterie. You are spineless and faint-of-heart, when I once thought you invincible."

"Yes, I'm a coward, Vauquelin hisses. "A worthless, weakened coward. Yet one you left to fend for himself. After creating Arsinée, how could I fathom repeating that error? I am incapable! I have meticulously designed my life for centuries to prevent it!"

Throughout his life, it had been fundamental for him to obscure any evidence of his vampirism, to protect the masses from his intrinsic horror.

Not to shield them from his violence — *no, no, god no, definitely not that* — but to protect and preserve *himself*.

While Yvain desired to multiply his brood and unleash vampires upon the world, Vauquelin had chosen discretion above all, even to his own detriment. Yvain's desires would lead to the obliteration of vampires: or worse, a vast population of egregiously irresponsible undead monsters.

Seclusion was (is) his eternal philosophy, his foundation, and nothing could ever change that. Not redemption, not becoming a human again ... nothing. His choices, he is confident, will remain the same, even should his years unfold once more.

Yvain hoists Vauquelin up by the throat, holding him above the ground until his face reddens.

"But it was your duty!" Yvain snarls. "It is the duty of all vampires! You were chosen to keep our line alive, and you have done nothing! You have created nothing ... you are nothing! So choose. Death or redemption!"

He releases Vauquelin and he tumbles to the floor, coughing, gasping, clutching his throat. Yvain kneels beside him and strokes his hair. Vauquelin stares at the ceiling, panting.

"The fact remains," Vauquelin gasps, "that I have no regrets about how I have chosen to live my life. I was left alone to make the choices I did. My terms. My only regret now is that you forced me to relinquish it."

"It was imperative for you to come back here. You will learn why. Do you remember these words? 'Your beauty is necessary for me. You are extraordinary, too sublime to leave this earth.' They are still true, my darling one. But you've sullied yourself."

"You are a paramount charlatan, Yvain. Again I ask you ... why did you abandon me? I called to you ... I prayed to you."

For a fraction of a second, Yvain looks old and shriveled. He was not a handsome man when he was created a vampire and the centuries have not improved his looks. He carries the rugged Gallic features of his ancestors, and now the pain of what he had wrought upon Vauquelin is entrenched across his countenance.

"I was silent, my dearest, because a half-year after your creation, Arsinée destroyed me."

"Destroyed you? Explain yourself!"

"I believe it would be more powerful to show you."

Yvain thrusts their foreheads together, empowering the abhorrent tale to tell itself.

PARIS, FRANCE | 1669 | LA CRÉATURE

Arsinée lured Yvain to a room, alone. She was seething, blinded by wrath. Yvain discovered a moment too late that he was trapped. There was but one entrance, and the lock had been triggered behind him. It was too late.

What a fool he was to allow himself to be ambushed by this beautiful but cunning vampire, whose very creation had been a significant oversight!

Yvain was unaware there was a traitor amongst his ranks: Arsinée's familiar whom she had newly enslaved, spellbinding him with promises of sex and money.

Loads of money, she told her stooge, *infinite money.*

Her maker (to whom she was wed) was rich, and he would be too if he would aid her in obliterating the only obstacle standing between her and her love.

Arsinée hatched the plan one evening at a masquerade at the Hôtel de Bouillon. The hostess, Marie Anne, Duchesse de Bouillon, was a neglected 18-year-old wife with a great deal of time and money at her disposal.

Her fêtes were glamorous and her desire for intriguing literary and artistic company was insatiable. A masquerade was a divine opportunity for vampires to orbit undetected within her circle.

Vauquelin disappeared weeks before, making it clear that he would not divulge his whereabouts. He was unresponsive to her pleas. For once she did not care. His absence was a blessing that night.

"Oh, madame, but your skin ..." a gentleman extended a gallant leg, took her hand, and kissed it. His eyes met hers, obscured behind a mask. "Surely this is the skin of a statue, and not a lady."

Arsinée snapped open her fan and swished it back and forth, remaining silent.

"I am Henri de la Trémoïlle. Could I entice you to take a turn in the gardens?" he asked, offering his elbow.

She acquiesced and he led her outdoors, the laughter and music growing fainter with each step.

"And you are?"

She hesitated, then whispered, "Arsinée de Vauquelin. But tell no one you saw me here tonight. It will be our little secret, yes?"

He arched his eyebrow. "Ah, madame is trifling this evening?" he asked, a devilish smile lifting the corner of his mouth.

"One might say that."

They walked deeper into the gardens. Arsinée said little, as he was willing to tell her his life story. He was unmarried, about to come into his fortune, and enjoying his life as a part-time soldier and full-time bon vivant.

Perfect, she thought. He could not be more perfect.

She let him prattle on, glancing at him on occasion and interjecting platitudes: "Oh!" "You don't say." "How fascinating!"

They seated themselves on a stone bench.

The other guests were far enough away as to be non-existent.

Perfect ... perfect.

She allowed him to kiss and fondle her and caress her cleavage. While he was distracted with getting his fingers under her stays, she took to his neck and drained the vivant just enough to weaken him.

As the night drew to its close, she vanished with her bewildered human prize through the garden and out of Marie Anne's unguarded gates, looking up at the sky and wondering if Vauquelin was gazing upon the same blue moon, wherever he might be.

She was captive to his anima: always, his perpetual shade was upon her face.

Back at Vauquelin's hôtel, Arsinée kicked in the scullery door. She had been shut out of the house for weeks: her few belongings were still trapped inside.

She dragged the man into her quarters and revived him with a glassful of sheep's blood. She did not complete the vampire creation ritual — she merely wanted him enslaved, so that he might do her bidding.

When he quickened, she lifted her skirts and rode him like a demon, spouting her rules and demands. The man was smitten beyond all hope and under her control.

The very next day, Yvain was ensnared, duped by an underling. And Arsinée's stooge was consigned outside the door, awaiting further instructions from his mistress.

Arsinée glared at Yvain, prepared to vanquish herself for the injustices brought upon her.

"You gave me to him and you took him away!" she wailed.

"I will not force Vauquelin to keep something he does not want. My mistake was not giving you to him ... my mistake was demanding that he create you. I should have let him bleed you dry and leave you to rot. I wronged him dreadfully."

"He has my heart! And I will never embrace him again because of you!" Rage surged in her chest.

"How can you be so simple?" Yvain said. "He despised you from the moment you were created."

Yvain turned his back to her.

Arsinée hurled a bucket of turpentine and a lighted candle at him, engulfing him in instantaneous flames.

Yvain shrieked as the conflagration spread across his body.

"Now, watch your demise, miscreant!" She thrust up a forbidden looking glass.

Yvain's melting face reflected back at him as his vampire blood fled his body. He aged at a frenzied pace.

The flames licked his skin.

His face shrunk and grew again, contorting into a mass of wrinkles. His spine went crooked and he hunched over, growing smaller and smaller, this imposing man who once stood over two meters tall. His hands gnarled and hair sprouted from his ears, burning off as it grew.

Yvain perished screaming, his skin shriveling until it began to pop and recede, exposing his muscles.

A blackened skeleton of cinders lay before her.

"This death is too good for you," she screamed. "I'll meet you again in hell!"

Yvain's cries summoned his coterie. They subdued and drained Arsinée's slave and knocked the door off its hinges, pouring forth into the room. What was once Yvain lay on the floor, a shapeless pile of smoldering ash.

The coterie descended upon her like crocodiles in violent unison and depleted her blood, leaving only enough to keep her alive.

Arsinée was thrown into a dungeon in the pit of the house, imprisoned in a rat-infested cell.

PARIS, FRANCE | 1668

"This, *cher* Vauquelin, is the explanation for your unanswered prayers, and for why her lamentations left your consciousness," Yvain says. "But you must remember that at this particular moment in time, she is alive."

Hearing this gives Vauquelin a chilling start. The entirety of his years had not been enough to assuage his revulsion for her.

He holds his hands up and backs toward the door.

"Oh, no. No, no, no. If you think I will make her vampire again, you are insane." He extracts his dagger and points it at his heart. "I will take my own life rather than give her immortality. Without my revenant blood I have the privilege of dying … and I will, right this instant. Where is she?" he demands.

"Patience never was your long suit, Vauquelin," Yvain says.

"I beg you to tell me. You owe me that, at least."

"It should come as no surprise that she is in this house."

Vauquelin's knees buckle.

Centuries and thousands of miles of distance from her, and now she is under the same roof as him.

In a dark, damp cellar, deep in the bowels of Yvain's domain, Arsinée paces the confines of her cell, tearing her hair, clawing her face, crying. She cannot sense the presence of Vauquelin, the man for whom she had left so much damage in her wake, for on this date she, like Vauquelin, is not yet a vampire.

Her once-elegant dress hangs about her body in blood-stained tatters. The ground is littered with moldy, stinking hay. A crude bucket sits in the corner for her waste.

A sliding panel opens in the door and a revolting plate of food is shoved in. Vampires know nothing of preparing human food.

She wails and kicks it away with her foot.

"I am dying! Bring me water! My father is a gendarme! He will have you drawn and quartered for this!"

The sliding panel opens once more. "You do not command me, filthy whore," the vampire guard growls. He steps aside and gestures for Vauquelin to have a look.

Vauquelin kneels outside the door, peering through the slot. The wretched vision of Arsinée, dispossessed of her vampiric strengths and living in her own filth, is one of the most gratifying sights he has beheld in ages, but it is soon overwritten by rage as he recalls all the misery she had inflicted upon him. He slams his fists on the iron door, emitting a resounding boom.

Arsinée jumps and throws herself against the wall.

He stands panting, with his forehead against the door.

The guard puts an arm around his shoulder and drags him away from the cell. Yvain meets them at the end of the corridor.

"Let me in there!" he cries. "I will strangle her with my own bare hands!"

"In due time, Vauquelin. In due time."

"Why did you not destroy her? How could you ever let her get the upper hand?" Vauquelin asks. But as the words leave his lips, it occurs to him that he could have asked himself the same question all those centuries ago.

He surrendered everything to her without ever considering he could have done away with her himself. How unsophisticated he had been in his early days as a vampire!

"I should have. But I hesitated ... and thus she ended me. I was a fool to let her live. Yet her imprisonment and imminent demise is, I hope, a small comfort for you."

"This makes no sense!" Vauquelin says. "If she assassinated you, how was it possible for you to observe my future?"

Yvain expels a heavy sigh. "Vauquelin, despite having lived so long, you still have much to learn, as do we all. I believe you can see that even several lifetimes is not enough to truly master all the secrets the vampire world has hidden in its folds. Our immortality extends far beyond mere physical being. Even if our bodies are eradicated, our spirits are indestructible by any force. I, as your maker, have the power to call you back through the centuries. I received your prayers, though it was not possible for me to answer you. Your anguish was my anguish, throughout your existence. These concepts are beyond a human's grasp, and indeed, difficult even for our own kind to comprehend. You are human again. So is she. I've brought us all together, to the time before these events occurred, so that we may rectify them. Fear not. Arsinée will be dealt with soon," Yvain says. "Can you now accept the reasons behind your traversal? I want to give you the redemption you so rightly deserve, and thereby to save myself. My desire is for us to save each other so that I may live, and that you may live again without torment. Die as a human, or live again with your dark blood. What is your choice?"

Yvain kisses Vauquelin, then pummels his mind with negative images of Delphine, pressuring him to face his own ignorance at the many times she ridiculed him.

He becomes the spectator, revisiting the precise moment he ends Delphine's life, swallows the next to last drop of her blood, and slides her body into his acid vat, deftly arranging her bones in his catacombs.

Yvain hovers over him, awaiting a response.

Vauquelin is unmoved.

"As you are quite aware, I eliminated her," he says. "That is now part of my history, and cannot be undone. You should be satisfied that there exists one less mortal to tempt me."

"Perhaps it cannot be undone, and perhaps it can," Yvain replies. "After all, you have the option to live your life over."

He waves his hand over Vauquelin's face, forcing him to live through Maeve's death ... again.

His desolation is resurrected by a tragic replica of her deathbed, extinction gripping her face as she thrashes on the bed, his tears of blood, his violent reaction to Death's indomitable thievery.

In response, fat human tears begin to roll down Vauquelin's face, streaming into his parted lips. Their unfamiliar saltiness startles him, and he whisks them away.

For good measure, Yvain forces him to relive the many times he let humans go, out of sympathy. *Sympathy! For mortals!* He lets forth a boisterous, mocking laugh as he ends the visions. "I must say, my dear Vauquelin, the catacombs were pure genius. I commend you."

Vauquelin grabs the lapels of Yvain's waistcoat.

"Enough! Let me relive the dignity of my life as a vampire, if such a thing exists. Show me what I did that is worth reliving perpetual night." He unties his neck stock in a frenzy, exposing his pulsating mortal veins.

Yvain lays a finger upon Vauquelin's neck, transfixed by the orgasmic ecstasy of a beating human heart. Unlike Vauquelin, he has not a remaining shred of human sympathy.

He could end Vauquelin in seconds.

But this is no ordinary human ... this is his progeny, his most beloved creation, pulled back through the labyrinthine arteries of time to be present at this very moment, with his beauty and vulnerability fully exposed.

Yvain resumes his deluge of visions: the exquisite essence of the vampire, the indescribable euphoria of drawing blood, of placing a human on the precipice of life and death, the godlike barbarity of making that human beg for its life or for immortality.

He unfolds history in Vauquelin's mind, all that he had lived through and acquired — only this time Yvain is there with him, experiencing and observing. Yvain had not been present for these events, yet he gives the impression of knowing them as intimately as he knows Vauquelin — inside and out.

Vauquelin envisions the possibility of a different life than the one he has lived, a life with Yvain and without Arsinée, one where Maeve survived, delectable and healthy, her youthful effervescence preserved for perpetuity.

The paths he had chosen were the wrong ones ... each of them.

Why did you let me suffer so long with this torment? Vauquelin thinks. *Why did you not heal my despair?*

Yvain hears him and softens toward his creature.

"It was necessary for you to live the life you did in order to prevail over your own destiny, and it was imperative that you return here — as a human — to comprehend what you must surrender. My only option was to force the naked truth upon you. Until I had you in my presence once again, I could not have shown you. You were consumed by your rage, and that was wholly my wrongdoing. I recognize and accept this."

Vauquelin hangs his head.

Yvain was speaking the truth; he had to admit it.

"But there is one last scandal, my dear Vauquelin, which I must bring to light."

Vauquelin grips the back of a chair till his knuckles whiten. He has had quite enough criticism for one evening, but he is woefully unprepared for what comes next.

"Your Maeve ... the fragile little human that you protected from your lethal reality, even to the point of letting her slip irretrievably through your fingers? You killed her. You were the one responsible for her death."

"You are mistaken!" Vauquelin roars. "I did not kill her! I lived to protect her from harm."

"Oh, but indeed you did. The sailors you fed upon during the American plague? You delivered the disease right onto your precious Maeve's lips. You brought the contagion to her doorstep, showered her with it. You were so blind, so incredibly naïve to think you could protect her."

All the robust color Vauquelin had regained that day drained out of his face and into his heart. "Maeve ..."

He had no other words. He had destroyed her.

"So, your choice. I must have your answer," Yvain said.

At last Vauquelin can admit to himself why he has chosen to return to this place. It is for one reason, and one reason alone: that he may be afforded the chance to have Maeve alive and standing before him once more.

He thrusts his neck toward Yvain.

"Let it be done," he says, his voice breaking.

Yvain snaps his fingers, summoning his coterie.

They reappear in the room, crawling all over the floor and the walls, surrounding Yvain and Vauquelin.

"Must you always have a fucking audience? Do it!" he spits.

Yvain grasps the back of Vauquelin's head and perforates his jugular, bleeding him with violent momentum.

Vauquelin screams. It has been centuries since another vampire has taken his blood and he is unrehearsed for the pain. He digs his fingers into Yvain's arms as he is drained. His mouth is pried open, and his body begins to quake as his maker's blood propels down his tongue, setting his windpipe aflame.

He plunges into the fathomless void, down through the floor, to the floor below, and the floor below that, his mind and body subverted by desolate morbidity.

It is a familiar journey.

It is considerably less frightening this time.

Vauquelin quickens and uprights himself.

Had hours passed? Days?

As it was the first time, he is unable to discern.

He has crossed once again beyond his mortal death, landing right back where he had before. His pores ooze, soaking his chemise through with bloody perspiration.

Yvain reclines in a large chair, watching him with half-lidded eyes, surrounded once again by his coterie.

He beckons to Vauquelin. "Come."

Vauquelin labors across the floor on his hands and knees, quailing at Yvain's feet.

The maker presents him with a small, silken box.

Vauquelin accepts it with trembling hands, fumbling to lift the cover. Inside is the same elaborate gold stiletto.

His self-confidence is shaken to its core.

Perhaps Yvain intends to kill him after all, or imprison him and leave him to decay, deprived of blood.

Vauquelin's arrogance has been his downfall, again and again.

Yvain removes the stiletto from the box and says, "I offered you a decision, a choice ... yes?"

"Yes," Vauquelin whispers.

"Your redemption is my redemption. If you reject my offer, take out my heart, and your troubles are over. It would be a pleasure to meet my destruction by your hand. Or ..." Yvain brings Vauquelin's hand to his throat. "You can drink."

Vauquelin glances around the room. If he makes an attempt on Yvain's life, his own will end in a heartbeat: the creatures will destroy him. His "choices" are meaningless.

There is no turning back now.

He places his hand over Yvain's and removes the stiletto, hesitating but a moment before he drives the dagger into Yvain's neck, drawing forth a line of blood.

His teeth lengthen and sharpen at once.

He hurls the stiletto across the room and laps the blood from Yvain's open wounds, gulping it in greedy slurps, driving his jaws harder and further into the flesh.

Turbulent spasms course throughout his body as his maker's blood merges with his own. His age-old, overpowering craving takes him in its clutches. He drinks until an enfeebled Yvain begins to slide down out of his chair with Vauquelin's teeth still embedded in his neck.

Yvain heaves him aside, coming to a rest on the floor, and arches his back in agony. "You are much, much more formidable than you were the first time, Vauquelin," he gasps.

The second creation has increased Vauquelin's strength — it is now immeasurable. He must learn to control himself again, and with unprecedented practice.

He collapses on the floor, panting and gasping, blood coursing down his chin. Almost in slow motion, a droplet falls from his chin, landing on the lapel of his justaucorps.

A flash of the museum impales his brain, to the scene where this very coat had been on public display three hundred and fifty years ahead in time, the droplet a cruel medal.

He looks from the stain to the face of his maker.

Yvain gropes his mangled neck and it mends in obeisance.

Vauquelin leans toward him, his eyes wide. This is the vampire gift he has always most coveted. It would have saved him a plethora of grief in his futurepast.

Perhaps he will inherit it this time.

"The sun will rise soon," Yvain says, his voice strained with exhaustion. His body is in distress, and he is in desperate need of replenishment. "Bring us the human."

The large, heavy doors open, and a woman in a hooded cloak is swept into the room. The doors close behind her. Yvain yanks the ribbon at the woman's neck and her cloak drops to the floor.

There stands Arsinée.

She makes no sign of recognition, swaying to and fro as if she is in a trance. The telltale signs are there: she has been fed upon multiple times. Her body is covered in blood-encrusted welts.

Vauquelin recoils, unable to speak.

He attempts to upright himself up on the corner of a table, which he topples in his struggle.

"Now that we are wise to the horrors this hellhound is capable of inflicting when given the dark blood, we will handle her accordingly," Yvain says, taking Vauquelin's hand and pulling him toward her. "She is ours to finish."

Yvain and Vauquelin descend upon her like beasts, devouring her, claiming all her blood.

Vauquelin is disappointed. He thought that when the day came, the act of ending Arsinée would leave him maniacal, euphoric. Instead, he lies exhausted on the floor.

It was just another kill.

It is over. He need dread her existence no longer.

"It is the first rule in the creation of a vampire: good judgment. Some humans are ideal. Others decidedly not. You were wise in your original hesitance toward her, my Vauquelin. Even so, I shall never regret choosing you. Now we must rest."

Yvain lifts him up and guides him into the crypt.

He settles into a luxurious coffin next to Yvain's, and slumber smothers him like molten lead.

He is full of the rich blood of his adversary.

She is no more, and never will trouble him again.

Vauquelin's path to redemption has begun. No longer will he let Yvain's unscrupulous cruelty be his animus.

The throbbing sound of history's movement fills his ears: its gears awaken and begin their creaking, heavy grind forward, triggering the recapitulation of his future.

He is uncertain whether he can endure it.

Vauquelin raises the lid of the coffin.

Yvain is awake, sprawled across an elegant scarlet sofa with his head in the lap of one of his creatures.

"You will want to be refreshed after your resurrection. Arise at your leisure, and we shall discuss your plans," he says.

Plans?

The entire world and all of time lies open before Vauquelin, waiting for him to come back through. He might as well spend his time draining the ocean one teaspoon at a time. How can he possibly conceive of what to do next?

He sits awhile in the coffin, irritable and disheveled, a petulant child who does not want to get out of bed. His mind boggles at resuming ordinary life.

He emerges at last, naked, and reluctantly accepts the vessel of blood offered to him by Yvain's valet. He turns a blind eye to the stares of Yvain and his pet. They both give him the once over, exchanging lustful glances.

"I suppose I must begin at the beginning," he says, draining the glass. "Will you join me?"

The air is surreal when Vauquelin walks through the doors to his own house with Yvain trailing behind. He hopes Olivier does not notice his bloody chemise — he keeps the lapels of his coat together to conceal it.

The faithful valet takes his master's personal effects while giving Yvain a subtle glare of elegant disdain.

"I require my bath and evening attire," Vauquelin orders, dashing up the staircase two steps at a time.

Yvain wanders into the library and amuses himself by playing the harpsichord.

In his bedchamber, he inspects the bed curtains.

They will suffice. Good.

He refuses to sleep in a coffin ever again. He hides all the looking glasses under the bed, feeds his bloodied chemise into the fireplace, and summons his servants for his toilette.

When he comes back downstairs, dressed for the evening, Vauquelin is somewhat surprised to find Yvain waiting for him on the sofa, drinking a glass of wine and holding a ribboned square box. Last night's events are a blur; he had already buried them away. He is far too accustomed to being alone.

Yvain places the box on a table. "A gift for you. Open it."

Vauquelin pulls the ribbon and the sides of the box fall away, revealing an immaculate human skull. He lifts it and turns it side to side in his hand.

"A souvenir from last night's festivities. Shall we dine out?"

A smile breaks out across Vauquelin's lips. He fully intends to indulge himself in some malicious amusement.

Although it is a Wednesday night, there are plentiful pleasures to be had in Paris, and so the two cavalier vampires disappear into the city in search of bloody fruit.

They arrive at the *hôtel particulier* of a bourgeois, M. de __, and play Lansquenet for several hours. They depart with one thousand gold *louis* and a male fop, whom they lure away with a flimsy promise to get him an audience with the Duc de Vendôme, whom neither of them knows.

Really, it is too easy!

Vauquelin cannot stop laughing as they drain the fop and leave him propped up against a stack of baskets in a corridor. They walk back to the carriage, arm in arm. It has been ages since he enjoyed himself with such vigor.

"How I missed you, my dear Vauquelin. We must do this more often," he says. "Until next time."

The house is quiet.

Vauquelin strips and falls into bed, Arsinée's skull ornamenting his nightstand. The evening had indeed been pleasurable, but the suffocating pressure of time falls upon him like an iron blanket. He is thrilled by the possibility of reclaiming his life and love, but anguished by the thought of millions upon millions of minutes unfolding once more.

He lies still in the deathly-quiet darkness of his chamber. He had grown accustomed to constant sound in the modern world: the profound depth of silence in ancient times is now foreign to him.

The outdoor noise, even here in the center of Paris, is minuscule compared to futurepast Los Angeles. No racing automobiles, no horns, no air conditioner whirr, no screeching car alarms, no planes or helicopters, no wailing sirens. No trains.

Inside the depths of his townhouse, far from the street, he can only hear the muted clattering of horse hooves, carriage wheels creaking on the earthen paths, and the increasing chatter of voices as the city comes to life.

There is a marked absence (to his futurist ears) of the innocuous hum of electronic noise. How he had loved electricity. Having lived for hundreds of years without it, he had never once taken the miracle of instant power for granted, available by the mere push of a button or flip of a switch.

Now he lies in the hallowed silence of a seventeenth-century morning. Myriad sounds occur elsewhere in the house, far from his bedchamber: the scrubbing of marble steps, the dull thud of laundry as it is pulled from wash pots and slapped on stones, the laughter and tomfoolery of the stable boys and the soft nickers and neighs of the horses ... a delivery of wine casks at the larder entrance.

Vauquelin's cocoon of tranquility isolates him from the soundtrack of an average morning at a fine house in Paris, manifesting far away from him on the floors below.

His mind is too restless for sleep.

He rings for Olivier, shushing him as he enters.

Olivier is a superior and steadfast valet. His family had served the Cavernays for generations. Now in his early thirties, he was but a child at the time of Vauquelin's birth. They had grown up together, in a manner of speaking, though their stations kept them in their places as master and servant. He is trustworthy, loyal to a fault, and paid handsomely. He is accustomed to and tolerant of his master's libertine conduct.

As he had to do the first time around, Vauquelin must edit the truth to maintain calm and order in the house. His prepared lie is one that had served him well after his original creation and multiple times in his futurepast.

Vauquelin parts the bed curtains so he can address Olivier man-to-man. "I must confide in you, but I do not want you to be alarmed. All is well. I will be well. First and foremost, you must believe that."

"As you decree, Monsieur."

"In recent days, I have been suffering from an affliction, but I have visited an expert. I now have a reason for my condition. I have developed a strange disease, the name and cause of which is obscure. I must apologize for my bizarre behavior. I did not yet know the cause of my malady."

He is aggravated by the necessary deception. He must either lie and preserve the façade for Olivier or dismiss the entire staff. In his echelon of society, in 1668, the latter is not an option.

"There are things which must change in order for me to remain comfortable and unharmed. These modifications must occur without any question."

"I am, as always, at Monsieur's service," Olivier says, bowing with his hand over his heart.

"I have developed a severe reaction to sunlight. I must never be exposed to it — it would mean my certain death. I shall rise at sundown and seek my slumber at sunrise. Therefore, I require you to alter your habits to accommodate mine. You run this house. It is under your command. I shall leave it to you to arrange the others' timetables to suit your own. I will henceforth dine outside of the house, as my surgeon recommends. You may continue to purchase victuals for yourself and the staff, but you must never bring me food. I shall rely on your discretion, Olivier."

The daylight issue washes off the valet like water off a duck's back, but the mention of food gives him pause. Monsieur le Duc has always been a voracious *gastronomique*.

Olivier gasps. "But Monsieur, this is devastating. I am sorry for you. How you adore your meals!"

Vauquelin presses the back of his hand against his mouth and bites his wrist, drawing forth droplets of blood. He flicks them away with his tongue.

The memory of the luxe meal he had consumed the day before, and the delirium of its indulgence, is fresh in his mind. But he is vampire once more, and his senses are twisted with joy and repulsion.

Vauquelin holds out his trembling hand, reaching for Olivier.

"Yesterday was my last meal as such, and I suffered dearly for it. It can no longer be so for me."

"Monsieur, fear not. I will ensure your safety and comfort."

Vauquelin withdraws his hand and retreats into the bed.

He recites the list of modifications he requires in the house and his life in order of their importance.

Olivier writes down each detail in his pocket ledger with a charcoal pencil.

"Thank you, Olivier. And now I must sleep. I will fend for myself for a few days to give you time to adjust. I realize this is much to take in. Please, go and take the time you need."

Olivier begins by overseeing the cataloguing and removal of all looking glasses in the house.

An odd request of his master — perhaps it has something to do with the reflection of sunlight.

No matter.

He always carries out his orders without fail.

Soon, all the looking glasses are sold and carried away by shopkeepers.

He crosses this item off the list.

Once the other critical tasks are complete, he takes to his bed, lying awake in the light of day, feeling peculiar. He should be up, attending to his normal duties.

Those duties will change, of course, as Monsieur ordained, but after an hour idle, he can stand it no longer and rises to dress.

He resumes his tasks and informs the other servants of the new rules dictated by their master, distributing gold coins to ensure they remain loyal and discreet.

One by one, each item on the list is struck through.

Dense, midnight-blue velvet curtains are hung over the many windows, enshrouding the house in complete and oppressive darkness, banishing the sunlight to remain outside its walls.

The weekly household candle order is quadrupled.

They must remain illuminated day and night to accommodate the staff and to protect Monsieur should he need to rise during the day.

Olivier stays awake for a full twenty-four hour period to prepare himself for the reversal of his sleeping habits.

Come to me.

Yvain's voice floods Vauquelin's awareness.

He does not disturb Olivier. He dresses himself, saddles a horse, and bolts through the streets of Paris to Yvain's château, located four leagues outside the old city gates.

The moment he walks through the doors, he is encircled by unruly vampires. Having a small gang of oversexed revenants at his beck and call is Yvain's absolute weakness.

"Begone, the lot of you!" he growls, shoving them aside.

Vauquelin makes his way to Yvain's den, oblivious to his fawning escorts. It is all so tedious.

The atmosphere is oppressive. A fierce pang of nostalgia strikes him — for his futurepast comfort and surroundings, his solitude, the myriad ways he had modernized his existence. He is unprepared (nor is he willing) to return to the dark underground of yore, and he certainly refuses to live amongst vampires.

His greatest wish is to be left alone.

"Master, let us taste him. Just one taste — " begs one of the creatures.

"Please, do try!" Yvain laughs. "It will be amusing to observe."

Vauquelin stands still as a statue while the creature flashes himself over, running his nose along his neck. When he opens his mouth to sink his teeth, Vauquelin snaps the vampire's jaw apart. It lies open, knocking against his neck. The creature backs away from him, shirking into a dark corner.

"Who else yearns to savor Vauquelin?" Yvain asks in a thundering tone, glancing around the room. They all skitter, vanishing into the corners.

Vauquelin saunters over to a chair and smooths his breeches, as if nothing had happened.

"Honestly, Yvain ... after all this time, I thought you would have learned about surrounding yourself with these sycophants. And yet you claim *I* made mistakes," Vauquelin says.

"At least I know how to put them in their place," Yvain replies, "a skill I believe you have yet to acquire. But please accept my felicitations for your reaction, *mon cher*. It was classic Vauquelin, and it sent my heart aquiver with pride."

Vauquelin narrows his eyes. He has lived near four centuries without a father, and disdains Yvain's patriarchal tone.

"Anyhow, it is good they have gone," Yvain says. "I have invited a tailor, just for the two of us."

The clothier is shown in.

He is in no danger.

As a rule, vampires do not feast upon humans who provide them with valuable services, and a private couturier is a splendid way to pass the time.

They spend the rest of the night perusing silks, satins, and brocades, commissioning outrageous embroideries and bespoke shoes ... Vauquelin is in his undisputed element.

After the tailor departs, they sit in front of the fire drinking from the coterie's finest vintage.

"In my ethereal state, I bore witness to your suffering," Yvain says, turning pensive. "I saw your modern life, but it was as if I were dreaming. From the first moment I initiated the process of returning you to your origins, I have asked myself many times: should Vauquelin choose this life again, will I be satisfied with hearing his stories or would I prefer to remain ignorant and experience it myself? You have an abundance of experience in the ways of the world."

"And?"

"I am, as yet, undecided."

Sitting in this room, candlelit, elegant, but still primitive, Vauquelin begins to ruminate. He puts his feet up on a table and regards his maker with sangfroid.

Numbers flood his head, leading him to analyze time's passage. According to his calculations, *he* is now the elder of this coterie, the most powerful one.

"When were you created?" he asks.

"It was the year 1456," Yvain says. "Betwixt and between the new age ... the Renaissance."

Vauquelin sits back hard in his chair. His tattered timeline has become clear.

"Then you are two hundred and twelve years old. Are you aware that you have allowed me to best you, my dear maker? You have made a grave miscalculation."

Yvain raises an eyebrow.

"You are responsible for bringing me back to this time," Vauquelin continues. "If I were not here now, you would cease to physically exist next year. I have walked upon this earth in excess of three and a half centuries, far beyond you and your experience. I am now the elder."

Yvain grips the armrest of his chair. "Were it thus, still I am your maker," he says through gritted teeth.

"Indeed, you made me, twice — but you have gravely underestimated the folly of bringing me back."

Vauquelin begins to pace, his hands pressed to his head, beguiled by his own realization.

"I never fucking asked for any of this," he said.

"Vauquelin ..." Yvain reaches out for him.

He backs away. "Do not dare approach me," he growls, resuming his angry pace.

Centuries ago, Yvain seduced him — forced him, even — into the life of the vampire. As he paces, he wonders what would have happened to him had his carriage not broken down on that calamitous night so long ago.

He would have gone on living his decadent, noble French life. He might have lived to a ripe old age, or died in his prime from the pox or syphilis, or been killed in a war, like his father or any other ordinary human man. He might have married, but likely not.

Instead, he crossed paths with a vampire, or the vampire had deliberately sought him out. His destiny was forged that night. Instead of living a routine, tormented human life, he had been forced to endure hundreds of years of an *immortal* tormented life, without the luxury of a denouement.

He has been condemned, for a second time, to endure an amaranthine life in the shadows. Even in his vampire state, he cannot escape the curse of human life. His options are few: live underground or live among humans.

Life underground is unbearable.

Life with humans is unsustainable.

He recalls Delphine and her refusals. Now he accepts that she never believed him, not until those final moments when she witnessed him take another human's life and subsequently take hers. He considers her assessment of him as damned, not blessed.

Vauquelin halts his pace and looks his maker in the eye.

Yvain has read all his thoughts. It is etched upon his face.

"Send me back! Return my original existence to me!"

"No! To live your years over again is a crucial component of your punishment," Yvain says. "Regardless, I have neither the will nor the strength."

"You are the cruelest of masters," Vauquelin says.

At once, the reality of what he just demanded blooms in his mind. Had Yvain been able to send him back to the twenty-first century, Maeve would truly be dead to him forever.

Now he can live with a mustard seed of faith that he will have the chance to reveal himself to her, even if she refuses him.

His life looms ahead, but with possibilities.

Profound change.

Rebirth, reconciliation.

"Where can we possibly go from here?" Vauquelin asks.

"I cannot answer that. I cannot predict the future ... I can only feel you there," Yvain says quietly. "But you are correct. Now you are indeed the elder."

Vauquelin is flummoxed by Yvain's onset weakness.

How did the tables turn?

"That I can answer, my dear Vauquelin," he says. "I was well aware of the consequences for bringing you back. Though I loathe to admit it, yes — I am now your inferior. I have given you my energy, my power. It was worth it for the possibility of living."

The living, the living — there is too much life ahead of him yet to be lived. The one he had been living was sabotaged. As Yvain pointed out, he would not have learned these lessons otherwise. Still, Yvain was responsible.

Should Vauquelin be grateful or resentful?

"You say that now, even having been the spectator to my lifelong despair? You have been alive for two centuries, but you are ignorant of the immense struggle life will bring for our kind in the future. You saw my choices, yes? But still you cannot fathom my reasoning for making them. Human intellect will grow beyond comprehension yet idiocy will become rampant. Superstition does not rule the future. Science and enlightenment guides all. Faith will be replaced by the desire for tangible proof. It will become increasingly dangerous for the vampire to live boldly as we are accustomed to now ... you shall see. The future has many impressive advancements to offer, but it will never be optimal for us. In fact, quite the opposite."

"Therefore, you do not think it is worth it," Yvain observes.

"There are powers we employ in this time that are worthless in the future. The police ... that is to say, the gendarmes ... they have all the control in society. We can be so easily detected," Vauquelin says. "There are substances which can harm us beyond belief. You criticize me for dwelling among humans, yet it is impossible to avoid it. I altered my life so that it became unnecessary to rely on them as victims."

"But why?" Yvain asks. "You shamed our ancestors and rejected our creed for the blood of mankind"

"Eh, *putain du sang!* I sustained myself on animals that I alone cultivated. They are pure. Human blood is not. You will recall the time in my life when I was incapacitated for weeks from drinking tainted human blood. It was the most frightening period of my existence. I called for you ... there was only silence."

Yvain buries his face in his hands. "It was torture seeing you suffer, yet being powerless to aid you. How pitiable that you had to resort to lowly animals!"

"Blood is blood. Clearly it kept me in function for decades. As you said to me when we were reunited, there are many things that cannot be explained, only experienced," he says. "I do not have the ancient French to accurately describe such futuristic tribulation." He resumes pacing. "I encountered no vampires in the New World ... perhaps they were senseless and were destroyed. If you had lived and followed me, that might have been our fate as well. We cannot know. I survived by my own design, with no guidance."

"One can only surmise that life ahead will be dismal for revenants," Yvain says.

"It can be ... but it can also be magnificent."

Vauquelin's future has already happened: it is now history, in reverse. It is not lost on him that his life could be severely altered as the centuries regenerate.

His heart sinks at the thought that he might not be afforded the inestimable privilege of knowing Maeve again. He wishes he could fast-forward the years like a tape player and be back in her arms once more. Even just once.

"You would choose her, and not Delphine?" Yvain asks.

"Not telling Maeve my truth, letting her slip through my fingers and delivering her to her mortal death, was my gravest error. Delphine was a mere lapse in judgment, as you so brutally made clear. I had a life with Maeve ... a normal life, above ground, almost in the sunlight. Can you even imagine that?"

Yvain yawns. Human life does not interest him in the least.

"Yet you threw it all away for blood and a fuck from a couple of tainted sailors. Consider it a blessing, dear Vauquelin. Had you been successful in inoculating Maeve the night she left this coil, you would have cursed her with her devastating human plague forever. What a heart-warming thought ... a feverish, blue-faced vampire coughing up her lungs for perpetuity," he laughed. "You remain shockingly ignorant, even after all this time. Have you not been curious enough to read our lore?"

Vauquelin flashes himself nose-to-nose with Yvain.

"How dare you? There is vastly greater wisdom at hand than the pitiable history of the undead! I assure you that it is possible to reap the benefits of our gifts and live in the mortal world. I did what was required to survive. Life itself is a disease, be it immortal or human! You are too deeply ensconced in your vampire existence ... you think you are above mortals. If I had not hesitated, if I had opened myself completely to Maeve, I know she would have embraced it!"

"You are eloquently arrogant for one so foolish, Vauquelin."

"Let me finish! You understand nothing about her ... nothing! I doubt with all my heart that you have ever experienced pure love. Your connections with your creatures are all born from intimidation and power. She loved me, as a man. A bizarre man, but a man nonetheless. Yet I would have her alive, even embraced by illness. You would surely toss anyone away who could not serve you, as you did me."

"I have tasted love," Yvain says, narrowing his eyes, "and many have loved *me*, deeply and often. I am cognizant of its power. You would not be standing here now if I did not. The sole difference between us, Vauquelin, is your inexplicable weakness for humans."

"Your lovers have all been under your control, intoxicated by your power," Vauquelin says. "Love cannot be forced, bought or enchanted. This you do *not* comprehend."

Yvain leaps from his chair.

"That is quite enough scolding for one night, Vauquelin. I must feed," he growls. "The bloodlust is upon me."

"Then let us go into the city."

Yvain snaps his fingers, and his young pet appears at his side.

"You have met Clément ... he will be joining us."

Clément — a porcelain, green-eyed wisp of a man-child dressed in resplendent purple velvet — stands with his hand encased in Yvain's elbow. Even so, his eyes linger too long, holding Vauquelin in a simmering gaze that can be mistaken for nothing but lustful mischief.

Exasperation swathes Vauquelin like a shroud.

He is not in the mood for companionship or games, but he is in the mood for blood.

So be it.

Vauquelin observes them both while the carriage makes its way to Paris. Clément fawns over Yvain while fluttering his long lashes at Vauquelin.

Exactly, he thinks. It is just as he had explained to Yvain. He calls Clément's bluff and returns his naughty glower, and all the while his maker pets his little creature, ignorant of their hot-blooded exchanges with one another.

The carriage hits a deep crevice, throwing Clément fast against

Yvain, who flings a protective arm across his chest. He strokes Yvain's arm while continuing to glance seductively at Vauquelin.

Yvain remains oblivious, lost in his lechery.

They come to a stop at a shabby theatre. Vauquelin clutches his walking staff and thinks for a moment. He has a flash of his desert adventure in California, as he sat in his own private mineral bath, cigarette in hand, palm fronds swirling over his head.

He recalls the intense feeling he had after the hot stones were placed down his back, and how they dissipated his anger.

The memory gives him a sense of calm, a center.

In that instant he decides how the evening is going to unfurl. He assumes control, descending the carriage first.

Yvain and Clément fall into step behind him.

The performance is a cast-off from Versailles, no doubt.

It is Molière, with considerably less financing.

Throughout the duration of the show, Vauquelin ignores Clément's accidental brushings of his leg and the thrusts of his too-loud laughter, yet the entire time Clément also worships Yvain — who still has not a clue.

At intermission, Vauquelin fakes a piss outside. Vampires rarely urinate. But it is a convenient way to bond with humans, and an excellent method for obtaining information. He asks his fellow pisser how one could meet the actors.

Having secured the location of a tavern frequented by the cast, he returns to his seat.

He did not kill the man.

His appetite is reserved for a more sumptuous feast.

"La Béarainaise," he informs his companions.

The celebration is in full swing when they arrive.

Vauquelin introduces Yvain to the male star of the operetta, who is dressed as a woman. He is captivated at once.

Good. It will keep Yvain out of his hair for the time being.

Vauquelin takes a chorus girl by the hand and leads her into a darkened corner. As he feasts upon her, he perceives a shadowy figure coming up the alley: it is Clément. Vauquelin holds out his hand, beckoning. Clément accepts it, and sinks his teeth into the other side of the girl's throat.

When they have relieved her of her blood, Vauquelin extracts his dagger and draws it across her neck, garnering a wide-eyed gawk from Clément, who cannot fathom the reason for cutting the throat of a dead human.

Vauquelin looks down and away.

Even now, his modern sensibilities plague him.

No self-respecting vampire in this age must worry about a bloodless victim. He licks the blade and sheaths it, aware that his cock is at full attention, as it always is after a kill.

He nuzzles Clément's cheek. "So ... you are Yvain's favorite."

Clément's bravado dissipates and he bites his lip.

He wonders if perhaps he has gone too far, as his little divertissement has suddenly turned serious. He knows Vauquelin is off-limits, and he witnessed his brutal reaction to the one who tried to drink from him. His eyes begin to dart about the alleyway, fretting for an escape.

"Drop the faux fear," Vauquelin says. "Your little scheme against Yvain is a dangerous game indeed, and you are quite mistaken if you think I am your pawn. I urge you to consider your position carefully, lest you yourself become the victim." He eases his voice into a whisper. "Is it truly Yvain you want? Or his power?"

Clément says nothing, merely fluttering his big doe eyes.

Vauquelin clutches him by the throat. *No wonder Yvain chose him*, he thinks. *He is disgustingly handsome.*

"What is it you want?" he repeats.

He looks Vauquelin in the eye and says, "You."

Vauquelin succumbs to his nature. He backs Clément against the wall, drawing his hand up between his legs. He lifts the young vampire's chin up for a kiss, and Clément melts into him. They unbutton their breeches with urgent frenzy, letting them fall to the ground, and Clément brings his hand up to clasp the back of Vauquelin's neck.

Vauquelin strokes himself against Clément. It is truly one of his most favorite acts: a kill, followed by a fuck ... something he had seldom experienced in modern times.

Now he will have it.

Vauquelin turns Clément around and eases himself in, running his hands over Clément's body, pulling his long hair back, brushing his lips against his ears. He has one hand against the wall and the other around Clément's cock, stroking it in sync with his thrusts.

Two beautiful vampires who will never have release find it the only way available to them.

Their bodies pressed together, their breeches still around their ankles, they grind in ecstatic unison.

Clément hurls himself around and lunges his neck forward.

Vauquelin enfolds him in his arms and drinks from him.

Out of nowhere, Yvain appears.

Clément sees him first and stiffens, yanking his pants up.

Vauquelin lifts his face, still dripping with Clément's blood.

He is prepared for this.

He tucks himself into his breeches and turns to face his maker as he buttons them up.

"You have bested me at all angles," Yvain says, turning five shades of crimson. "I am beginning to think you were right ... bringing you back was an enormous mistake."

"I would that you had not! You have upended my life in ways I never would have thought possible!"

"*Alors*," Yvain replies, "I cannot say I blame either of you for giving into your desires for one other, my two most beautiful animals." He walks toward them, reaching for his fly.

"You will never have me. Never!" Vauquelin says. Now is his best and only chance. "Since you have done your best to destroy my peace of mind, I insist that you liberate me. Let me go! It is imperative that you sever your ties to me."

Yvain's face blazes with wrath. Vauquelin, his greatest creation and his favorite, has been nothing but a disappointment, time and again. But to unshackle him without a fight? Not a chance.

"You are indeed an imbecile if you think I would relinquish you so easily."

"Your habit of collecting and discarding pets must stop, Yvain." Vauquelin gestures to Clément, who regards them in slump-shouldered silence, too frightened to speak. "It is only a matter of time before you abandon this one too, and send him straight into the same hell you plunged me into."

They lock eyes, each daring the other to make a move.

Yvain flashes behind Vauquelin, drawing his stiletto against his throat. "I could end you right now, dearest," he growls into Vauquelin's ear. "Taking you from this earth is preferable to having you walk upon it without me."

"Please, indulge me. End my suffering and avail me from the torture of navigating the fathomless abyss of my history once more. I shall embrace Death and welcome her," Vauquelin cries. "Believe me, the earth shall be neither better nor worse without my tread upon it. I have had quite enough of living. Of this you can be sure. You have already broken me ... finish it."

Yvain sinks to his knees, pulling Vauquelin down with him. He had not anticipated this — he presumed Vauquelin would fight for his life.

Yvain's vainglorious swagger dissipates into defeat.

He touches Vauquelin's cheek and bites into his neck. He takes a small amount of blood, which he promptly spits on the ground. "I renounce you. You are free of me. You will never know me again, nor I you. I shall regret this for all of my remaining days."

Vauquelin takes Clément's hand and flashes him away, looking back at Yvain over his shoulder.

The old master stands impotent, powerless to react.

Vauquelin and Clément arrive at Vauquelin's hôtel and rush into its shelter, anxious to get as far as possible away from Yvain.

As they enter, the clock chimes four.

"Look, we haven't much time," Vauquelin says. "Yvain will be searching for you. Come."

They sit in the library. Clément opens his mouth to speak and Vauquelin holds up his hand. "I am sure you have many questions, but now I must think."

He begins to pace. It is a habit he cannot shake of late.

His mind is working in overdrive.

He has gotten himself into a bit of a quagmire with Clément, and now he must decide whether to drag the poor youth further into his unfolding disaster or let him fend for himself.

Throughout the time-shifts, Vauquelin's behavior has been — and is, even at this moment — abominable, but it appears he is unable to stop himself.

He had not been the most exemplary person in his futurepast. He was selfish and self-indulgent, but for the majority of his existence he has had no one to rely on him and no one upon whom he could rely. His isolation from all beings, human or vampire, is deliberate.

But is not it preferable for vampires to remain clandestine? Humans would be incapable of coming to terms with vampires running rampant in the world. Chaos and mass death would ensue. It is best for all if they remain underground, obscured — the fodder for nightmares and fiction.

He is stranded in the raging seas of his own history, but he is free. It will take decades, perhaps even centuries, for him to learn to savor his independence and for Yvain's release to fade from his mind. He had advanced as an ancient man in the modern world and that world had been capsized, submerging him in the deepest recesses of his past.

All he can do now is navigate the nightmarish vortex of time.

Vauquelin halts and buries his face in his hands.

Yvain's centuries of silence are now accounted for, and he needs wonder about him no more. In his futurepast, the possibility that Yvain was merely ignoring him still gave him hope, someone to call out to. Now he has no one, absolutely no one ... and he has only himself to blame.

The distinct halves of his personality are battling to the death, and only one must prevail. If he is to be the same man Maeve once loved, he has no choice.

If he retraces each step of his life in the precise manner as he did the first time, will those steps get him back to Maeve in another two and a half centuries? Or has he already altered events so that could never be?

Only time (his true enemy) will tell.

His thoughts come crashing down upon him.

He does not notice Clément cross the room, and when he feels his hand on his shoulder, he jumps.

It cruelly places him in the here and now.

"Clément, I must apologize. My behavior has been aberrant. And if you say you love me, I will tear you to pieces."

"Should Yvain cast me out I will be alone, and I will have no home of my own."

"He did the same to me. I was created and left to fend for myself. I assure you, it is possible to live a good life on your own. Six months ago, I was living in the twenty-first century, until Yvain abducted me from my comfortable existence. I doubt you could even fathom the ways in which humanity has evolved."

"Yvain told me you came from the future," Clément says, "but I did not quite believe him. How can that be so?"

The current year is 1668. Clément has been a revenant for twelve moons. His age will be twenty forever. He reveals to Vauquelin how he was created — not by Yvain, but by one of the other vampires in the coterie. Clément had been groomed by Yvain, and became his lover at once. Yvain doted on him.

"But do you love him?" Vauquelin asks.

"He protects me. My maker is weak, a vampire of no consequence. Yvain has become my sun, moon, and stars, and I am his. No one has ever cared for me this way."

Yvain had royally fucked up Vauquelin's life, and he wants to make him suffer for it. But now, looking at this young, naïve vampire, he realizes that taking Clément away from him is a cheap move. Perhaps they really did love each other …who was Vauquelin to say?

"I am sorry that I forced myself upon you," Vauquelin says.

Clément takes his hand. "No, it was I who taunted you, because I wanted a taste of your beauty. I admire you greatly but I do not love you, although I believe I could in time."

Relief washes over Vauquelin. In his rash behavior this evening, he had not intended to ignite a love affair. Nonetheless, a significant bond has manifested between them — he must honor it.

"Drink from me. I want to strengthen you. You are aware that all of Yvain's creatures want my blood … it is rich with his original potency, but they are unaware that my strength is now sevenfold."

Clément licks Vauquelin's neck, takes him in his arms, and sinks his teeth.

"That's enough," Vauquelin whispers. He pushes Clément away. "No one has partaken of me, with the exception of Yvain and another vampire who is no more. I hope it serves you well."

Clément springs a massive erection. They both look down at it and Vauquelin laughs, raising an eyebrow.

"*Putain d'enfer* … I've gifted you with my own personal affliction. May you come to enjoy it, my friend."

The clock chimes six. There is still no sign of Yvain.

"Come, let us rest. Our worries will still be here tomorrow night, and so will he."

Vauquelin leads him to the bed.

"You do not sleep in a coffin!" Clément exclaims.

"You must open your mind, *mon petit* ... the world is much greater than you've been led to believe. Anything is possible."

He secures the curtains, shielding them against the burgeoning light of day. Turning onto his side, he twirls a lock of Clément's hair in his fingers, drops kisses on his shoulders, strokes his cheek with the back of his hand.

They make love again, this time with more care and intention, and fall into their slumber naked, limbs intertwined.

It is an intimacy that he has not experienced since Delphine, and it is a comfort.

Despite the violent beginning to this night with Clément, Vauquelin at last has a friend — one who understands his struggles as only another vampire could.

It is strange and soothing.

Upon waking, Vauquelin's first sight is a sound-asleep Clément.

His pulse quickens at the spectacle of Clément's dark, curly hair tumbled out on the pillow, with those devilishly long lashes resting against his cheeks ... it stirs something that has been long-dormant in his soul.

Clément looks so virtuous, so pure.

Vauquelin could lay there for infinity gazing upon him, but the sun is down.

He nudges him, whispering, "We must dress. If Yvain does not come to us, then we shall go to him. It is the right thing to do. All will be well ... you have my word."

Vauquelin smooths Clément's hair and puts an arm around his shoulders, guiding him out of the room.

On the journey to Yvain's château, Clément pummels him with questions about the future.

Vauquelin deflects them all.

"*Mon chéri*, if I were to answer these inquiries, you would be robbed of the gift of living life as it unfolds. There is much I could tell you, but it would be a prison sentence for you. Without facts you may think me a fraud, but please believe me. It is much better to live life as it presents itself, without thinking of how different things could and will be. I am living that in reverse now, bereft of a life I cannot touch. I assure you, to tell you the whole truth of it would cause your imagination to fester and rot. You cannot possibly comprehend, and you must experience it yourself. That is one lesson from Yvain that I learned on my journey back here, and for that, perhaps it was worth it. But know this: you are alone, and will be perpetually alone. No other being, human or vampire, can give you solace for that."

In Clément, he has a benevolent audience for perhaps the first time in his life: a comrade, a sympathetic soul who passes no judgment on his unorthodox ways.

He has never spoken about himself with such candor, not even to Delphine, and it is powerful.

"In the future, you will find no forgiveness, no redemption. If you think Yvain will prepare you for this, consider yourself deceived. He will continue to beguile you with delusions of grandeur and obscure vital wisdom from you. You must take it upon yourself to learn. As you progress through the years, it will become increasingly difficult to find sustenance. Your nature will begin to suffocate you. There is no respite but to live alone, isolated. You have all the time in the world. You can use that time wisely to learn and expand your mind or you can live as a monster, like Yvain and his other vampires, including me. I found my comfort on the fringes of society, but from my chosen refuge I gave laughable amounts of money to humans who could create wonderful things in the visible world. I did not make anything of myself, nor did I conceive of any ideas that could change the world. I could have. Perhaps you can."

Rain begins to lash the roof of the carriage, and Vauquelin parts the curtains, watching the droplets slide down the glass.

"We are accursed, but you do not have to concede to evil. It is possible to live a good life, even as a vampire, and to experience the love and life of a human man. You can live in darkness and still seek light elsewhere in your life. I believe I am a testament to that, despite what Yvain must have told you about me."

Clément reaches for his hand. "You are not a monster."

"There are humans that are vastly more monstrous than we. I still have the soul of a man, and so do you. I cannot tell you what your future will be, but I can hope that you will surrender yourself to it. Be a collector of wisdom."

The carriage clatters to a stop in front of Yvain's château.

Vauquelin anguishes at parting from Clément and surrendering his newfound kinship, but surrender it he must.

The coachman opens the carriage door, and Vauquelin snatches it back, pulling it shut.

"Clément, can you assure me that you are content to remain here in the coterie, with Yvain?"

"Yes, I am content. I must not think about the future. I will keep your words with me forever."

"Forever is another human concept. A sweet word that cannot carry the weight of its meaning. But you, *cher* Clément, will remain in my heart for all my days."

He presses his face to Clément's, inhaling the fragrance of his hair, imprinting the memory of it.

"Be good to yourself. I shall not go in."

Vauquelin is quite sure they will never meet again.

Clément casts him a wistful look and embraces him one last time. "Farewell, my friend."

Vauquelin shuts the carriage door and raps the ceiling with his staff. His heart surges, and it causes him physical pain. The closest he has ever come to feeling such wretchedness was the night Maeve died.

Another loss.

Once again he is the victim of his own precarious shadow love.

If I could live my entire life over — how many times had humans uttered this phrase?

He laughs.

What a concept.

Trust me, you would not want that, he says to himself as the carriage takes him back home, alone.

30

It is Christmas Eve.

A little over a month has passed since his second resurrection.

The logs in the fireplace pop and hiss, sending bursts of cinders up the flue. One year ago, on this same night in 1959, he hunted down a hapless human in a Santa hat outside a dive bar in Los Angeles.

The Demon of Repetition rides upon Vauquelin's back, and his terminal ennui has followed him back through the centuries.

Yvain has kept his word to stay away, and Vauquelin has not sought him out. But this also means absence from Clément: Vauquelin misses him profoundly.

He recalls his maker's pedantic apologies and his sorrow at abandoning him, his regret for Vauquelin's lifelong misery.

They were just words. Although Yvain might have been genuinely remorseful, the damage is done.

Vauquelin's journey back to his origin as vampire has solved none of this, and in fact, heaped him with more guilt by informing him he had been responsible for Maeve's death twofold.

The knowledge weighs upon him like an anchor, but he cannot

allow it to drag him down to the bottom of his darkest trenches.

Taking languid draws from a bottle of claret, he fantasizes about his futurepast pleasures. If he is patient and can persevere, they will be his once again. But now all his desires are locked away on the opposite side of time.

Here he abides, in the most extravagant surroundings available to a man of his station in 1668, waiting for the ax to fall. In fourteen more years (the blink of an eye for Vauquelin) this house and the majority of his possessions will be confiscated and possessed by the crowned head of France.

He was woefully unprepared and did not see it coming the first time around, but perhaps now he can alter the outcome.

Soon, Louis XIV will move his entire court to Versailles and call forth on the highest French nobility to relocate to the palace, to become permanent residents. He will assemble his planets and stars into their proper place in his magnificent orbit.

The totality of the aristocrats of France will be summoned. And if any of them refuse or fail to respond, they will be stripped of their titles and their properties seized.

XIV was fearful and paranoid after the Fronde rebellion of 1648 during his minority. The rebels threatened to dethrone him. Therefore, he wanted all the nobility under his thumb, so he could monitor their every move.

Vauquelin was not then and is not now in a position to blame him, but he is determined to be the sovereign of his own life.

If he enjoyed taking orders and living under scrutiny, he would have pledged his fealty to Yvain's coterie — certainly not to a capricious king.

On his original journey through time, Vauquelin was among

the nobility who rebuffed the Sun King's demands. He had no intention whatsoever of vacating his properties and taking up residence in the château of Versailles.

He could not survive in such a microcosm: it would be impossible for him to exist as a nocturnal creature and conceal his haemovore nature.

Before XIV's sweeping accounts of the nobles, he had been able to live a comfortable life far from the extensive espionage of the court. When Louis called the nobility to heel, the results would be devastating to the country. How different Vauquelin's life would have turned out if he had complied!

Imagine, a vampire living in Versailles ...

Preposterous.

In 1668, Vauquelin's holdings were/are:

> *One title, Le Duc de Vauquelin, with a duchy income of over 100,000 livres per annum, inherited from his father*

> *One hôtel particulier, L'hôtel du Coquillage, acquired by his father in 1601, located in Paris, in which he now sits ruminating, comprised of: three floors, one stable, six horses (four mares and two stallions), one barouche, one post-chaise, one phaeton, one 1ᵉʳ valet de chambre/head of household, one chef (dismissed), two sous-valets de chambre, one head groom, two stable boys, two coachmen, four chambermaids, one house musician, three scullery maids (dismissed), and one sommelier*

> *One Château de Renonçeau, located in Rueil, Hauts-de-Seine*

One Château du Cavernay, located in Annecy

900,000 livres in currency and jewels

500,000 livres in furnishings and art

300,000 livres in clothing

5,000 livres in weaponry

1,854 books

His wealth is vast, his family name ancient. He is the end of his line, a Parsifal: a rare only child and the sole male heir. And now that he was vampire, he could have no offspring. Regardless, it had never been his desire to procreate and give himself an heir.

All his worldly possessions could (would) be seized by the King at His Most Christian Majesty's pleasure. If he does not comply this time, his title will once again be taken and sold to another nobleman or given to a mistress of the King.

There will be no possibility of retaining it.

He knows what will happen to anyone with a title: he already lived through France's lust for noble blood during the Revolution. He was then, and will be once more, frankly delighted to let it go, although the duchy revenue is substantial.

On his original journey, he managed to get the majority of his monetary wealth and a smattering of personal effects into hiding or out of the country altogether.

He traveled to London and placed his currency and jewels in a bank, retaining only the services of Olivier and the few material objects that he was able to fit into trunks.

He remained in England for almost a decade.

From London he traveled to Italy, where he found the landscape and the culture much more suited to his tastes.

After seventy-two years on the throne, the seemingly immortal Louis finally met his death in 1715.

Only then did Vauquelin return to France and resume his life.

This time, he is determined to stay put.

Vauquelin stands and stretches.

Right now he wants only amusement and fulfillment, immediate gratification ... he has no mind for the future.

He knows well enough what is coming.

The unwavering clacking and pace of the horses' hooves on the road lulls him, and he sways his body in rhythm with the coach. Though luxurious, it cannot hold a candle to his futurepast Pagani, but it is the greatest horsepower he has at his disposal. He pounds on the roof, urging the coachman to go faster.

During the journey, Vauquelin recalls all he said to Clément. He splashes the thoughts around in his head, aware that he could also be speaking to himself.

His future self, addressing his ancient self.

Vauquelin had once been a novice vampire like Clément.

The only thing separating the two of them is some three hundred and fifty years' worth of time.

Otherwise, they are much the same.

He wishes for Clément the strength to detach himself from

Yvain and experience life as he had, on his own terms, but the young vampire must follow his own path.

If only Clément were with him now ... they could have a bit of fun. Alas, it is not in the cards for them to be together.

Arriving in the village of Versailles, Vauquelin descends from his carriage and is at once surrounded by threadbare beggar children. He distributes coins to them as he surveys the streets. They are sparse of people, but he will find his way.

Children are off limits.

He locates the tavern and causes a stir upon his entrance. It is out of the ordinary for aristocrats to appear in the sole drinkery in this little village, let alone on Christmas Eve.

It will be many years hence that the mighty château will bring them business and prosperity.

The patrons remind Vauquelin of his time among the beatniks in futurepast Los Angeles. This is no different. Common folk are far more colorful than the vapid aristocracy, of which he is once again a member.

He has always preferred low company. It is a trait he shared with Maeve and greatly appreciated in her.

His attire gives him away at once. It is too dark for them to notice his freakish visage, but even so, all aristocrats are pale. Porcelain skin is a hallmark of western European nobility, accentuated even further with powder; therefore he raises no suspicions. Indeed, they are honored by his presence, that a nobleman would deign to descend upon their humble, unsophisticated establishment.

Right away he rounds up a raucous game of whist, allowing all his opponents to triumph over him.

Currency is flowing.

He pays for everyone's wine.

They love him.

But he is not here out of sheer generosity.

As the hours march on, his hunger intensifies. He has earned their favor — now he will take his reward.

It is time.

Vauquelin makes a sly departure out the back door and waits, entertaining himself by balancing his walking staff on his palm until he hears a door open. He drops the point of the staff to the ground and leans on it in anticipation.

He resolves to use no tricks, no enchantment.

This is pure sport.

Who will this star-crossed human be?

As fate would have it, it is the barmaid. She carries a lantern in one hand and a basket of garbage in the other.

Vauquelin flashes himself to her side, his hand clutching the small of her back. He locks her in his gaze, and she drops the basket, scattering rotten food onto Vauquelin's finely-shod feet.

"Begging your pardon, Monsieur," she says, giving a small curtsy. "You startled me."

Disgusted, he shakes the filth off as best he can.

The disruption rattles his game, yet he regains his bravado before she can blink. Snatching the lantern from her hand, he lifts it high and bares his teeth in a seductive snarl.

She gasps.

Terror erupts across her face and, grasping a small pewter cross, her hand flies to her neck. In desperation, she hoists her neck towards him, cross first.

"And what do you call yourself, *mon trésor?*" he whispers.

She is frozen, terrified, and still thrusting the cross forward with a trembling hand.

"I will not tell you, *maléfique!* Leave me be!"

He snatches the ribbon off her neck and dangles the bauble just above his lips.

"I have always loved crucifixes," he says, dropping it into his mouth and swallowing it with an elaborate gulp.

She is too horrified to scream.

Vauquelin covers her mouth and bleeds her, licking the last of her blood from her throat. He strokes her neck as one would caress his beloved, and his fingers erase the puncture marks he made.

His eyes bulge.

Yvain's unique skill has become his at last!

Holding the deceased barmaid at arm's length, Vauquelin studies her face for a moment and brings her gently down to the ground, closing her dead eyes.

Death has made her beautiful.

Still, he hates it when they die with their eyes open.

A futurepast industrial song is stuck in Vauquelin's head on an endless loop, driving him mad.

He would love nothing more than to blast it through a set of not-yet-invented wireless speakers, as he saunters around his glorious seventeenth-century domain in lace and embroidered silk. It would be so appropriate for his nouveau surreality.

Oh, well.

His only option is to hum it to his house musician, who attempts to tap it out on the harpsichord in the library.

It is an interesting sound, but the combination of bizarre notes baffles the poor musician. Regardless, Vauquelin is pleased with the results. The dissonant, unholy union of baroque and darkwave is delicious to his ears.

The musician's skills are being stretched beyond his capacity, and so Vauquelin dismisses him and settles for saddling up his favorite horse: a black Friesian mare called Geneviève.

The song remains in his consciousness — it is an ironic, infernal soundtrack for a damned modern soul riding horseback through the midnight streets of Paris in the *ancien régime*.

In his futurepast, he adored driving automobiles to clear his head. Now, his only travel options are horses, carriages and coachmen. As much as he laments the technology that modern life afforded him, he has missed ancient, feral moments like this.

Someday, when he gets back to the time of automobiles, he will keep horses again. Why had he never thought of doing so before? He strokes her curly black mane and kisses her velvety muzzle.

"What a pity one cannot turn a horse into a vampire," he whispers. If only he could keep Geneviève with him forever.

Vauquelin settles into the slow, rolling motion of her gait. His thoughts are a bizarre cocktail of the recent past, future, and futurepastpresent memories. He was living in Southern California mere months ago.

What a peculiar fucking trip this has been.

The concept of time is crushing: nanoseconds and milliseconds and seconds and minutes and hours and days and weeks and months and years and decades and centuries without end lie ahead of him.

The thought of enduring them over again cripples his mind.

But Maeve is waiting out there somewhere, tucked in the wings of the future. Maeve's family origins were in Ireland. Her ancestors are alive now. He wishes he knew who they were — that he could observe them and tell her about them someday — but even if he knew how to find them he must not do anything to impede their natural progress.

Stage upon stage is being raised and torn down and replaced so that she may make her appearance in the world.

Vauquelin has no reason to believe that his re-emergence in the past will alter her ancestry in any manner, but nevertheless, he resolves to keep his feet firmly on his side of the English Channel until the day of his departure for America arrives. And when the need arises again, his money will go to a Swiss bank, not an English one.

He will do anything to get back to her, to revise the ending of her story, even if it means suffering through two more interminable centuries. She is the only aspect of his futurepast he does not want to alter. The rest can go to hell as far as he is concerned, and this time he will not repeat his tragic error.

He has abundant time to decipher a way to convince her, and he must not fail.

One thing is clear: the recent brutality he has been exhibiting is untenable. If he continues behaving this way, he will no longer be the man that Maeve fell in love with. It is imperative that he be the same as he was the day they met: there is no alternative.

But how can he guarantee anything now?

He had surrendered himself to a sickening and comfortable descent down, down, down into his old mode of malice, enraged by the time-shifts, furious at being ripped out of the untroubled existence he had designed for himself. It is his natural reaction, but he must keep his darkest recesses at bay.

He is here now and there is nothing he can do to change the circumstances. It was his calculated choice to become vampire once more. He was given another chance to set things right that had gone horribly wrong as he fumbled his way through his futurepast, to end what he had begun.

Extending his spine and throwing his shoulders back, he pulls Geneviève to a stop.

His anger becomes white hot and crystalline.

It evaporates from his chest like steam, and just like that, he is unburdened.

He urges Geneviève back into a gallop.

His parallel psyches, one of ancient origin and one born in the future, have merged at last. He embraces his newborn strength and power, and now he can confirm that Delphine was mistaken: this life of his is indeed a gift, not a damnation.

He laughs exuberantly as he guides Geneviève through the gates of his house. It has been a lifetime since he held such happiness in his heart.

He is purified and resurrected indeed.

Vauquelin hands Geneviève off to the groom and bolts up the stairs two at a time. He peers under his bed.

The satchel and his 1936 suit are missing.

Panic splays through his heart as he opens a trunk and rifles through it, creating a monumental mess on the floor with the sundry chemises, jabots, and stockings stored in its interior.

At last he locates the jacket and clutches it to his chest, eyes rolling back into his head in deep relief, for inside the pocket is a small, leather-bound case containing the sole existing photograph of himself and Maeve.

He has not looked at the photo in perhaps a hundred years.

It is no small miracle that it is still in his possession.

He placed it in his pocket at the eleventh hour when he packed for his ocean voyage out of New York, and he did not have the heart to open it even then.

Vauquelin's decision to keep the satchel in bed with him during the last time-shift was prudent.

Aside from the photograph, his newly-acquired pocket watch, and the suit and shoes he had worn in the coffin when he went into his extended slumber for travel, he retains no other objects from the future.

The suit had been cleaned, folded and placed in the wardrobe. No doubt Olivier was mystified by it. Compared to the fashions of this era, it must have appeared utterly plain and bizarre.

Ankle length trousers? *Unheard of!*

Dull wool tweed? *Appalling!*

Even the servants' garb is more extravagant than this expensive mid-1930s men's suit, yet Olivier safeguarded it without question. He is worth his weight, and then some, in pure gold.

If Vauquelin had lost the photograph it would have been unfortunate indeed: but regardless, her face is imprinted in his mind. It is impossible for him to forget how she looked.

He flicks the small gold clasp and opens the case at last.

Maeve's serene smile crushes him.

He extracts her copper curl, tied with a segment of black lace ribbon. It no longer carries her scent, but still he sweeps it across his lips, closing his eyes and inhaling it. He carefully re-latches the case and places it in the drawer of his mother's jewel box.

Vauquelin is bound and determined not to sway too much from his first journey. Even the smallest altered detail could keep him from meeting Maeve again.

The sum of his existence hinges on one date: August 11, 1900, an evening in his futurepast that began like any other evening but ended up turning his world on its ear and illuminating it with blinding light.

It was the day he met her.

He must replicate each exact scenario, down to the last letter, that will once again place him at her feet.

His anticipation of their reunion is akin to (im)patiently enduring a life sentence in prison, with freedom (and her) awaiting him on the other side of his impenetrable walls.

Vauquelin lies across the foot of the bed and scrutinizes his portrait. Painted during his first year as a vampire, it lords over his bedchamber in its original spot. In his futurepast, it was hanging next to his bed in Los Angeles and once mystified Maeve.

His newfound self-realizations have inspired him to commission a new portrait as a commemoration of his reinstatement, his fourth life. Twice human, twice vampire.

He calls for Olivier and instructs him to send for Monsieur Le Brun. Time is of the essence: in less than a year, the renowned painter will be unavailable, tasked with the gargantuan assignment of decorating Versailles, and only the best will do.

Vauquelin stands in front of his elaborate marble fireplace as Monsieur Le Brun begins his work. The chandelier has been lowered as much as possible over his head to afford the artist sufficient illumination in the funereal house.

For his original portrait, he had worn an ensemble typical of the nobility at the time. Now he has chosen something significantly more malevolent, something befitting a vampire.

He is adorned in head-to-toe black: in this era, a color reserved for clergy and members of high office.

He worked for weeks with a couturier to create this costume: an embroidered, watered-silk justaucorps and a voluminous chemise crowned by a double lace collar, with *canions* embellished by vermilion metallic scrolls and yards of gossamer ribbons.

His legs are swathed in scarlet silk stockings and his feet shod in ebony leather shoes, red-heeled with elaborate silk and diamond encrusted bows.

A black fox fur adorns his neck and shoulders.

His dark hair has been curled by hot iron, framing his face with perfect raven ringlets. His new walking staff is crowned by a silver horned devil's head with garnet eyes.

The carved shaft is enameled in crimson.

The ensemble is a bold move, yet one that will raise no eyebrows. Portraits are often theatrical in this period. It is the first time in his long life that he voluntarily — not to mention outwardly — proclaims his vampirism, preserving it for the years to come.

The new painting is a testament to the cataclysmic reversal in his perception. If he can learn to venerate his reality, perhaps his life will be easier.

Perhaps.

The universe has bequeathed Vauquelin with merciful amnesty: his time begins to surge forward in hyper-speed.

When he awakens at night it feels as though a mere hour has passed before it is time for him to go to his rest again.

Seconds and minutes and hours and days and nights and weeks and months speed by.

Is time really so fast-moving, or is it like repeating a road trip where one is familiar with the surroundings? Or watching a movie or reading a book for the second or fifth time, when time unfurls much more quickly than the first?

We cannot know.

After his original creation, his fascination for the mundane intensified: he could stare at a candle for hours, examine every single fiber of a feather, memorize each note on a musical score ... and thus his minutes passed.

It had become such a custom for him that he took this unique skill for granted. He must cultivate it once more to soothe the losses of his futurepast technological amusements.

He resumes his old habit of imagining himself in a looking

glass when his staff finishes dressing him each evening. His recent, all-too-brief glimpses of his human self have inspired him. He has only his memory and his portraits to confirm his physical appearance, and each person who sees them exclaims at the incredible likeness Monsieur Le Brun has captured.

He is performing a role in his own movie, and he witnesses the aristocracy's clothing and manner of dress evolve at full throttle. Soon, it is 1680. The King has begun losing his hair, and, in the twinkling of an eye, massive wigs in the style of XIV's luscious, god-given locks become *de rigueur* for men.

Olivier, standing on a stool, places the latest model upon Vauquelin's head.

The wig is heavy and thick with a waterfall of midnight curls, weighing no less than four and a half kilograms.

Vauquelin is humbled a bit at first by its burden.

With the wig, his *rapier*, and the combined weight of the fabric and precious metal threads, buckles, and buttons on his clothing and shoes, he carries some thirty kilos of contemporary dress and accessories upon his person.

Vauquelin stands erect in his red-heeled leather shoes, majestic and elegant in the height of late seventeenth-century fashion. He is abnormally tall for a man of his era. Were he to stand next to the King, he would rival the monarch's appearance, towering above him in both height and finery.

This is one of the many reasons he would be suspect amongst the nobility. No one, not even Vauquelin, should dare have the audacity to outshine the Sun King.

The conspicuous change in fashion is a harsh reminder that the upheaval of the French nobility is nigh. He requires an elaborate, well-developed plan to preserve his holdings.

He must take action for his future, or he will lose his homes and possessions in the same manner he lost them the first time.

It is a critical juncture that calls for proactive measures.

Olivier's imminent death is another subject he must address. Olivier is one of the most important humans in Vauquelin's history ... he cannot let him go again.

Of the many lessons Vauquelin has learned throughout his travails, one in particular rises to the top:

BEWARE THE DANGER OF HESITATION

The clock chimes half-past six.

Vauquelin orders all the servants out of his chamber with the exception of Olivier.

PARIS, FRANCE | 1680

Vauquelin motions for Olivier to sit next to him on the chaise at the foot of the bed.

The valet hesitates, swallowing hard and stretching his collar with a finger. All of a sudden the room is airless, stifling.

Although his intimacy with Monsieur runs deep, he has never been this personal with him and he has not once been seated in his master's presence, let alone by his side. Nevertheless, he arranges himself, stiff-backed, on the very edge of the chaise.

Vauquelin has made somewhat of a rash decision. His guilt over Maeve inspires him to do what he is about to do. It is a gargantuan risk, but one he must take.

"Olivier, what is your age, my friend?"

Friend? *Friend?*

A muscle in Olivier's cheek begins to twitch. Monsieur's recent behavior has been erratic, but this is confounding. Perhaps Monsieur intends to dismiss him. After all, he is not quite as robust as he once was. In a quavering voice he replies, "I am forty-eight years old, Monsieur."

How curious! Vauquelin thinks. *If I were human, then I would now be forty-four.*

After his creation as a vampire, awareness of his human age faded away; this new realization amazes him. But there are more important tasks at hand. He clears his throat.

"What if I told you that by this time next year, you will be dead of smallpox?"

The valet nearly falls off the chaise, and braces himself with a foot. "How could Monsieur know how and when I will die?"

"You must call me Vauquelin. No more Monsieur. I insist."

He stands and begins pacing. There is no retreating now: he has ambushed his poor, beleaguered valet, and he is in too deep.

"You have been inordinately loyal to me," he begins.

Olivier's eyes begin to well up with tears.

His chin is set aquiver.

How undignified! What will Monsieur think?

He has now convinced himself, in his heart of hearts, that dismissal is forthcoming. His mind races with thoughts of how he will live, where he will find work, how he will ever find another family so worthy of his respect. His entire lifetime has been spent in Monsieur's service, from the day Monsieur was born. There has been no other way of life for him.

"Olivier! Forgive me for agonizing you. I beg you, allow me to remedy this." He takes a deep breath and begins again. "You have been inordinately loyal to me, but you *will* die from the pox next year. This is not speculation — it is a certainty. The reason I know this is that I lived through your death and hundreds of years beyond, well into the twenty-first century. I despise the thought of experiencing your demise a second time. I would like for you remain with me always, as my friend, as my brother."

Judging by the incredulous expression on Olivier's face, this is not going well at all.

As he had with Delphine and the mobile phone, he relies on a relic of the futurepast to help illustrate his cause. He retrieves the 1936 suit and the photograph from the trunk.

"What went through your mind when you found these objects, Olivier?" He hands them to the valet. "Inspect them closely."

Olivier opens the jacket.

"Read the label," Vauquelin says.

Olivier does not speak English. He struggles to enunciate *Bullock's Wilshire, Los Angeles, Calif. USA.*

"Monsieur, what does this mean?"

"This suit of clothing comes from a city and country that does not yet exist, across the Atlantic Ocean. I lived there, and I purchased it in the year 1936. Now I will ask you to open that small case."

Olivier opens the photograph and goes pale. It is his own Monsieur standing in a much different suit, but still obviously not of this era, with a woman.

Scrawled across the bottom, in white handwriting, are the numbers *1901*. Myriad questions tumble out of his consciousness and through his lips.

"Monsieur, this is such a detailed painting to be so small. How is this possible? Why is there no color? What are these numbers? And who is this lady to you?"

Vauquelin takes the photograph from Oliver, holding it against his chest before re-clasping it.

"There is no one walking this earth who knows me as well as you do, Olivier. Yet there are essential facts about me that I was warranted to conceal for your own protection. I have asked you time and again for blind faith and you have not once failed me." He hangs his head. "The strange gentleman who visited our home? He is a vampire, a revenant — the undead, and he made me one of his own. I have lived well beyond the year 2020, yet I have been condemned to live my life over again. Alas, I have no further proof of the future to show you. These objects are the sole existing souvenirs of my improbable journey."

Vauquelin opens his mouth in the most non-threatening manner he can muster, exposing his elongated teeth.

Olivier's eyes distend as he extends his head for a closer look. When Vauquelin touches his shoulder, he flinches.

"Surely you do not relish the idea of being a servant for the rest of your life. I would like you to be free from your work and, most importantly, to be *alive* ... and to be my companion. Could you fathom becoming vampire, as I am, and living an eternal life?"

Olivier springs from the chair, his breath coming in spurts.

He stammers, "Monsieur, you have been nothing save kind and generous to me. But the vampire is evil incarnate! You are by no means evil. What you are telling me cannot possibly be true! I will not believe it!"

"My dear Olivier," Vauquelin says, "evil is but a fairy tale, an invention of man, a way to keep his supposed inferiors under his control. Evil is purely a matter of perspective. Permit me to explain further. If I transform you, you will never age ... and you will never die. You will never become ill. I need you. You are already accustomed to living in the night, but ... the vampire must kill in order to survive, Olivier. I subsist solely on the blood of the living. Is it evil to do what one must do to survive? Is the wolf evil? The hunter of meat, the farmer of flesh for your plate ... are they evil? When I told you I would take my meals outside the house in the evenings, this is what I meant. I hunt for my human victims in the dark of night."

Olivier begins to weep in earnest.

"I am sorry I lied to you. I wanted to protect you. I could not bear for you to think me a fiend." He leans down and helps Olivier back to the chaise. "However, Olivier, I must warn you: should you decline my offer, I will take your life this night. My hands are now tied. No human must know my true nature. You will die tonight or become vampire. Both choices will spare you from disease ... one will allow you to live forever."

"What shall I do?" Olivier asks.

"Let me serve you. Let me conduct the ritual of the toilette as your valet. I will call the servants, but you must not reveal one single word of this. You must play along and follow my prompts. It is my desire for you to indulge yourself. Let the servants groom you exactly as you wish. But I must emphasize: how you look tonight will be your physical appearance for eternity. Your hair, your nails, your entire body. Think carefully on this, for once you are vampire, any alterations you make to your person will revert during your slumber."

"Let it be done, Monsieur," Olivier says, tripping over his tongue, "but I must admit I am both intrigued and terrorized out of my senses."

Vauquelin pulls the servants' sash, and within minutes the doors to the bedchamber open. He orders a sumptuous meal, glancing at

Olivier for approval of his choices.

The servants are befuddled. Monsieur has not taken a meal in years! Fearful of disobeying him, they return an hour later bearing a cart teeming with plates of food.

Vauquelin waits on the other side of the room for Olivier to enjoy his last supper. When the staff returns for the dishes, he says, "You will bring my bath and begin my *lever* ... for Olivier."

In a whirlwind of activity, the necessary accoutrements are gathered and the bath is prepared. The servants stand in formation, giving each other subtle looks of dismay, until Vauquelin dismisses them with a wave of his hand.

"I will summon you when we are ready," he says, closing and locking the door.

He orders Olivier to undress and get in the bath. When he is submerged, Vauquelin pours a glass of wine and hands it to him. "Relax, and enjoy, my friend. Take your time. There is no need for you to rush."

He sits at his desk and begins composing a letter.

The clock chimes the quarter of the hour. Olivier bathes, takes approximately one sip of wine, and announces he is done.

The surprised chamber musician stops mid-performance.

"A ten-minute bath?" Vauquelin remarks , furrowing his brow. "That is hardly luxurious. As you are well aware, my baths can last for hours."

"I can conceive of no reason to delay, Monsieur."

Vauquelin hesitates. He doubts himself: has he sufficiently enlightened Olivier, or has he merely frightened him into yielding to his wishes? Nonetheless, he recalls the servants. He points to the naked valet who stands shivering before them, covering his genitals with his hands.

"Olivier is to be treated as your master now. Perform the toilette and bring him a selection of my garments from which he may choose."

The servants are aghast.

Has Monsieur well and truly lost his senses?

"Do not stand there like apes!" he bellows, snapping his fingers. "Attend to your duties!"

While answering questions throughout the ritual, Olivier deflects to Vauquelin, seeking his approval and reassurance.

"Give them your orders, Olivier. This is all for you ... you must be absolutely satisfied."

The soon-to-be-former *première* valet is mystified as his own long list of *lever* duties, meant for Monsieur and Monsieur alone, is carried out upon him. When it is done, he assumes an awkward stance in one of his master's finest suits of clothing, which will need alteration considering he is a good fourteen centimeters shorter than Monsieur.

With Vauquelin's goading, Olivier turns his head to the servants.

"Leave us at once," he says, pointing to the door.

Dumbfounded, they shuffle out, and the last one closes the door behind him.

Vauquelin applauds, striding across the room and locking the door. "Well done, Olivier. Are you pleased with your appearance? I regret that you are unable to see how magnificent you look. But I assure you, you cut a splendid impression."

"I am humbled, Monsieur." He extends a gallant leg and bows.

"If you are to be my companion, I must insist that you address me as Vauquelin. Please. No more Monsieur."

Vauquelin stands behind a large object concealed beneath a drape. With a grandiose flourish he pulls a cord, revealing a fine upright looking glass that he had purchased for this very occasion. He moves behind Olivier, resting a hand on his shoulder.

Olivier nods and glances at the mirror, astonished by the absence of Vauquelin's reflection, while he himself reflects as expected, with clarity.

"But, Monsieur ... Vauquelin ... why can I not see you? Is this why you ordered the removal of all the looking glasses?"

"Correct. Even so, I have no explanation for why a vampire's reflection does not manifest. Legend has it that vampires have no souls ..." Vauquelin pauses a moment, witnessing fear spread across Olivier's face, "however, I disagree. What is a soul, my friend? Can it be weighed, held in the hand? Can it be preserved, sold, or given away? It may well be that vampires are damned, but show me a human man who is truly worthy of eternal salvation by an imaginary god. Damned or not, vampires shall go on living without end. Perhaps our final destination is hell ... perhaps we bypass hell while a mortal man lives it on earth. A looking glass is a human invention. We are merely passing through this mortal coil. I suspect the glass cannot capture our image because vampires are preternatural. The soil captures the imprints of my feet as I walk upon it. Therefore, I know I exist. That is more credible to me than the phantom manifestation of my appearance. I merely am, and I will continue to be for an infinite number of years to come." He placed a finger on his temple. "What is inside here," he said, moving his fingers down his face and body, "is more important than what is outside here, and no mirrored image can capture that. Do not despair."

"What will happen next?" Olivier asks.

Vauquelin leads him to the bed and parts the curtains, indicating that Olivier should go inside.

Does Monsieur mean to have intercourse with me? he wonders, dismayed. Monsieur has disappeared into his bedchamber with men many times before. But he obeys.

Vauquelin attempts to keep a straight face: still, an embarrassed laugh escapes his lips. "No, no, Olivier. It is not my intention to seduce you," he says, climbing into the bed and closing the curtains. "Lie down, and I will explain."

Olivier is mortified that Monsieur is able to read his thoughts, but his chagrin turns into trepidation and his limbs become stiff with terror.

"Now I will pierce your neck and consume your blood," Vauquelin explains. "You will die, but only in a manner of speaking. You will have the sensation of falling. I must warn you. It is a ghastly and soul-crushing experience, but please remember, it is only temporary. You will plummet into the blackest blackness, and you may believe you are done for — yet you will survive this horror, I assure you, and rise again in immortality. Your teeth will become like mine. You will use them to take blood. This will be repulsive to you at first, but it is the gateway to your nourishment."

Vauquelin takes a deep breath. He hopes to the depths of his being that he does not fuck up his first intentional transformation.

"Shall we begin?"

Olivier gives a timid nod.

"I beg you, do not be afraid," Vauquelin whispers. "I promise it will not last long and you shall emerge stronger than ever, immune to disease or death." He wills silence upon Olivier and moves his chin aside, burying his teeth in his neck.

Olivier whimpers — thick tears stream down his cheeks.

Vauquelin drinks as much as he can.

With his stiletto, he cuts the back of his hand and streams his own cursed blood through Olivier's parted lips.

Vauquelin releases him and recoils on the bed, slack-jawed with awe as the future vampire begins his initial descent into eternal damnation.

Olivier tosses from post to pillar, soaked with perspiration, his entire body wracked by apoplectic tremors. He curls himself into a fetal position one moment and tautens straight as a board the next. He rises from the bed, levitating and sinking again into his own obsidian hell.

When Olivier begins to scream and wail, Vauquelin, terror-struck, smothers his cries with a pillow.

He gets up on his knees, rocking as he clasps his hands.

Please, please, please let the servants be in their quarters and not listening outside …

He flattens an ear against the door.

There are no knocks, no scratches, no footsteps.

The room falls silent once more.

For a brief moment, he is reminded of a documentary he once saw in his futurepast about a drug addict going through opiate withdrawals. The vampire creation ritual is much the same, and quite horrifying to witness.

Hours of violent thrashing pass before Oliver becomes still.

Vauquelin observes the former valet's complexion drain into the exsanguinous pallor that will be his perpetual skin tone.

He has no conception of how long the rite is meant to last. In both of his own experiences, he lost all sense of time. But the sun is due to rise, and Olivier has not yet stirred.

His body is rigid and cold.

Vauquelin has not spent so much time with a corpse since the night he lost Maeve, and then he knew in no uncertain terms that she would never rise again.

A knock rips through the silence, startling him, and he rushes to the door, leaning upon it with his full weight.

"Monsieur, we are here for your *coucher*," comes a muted voice.

"Leave us be!" Vauquelin thunders. "Do not approach my door again until I call for you!"

He turns back to Olivier.

What if he has killed the poor man?

Vauquelin is unskilled, a novice maker.

He extinguishes the candles in the room and lies down, pulling the bed curtains closed.

He can do nothing but wait.

The house is tranquil — it is early morning. He creeps down to the library and retrieves several books. In the midst of reading, his thoughts meander to the night of his primeval creation, when he had been so utterly alone and unaware of what would become of him.

He is consumed by remorse: watching the rite with his own eyes is proof that he had not girded Olivier for this devastating blow. It is too late now, though.

The experience will shape Olivier as it shaped Vauquelin.

He is near the end of his last book when Olivier triumphs over his mortal death and lunges forth from the bed. All in all, it had taken Olivier three days and nights to rise again.

Vauquelin rushes to his side.

"Your teeth," he says, "show them to me."

Olivier opens his mouth wide.

There are the daggers.

"Take heed! They are weapons. You will grow accustomed to them in time."

Vauquelin sinks back into his chair, astonished beyond all belief.

Had he also lain dead for three days?

It must be so.

No wonder vampires are perceived to be evil: they rival Christ and his rise from death. The entire wretched experience is at once horrifying and fascinating, and there are no humans alive who could inspire Vauquelin to repeat it.

Not yet.

But there is more work to be done.

"Now, my brother, it is your turn to be replenished. I will provide your first blood. My strength will become your strength." He elongates his neck and taps his jugular vein with two fingertips. "Go on."

Olivier yields to his vampire-birth-bloodlust, tearing into Vauquelin with fervor.

"Swallow it all," Vauquelin commands, gritting his teeth through the pain. "I will push you away when you've had enough."

But what if he cannot judge?

What if Olivier drains him to death, like an infant rattlesnake lacking the instinct to stop releasing its venom?

His heartbeat deteriorates — terror courses through his veins in place of his haunted blood.

"Stop, stop, STOP!" he cries.

The new vampire's teeth rend his flesh on withdrawal.

Vauquelin strokes the wounds and they heal with his touch, filling Olivier with awe.

They both collapse on the pillows, gasping for air.

When his breath returns to normal, Vauquelin bursts out of bed. The clock chimes seven.

"Come now, my friend," he says, pulling Olivier out of the bed and almost causing him to lose his footing. "We are venturing out into the night. There is much for you to learn and we must begin immediately."

Vauquelin rubs his hands together.

He is giddy, excited.

He still does not feature the idea of creating vampires, but if he must, he believes Olivier is an excellent choice.

They journey to Croissy-Sur-Seine, a small village near Vauquelin's château at Rueil, and enter a tavern.

"Enjoy yourself, Olivier. You are now in possession of a lethal secret, one which you must keep carefully guarded. You are the king of discretion, but you must remember that our discovery means our destruction. If I teach you anything, that is perhaps the most important. And now, perhaps, you can understand the rationale behind my bizarre quirks and requests."

They consume cask after cask of wine while Vauquelin instructs his new progeny. He reveals everything he can think of to Olivier, instructing him in the etiquette and conduct that he had been forced to learn on his own, or by error.

He pledges to be a maker of principle, unlike Yvain, and to ensure that Olivier becomes a gentleman vampire, not a rogue.

Together, they share Olivier's first victim.

They lure a loud-mouthed gambler outside with promise of payment for their debts, and drain him behind their coach. Vauquelin instructs Olivier on the finer points of making a kill, and hands him his stiletto to disguise their evidence.

"We are bonded by blood now, Olivier. We are brothers. If ever we are apart and you need me, I will hear you, and I will come to your side without fail." He glances at the clock; it is almost five. "You must always be aware of time. You must never greet the sun. You will learn to internalize time's passage. Few things can harm us, but the sun will burn you to ashes in an instant. You will sleep with me until we can outfit a bed like mine for you."

The carriage returns them to Paris and they head straight to Vauquelin's bedchamber, ignoring the curious stares of the servants.

Later, in their own quarters, the servants gossip that Monsieur has taken Olivier for a lover.

They have long suspected that Olivier is in love with Monsieur. After all, neither of them had ever taken a wife, and they always deflect the flirtations of the female staff.

As they drift off, he pats Olivier's hand, overcome with joy.

"Now the pox cannot take you from me," he whispers.

Vauquelin, the spoiled only child, has a brother at last.

PARIS, FRANCE | 1682

"My title, along with its château and duchy, will be lost in five years' time, Olivier. I will no longer be Monsieur le Duc … I will be a mere *haute* bourgeois gentleman. The only way I can retain it is to move into Versailles and keep you as my servant, at least in appearance."

To a man of Olivier's humble origins, the thought of living in the chosen home of the Sun King is a dream, and he says as much.

"No. Absolutely not. One day, perhaps, we will go there, so that you may draw your own conclusions."

Louis XIV's dreams of excessive grandeur will soon seduce the nobility. The outside world will know nothing of the sinister contrivings arising behind its gilded gates.

Vauquelin does not want to deprive Olivier of experiencing an authentic life, and he knows better than most that the element of surprise is essential to surviving an eternal existence. But in such drastic periods of unfolding history, he cannot afford to leave Olivier in the dark.

It is his duty to disclose the truth of dangerous events that could harm either of them.

"Versailles will be no better than a decorative prison. Take this beautiful hôtel we are living in." He gestures around the room. "A finer home could not be found in Paris, no? If we were to follow the King's edict and relocate to Versailles when the time comes, we would be living in a room the size of this library, likely smaller. Rarely would we be permitted to visit this house. Perhaps only once or twice a year, and even then, only at the week's end. We would be prevented from traveling to the châteaux. Any journeys away from Versailles must be sanctioned by the King. We would be unable to leave the grounds to find our sustenance … if we were discovered hunting among the nobility, they would sentence us to burn at the pyre, or separate our limbs on a Catherine wheel. The court has always been suspicious and false-hearted, but it will amplify once they are imprisoned by copious gossip and ruinous idle time, scrutinizing each other's every gesture. It would be an impossible situation for us to live in as we are. We could not take our slumber during the day. Imagine living in a glass dome where you are kept under surveillance by the King's spies, and all your correspondence is opened and read. I have sheltered you from the cruel reality of the nobility. This is the beginning of the fall of the monarchy, my friend. One hundred years from now, the royal line will come to its halt in France. The populace shall rise up. A revolution is coming, and the aristocrats will all lose their heads."

"But the château in Annecy — could we not go there to avoid His Majesty's call?" Olivier asks. He cannot conceive of a France without a King. "I have heard tell that he has little interest in the provincial nobility."

"It is too far from Paris. You are a free man, Olivier … relocate if you wish. As you are aware, I have not been to Annecy in years. I prefer to remain here. The provinces are too dull for me and the populations are too small. Trust me when I say that it would be difficult for us to remain hidden in a *petit village*. I shall soon purchase another château, one which the King will be unable to take from me. This is what I did during my first journey through time. It will all execute flawlessly, I assure you."

Seated at a table in the library, Vauquelin and Olivier prepare to thwart the seizure of his possessions. His lawyer, Monsieur de Subligny, has been summoned and now sits before them, paper and quill in hand.

"All my properties with the exception of the Château de Renonçeau shall be transferred to Olivier Boucher," he says, gesturing to his fledgling vampire companion.

"But, Monsieur! This is most unusual! It is my opinion that you should undergo an examination to determine you are of sound mind to make such a decision!"

Vauquelin casts a deep enchantment over him.

Be silent and obey.

The documents are composed. Arrangements are made for the majority of Vauquelin's currency, jewels, and gold to be relocated to a bank in Geneva.

Vauquelin and Olivier sign the papers, finishing them with Monsieur le Duc de Vauquelin's Baphomet V-monogram wax seal and crimson ribbon.

Olivier rings the servants' sash (an act he is still becoming accustomed to), and orders the lawyer to be shown out.

A few days later Monsieur de Subligny is en route to Évreux with a trunk full of gold, traveling in a carriage protected by four gendarmes on horseback.

The purchase of the Château d'Evelines in Évreux in the name of Olivier Boucher has begun, and the furniture and objects Vauquelin desires to keep from Renonçeau will be relocated to his new abode.

The Paris hôtel will be his forever.

His future is secure.

PARIS, FRANCE | 16 OCTOBER 1793

The Queen was beheaded today.

Reliving this event a second time is abhorrent to Vauquelin. He briefly considered attempting an intervention to save the dear scapegoat Queen and her family, but it was far too perilous. The citizens were determined to take the head of Antoinette and they would not be swayed. He was incapable of stopping her execution, and regardless, he is ever-fearful of toying with major historical events.

Vauquelin fled France in 1791 during his first trip through time — now he has chosen to stay and observe the horror unfold.

When he quickens, he takes his phaeton to Olivier's *hôtel particulier*, located mere blocks from his own.

The hôtel was purchased for him in 1718. He had never owned a home before; he had always lived with Vauquelin's family. Olivier is now independent, having been a vampire for over a century.

Their kinship remains steadfast.

Olivier opens the door himself. He has no servants. They have all left him, none so faithful as he himself had once been, and domestics are scarce during the Reign of Terror. They are all fighting on the streets and in the barricades, calling for the bloody heads of their oppressors.

"Let us go out for the hunt, my brother," Vauquelin says.

The vampire companions have altered their clothing and appearance to a drastic degree. Hidden away are lace, silks and satins. Stockings and fine leather shoes have been cast aside. In this barbarous landscape, one's sartorial selections are of utmost importance.

Instead, they are clothed in the garb of *les citoyens*: loose trousers down to their ankles and simple cotton blouses, sporting the precursor of the beret with prominent red, white, and blue cockades. Their long seventeenth-century hair is absent of patrician white-powdered wigs and drawn into queues with simple ribbons to hold them fast.

Olivier is embittered by the new mode. After his transformation, he had evolved into quite the clothes hound.

"Fear not," Vauquelin says. "The Revolution will soon find its completion, and our wardrobes will be reinvented once again with elegant vengeance!"

He hates the style too, but at no other point in history has it been so crucial for him to be inconspicuous. Aristocrats in denial were snatched away left and right and given a prompt trial at the base of the National Razor. They were — without fail — found guilty of treason against the Commune.

The air in Paris is fervid with the fragrance of *le sang perdu*.

The Reign of Terror is altogether a glorious and depressing era for a vampire.

Blood, blood everywhere ... and not a drop to drink.

When they reach La Place de la Révolution, Vauquelin stops the phaeton, securing the horse to a post, and they begin their grisly promenade.

Late as it is, the cries of Madame La Guillotine ring out with murderous glee, followed by the dull thunk of the victim's head after it is separated from the body and deafening cheers from the bloodthirsty spectators.

Even as a creature well-versed in carnage, Vauquelin finds it revolting. He may subsist on the blood of humans, but these revolutionary humans have a bloodlust that far exceeds his own.

La Guillotine was indiscriminate, even to immortal nobles, and the Terror afflicts all who walk upon French soil.

They approach the crowd, remaining on the edges, and Vauquelin spreads his arms wide.

"Behold ... the glory of France."

Olivier covers his mouth in revulsion and says, "It is precisely as you described, only much more gruesome. How tragic for you to witness afresh! I doubt you could have exaggerated the despair and depravity unraveling before us."

"Yes, but then I did not stay long enough to observe with my own eyes how it had escalated to this level of barbarity. This, my brother, is proof that humans are more monstrous than we could ever be. As haemovores, we take the blood we need to merely survive. Their need for blood is immeasurable."

In the wee hours of the night, the masses begin to disperse and seek their beds at last, only to resume their diabolical enterprise upon daybreak.

Vauquelin and Olivier step up to the scaffold. Their shoes are besmirched by blood; the ground beneath is saturated with savage noble gore.

Navigating through rivulets of blood that they cannot consume is both fascinating and repulsive. But in the midst of all the carnage, still they must feed themselves — and they are surrounded by unfit dead blood.

Thousands of aristocratic names populate the death rolls: they will become vampiric prey. It will be one of the rare times Vauquelin will interfere with history on his second passage, writing himself into the story a bit.

Instead of meeting their fates beneath the blade of the guillotine, they will meet him.

Alone, he cannot stop the Revolution, but he will take full advantage of the easy hunting field.

Armed with a ledger full of names and addresses enchanted away from a *sans-culotte*, whom they consumed and left dead in an alleyway, Vauquelin and Olivier launch their own reign of terror.

Dressed in their aristocratic finery in brazen defiance, they knock on the door of the Comte de __ and drain his wife, the Comte himself, their daughter, and one maidservant.

They continue their blood feast for a full year, until they begin to hear whisperings of vampirism around Paris.

With the demise of Robespierre, who met his death at the very blade of the death machine he had championed, they vanish: Vauquelin to Évreux, Olivier to the Château du Cavernay in Annecy, Provence.

They will not see one another for fifty more years.

PITTSBURGH, PENNSYLVANIA | 1886

For a girl of sixteen, the receipt of a letter was a boundless source of joy and the letter Maeve held in her hands was about to change her life, though it would be many more years before its purpose became clear.

Maeve was a bright girl, but sullen and prone to bouts of loneliness. She was an only child and preferred to find her companionship in the world of books, despite her father's gentle urging toward social activities.

People disappointed her on a regular basis, leading her to wonder if perhaps she had been born in the wrong time. She despised the endless functions of the season with a passion, and abhorred being paraded in front of potential suitors like a prize heifer.

There must be a more valuable life for her, something beyond becoming some man's wife and doing his bidding.

Her father had promised that she alone could choose her husband, that she needn't hurry or settle, but that she *must* marry. He was determined to secure a reliable man to care for her should something ever happen to him, and to continue their family line.

His work was dangerous, he reminded her, and with what was left of their kin so far away in Ireland, it was imperative that she be looked after.

She found herself unable to argue with this. The thought of being left alone was quite terrifying at her age. But even more terrifying was thinking of a life without her dear Papa.

Maeve carried the unopened letter in her pocket for several hours before opening it. The anticipation was too much! She wanted to savor its enigmatic delights as long as possible.

There was no envelope: it was a single folded sheet, embossed with an esoteric black wax seal bearing the head of a goat-man inside the letter V. She had never seen anything like it.

The mysterious stamp gave her a delicious, taboo thrill, as if it were a museum relic she had stumbled upon — something that should be hidden away from her eyes.

The laid paper was elegant, the handwriting elaborately scripted, even calligraphic. It looked a bit more primitive than the fountain pen she used. Perhaps it was written with a quill.

And it was from Paris! Magnificent!

Someday she would travel there, to the city of her favorite author, George Sand ... someday.

At last, she broke the seal and read the words within.

Paris, 3 May 1886
Dearest Maeve,

Please remember my name — for one day, when the time is right, we shall meet.

M. Louis-Augustin du Cavernay de Vauquelin

How exhilarating! Who was this strange man, and how did he acquire her name and address?

Maeve constructed an elaborate fantasy based on Monsieur de Vauquelin: his letter ignited her imagination.

In her mind's eye, he was fine-boned and slight of build, with midnight hair and penetrating eyes. He was tall like her, even taller though, and what a pair they would make!

If only he were real ... she would not feel so awkward and out of place with such a man by her side. He would understand the secret stories in her soul, the ones she could utter to no one else. He would finish her thoughts, know her better than she knew herself.

She awakened time and again in the middle of the night, impassioned and breathless, with her imaginary suitor's name on her lips and the diaphanous chill of his touch stealing across her skin.

His name was aristocratic (so many names!), and so must he be. A wealthy Parisian, he would come to her rescue one day and sweep her off to his glamorous city, where she would meet artists and writers, listen to famous pianists perform in person at a glamorous salon, and live *la vie bohème*.

She would visit the storied Parisian dressmakers and amass a wardrobe of the most elegant gowns Paris could offer. She would keep his splendid house and invite the brightest minds of the city to supper!

Madame Maeve de Vauquelin! It sounded perfect to her ears.

These elaborate fantasies carried her through some of the darkest periods of her life.

Imagine her disappointment when, three years later at the ripe old age of nineteen, she made the acquaintance of one Mr. Gerald Sullivan at an Independence Day celebration, and he began calling on her. Within weeks he had proposed marriage, and her tender-hearted father urged her to accept.

But Gerald was no Louis-Augustin. He was a plain old Irish-American business partner of her father's, quite dull. And he was a good two inches shorter than her to boot.

"Gerald is a decent, reliable man, Maeve, and he will be good for you," her father said.

To her dismay, no other men had come calling.

She was out of options. The fatigue of age and hard work was upon her father's face: she could not deny it. He was protecting her and she conceded to the marriage in doleful defeat.

The time had come for the dream to end. She would not live in Paris but Pittsburgh, with short, predictable Gerald.

She must accept her fate.

They were wed in 1889 at the Cathedral Basilica of Saints Peter and Paul in Philadelphia, Gerald's family church. She wore flat slippers instead of the creamy ivory heels she had coveted for her wedding day, and the groom wore lifts.

The bride was given free license and a large spending account to embellish their dignified row-house on Liverpool Street in Pittsburgh, and when she was not busy fussing over silks and satins she was thinking about Monsieur de Vauquelin, where he was and what he was doing, and practicing what she would say to him on the day they met at last. Maybe he would whisk her away and cause a scandal!

He had penetrated her conscience with a single letter.

Its power held her fast in its clutches for years.

Six months into the marriage, Maeve's dear Papa took his last hard-earned breath, plunging her into the depths of melancholy. She began to feel more alone *with* Gerald than she did when he was not at home.

She withdrew into her imagination and cultivated her eccentricities. She never stopped wearing her mourning black, which disgusted Gerald, distressed the ladies and raised the gentlemen's eyebrows.

She redecorated the entire house in dark tones. She wanted her surroundings to reflect her pathos, which grew bleaker and blacker by the day.

Maeve was unaware that she was developing qualities that would befit her future, that she was becoming the paramount mistress of her clandestine suitor's affections — because she, too, was macabre and misunderstood and chose to close herself off from society.

For hours, she sat reading and rereading her Tarot cards, searching in vain for clues to an improvement for her dreary existence.

She visited a clairvoyant each week, grasping for any indication that Monsieur de Vauquelin might be heading her way.

The answers were always foggy, unreliable.

And so the days unfurled … slow as molasses for Maeve, and quick as lightning for Vauquelin, for he had been on this journey once before.

At that moment they were on opposite sides of the Atlantic ocean, waiting.

When Maeve buried Gerald, she did not grieve for him ... not even for a moment. Instead, she grieved for the years she had lost to her dismal marriage.

He was a good husband for a while.

After three years wed, it was clear she was unable to conceive. Gerald was ignorant of the fact that Maeve did not want to be a mother, that she visited a mystic and took potions to prevent it.

It was a sin, she knew, but it was necessary for her. There would be no heir to his name, and Maeve became the target for Gerald's bitter resentment.

He was never home — it was no secret that he had a mistress. This was fine by Maeve, as it meant that he called for her in bed less and less often, but her life had become meaningless and dull: just as she suspected it would.

She was confident that if her poor Papa had lived to see what her life had become, and how her "decent, reliable, kind" husband had treated her, he would have strangled Gerald with his own bare hands.

Ever isolated, Maeve retreated back into her comfortable world of dark dreams, and pervasive thoughts of Monsieur de Vauquelin returned with a vehemence.

The possibility of such a man's existence was a salve for her weary mind.

There still had only been the one letter, but as the time passed, she stoked and tended her last remaining cinder of hope for another word from him.

She refused to let it die.

Her final visit to the seer yielded another portentous forecast.

"A tall, transcendent man stands in front of a house, gazing up at the windows with sorrow in his soul ... I believe it is *your* house," the crone said, tapping her crystal ball, "but it is raining, and he walks away. He will not reappear."

Maeve dropped some coins on the table with her chin on her chest and shuffled out, never to return.

The ceaseless and rainy Pennsylvania winters began to take a toll on her. She was often forced to take to her bed, felled by congestion and a persistent chill that could only be half-assuaged by the humid summers. The dampness took up residence in her chest and would not let go.

In 1895, widowed for just over a year, Maeve executed the full measure of her liberation. She saw a magazine advertisement about the new state of California, and the plentiful sunshine and health benefits of its southern half.

She was intrigued by the chance to escape the oppressive society matrons of old-money New England, none of whom ever accepted her in their circles. So she threw caution to the wind and within weeks both of her houses, Gerald's and her papa's, were sold and her belongings in transport to the West.

She was a rarity — a widow of means. She could do anything her heart desired. There was no one, and before all else no man, to stop her.

Society tongues wagged all over Pittsburgh.

Mrs. Sullivan had lost her senses! She had no one to advise her!

She would be slaughtered in transit by the red-skinned savages! She would be back in Pittsburgh in less than a year!

In fact, they gave her six months.

Then she would find out that she should have listened.

The rumors were inconsequential, because Maeve was her father's daughter and a stubborn Celt.

Let them talk.

She boarded a train to California with her family manservant, Charles, and never looked back.

The train carried her across the country and her spirits flourished with each burst of steam.

She was taking control for the first time in her existence, and never again would she be ordered around.

As the great machine of steel gobbled up the many miles ahead of her, she was frightened and exhilarated in unison. Her one fear was that with her departure, Monsieur de Vauquelin would never be able to find her ... but it no longer mattered.

She was grateful to him for keeping her imagination and self-confidence well-fed.

Now she must think of herself and herself only.

Maeve allowed her fragile cinder of hope to snuff out at last.

PARIS, FRANCE | 1900

The hôtel is packed with crates full of the belongings Vauquelin will transport to America. The remaining furnishings are covered in linen and the servants have all been dismissed, with the exception of a caretaker. He will not sell the hôtel; it is his intention to return to it someday with Maeve.

She will adore it.

There is a knock at the door. Vauquelin opens it and admits Olivier, who had received a letter.

"So it is really true, Vauquelin. You are returning to America."

"There is no alternative for me," Vauquelin says. "My entire existence relies on the possibility of reuniting with Maeve. If I do not attempt it, I might as well walk into the sunlight and be finished. Have you decided to join me?"

Olivier has spent a great deal of time turning Vauquelin's invitation over and over in his head. He is the consummate European. Cross-ocean travel holds little appeal for him, especially to an unsophisticated young state populated by wild savages.

His greatest joy is taking train journeys across France, and, when he is in Annecy, to Italy or sometimes Spain.

But this satisfies his feeble wanderlust.

Olivier's vampire life has afforded him adventures he would never have been able to experience as a common servant, not to mention one exterminated early in life by contagion.

"I believe this journey is once more yours to take alone. My presence could alter your path. Perhaps I will join you one day when you are settled with your Maeve," he replies.

A broad smile spreads across Vauquelin's face.

By now Olivier and Vauquelin are quite accustomed to being parted for long periods. They always pick up right where they left off with one another, as only the most faithful of friends can.

"Are you happy, being alive for so many years?" Vauquelin asks.

"The years have been a marvel. My life is a pleasure. You know well that, like you, I am a solitary man. But I may take a wife. The seclusion assails me at times. I have many years to plan this properly," he says, with a rueful smirk.

"Choose carefully, my friend. You have not yet created another vampire. May you avoid my own nuptial woes."

They erupt in laughter, falling into a hearty embrace.

"I shall miss you, my brother."

It is a bittersweet parting of maker and progeny — to this date, Olivier remains the only vampire Vauquelin had deliberately chosen to create. But Olivier can protect himself: he has been well-educated in safeguarding his existence.

Vauquelin knows they will meet again.

LOS ANGELES, CALIFORNIA | 1900

Tomorrow's date: August 11. He will see her again at last, universe willing. His entire body is aflame with anticipation.

He has crippled his mind multiple times trying to calculate exactly how many days — nights — years — it has been since he last touched her. He lived one hundred and twenty-nine years without her in his futurepast, and another two hundred and twenty-two to reach her once more. Hundreds of thousands of monotonous nights, give or take a few.

Two hundred and twenty-two years to execute his plans.

Even so, he remains unsure.

As of today, including the repetition of his past, he has been alive for six hundred and twenty-four years.

Vauquelin wrestles with whether to appear at the theatre tomorrow night and let fate play out as it will, or scheme another way to find her.

The fragility of a moment frightens him still.

One wrong move, no matter how slight, could unravel the finely woven cloth of history. His stay on earth is ironclad, yet the merest false step might erode his yearned-for future as a crushing wave can decimate a sand dune.

Tonight he rides by her house in a carriage like a lovesick schoolboy, beseeching any sign of her existence. A shadow moves across the window in her room, sending his heart aflutter.

He is quite certain it will leap through his coat.

He sits staring at her house, their house, his house, which had provided him with such beautiful shelter from society and had once been filled with abundant love and acceptance.

Pain and melancholy at once subdue him.

None of the skills afforded a vampire can affect the outcome for him. He must rely, as he has so often in his journeys, on fate.

There are no guarantees that he will regain all that he has lost, and he cannot bear the thought. It is all he can do to not eject himself from the carriage and attempt a flight into her arms.

Instead he knocks on the ceiling of the carriage, stops at Turnverein Hall to purchase a ticket for the next evening, and returns to his shack: not the same derelict little cottage he had rented during his first journey to Los Angeles, but right next door.

He climbs up the steps and sits on the landing. Time slows like the violet syrup he so loved as a boy.

He is without her because he lied. He never afforded her the opportunity to judge him: he condemned himself before she could. It remains the most foolish (and the most definitive) choice he has ever made.

Should he be granted the miraculous fortune to cross paths with her again, he will forbid himself from enchanting her.

He wants to give her only his pure, unadulterated truth.

And so he sits on his crude little stoop, at long last back in his true city, Los Angeles, with his true love in her house mere miles away from him, living and breathing.

Alive. Alive. Alive.

The moon rises and the ladies of the night begin their parade down his street, and he continues sitting until the early morning vendors begin to appear with their carts and the sky turns from black to a deep, dark purple.

He drags himself inside to his coffin, tormented by wakefulness. His heart stills, but his fingers agitate upon his chest, unable to rest.

The centuries have spoken and taken their due.

His coveted moment has, at last, arrived.

Vauquelin dresses in the exact manner he dressed on this night once before, down to the most minute detail.

He arrives at the theatre. The same terrible burlesque is on the bill, the same hand-painted posters hang on the walls.

His arrival is late — it is his intention to be there after the performance begins, to avoid any accidental encounters.

Pacing about, hearing snippets of the actors and the musicians and the audience, he pictures her laughing at the absurd comedy, sitting beautifully erect in her box seat, raising her opera glasses for a better look, right where he once sat by her side that fated night of their acquaintance.

He purchases two glasses of champagne and waits at the bar until he hears applause for intermission, assuming a position where the doors are in plain view.

His heart flogs his chest.

His lungs struggle to find their air.

Well-dressed patrons begin to stream into the lobby, and he jerks his head about, searching for her with frenetic eyes.

Maeve is nowhere to be seen.

A crowd forms in a queue at the bar, their programs in hand, impervious to his anxiety and despair, laughing and enjoying themselves as if the most crucial day in Vauquelin's long life is not in danger of being destroyed in the blink of an eye.

The din of the chattering crowd is intolerable.

Every patron is screaming.

Their cruel laughter pierces his eardrums ... their inane conversations all enter his head at once.

He believes he might lose his sanity at last.

Flinging the champagne to the floor he races through the lobby, jostling anyone who dares cross his path.

A door slams him in the face.

His eyes are blinded by stars, and the world goes silent.

The patrons begin to move in slow motion.

Their mouths are agape as they point and watch him falter (are they mocking him and his pathetic hope that his destiny could be fulfilled?).

Such a fool he has been!

The walls begin to melt and shrink, crushing him, closing him in. A muted scream erupts in his brain.

Without warning his eyes regain their focus, and he finds himself looking into the blurred, dark gaze of Maeve.

Her hand is on his elbow, a fan dangles from her wrist.

"Sir, I beg your pardon! Are you quite alright?"

He cannot breathe. "Mev."

She cocks her head in confusion. "My name is not Mev. Perhaps you have mistaken me for another?"

He blinks repeatedly, unable to speak.

This is an unmitigated disaster.

He focuses again ... indeed, this woman is not Maeve.

Blood tears fight their way to the surface.

He fumbles for a handkerchief in his pocket and presses it to his face. "Forgive me ... I ... "

Time ceases to exist. All sound again drains from his ears and he stands deafened, staring at this wretched woman who dares have the audacity to not be Maeve.

He flees out the front door of the theatre.

The streets are dark.

A rare Southern California rain begins to fall, causing a flash flood to deluge the roads and turn them to thick, malodorous mud. He walks and walks and walks, his feet becoming drenched and swollen.

Everything is ruined.

History has failed him — or else some treacherous thread has been pulled, transforming the pattern into an altogether different design. He had destroyed it, despite his mindfulness to avoid any miscalculations.

Perhaps she did not move to California after all and is still living in Pittsburgh ... perhaps she is not even alive.

He arrives at Pearl Street.

Maeve's street.

Their street.

His street.

Vauquelin stands outside the elegant, scrolled iron fence that segregates the house from the road, gazing up at the windows.

Seedling palm trees, palms that will one day sway and tower impossibly high, as high as the roofline, begin their ascent on the perimeter of the lawn.

He is overcome with longing.

Not for the house itself, but for the love and comfort that had blossomed within its walls.

Is she there, inside?

He wonders what she is doing instead, why she did not go to the theatre. Is she unwell? Is she sitting in her library, drinking cognac, reading a book?

A shadow passes a window, and it makes his blood tingle.

He cannot go to the door.

He looks a mess: he is thoroughly soaked by the rain.

Slump-shouldered, he turns on his heel and walks on his destroyed feet the several miles back to his own little hovel, absorbing the pain he so rightfully deserves.

How gullible he had been, to think he could reclaim this golden, light-ridden life.

Maeve's absence at the theatre was an omen.

All those years of life and planning have resulted in naught.

Once inside, he strips off his soaked clothes and sits at his small desk with his bedraggled feet in a basin of hot water.

A blank sheet of paper stares at him in defiant, empty silence, begging to be scratched and imprinted with the tip of his quill.

It takes hours for the words to come forth.

Vauquelin looms over the front steps of Maeve's house, holding a small parcel and a letter bearing his wax seal.

Wax seals have long been out of fashion, but so has he.

His hands tremble as he advances and strikes the massive brass door knocker. Charles opens the door.

He lifts his top hat and says, "Good evening to you, Charles. Is Madame Sullivan at home?"

Charles squints and draws back. He has never laid eyes upon the gentleman who stands before him speaking of his mistress with such familiarity. How does this man know his name?

Maeve comes scampering down the stairs holding a gargantuan vase of flowers, and Vauquelin leans aside so he can see her. She is radiant: the sight of her nearly melts his cold flesh, and sends his heart pounding in a volatile collision of exultation and terror.

"Who is it, Charles?" she asks.

At the sound of her voice, Vauquelin believes he might be reduced to a puddle right here on her front porch. Removing his billfold, he extracts a scripted calling card bearing his name, bowing as he hands it over with an unsteady gloved hand.

the many questions you no doubt have for me, and indeed, it may bring new ones to light."

She raises an eyebrow and begins reading aloud.

"Once upon a time, a beautiful young lass was born ... "

As she begins, Vauquelin sits at her piano and begins playing Liszt's Standchën in D Minor.

It was always their favorite.

Maeve blanches. What a coincidence that he should choose to play her favorite piece! She looks to the ceiling and takes a deep breath, returning to the letter.

> ... and given the name Maeve. She was a solitary
> individual, much like myself. Her father was not a
> wealthy man, but he found the means to whisk her
> away from a life of poverty and famine in Ireland and
> begin life anew in Pennsylvania, far away from their
> ancestral home. She grew and grew, blossoming into
> a headstrong young woman. Her father called her
> *A Stór* — "my little darling".

Maeve choked up. But she persisted.

> Surrounded by men, and with the lack of a mother's
> guidance, she came to believe that there was simply no
> acceptable reason why she should not live as they did,
> free to do as she pleased.

She existed quietly, doing the minimum that society required of her, until the day she found herself widowed and quite alone, sitting upon a fortune that the men had amassed. Fearlessly, and quite unlike the average woman of her time, she made a bold decision — she packed her belongings and moved to the wild lands in the West called California.

The elite of Pittsburgh begged and pleaded with her not to go. They plied her with tales of danger. She was shaming her father and spitting on his grave! Women should not travel alone! She had no people in that godforsaken land! She would be dead within the year!

Yet she went despite their warnings, and she created a beautiful existence for herself alone. She built a fine house. She traveled to Europe without an escort. She read books, she walked in her gardens, inhaling the intoxicating fragrance of once-exotic citrus blossoms. Each night, prior to sleep, she would remove a blue heart-shaped sapphire from a drawer in her night stand and kiss it. Her mother wore this stone as Maeve made her first entrance into this world.

Maeve's new life was glorious, meticulously designed to be only what she coveted. She had no need for companionship, but hesitated not if she desired to find solace in the arms of a man. She was not looking for any man to become a permanent part of her existence.

Her world was tranquil and lovely. She found her
amusements when and where she wanted them. She
had fulfilled her obligations to society and married as a
dutiful daughter should, but now she was free.

She loved the theatre and music and opera, but there
was precious little before her arrival. Her generosity to
fledgling Los Angeles was legendary. Her efforts helped
arts and culture to take root in this vile village.

Yes, Maeve, this story is about you.

But you do not yet know how your story will end. I do,
and there is a possibility that I may affect the finale if
we are so fortunate. Now I speak about your future in
the past tense ... how is that possible, when it has not
yet happened?

How odd it seems to be the author of your future in
this story, but author I am not. I am a mere participant,
a figure who once played a significant role in your life,
far, far into a future that must be lived again.

I loved you — indeed I have always loved you —
fiercely and with a love I did not think possible.

You did not need anyone, but I came into your life and
you beguiled me. You wanted me, and I tasted love for
the first time in my long, repetitive life.

I am a man, yet something more or less than a man.
I am quite unlovable, you see. I am an aberration,
undeserving of love. What I deserve is a life spent
underground, away from the complications of humanity,
yet you gifted me with a wealth of light. Your loss was
too great for any average man to bear. Alas, I am a far
from average man ... I had no choice but to carry it
upon my shoulders for all my infinite years.

Like you, I have lived alone for most of my life.
I exist only in darkness. I did not feel the sun upon
my face until that fateful night I met you in a theatre,
so long ago in the fullness of time ... but last night,
the appointed night, you were not there, and I must
concede to the possibility that I may never feel that
warmth again.

Because of my failures, you died a horrific death,
one I could have prevented had I not been so steadfast
in my desire to protect you from my own violent reality,
had I not delivered death to your lavish lips.

I have traveled backwards and forth through the
centuries to reach you again. And now, I cast my last
remaining hope to you, for you are the love of my life.

All that is left for me is to tell the truth. I cannot
fathom a life without you again. Your absence created a
hollow in my heart, a savage and black place devoid of
hope and filled with nothing but drudgery and despair.

My epic journey may well terminate in dust, heartbreak, and torment the instant you complete this letter. I fear I may be doomed to again pay the price for the gravest error of my existence.

Please, I ask you to open the small box that I have included with this tale, and, after you have inspected its contents, to return to this page.

Maeve is mystified ... but this is fantastic!

Nothing so extraordinary has happened in her entire life, with the exception of receiving his original note. And his talk of her death! And the Standchën! How could he possibly know when she would die, and this music?

She opens the satin box with trembling fingers.

Inside is the photograph, dated in white handwriting across the bottom: she is seated, wearing her favorite Worth dress (which she wore for the first time just last week and hangs in her closet as they speak). Monsieur de Vauquelin stands behind her with a devilish closed-lip smile, his hand resting placidly on her shoulder.

Maeve lifts the lock of her hair and holds it up to the light, fear spreading through her eyes.

She hurls the photograph to the floor.

"What trickery is this? Who are you, sir?"

She abruptly stands, and he leaps up from the piano, taking her by the wrist.

The color drains from her face.

"Maeve. This is you, and it is I. It is us. It was taken in 1901 ... which is next year. You yourself can read the date on the bottom. No one should be expected to believe what I am telling you, but I implore you ... please finish reading the letter."

Her chin is thrust out.

Vauquelin's heart swells.

He knows she is terribly frightened, pretending not to be, and on the verge of becoming angry. Her temper is like that of a volcano. He always loved her volatile disposition: he had witnessed it a mere handful of times, so even-keeled was she.

"Please, *bien-aimée*, I beg you ... do not be afraid." He reaches out to her, smoothing her hair, drawing a finger across her lips.

Her face softens and her breathing slows, so he places the letter in her hands once more.

> Maeve. My Maeve. We lived as man and wife, and we
> loved one another madly. It was another time. We have
> been here before, though one night removed, but the
> circumstances were different. We met by happenstance,
> at the theatre. You brought me here to your home,
> and we sealed our fates that night. I will tell you more,
> but the words must come from my own lips and not
> this quill. If you disavow me, I will depart at once and
> trouble you nevermore. I give you my word of honor.

Maeve drops the letter in her lap and fixes her eyes upon the wall. What she just read was her secret story, the one she had kept in her heart for so long and never uttered aloud to another soul, but with an ending she had not anticipated.

"I must ask you," Vauquelin says. "Aside from thinking me insane, are you drawn to me?"

She rises and turns to face him, locking him in a peculiar gaze, then extends her hand, beckoning to him.

"God help me, I have been infatuated with you since the moment I opened your first letter. I never thought you would stand before me in flesh and blood. I had convinced myself you were a mere figment of my imagination. You have been a fixture in my dreams, and now you deliver me magic."

Vauquelin takes her hand, pulling her close, and buries his face in her hair. Her familiar scent, vetiver, the fragrance of her skin, which is Maeve's scent only and no one else's.

His irrepressible memory meets his senses at last.

It is intoxicating.

He pulls away and retrieves the photograph from the floor, pressing it into her hands. He flashes himself across the room from her, startling her with his swift movement, and she gazes at the photograph again.

"*Ma bien-aimée*, I did stretch the truth to you before, but there is a crucial dimension to my life that I did not reveal to you. I must tell you now because I cannot lose you again. By omitting the truth about myself, I allowed Death to steal you from me when we could have remained together for innumerable years. In fact, I invited her through our doors. I could have prevented the immense suffering that will take you again in the not too distant future, my love. A plague is coming ... it will carry you away. It was my own insecurity that prevented me from saving your life and giving myself wholly unto you. I convinced myself that if I told you the truth, you would abandon me. But I lost you regardless! I failed you, and thereby I failed myself! My existence was mutilated by your absence. The torturous passage of time has led me to this moment once more. But if you choose to reject me now, I will respect your wishes."

Her face is full of empathy and curiosity.

Maeve, absolute, pure Maeve.

They stand merely looking at each other, and Vauquelin uses the silence to bolster himself for what he must say.

No more lies.

His creed must be emancipated.

"My darling ... I am immortal. I am the undead. I am vampire, and I was such when I knew you."

Maeve gazes at him with glassy eyes.

Vauquelin might as well have said, "I am *hfowqihgqbnv*."

She is innocent, unsullied by the befouled existence of such grotesquery: exactly as he had once wanted to keep and protect her, but he can do it no longer.

All the hundreds of years he had been given to prepare for this moment, all the thoughts and schemes he had conceived ... it all evaporates into thin air.

He is left raw, almost human, reduced to the pitiable emotions of a common mortal.

He fumbles for words and explanations that are not forthcoming. All he wanted was to deliver her truth, but no more words will rise to meet his lips — and even if they did, they would be just that: meaningless words, nothing more.

One of the many lessons he has learned on his journey back through time is that he cannot expect humans to empathize with his state of being. It is beyond their grasp.

So he takes her face in his hands, pressing their foreheads together. He had not wanted to do so, but stark desperation grows within him and he can conceive of no other option.

He transfuses his memories into her mind.

In mere seconds, Maeve sees the eighteen years of their life together unfold. Their delights. Their joy, their beautiful experiences. Their quiet, unremarkable moments of being alive in each other's presence.

The vision crescendos into her horrific, painful death, followed by his suffocating grief. Her (his) house in the future, its walls suffocating him with her absence. His anarchic void. Vauquelin taking human blood and leaving countless bodies in his wake. The catacombs in the cellar, her own coffin and her memento mori. Vauquelin advancing through the future, alone, and his journey back through his own already-written pages ... culminating in his choice to live it all over again, all for the fracturable possibility of standing before her in this moment.

At last, Maeve sees her imaginary life with Monsieur de Vauquelin manifest before her eyes. It was the authentic life she had once imagined for herself, the one she was denied. The fine house, her elegant partner, her cultivated life of solitude with another individual who understood her hidden soul. A dark, solitary man, whose deep sadness matched her own, and whose demons she knew she could embrace.

She devours it all in an exquisite melding of inexplicable terror and rapture.

The transmission ends in her tears.

She recognizes the suffering and pain reflected on his face, and at once she is no longer afraid of him.

"I lived well over a hundred years beyond your death. I relived hundreds more in the past in order to return to you. The sum of that time was crippling without you," he says. "I did not give you the opportunity to know me completely and form your own decisions about me. And thus you met your death, which I could have prevented. This alone is the greatest failure of my existence. But I will release you if that is what your soul requires."

"Put your hand on my heart," she says.

Vauquelin obeys. He tilts his head back, enthralled by the rhythmic euphoria of her healthy beating heart.

"Can you feel what I want?" she asks. "Can you see that I have any choice left to me now?"

"Please, Maeve," he whispers. "Let our souls collide once again. I am your servant, Madame. I have been for centuries and will be for eternity. But this is not an easy life I offer you. I am a *voleur* ... I will steal the very sunlight from above your face, something you adore with all your spirit, and enfold you within the depths of my own impenetrable midnight."

She presses herself against him and thrusts up her chin.

He draws his fingers down her pulsing jugular, taking one last pleading glance at her face.

Her choice must be indisputable.

"I shall find my sunlight in your eyes," she said, "if you will promise to never stop looking at me as you are now."

Guiding her head, he circles her waist with an arm and places his lips upon her neck. The pop as his teeth pierce that ivory skin is altogether ghastly and sweet.

It is pure torture for him to inflict pain upon her, but soon there will be no further pain.

No death.

Maeve's blood electrifies him.

Oh, the taste of her!

He counts the beats of her heart.

When it slows, he bites into the vein on his hand.

His dark blood courses through her parted lips.

She loses consciousness, and he clasps her body.

He falls with her through the floors.

He waits. Time has no meaning now that he is holding her.

An eternity could pass, and indeed it feels as such.

Being the spectator to her death once more is agony married to ecstasy — because this time, she will rise again, nevermore to be touched by Death's indomitable hand.

He will hold her until time ends.

He is confident of the hours required, but morning is imminent.

He panics and drags her down into the cellar.

She is still, so still.

Her face is ashen and her rosy lips have lost their blush.

Vauquelin's breath becomes shallow ... he gasps for air, sobbing.

His many days on earth have been distilled to this moment.

What if he has failed?

It is taking much longer than it did with Olivier.

Vauquelin sits by her wilted body, rocking to and fro, cradling his face in his hands, streaking them with blood tears.

He was wrong to attempt to turn her.

Instead, he could have rebuilt the façade and lived another eighteen years with her, instead of this one wretched night.

To come this far and lose her again ...

He is doomed to live alone, accompanied only by his lies.

His guttural wails echo through the cellar.

With both hands she grasps Vauquelin's wrist, startling him.

Her hair becomes aflame, and she rises from her ashen state like a phoenix. Her skin sheds its deathly hue and assumes a luminescence that astonishes him.

Her beauty had stumbled him in life, but now, in her eternal death, she is resplendent beyond all reality and all dreams.

Vauquelin is humbled by her metamorphosis.

He bows to her, offering her his jugular, his precious artery, and she drinks from him. He falters, struggling to remain upright, but he cannot push her away, will not ever.

Oh!

He presses his lips to hers, and her lips respond. His blood has restored her as he had wanted so many years ago, when the price of his hesitation was her life.

Now, she cannot be stolen from him.

Her iron-fragranced breath mingles with his and her resurrection is worth more to him than any measure of blood.

Taking her by the hand, he guides her back down to the floor. They go to their rest in absolute darkness, his arm curled around her head, twirling her curls, just as they had always done.

They are still alive.

ACKNOWLEDGEMENTS

My most gracious thanks go to my husband, Franco, who endured a great deal of torture during my writing of this book and always gives me his utmost support and encouragement.

To my mother, Sheila, who gifted me with a deep imagination. We've always loved the dark side.

To my early readers:
Paulette Kennedy, Sharolyn Poli, Nadia Khansa, Miranda Caudell, Lorena Michelle, and Julie Sinclair.

To Michael Murphy (RIP), who always knew I had a book in me, even when I didn't know it myself. I only wish he could read it now. I know that he is congratulating me from afar. He would love the cover as much as I do.

To The Binders writing groups, who have given me a wealth of knowledge and inspiration.

To Polidori Press, who made the telling of Vauquelin's story possible. It's a tough world for vampires these days.

Without the above, *Beguiled by Night* would not exist.

ABOUT THE AUTHOR

Nicole Eigener is a lifelong student of French history and the macabre. Her fascination with vampires dates back to the age of eight, when she saw *'Salem's Lot* on television. Many years later, her love for haemovores became a beautiful marriage to her obsession with French history and culture, specifically of the seventeenth-century.

Beguiled by Night is her first published novel, although she has been writing since childhood. Growing up, the words of Toni Morrison were always bubbling beneath her dark surfaces: "If there's a book that you want to read, but it hasn't been written yet, then you must write it." And so she did. She hopes you love Vauquelin and her French vampire world as much as she does. Nicole lives in Southern California with her husband.

Twitter and Facebook: @NicoleEigener
Instagram: @beguiledbynight

Visit *thevampire.org* to experience more of *Beguiled by Night*, including French pronunciations and a soundtrack.